LEAVING EASTERN

PARKWAY

LEAVING EASTERN

PARKWAY

a novel

MATTHEW DAUB

Delphinium Books

LEAVING EASTERN PARKWAY

Printed in the United States of America

For information, address DELPHINIUM BOOKS, INC.,
16350 Ventura Boulevard, Suite D
PO Box 803
Encino, CA 91436

Library of Congress Cataloguing-in-Publication Data is available
on request.
ISBN 978-1-953002-29-7
ScoutAutomatedPrintCode
First Paperback Edition: September 2023
Jacket and interior design by Colin Dockrill, AIGA

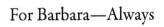
For Barbara—Always

A glossary of Yiddish and Hebrew
words and phrases appears on p. 329

PART ONE

EASTERN PARKWAY:
CROWN HEIGHTS, BROOKLYN, 1991

My father died almost instantly. At least that is what they told my mother. She was standing right next to him when he was hit, his black fedora and shoes left at her feet, his body landing many yards down Eastern Parkway. The driver of the blue Chevrolet did not stop. The investigators said the impact speed was close to fifty, judging from the lack of skid marks and what they called the pedestrian throw distance.

This was my fault. My father would be alive today if not for me; I am certain of it. My father would be alive, and my mother would not have had her fourth mental breakdown. I would still be an observant Jew, not living as a goy. This is the guilt I bear.

I blame myself, but more than that, I blame Hashem for my love of handball. My gift. It was Hashem who gave me the ability to play with either hand, my right as strong as my left. I felt the pure joy of it from the very first time I hit the ball, as natural to me as breathing. Why would Hashem give such a gift if he did not expect me to use it? To this day I blame him, but this is not something a boy tells his Rebbe, especially when he should be in shul on Shabbos.

I was at the handball courts when my father was killed. I heard the sirens wailing in the early afternoon, first one and then another, but it was like any normal day in Crown Heights and I was distracted by the clamor of the crowd, gentiles watching in amazement as the Hasidic boy in his undershirt and yarmulke sent the favored players home in defeat. I paid no attention to the sirens announcing my father's death.

I was too busy concentrating on my opponents' weaknesses, the holes in their game, and determining how I would systematically take them apart.

This was not the first time I played handball on Shabbos and it would not be the last, though it was the first time I did not attend shul with my parents. And this was only the beginning of my transgressions. I picked up a pen to fill out the registration forms. Money changed hands. I tied and untied my sneaker laces. I ate treif from a hot dog vendor. I committed many more sins that day, perhaps more than I should disclose.

Some would say an observant Jew showing such public disregard for Torah is a desecration of the name of God. A chillul Hashem, they would say, and there cannot be full atonement for these willful sins, not even on Yom Kippur. I am telling the truth; this is what the rabbis teach.

I will not make excuses for those things I did, but I am in deeper communion with Hashem on the handball court than I am in prayer or Torah study. This is another thing a boy does not tell his Rebbe.

My obsession began harmlessly enough with the Ace-King-Queen games we played behind our apartment house. I was no different than the other Hasidic boys except none of them stood a chance against me. I will confess, I liked to win then as I do now. I enjoyed vanquishing my friends and soon started playing against other boys in the neighborhood.

Mendie Resnick and Yossi Teitelbaum walked for blocks to watch me hit the pink Spaldeen low and tight against the corner of the chalk box while putting an unpredictable spin on the ball. They cheered me on in Yiddish while my opponents cursed in American and Italian. The losers of our street games had to go *cans up*, bending over against the apartment house wall while the winner throws the stinging ball as hard as he can at their tuchuses. I seldom had to face the wall. If you are not Jewish, you have no idea what this means.

We are said to be good with money. Jews make good furriers, diamond cutters, salesmen of household goods and the like. In Crown Heights we are scholars. We study Torah and Talmud, we do not excel at sports, we are not dominant handball players. A Hasid in his black suit and hat and wearing handball gloves is an image straight from the Sunday funnies, but I wore my white calfskin gloves with pride, both palms showing equal evidence of hard use.

I am not the only Jew to ever play handball, far from it. Handball was practically a Jewish game at one time. We've been champions, dominant in the older days, with names like Hershkowitz, Orenstein, Lewis, Sandler, Eisenberg, Rosenfeld, Jacobs, Haber . . . I could go on and on, although I am surely the only Hasid, the only pious one. I suppose I should say I *was* the only pious one. Some would deny I am even still a Jew, and I would have a hard time making a case for myself.

Certainly, frum Jews do not play handball for money on Shabbos; of this there is no debate and I cannot justify what I did. At fifteen, I was no longer a child. I made my choices. But this was a special day on my home court. Players would be coming from all over the city and beyond for this tournament. I am sure some had already heard of me, the wiry little Yid who plays in secret on Shabbos, the Yid with his payos scotch taped behind his ears, the Yid who does not talk trash like the other players do.

There is always much trash talk in handball. Talk is a big part of the New York game, the swagger and intimidation, the street tradition. Imagine what they were saying at the sight of me forking over my entry fee in my black suit and wide-brim fedora. I signed up for the Men's Open Small

Ball instead of the under-seventeen group because I wanted a chance to play against the best of them.

I knew nothing of tournament play then. My only strategy was to win, to beat my opponents as quickly and devastatingly as possible, and that is what I did. In the 32s I went up against an Asian from Queens who was obviously humiliated to be sharing the court with a fifteen-year-old Hasid. There were jeers and taunts, put silent as I destroyed him quickly, 21–3 and 21–5.

In the 16s I faced a big Hispanic guy who came with an entourage from the Bronx. I had heard his name before, supposedly a macher. Many bets were placed in his favor. He was stronger and far better schooled than I was. I do not mean to sound boastful, but I read his game and played him like a Klezmer fiddle. By late afternoon, they all knew the rumors of my game were true.

I saw the expressions on the faces in the crowd. These were not the faces of gentiles mocking because a Hasidic boy had desecrated the Sabbath. Quite the opposite. Some would tell their children of the first time they saw me play—the prodigy who would one day rank with the great names of old. They would remember when Zev Altshul stepped from his eruv and into the world on Shabbos to play for the glory of Hashem, the God of the Jews, who was not the giver of unkeepable commandments but of joyous gifts.

I stayed to watch the other games finish, eating a hot dog with mustard and sauerkraut while peering through the chain link, when a man, I would say somewhere in his fifties, came up to me laughing.

"Those aren't kosher, you know," he said, pointing to my Sabrett hot dog. "They say they're kosher-style, but it's treif."

So this man was a Jew?

I was embarrassed and did not know what to say. I held

up my can of Dr. Brown's Cel-Ray soda.

"Oh, so we have a tradeoff, eh? A Dr. Brown's nullifies a Sabrett?"

He laughed aloud again.

"I can get behind that," he said. "Listen, kiddo, just so you know, I'm going to put some money on you for the quarters tomorrow. The odds are steep so I'm not risking that much, but I'll make a bundle if you can step up. You think you can do that?"

I shrugged, trying not to seem cocky.

He said, "I think you've got a chance, at least of making it through the quarters."

I smiled for the first time all day before he dumped a cold bucket of reality on my kindled confidence.

"None of them know you yet, and it'll take them a while to figure you out, but once they do, you're toast. You've got arm, kid. That's what Vic Hershkowitz told me when I was younger than you. Vic Hershkowitz, you know who he is?"

Of course I did.

"You're a natural," the man said. "You put a lot of stuff on the ball and you're tough to return, but you'll never be great until you can hit harder. That's what Hershkowitz told me, too. Your tap shot to the corner worked pretty well for you today, but they'll be on to it soon enough, and you're not so great at reading hooks. That's where I'd work you over. And you could do a lot better job blocking. You're making it much too easy for them. Take up more of the court. You understand what I'm saying to you?"

I nodded.

"And you need to start playing the tournaments," he said. "You should've been playing them already at your age. You won't get any better till you play the tournaments."

I nodded again. Always a lot of nodding.

"Do you want to learn how to play handball?" he asked.

I told him I did and he handed me his card—Harry Rosenfeld. The man was a legend from the Brighton Beach Baths, a national champion.

"You call me," he said. "You call me if you want to get serious about your game."

This I could not believe. I left the courts for home on the happiest day of my life, ready to face some of the best players in New York the next morning and elated that Harry Rosenfeld had seen my game and thought I stood a chance.

But I did not connect those sirens with the devastation waiting for me at home. I had no idea when I shook Harry Rosenfeld's hand that I would not play handball on my home court again anytime soon, and that my failure to return for the quarters would only add to the mystique surrounding me in the coming years.

The spring flowers were in glorious full bloom as I made my way home along Eastern Parkway, with the lowering sun and lengthening shadows bathing the parkway in blue. The tops of the apartment houses turned a fiery red-orange in the last licks of sunlight.

I suddenly realized I had forgotten to remove the tape from my payos, so I discreetly stepped between two parked minivans to put myself in order. I made no eye contact with other Hasidim passing by on the walk—families, the women pushing baby strollers, so many children. I hoped they would not notice the white sneakers poking conspicuously from beneath my pant legs, the black trousers that now sported a fresh hole in one knee. I worried about explaining this to my parents. My mother mended my torn pants so often, she must have thought I was the clumsiest boy in Brooklyn.

I arrived at our building to find the lobby empty and the

elevator in Shabbos mode, running continually and stopping at every floor so observant Jews would not have to push the buttons to complete an electric circuit. I rode the elevator to the fifth floor and took the stairs up one more flight to the roof landing, where I'd left my slip-on Shabbos shoes. I untied my sneakers and set them neatly side by side, then took the stairs down to the fourth floor. I paused in the hallway outside our apartment to gather my thoughts and rehearse what I was going to say to my father, how I would lie to him about where I had been and how I tore my pants.

I turned the lock, then placed my hand over the mezuzah on our right doorpost and touched my fingers to my lips before entering. The lights in the living room had been left on since Friday evening before sundown. My parents were not in the apartment, but a familiar figure was sitting on our sofa with his face illuminated by the yellow glow of an end-table lamp.

"Come sit, Zev," Rav Feldsher said to me in Yiddish, patting the cushion next to him and setting his prayer book aside.

I expected to be in trouble for what I had done, but nothing like this, at least not so soon. Rav Feldsher was a rabbi of great stature, an emissary of the Rebbe and mentor of my father, an important man in the Lubavitcher community.

When I was three years old, Abba took me to the cheder for my first day of religious instruction. It was a memorable day, so special because Rav Feldsher was there, and not just the regular teacher. Abba drizzled honey on a sheet of paper with letters of the Hebrew alphabet written on it. He guided my hand as I dipped my finger in the honey and tasted it twenty-two times while he helped me pronounce each letter from aleph to tav. Rav Feldsher smiled proudly at my first lesson in the sweetness of Torah study—a boy with such promise!

"Zev, come sit," he said, patting the cushion again. "Please, come sit by me."

I sat down next to him with my keys rattling in my hand, taking inventory of the many sins I'd committed since leaving the apartment that morning. Carrying my house keys outside our eruv on Shabbos was just one of the many. Surely Rav Feldsher could not know all those things I had done?

"There has been a terrible tragedy today," he said, stroking my shoulder gently. "It is your father; may his memory be a blessing."

I had heard that honorific used before, only in reference to the dead. My throat tightened. Even the simplest mutter would have taken far greater effort than any I had expended on the handball court that day. I sat staring at a dark spot on the carpet where my father once spilled the Kiddush wine, leaving an irregular purple-red stain. I must confess, my first emotion was relief that Rav Feldsher had not come to discuss my Shabbos transgressions. It is my greatest shame to admit this.

"It is very difficult to lose one's father, I know this," he said, speaking in the philosophical manner of all rabbis. "We cannot always understand the ways of Hashem. The work of his hand is a great mystery."

I said nothing, but Hashem's hand was no mystery to me at all. I could see it in this judgment as clearly as I saw the flaws in my opponents' games earlier in the day.

"We must trust in his goodness," Rav Feldsher continued. "It is written: '*He does not willingly afflict the sons of men.*' There is always a divine purpose in suffering, no matter how difficult this is to understand."

"*Difficult to understand?*" The only thing I did not understand was why Hashem would take my father and not me. It was not my father who profaned the Sabbath, who violated the commandment to keep the day of rest holy. My father did not eat treif from the hot dog cart. Why would God punish him? And what about my mother? How would she survive without my father to take care of her? She was not strong. Was she also being punished for the sins of her son?

Rav Feldsher sat next to me in silence, his hand still resting on my shoulder. In yeshiva I'd read of the friends of Job, who came to him in his misery and stayed seven days without saying a word. We sat together for many minutes before the rabbi spoke again.

"Your father did not suffer, so this is at least a small blessing," he said. "I heard the policeman tell this to your mother."

"Where is she now?" I asked in English.

The rabbi answered in the mix of English and Yiddish common to Lubavitchers.

"Rabbanit Feldsher is watching by her. Some other women also."

"Is she OK?" I asked.

"Your mother is not so well. She has not spoken already since the police."

"Is it like before, like last time?"

"Nu, is too early to tell. Your mother was not well before, and the accident has been a terrible shock from her. We can only pray."

"Can I see her?"

"Of course . . . and I will call your sister after Havdalah."

My sister? I had not seen her in years, not even heard her name spoken in the apartment. Frayda was the first to go *off-the-derech*, to abandon Torah and bring shame to our parents. I was still a child, but I remember the calamity well, the terrible upset it caused in our household. I could not imagine seeing her again, although we now had more in common than I realized when she left Crown Heights almost eight years ago.

9

"How did you know where to find her?" I asked.

Rav Feldsher removed his glasses and huffed on the lenses, wiping them with a tissue. I was not sure this was allowed on Shabbos.

He said, "The Rebbe has many contacts in the world, kinehora."

"Will she come back here to Brooklyn?" I asked.

"This will be up to your sister," he said. "But I will call when Shabbos is over."

Frayda never fit the mold of the typical Lubavitcher girl. She was too inquisitive, always seeking something beyond the role assigned to her by our traditions. As a very young child she kept a confetti collection, carefully tearing small bits of colored paper into tiny, near-equal parts and then sorting them into the egg cartons our mother saved for her. My parents made jokes about her odd creative ways until it became apparent she was drifting away from us. By the time Frayda announced she wanted to go to art school, it was too late. Her behavior was incomprehensible to me at the time.

I was not quite eight years old when she took me to the Brooklyn Museum. I had passed it hundreds of times but had never once been inside this grandest of buildings on Eastern Parkway. Neither my parents nor I had any interest in art, although it is not forbidden in the Torah or our traditions. Probably every home in our community had at least one painting of the Rebbe, or some religious picture, or shtetl scene on the wall.

"Those things are not art," Frayda stated definitively as we climbed the impressive cascade of steps together. "In here you will see what real art looks like."

Honestly, I did not see anything so wonderful in the Brooklyn Museum. I could not tell much difference between Frayda's "real art" and the painting in our dining room of

Hasidic men dancing with the Torah scrolls or the smiling Rebbe staring down at me from his place of honor on the living room wall. Yet Frayda seemed so sure of herself, which both fascinated and frightened me. At eight years old, I was sure of nothing except my duty to obey the commandments of Torah, our parents, and the teachings of our rabbis.

"This is a Georgia O'Keeffe," Frayda said excitedly, pulling me in front of a particularly strange painting I could not even begin to fathom.

"She's old now and lives in the desert, but she's a very famous artist. A pioneer."

"I do not like it," I said.

"Well, you just don't understand. Maybe when you get older . . . This whole show is of art made by women. Isn't that amazing, Zev? Things are changing in the world."

"What do you mean, why do things need to change?" I asked.

She rolled her eyes as if she were trying to carry on a conversation with an idiot.

"Women can do most of the things men can do now," she said. "Isn't that obvious?"

Frayda had answered me in English, and I found her matter-of-fact statement far more shocking than any of the art hanging on the walls of the museum.

"No, they can't," I said in Yiddish. "Why would you say something like that?"

"Because it's true," she said, in English again.

My sister had always been good to me—in fact, she practically raised me when our mother went into the hospital the first time, but we had never spoken of such things before and I was afraid of her ideas.

"So if I were to become an artist, do you think I should have to spend my life painting pictures of the Rebbe over and over again? Look at the world God created. Crown Heights is not the whole world, you know. Look how we dress here in the nineteen-eighties, like we're still in Russia or Poland a hundred years ago."

"So?"

"So there's never any change here, that's what I'm saying. We live only for the past, no matter how crazy the past was. When I'm married, should I have to let a rabbi inspect my underwear after my period and go to the mikvah before I'm declared clean again?"

"What do you mean?" I asked.

Frayda had forgotten I knew nothing of a woman's period or the laws of marriage purity.

"Never mind, it's not important right now. Do you see that painting over there?" she asked, pointing to a colorful mish-mash across the room. "That artist is Jewish, or she was . . . Sonia Delaunay was her married name. She was born Sarah Stern."

"How do you know all this?" I asked. We were never taught such worldly things in our schools.

"I have a friend," she said in English. "And I've been reading."

"Abba would be worried if he knew what you were doing," I said.

"Well, he doesn't have to know, does he? There's nothing wrong with new ideas, Zev. This is how we make progress. There are other Jewish women in this show and none of them paint pictures of the Rebbe."

I was terribly confused. We had been taught to love and revere the Rebbe. Many even believed he was Moshiach. I had never heard anyone speak of him this way before. Frayda would never talk like this in front of our father.

"Why are you saying these things?" I asked.

"Because all people should have the right to think for themselves, but here in Crown Heights we must do exactly as we've been taught. The rabbis think for us, they answer all our questions. If you want to know if something is right, you ask the rabbi, and an old man will tell you if it's permissible to scratch your tuchus and which finger to use."

"Frayda! Stop, you're scaring me."

She smiled at me caringly.

"You're right, Zevi, so let's not talk about this anymore. You're right, it's not good for you."

Frayda was speaking Yiddish again, which was reassuring.

"I'm sorry," she said. "Let's look at some more paintings and then we can go home. We can stop for a sweet on the way if you like, all right?"

I still lived in a small and simple world, and the mention of stopping for a sweet instantly calmed me. I had no idea our conversation was a foreshadowing of my own future and that Frayda's "friend" was Paul Griffin, a graduate student at nearby Pratt Institute, and the man who would become something of a de facto stepfather to me.

She was nineteen years old at the time and destined for marriage to Rav Feldsher's middle son, Dov. She was not happy about the proposed arrangement, but the match had already been made and both families were enthusiastic. She could have said no to Dov Feldsher, but when she finally spoke up, Frayda's *no* went well beyond rejecting an arranged marriage. She said no to Hashem, to the community of her birth, to life in Crown Heights, to our parents, and to me.

When Rav Feldsher spoke her name, it was like a resurrection of the dead. My mother had already sat shiva for Frayda after she left us for her gentile boyfriend. Eema mourned her eldest daughter then as she mourned the two daughters she miscarried before I was born, and would now mourn my father.

Rav Feldsher stood up from the sofa and carefully placed his hat on over his yarmulke.

"So now we will go see your mother, yes? I believe it would be wise not to mention your sister to her unless she inquires. Let her rest tonight and perhaps she will be stronger tomorrow. There are other things we must discuss, too, Zev, but we will leave this for another time, yes?"

I nodded. Again with the nodding.

I was unsure what *other things* Rav Feldsher might be referring to, but feared it was my wayward life as a handball player, a life I did not want to give up. Then I realized I had not yet inquired of my father's death, nor had I shown any outward signs of grief. For this also I was filled with shame. I gathered my courage and asked the rabbi how my father died.

Rav Feldsher stroked his white beard and tilted his head slightly to the side, as if he were examining an arcane Talmudic verse or perhaps wondering what kind of boy does not cry for his own father.

He said, "Your parents were on their way home from shul, about to cross the parkway. The police said a car was speeding and did not stop by the red light. Was nothing to be done from your father; may Hashem avenge his blood."

"Where is he?" I asked.

"At Shomrei Hadas, the funeral chapel."

"And my mother was not hurt?" I asked.

"She is not hurt physically, but your mother has not spoken for hours since the police. Perhaps seeing you will be a comfort, yes?"

It was dusk when we left the apartment. Lights left on the entire day now glowed from windows all along Eastern Parkway in the approaching evening. Rav Feldsher gently placed his hand under my arm and guided me the wrong way down the sidewalk.

"I thought you said my mother was at your house?" I asked, confused by this change in direction. Rav Feldsher lived on President Street, close to the Rebbe. We should have turned to the left, not the right.

"Yes, we are going to my house," he said, offering no further explanation.

Then I realized he was taking us around the block to avoid passing the spot where my father died. This is when the tragedy of my devastated family struck me like a kill shot: fast and low against the wall, impossible to return. Only a few hours earlier I covered the entire handball court with ease; now sweat gathered under the dam of my hatband and a sizable bead drizzled down my cheek. I could barely place one foot in front of the other, as though the weight of my father's struggles in life had suddenly descended upon me.

His yeshiva training did little to prepare my father for making his way in the modern world. He studied Torah and Talmud, acquiring only rudimentary skills in English and mathematics. He was one of the gabbaim, a respected layman in our synagogue, yet he serviced dry-cleaning machines all over Brooklyn and Queens during the day and returned home in the evening, a weary Torah scholar reeking of chemicals. And on top of all this, on many nights he left us to work for the Rebbe and Rav Feldsher at 770, the Chabad-Lubavitch World Headquarters.

The rabbi had walked a few steps ahead before he realized I was no longer following him. He turned back to see me doubled over with my hands on my knees and my chest heaving. A sound, almost like the cluck of a chicken, leapt from my throat. I caught it and stuffed it back down, but the cluck emerged again, followed by another and another, along with

15

chicken-like neck jerks that culminated in an uncontrollable cackle of grief.

Rav Feldsher placed his hand on my back and patted it gently.

"Is good, Zev, is good to cry. Do not hold this inside. Do not hold this in."

That's when I vomited all over the rabbi's nicely polished Shabbos shoes, the half-digested treif of my hot dog lunch splattering pink up his black pant leg. He stepped back, expecting to be the target of another violent heave, but I stood upright and wiped my mouth on my coat sleeve, then spit several times in the grassy strip next to the sidewalk.

"I'm sorry," I said, spitting again. "I am sorry for everything."

Rav Feldsher looked down at his defiled Shabbos shoes and pants.

"We will go see your mother now," was all he said.

The rav and rabbanit's house was one of the grandest affairs on President Street, what they used to call "Doctors' Row." It was just the two of them, with their nine children all married. Surely they could have done with a smaller place, but the house was a testament to their position in the community, being so close to the Rebbe's.

I had passed it a thousand times, imagining how elegant the rooms inside must be, but when Rav Feldsher opened the leaded glass door, we were greeted by a stale blast of mildew. The place smelled as if it had not been aired out in years. The gold brocade wallpaper in the vestibule was faded and the velveteen furniture in the parlor looked sadly careworn.

The three women chatting away inside went silent as soon as the rabbi entered. Miryam Resnick, one of my mother's few friends, came rushing toward me. She had taken care of me twice before when my mother was ill. She stopped short, as though an invisible wall had suddenly sprung up between us. Rav Feldsher motioned to her and she stepped a little closer, extending her condolences and assuring me she would do whatever was necessary to help during my mother's recovery.

Mrs. Resnick stared at the rabbi's pant legs and shoes before he headed to the kitchen to clean my vomit from them. I heard water running in the sink. Although Shabbos had not yet ended, it was probably permissible for him to wipe his shoes with water because they were made of leather; however, he could only scrape the solids off his cloth pants with the back of a knife. I was certain Rav Feldsher would be careful not to violate the Shabbos laws as I had.

Mrs. Resnick reached out to touch my forearm, but immediately withdrew her hand. She said, "We will take good care of you, Zev. There is no need to worry."

I wanted to tell her I had every reason in the world to worry, but kept this to myself.

She then led me upstairs to a tiny room where my mother was lying facedown on a narrow single bed. Her sheitel, the wig married women in our community wear, was askew and short strands of her own shorn hair poked out on one side. Rabbanit Leah Feldsher was sitting in a chair next to the bed. She motioned for me to come sit next to my mother. I sat down on the bed, but had no idea what to do next. The rabbanit gestured again, encouraging me to speak up.

"Eema," I said, barely above a whisper.

My mother did not respond, so I raised my voice a bit.

"Eema . . . Eema, I'm here."

This time I cautiously touched her arm. When she did not stir, I poked her shoulder a little harder, perhaps harder than I should have. I had seen my mother in distress before, but never like this.

I turned toward the rabbanit and asked, "So what, then?"
She shrugged and said, "The Rebbe is praying."

Even at her best my mother was a fragile soul, unable to work outside the home as many other Lubavitcher women did while their husbands studied. Simple household chores were as much as she could bear. Sometimes I would return home from yeshiva to find the apartment just as I had left it in the morning, breakfast dishes still on the kitchen table and my mother humming softly in a chair by the window.

When she was healthy, she kept a neat house. She would sing to me and call me her tatellah and make me special treats. But the darkness was always lurking—her spells, as my father called them, her mahalat nefesh, my mother's sickness of the soul. She would go for periods of near normalcy only to drop into the abyss again. Those were the most terrifying days of my childhood, never knowing which mother I would find when I came home.

The shades in the Feldsher house were drawn, so I was not aware the sun had set. A woman knocked on the partly closed bedroom door and peeked inside, saying it was time for Havdalah. Rabbanit Feldsher rose slowly from her chair, her joints popping and creaking.

"We cannot leave Rayna alone," she said. "Someone must stay here by her."

The woman at the door volunteered. I did not want to leave my mother's side, but the woman quickly ushered me out of the room right behind the rabbanit.

Rav Feldsher was waiting for us downstairs in the dining room. He had changed his pants and was preparing Havdalah to mark the end of Shabbos and the beginning of the new week. This service had always been one of my favorites. It lasted only a few minutes and I enjoyed lighting the braided candle and passing the little bag of spices around. But I could not concentrate on Havdalah this night with my father lying in the funeral chapel and my mother suffering alone upstairs, watched over by a stranger.

Rav Feldsher extinguished the Havdalah candle by laying it on its side and pouring wine over the wick. We then dipped our pinkie fingers in the wine and lightly wiped our eyebrows, wishing each other a good week. I could not imagine a more inappropriate blessing. It was not going to be a good week. How could it be?

Rav Feldsher left the dining room. I listened as his footsteps faded down the dimly lit hallway, followed by the cawing of a rusty door hinge and the clack of a latch.

Mrs. Resnick said, "This has been a very sad day for you, Zev. So you will stay by us tonight, yes? We will go to your apartment and gather your things and I will bring some clothes back here for your mother."

The last time I stayed with the Resnicks was about two years ago when my mother was hospitalized for the third time. I did not want to return there. This is what I dreaded most. I politely told her I wanted to stay with my mother. Mrs. Resnick said she did not know if that would be possible and then looked to Rabbanit Feldsher. The rabbanit told me I should go upstairs, so I did. I heard the two of them speaking in hushed Yiddish as I climbed the steps.

In the bedroom, the woman who was supposed to be watching my mother was sound asleep, snoring loudly. I stepped lightly past her chair and knelt next to the bed. My mother had not moved since I left her.

"Eema, it's Zev," I whispered. "Eema, please talk to me."

She did not respond.

I lay down next to her and brought my lips close to her ear. I could smell the stale sweat rising from under her sheitel.

"Eema, please, it's Zev. Please say something. I am afraid."

With that she rolled slightly onto her side, her head still partly pressed into the pillow. My mother was beautiful, even in this disheveled state with her red eyes and the wrinkled imprint of the pillow on her smooth skin.

Indeed she was a remarkable beauty, and of this I was always aware. As a young boy I saw the men stare at her as we walked down Kingston Avenue. Hasidic men are taught never to make eye contact with a woman who is not their wife, lest they be tempted into lustful thoughts. They are taught to always keep their distance, not permitted even to shake hands, and yet the men stared. The women stared, too. It was not my mother's fault. She had the kind of face and figure impossible to conceal beneath a polyester sheitel and the most modest of clothes.

She had been smuggled from Poland as a baby at the start of World War II and had no memories of her parents, or of the British camp she was sent to, or of the succession of foster homes she was placed in. She was a soul with no past, but whatever horrors my mother experienced followed her to Canada, and eventually the United States. Beauty was Rayna Altshul's curse and saving grace. She had been a paradox since childhood—this amazingly lovely girl who would almost certainly bring any man his share of heartaches.

Her beauty proved irresistible to my father, who followed his heart and not his head, ignoring the advice of the matchmakers. He was part of the Kindertransport. His parents and immediate family all perished in the Nazi Holocaust, so Meir Altshul had only his better judgment to struggle against when choosing a wife, and struggle he did until this very day of his death.

"Please talk to me, Eema," I pleaded.

My mother opened her eyes.

"Nisht mer," she muttered softly in Yiddish. "Nisht mer."
I could barely hear her.

"What are you saying, Eema?"

"Nisht mer," she said again, much louder this time.

"What do you mean, *no more*? Why are you saying that?"

"Nisht mer ... Nisht mer," she repeated, raising her voice almost to a shout.

"Nisht mer."

The woman in the chair stirred just as Rabbanit Feldsher entered the room. My mother went silent.

"Ah, so Rayna is awake?" the rabbanit said. "Das iz gut."

The woman in the chair stood up, looking both confused and embarrassed. The rabbanit approached the side of the bed and stroked my mother's sheitel, which shifted under her touch.

The rabbi would like to speak from you," she said to me. "Mrs. Perlow and I will stay by your mother now. You should go downstairs to the rabbi."

I did not want to leave, but did as I was told. Rav Feldsher was sitting alone in the parlor reading a Jewish newspaper.

"You have had nothing to eat this evening?" he asked.

I shook my head no.

"Then we should fix you a little something," he said. "Is some cold chicken in the icebox, perhaps some kasha."

I nodded, although I was not hungry.

"The service is tomorrow at two o'clock and we will sit shiva in your parents' apartment before sundown. Your sister is driving here. I don't know from her husband, but is best for her to sleep in the apartment. So tonight you will stay by the Resnicks, yes?"

Alarm spread across my face. Rav Feldsher seemed puzzled and annoyed by my reaction.

"So what is wrong from this?" he asked.

"I don't want to stay with the Resnicks," I insisted, practically in tears.

The rabbi's eyes narrowed, and who could blame him? The chutzpah of this arrogant little Shabbos breaker, so ungrateful to those who had been so kind to him.

"And why is this?" he asked, again stroking his white beard in the habit of the men of our community.

I answered the rabbi with a half-truth. I would not tell him the real reason.

I said, "I want to be near my mother. I can sit with her during the night and be a help to the rabbanit."

"Is all well and good," he answered, "but Mrs. Klein and Mrs. Perlow are here. Your mother will be cared for and tomorrow we will see if she is doing better, yes? So is best you should stay by Mrs. Resnick tonight."

I don't know where I found the nerve, but I continued pleading my cause.

"Please, Rabbi," I said in Yiddish, trying to evoke as much sympathy as I could. "Please, it would make me feel so much better to be close to my mother tonight."

He did not answer me immediately, but his head subtly bobbed up and down, if not in agreement, at least giving consideration to my request.

Finally, he said, "So I should speak from this by the rabbanit. I suppose you could use our Yaakov's old room across the hall from your mother. Now go by Mrs. Resnick and collect your things from the apartment. We should decide this when you return, yes? Now go in the kitchen and eat something."

I thanked the rabbi profusely and did exactly as he told me.

Mrs. Resnick did not look at me while she fixed me a plate. I thought she must have been upset because I did not wish to stay in her apartment. I was sorry, but the insult could not be avoided. I was not about to tell her the truth, just as I did not tell Rav Feldsher the truth. In fact, I have told no one what I am about to disclose and I am revealing it only so you may better understand the actions I would take in the coming days, to judge if I was wise or foolish, if I sinned or acted reasonably.

I was nine years old when I stayed with the Resnicks the first time. I would have preferred to stay at home with my father, even though I knew this was impossible with his work and evening duties at the shul. They took me in again when I was thirteen and I stayed with the family for nearly three months that time. Their apartment was already over-crowded, so Mrs. Resnick made a bed for me on the floor in the living room. When the lights went out, there was only the china wall clock to keep me company with its incessant tick-tocking and loud chimes on the quarter hour.

This I got used to.

Mr. Shmuel Resnick I never got used to.

He was big and rough and I was afraid of him. He paid almost no attention to me when I stayed with them the first time. I did not expect him to treat me like one of his own children, but he barely acknowledged my existence, as though he resented every breath I took in his home. I felt like such an intruder, tiptoeing around the apartment, always on my best behavior, not daring to even open the refrigerator without first asking permission.

The troubles began the last time I stayed with them. Shmuel Resnick pretended to be kind but cursed me when no one was around, calling me schmendrick and hoizer gaier, all sorts of insults, saying he should make me clean his toilet to pay for all the food I ate. I did not dare speak up or complain. Shmuel Resnick was a direct descendent of the Baal

Shem Tov on his mother's side, respected by all in our community, a man of many responsibilities. He was in charge of the Rebbe's Sunday Dollars.

The stacks of dollar bills were brought to 770 from the bank before Shabbos, and every Sunday thousands of visitors, Jews and non-Jews, lined up to receive a freshly minted bill from the Rebbe's hand along with a blessing. The long lines moved fast and lasted several hours, with bills peeled rapidly from the stacks like playing cards shuffled from a deck. The Rebbe often gave more than one bill to a person— sometimes three, four, or five to a child. It was impossible to know exactly how many dollars were given out.

One Sunday, I caught Shmuel Resnick stealing from the Rebbe. I was sick and did not go to yeshiva. He must not have known I was in the apartment when he came home with the paper grocery sack he had set aside for himself. He tried slipping the bills back in the sack when he saw me, saying he was only counting them and keeping them safe for the Rebbe, but the guilty look on his face told me what he was really up to. Even at that age I was good at spotting liars, having had so much practice myself.

He said, "So what do you think? Is none of your business here."

I stood in the doorway staring at the money in his hands.

"So go already," he shouted.

I swear, I was not trying to be obstinate, but for some reason I could not move. Without warning, Shmuel Resnick lunged from his chair and grabbed me by the throat, lifting me off the floor and pinning me to the wall. I tugged at his wrists, struggling to pull his hands away, but he was much too strong.

"So you should shut up your big mouth," he snarled through clenched teeth. "If you say anything from this, I will kill you and your meshuggeneh mother too. Your father would be better off without the both of you."

He tightened his grip and pressed his thumbs deeper into my windpipe. I was afraid my eyes were about to pop from their sockets when he suddenly let go and I dropped to the floor, desperately sucking in air.

He said, "It would be a mitzvah to kill you, Hoizer Gaier."

This was not the end of the cruelty I endured in his house and I have been terrified of the man ever since. So this is why I did not want to go to the Resnicks, and why I was so relieved when Rav Feldsher agreed to let me stay close to my mother that night.

Miryam Resnick accompanied me to my parents' apartment, where I filled my school backpack with clothes and underwear and she packed a small suitcase with things for my mother. On our way back to President Street she told me how proud my parents were of me, how my mother was always talking about her little Zevi. I know Mrs. Resnick was trying to comfort me, but this only made me feel worse.

We rang the doorbell at Rav Feldsher's house and Mrs. Perlow escorted us into the parlor. She then directed me down the dark hallway to the study, where the rabbi was waiting. He was shuffling through papers on his desk, although I got the impression this was not so much business as the appearance of business. He asked me to close the door behind me. Rav Feldsher cleared his throat, then took a sip from his wineglass and cleared his throat again.

"I have given this matter much thought," he said. "I have spoken by the rabbanit and we believe it is best you should spend the night by the Resnicks."

"But you said I could stay here in Yaakov's room," I protested, using a tone of voice the rabbi was probably not accustomed to hearing.

"No, I did not say this, only that I would consider it. Now we will not discuss this matter further. Is in no one's best interest and is only a distraction from the difficulties ahead. Your mother is very ill and will be going to the hospital tonight. Is obvious we cannot care for her here, and we cannot postpone this, not even until morning. Tomorrow we should discuss a more permanent solution, and if for some reason the Resnicks are not suitable, we will find another place by you. Can you agree, Zev? Is what your father would have wanted, no?"

I nodded in submission.

"The Rebbe is very aware of your needs right now and is praying. Is nothing else to be done at the moment, do you understand?"

The decision had been made and I had to face facts. My mother was going back into the hospital and I was on my way to the Resnicks again. I had naively hoped she might be well enough to come home after a good night's rest. I see now these were the foolish wishes of a child.

Shmuel Resnick was in a foul mood when we arrived at the apartment on Kingston Avenue. He greeted me coldly, having already been inconvenienced enough by having his wife yanked away on Shabbos. Now the interloper had returned, my unwanted presence reminding him he was not nearly the pious Jew he pretended to be.

Mrs. Resnick began making up my little pallet on the living room floor. Her son, Mendie, my classmate, pulled me aside and the other boys gathered around. I had reluctantly achieved some fame within the yeshiva and the boys wanted to know how my tournament went. I begged them not to mention it again, especially not in front of their parents.

We played Scrabble until bedtime and then I waited my turn as the seven family members used the apartment's single bathroom. I spent what seemed like hours listening to the endless ticking of the clock and the clanging of steam pipes. I lay there in the dark, begging Hashem to let me take my father's place in the grave, trying to will him back to this world, envisioning him knocking on the Resnicks' door, saying, "*Come Zev, we are going home*," yet knowing full well Abba would never be taking me home again.

I was used to waiting for him, all those nights alone in my bedroom, listening for the sound of his key twisting in the lock, signaling his return after working late into the evening for the Rebbe. One night, as he was preparing to leave for 770, I asked why he had to be away from us so often. I was very young and Abba answered gently. He tilted his head slightly to the side and smiled as he explained.

"There is always work to be done, Zevelah. The world must be made ready for Moshiach and the Rebbe cannot do everything from this by himself. As great as he is, he needs many hands. Yours and mine. Our hearts must be willing. We await Moshiach, but that does not mean we sit passively. If we sit and do nothing, Moshiach will not come, so we do acts of charity, perform the mitzvot. We plow the field so when the soil is ready, the plants may spring up. Do you understand what I am saying to you? If the ground is hard, nothing will grow, so we must follow the Rebbe's example and till the soil."

"But can't you stay home with us tonight, just this one time?" I asked.

"Yes, I could stay home. I can always stay home; this is a choice, but the world will be a better place when Moshiach comes—better for you and Eema, better for all Jews, better for the goyim too."

"Can I come with you tonight?" I asked, making sure to wear my most convincing pout.

"On most nights it is not possible, but tonight we will see, yes? Tonight, it may be possible."

Abba told me to wait in my room as he lifted the receiver of the kitchen wall phone and began dialing. A moment later he came to the bedroom door and told me to put on my jacket. We left my mother standing at the sink with the dinner dishes. She uttered a weak goodbye, her sad eyes brimming with disappointment.

Abba held my hand as we walked along Eastern Parkway, the night air so chilly for early spring. When we passed 770, I asked why we were not going inside.

He said, "Our business is elsewhere tonight. It is almost Pesach, and there are many families with no means to prepare a decent Seder."

On the next block, Abba pointed to a cramped passageway between two red brick apartment buildings.

"This is where we are going," he said.

We descended five worn concrete steps below street level. It was dark and I was afraid. I squeezed my father's hand tightly as we threaded a narrow gauntlet of smelly garbage cans on the way to a low-ceilinged basement alcove lit only by one dim lightbulb. He knocked on a thick metal door but did not wait for an answer as we stepped into a large well-lighted room full of men packing boxes with groceries. They greeted my father warmly.

"So I see you've brought a little helper with you tonight, eh, Meir? I'm sure we can find a job for him," the gabbai, Shlomo Gittelman, said.

One entire wall of the room was stacked with cartons of Osem Israeli Matzah. My father opened several cartons and told me to make sure I kept the tables where the men were assembling the food boxes well stocked. I felt so proud to be working alongside them.

At about eight o'clock the metal door creaked open and the Rebbe entered the room accompanied by his secretary and five men who were not wearing yarmulkes. Two of them took notes, another took photographs. No one was expecting a visit from the Rebbe, and work in the basement came to a halt. This was very unusual.

The old tzadik slowly raised his hand, not in a gesture of authority, but graciously, as if offering a benediction.

"Please," he said, "do not stop what you are doing. This is not a menial task. Pesach is almost upon us and we are about to celebrate the liberation of our people, our freedom from four hundred years of bondage in Egypt, but we cannot celebrate fully as long as there are Jews who are hungry and cannot keep a kosher Seder. In the Haggadah it is written, *All who are hungry come and eat; all who are needy come and celebrate Pesach.*' So, you see, what you are doing is a great mitzvah. It is no small thing. You are working on behalf of all Jews everywhere."

The Rebbe fixed his gaze upon me and smiled at the only child in the room. He approached and kissed his hand before touching it to my forehead as one might kiss a mezuzah. I do not believe he recognized me as Meir Altshul's son.

He said, "As our sages have pointed out, it is only because the Hebrew children in Egypt received a proper Jewish education that our entire nation was liberated from slavery. It is because of these very children, and Jewish children of every generation, that the Torah was entrusted to our people."

The Rebbe bent forward, lowering his head almost level with mine. His eyes were the deepest blue, somewhat clouded by age, yet sharp and clear. He gently grasped my chin and said, "Mazel tov, young man. May Hashem grant you and your dear family true liberation from anxiety and want this Pesach."

At that moment I desired nothing more in life than to serve the Rebbe and do mitzvot like my father. He was kvelling with pride as we walked back to the apartment later that night. It was well past my bedtime, but Abba did not seem to mind.

"Won't Eema be angry with us?" I asked.

"She will get over it," he said. "You received a special blessing from our Rebbe tonight, a blessing for our entire family. This is more important than a few hours of sleep."

"Can I come with you again next time, Abba?"

"I cannot say at the moment, Zevelah. It may not be possible next time. Some tasks are not suitable for a child. Nothing is more important than doing mitzvot, but there are also things I must do that are not so pleasant as making Pesach boxes. I do this for you, and Frayda, and Eema, to provide for our family. This is a mitzvah too."

I pictured my father's gentle smile, a tenderness that was not always so obvious. This sweet memory came rushing back to me as I lay on the floor of the Resnicks' living room after skipping shul to play handball. My sins of the day returned in a wave of remorse, and my grief finally found an outlet in tears for my dead father and helpless mother—and for my wretched self, the worst of all faithless sons.

The phone rang in the early morning hours, sounding like a faraway alarm bell. It rang for quite a while before Shmuel Resnick answered. I could not make out any part of his conversation, but he soon came into the living room and told me to hurry and get dressed.

"We are going to see the Rebbe," he said, none too happily.

"The Rebbe?" I replied in utter disbelief. "Why are we going to the Rebbe?"

"Just get dressed," he said. "The Rebbe wants to talk with

you and I need to take you to 770."

770 Eastern Parkway was, and is, considered a holy place. To be summoned to 770 by the Rebbe was like being called to Mount Sinai by Moses. You cannot imagine it. The Rebbe was the embodiment of God on earth, morally perfect, infinitely wise. When he spoke it was like the voice of God himself. What could the Rebbe possibly want with me?

Early on Sunday morning the streets of Crown Heights were not empty as one might expect in other neighborhoods of the city. Jewish businesses were opening for the week and children were on their way to cheder and yeshiva. I walked next to Shmuel Resnick in silence with the tension between us like a frayed tefillin strap, the leather stretched to the point of snapping. At that moment I realized two things about the man who might once again have charge of me until my mother got better. First was how much he despised me, and second was how much I terrified him. I had not seen that fear in him before.

At 770, the Rebbe's secretary, a white-bearded rabbi of some stature, greeted us. I was immediately separated from Shmuel Resnick and escorted to the Rebbe's office. Rav Feldsher was seated in a straight-backed chair, and the Rebbe sat behind his heavy wooden desk, which was piled high with books, papers, and religious tracts. A metal folding chair had been placed between the two rabbis. Rav Feldsher pointed to it and invited me to sit.

I surveyed the room with a mixture of awe and bewilderment, marveling at the modesty of its oak floors, dark paneling, and simple bookshelves running most of the way to the ceiling. It did not at all look like the mystical inner sanctum of the holiest man on earth.

The light streaming through the upper row of leaded glass windows was as clear as the Rebbe's eyes, but the lower windows were protected by wire security grates, reminding me that *Gan Eden Ha'Elyon*, as the Rebbe's study was known—*The Highest Garden of Eden*—was in Crown Heights, Brooklyn.

The Rebbe stroked his white beard just below the corners of his mouth while making a chewing motion, as if trying to loosen food from his teeth. He spoke to me in Yiddish, his voice radiating kindness like the warmth of the sun on an early spring day.

"I was deeply grieved to hear of the loss of your father, may his soul rest in peace, but the ways of Hashem are not for us to question."

I nodded in agreement, although Hashem's judgment did not seem very fair to me.

"As you know," he continued, "a created being cannot fathom the ways of its Creator. It is impossible, just as a very young child cannot comprehend the teachings of a learned scientist. However, the great scientist was at one time a child himself, and the present child may one day grow up to become an even greater scientist. Do you understand what I am saying to you, Zev Altshul? We are created in God's image, however a created being has nothing in common with its Creator in regards to knowledge and intelligence. The Creator completely transcends the created, so it is not surprising that a finite being cannot comprehend the infinite."

I think I understood the Rebbe's analogy.

"I know this does not minimize your loss and pain," he said. "It is never easy to accept the passing of a near and dear one, and now I must add further to your sorrows. It grieves me beyond measure to tell you. . ."

The Rebbe's blue eyes were moist.

"There will be two burials today," he stated plainly. "Your mother . . . may Hashem grant her peace."

These words set upon me with the ferocity of the Angel of Death, tearing apart what was left of my tattered soul. I could scarcely believe what I was hearing. My mother was supposedly being looked after in Rav Feldsher's home.

"But they told me she was going to the hospital," I said.

"Your mother took her own life. A great tragedy, and it is better we do not dwell on such things," the Rebbe said, passing me a box of Kleenex.

"It is our duty as Jews to spread the light of Torah and do mitzvot in this world. This morbid topic is not conducive to the good works that should fill one's life, especially a young man whose entire life is ahead of him."

"But how could this have happened?" I asked. "They were supposed to be watching her."

"The answer will not be helpful to you, and these are not matters we generally speak of," the Rebbe replied.

"Please, she is my mother. I need to know what happened."

The Rebbe stroked his beard, making that chewing motion again while considering my request.

"Some hidden things are best not brought to light, Zev Altshul. They only distract us and cause us pain and burden our hearts. But so as not to leave your question completely unanswered, I will tell you she did this quickly."

"But how did she do it? Please tell me."

The Rebbe seemed troubled by my persistence, but turned to Rav Feldsher and nodded slowly, granting him permission to elaborate.

"I do not know another way to say this." The rabbi paused as if trying to find the words to continue. "Your mother, may her soul find peace . . . your mother hung herself in the upstairs bathroom of our house. The rabbanit found her hanging by one of her stockings. The police were called. They did their investigation and your mother is in Shomrei Hadas with your father. There is no point in saying more."

I slumped forward in the chair, my head resting in my hands, overcome with memories of my parents and the realization that I was now an orphan. Nothing more was said as I wept, the two older rabbis sitting silently for several minutes in the highest tradition of Jewish mourners.

When I regained my composure, the Rebbe spoke again.

"One who willfully takes his own life has no share in the world to come. You know this, yes? We are commanded not to mourn for them. We do not sit shiva. There are few transgressions that carry so great a judgment."

A sudden fury began rising within me. I believe the Rebbe may have sensed this as he continued speaking.

"However, of this the most learned rabbis are all in agreement: a person must be of sound mind in order for such an act to be considered willful. Your mother, may Hashem have mercy on her soul, was clearly not of sound mind when she took her life, so we will mourn for her as we mourn for your father. May Hashem have mercy on both of them."

I did not find the Rebbe's words comforting. I know it is a further sacrilege for me to admit this. How dare I, a snot-nosed little Yid, barely beyond my bar mitzvah . . . how dare I not esteem our Grand Rebbe's every word?

Rav Feldsher spoke up again, saying, "Arrangements have been made at Shomrei Hadas and the burial is at Montefiore later this afternoon. Everything is done and paid for and we will begin sitting shiva in your parents' apartment before sundown. Mrs. Resnick and the others will provide everything you need. The Hasidim mourn with you."

"And what about my sister?" I asked.

"Your sister can stay in the apartment when she arrives. . .If she arrives

"Can I stay there with her?" I asked.

"No," Rav Feldsher replied, leaving no room for bargaining. "This would not be good for you. Frayda is off-the-derech and no one has seen her in many years. Is no telling . . . and you do not need any more distractions right now. You should better stay by the Resnicks, at least until a more permanent arrangement can be made."

"But I don't want to go to the Resnicks," I said, fully aware of how whiny I sounded.

Rav Feldsher exhaled forcefully in a loss of patience. He asked me to explain myself.

"The Resnicks have been good to you in the past, no? This does not seem reasonable."

I stared down at the floor, not knowing how to answer. The Rebbe interceded.

"It is difficult to make important decisions under such circumstances as these. I am confident a little time will be of great help to you, and you will see many things in a different light in the coming days. But it is most essential that you see in the light of Torah and not in the wisdom of the gentiles, which is darkness and not light at all."

The Rebbe's next statement knocked the wind from me.

"I have heard of your prowess with the game of handball," he said, as matter-of-factly as if he were acknowledging the sky is blue.

Many Lubavitchers believed our Rebbe was as omniscient as Hashem himself. Others said he had eyes and ears everywhere. Either way, nothing happened in Crown Heights without him knowing of it. So the Rebbe knew of my handball playing? Did he also know I desecrated the Sabbath yesterday and ate treif at the handball court? He leaned closer as he continued his discourse.

"Some Jews have particularly sensitive souls, and with

those even the most minor of infractions will produce great anxiety, but even the ordinary soul of the average Jew is troubled by failure to observe the fundamental mitzvot. To rectify matters, one must bring one's daily life and conduct into complete harmony with the essence of the Jewish soul through strict adherence to Torah and mitzvot."

And then he asked me the most puzzling question:

"So do you like baseball?"

I told him I did. But how would our Rebbe know anything about baseball, and why would he care if I liked the game or not?

"Then you know of the great pitcher, Sandy Koufax? He was the youngest player ever inducted into the Hall of Fame."

Of course I knew about Sandy Koufax. Everybody did, especially Jews. Koufax was a hero of our people, but I was still surprised the Lubavitcher Grand Rebbe knew so much about baseball.

"And so you know Sandy Koufax refused to pitch in the first game of the 1965 World Series because it was being played on Yom Kippur, yes? Sandy Koufax is not a frum Jew, but he is a Jew nonetheless. Hashem bestowed a special gift upon him, but Sandy Koufax knew that the mitzvot take precedence, even over such a gift. Do you understand what I am saying to you, Zev Altshul?"

I understood.

I felt the warmth of the Rebbe's palm spread across my forehead as he blessed me, and left 770 on the day of my parents' burial feeling somewhat better after talking baseball with the holiest man on earth.

"You were a long time from in there," Shmuel Resnick said as we stepped out onto Eastern Parkway. When I did not respond, he probed further.

"You were more than an hour. So what did the Rebbe want from you so long?"

When I shrugged off this question too, Shmuel Resnick grew impatient.

He said, "So what are you, a big macher now? You would not have been to see the Rebbe if your parents were alive. Nu? It takes many months to have yechidus by the Rebbe. One must make preparation first. Little pishers with big mouths do not have yechidus by the Rebbe."

I could almost smell the nervous fear on him.

I said, "We spoke of other things too, not only my parents."

"Oych a beshefenish!" Shmuel Resnick snickered, quite proud of his great wit. "So what then, you were debating Talmud by him? I am sure it must have been very enlightening. Two great scholars, I could just see it!"

"No," I said. "We were not speaking about religion."

"So what then?" he asked.

His weakness gave me an opening.

I said, "The Rebbe wanted to know about all the money you stole from him."

The sun was very bright on this Sunday morning, the sky a most translucent shade of blue. I smiled to myself as the darkest of clouds gathered around Shmuel Resnick's head. He stopped laughing and turned away from me, fixing his eyes straight ahead.

I have no idea what prompted me to say what I did, but my timing was perfect, delivered as naturally as truth, as convincingly as if I had planned it in advance. At least in Shmuel Resnick's mind, he had just been exposed as a thief and shamed before our Rebbe, disgraced before God.

We continued along Kingston Avenue in silence. An orthodox man swept the sidewalk in front of his kosher market, and the scent of fresh-cut lilies wafted from the open door-way of Crown Flowers as we passed. We were in the middle of the next block before Shmuel Resnick spoke again.

"The Rebbe would never believe you," he said in a more sober tone, still avoiding eye contact. He was desperately try-ing to appear confident, but his slack-jawed expression told me everything I needed to know.

There are great lessons to be learned from handball. It is more than just a simple game. You learn to observe your op-ponent carefully. You learn when to feign weakness, when to show strength, and when to strike with lethal force. You must always play your opponent three steps ahead, setting him up, placing him in just the right position for the kill.

I said, "I would not be so sure what the Rebbe believes if I were you."

I did not know where my boldness came from. Shmuel Resnick struck an even more aggressive posture, a complete-ly false show of bravado. Many players talk trash when they know they are in trouble.

He said, "Do you take me for an idiot? You would never tell this to the Rebbe, and if you did, I would kill you and you can go join your father and meshuggeh mother in the grave at Montefiore."

Shmuel Resnick was a powerful man, but I had defeat-ed stronger players before. Quickness and agility are better weapons than strength, but the best weapon of all is cunning, and in this Shmuel Resnick was no match for me.

We were about to pass under a blue banner spanning the street between two light posts: MOSHIACH IS ON HIS WAY—LET'S BE READY!

I said, "The Rebbe is aware of everything you did. He will be watching you from now on."

"Feh," Shmuel Resnick replied, trying to disguise his unease with a gesture of utter disgust before pivoting and heading off in the opposite direction down Kingston Avenue.

By two in the afternoon a sea of black hats filled 38th Street in front of Shomrei Hadas, more than the chapel could hold. Two white-draped caskets sat side by side at the entrance. A lectern and microphone had been placed at the foot of the caskets, where rabbis, gabbaim, and other important men were milling about.

I stood off to the side near the loudspeakers, scanning the crowd for my sister, searching for any woman dressed in worldly clothing, unsure if I would even recognize her after all these years. Beyond the spreading circle of men, scarved and sheiteled women, many clutching handkerchiefs to their faces, gathered along the sidewalks. They kept their distance, not allowed to press in. I did not see my sister among them.

Rav Feldsher stepped toward me and firmly grasped the left lapel of my suit jacket. He reached into his pocket, took out a single-edge razor blade, and made a small cut in the jacket's lapel and another in my white shirt.

I recited the Keriah prayer in Hebrew: *"Blessed art thou, O Lord our God, Ruler of the universe, the True Judge,"* and then tore both garments as we are commanded to do, hoping their rending might also open up a tender place in my heart.

Rav Avram Koretz took to the podium and read psalms and blessings. I was standing directly in front of one of the loudspeakers, but the prayers sounded far away, like entreaties for someone else's parents from somewhere on another Brooklyn street. I continued to search for my sister amid the swelling crowd that had now closed down 14th Avenue.

Reb Dovid Greenberg, my father's friend since yeshiva, stepped to the microphone and delivered his eulogy in a quavering voice:

"Meir Altshul's entire life revolved around the Rebbe and mitzvot. If the Rebbe asked something of Hasidim, it was Meir's duty and pleasure to fulfill it, whether this meant hanging a Moshiach banner in front of the yeshiva or in his faithful service as one of our most beloved gabbaim . . ."

Reb Greenberg went on for several minutes without once mentioning my mother, other than to say my father remained devoted to her despite many difficulties.

Anger once again overwhelmed my soul. Was it because my mother was ignored, treated as an appendage of my father, or was it because I was such a deficient son, unable to properly mourn my own parents?

I stared down at my hands and the thick calluses I had earned by smacking the hard rubber ball millions of times. At Coney Island I once saw an older player put a cigarette out in his palm to win a bet. Back then I could not wait for my own palms to become as tough as his. I hit straight through the pain and bone bruises until my hands became like bricks, although, on this day of my parents' funeral, I was less proud of the calluses covering my heart.

The pallbearers hoisted the coffins onto their shoulders and the sea of mourners parted for the two hearses. I kept searching for my sister as the procession solemnly made its way up 14th Avenue. We had been estranged for so long, perhaps she decided not to make the long journey to Brooklyn after all?

When Frayda left, I believed she had disgraced our parents. I could not comprehend what had drawn her away from our family, why she wanted to attend art school or, worse yet, marry a gentile. The last I heard she had changed her name and no longer lived as a Jew.

What strange gods ensnared the hearts of these Altshul children, as if Sodom and Gomorrah lured us away from either end of Eastern Parkway? Frayda's Sodom was the Brooklyn Museum near Grand Army Plaza, and my Gomorrah, the handball courts in Lincoln Terrace Park. This was not how our parents raised us. I was almost relieved they were no longer alive to be disgraced again, this time by me.

I sat between Rav and Rabbanit Feldsher in the back seat of the funeral car as the procession made its way down Ocean Parkway through Gravesend to Coney Island. We passed within blocks of the Seaside Courts, the 770 of handball, no more hallowed ground in the city for a one-wall handballer. I had snuck away many times to watch the greats play there.

As I gazed out of the limousine window, I wondered what was happening at the tournament I had forfeited yesterday. The finals would probably be wrapping up about now. Did anyone there ask what happened to the little Jew in the yarmulke? Could they know he was about to bury his parents?

It took almost an hour for the procession to arrive at Montefiore Cemetery in Queens, the number of mourners only a fraction of what it was in Brooklyn. I followed the pallbearers to the freshly dug graves, again searching faces for any sign of my sister. A silver car slowed at the road closest to the gravesite and my heart began beating faster. I could not see inside the car because of the glare on its windows. *This must be her*, I thought, but the car continued on its way without stopping.

"You said Frayda was coming," I whispered to Rav Feldsher, who was turning pages in his prayer book.

"Nu, is what she told me," he responded. "Who knows? There could be many reasons."

"Can we wait a little longer?" I asked. "What if she is on her way?"

"Is impossible," the old rabbi said, shaking his head. "Shiva must begin before dark, otherwise it will be an extra day.

Mrs. Resnick is preparing the apartment for us now. Are you ready to recite the Kaddish?"

As the only male family member, I was responsible for leading the mourners' prayer for the dead at the end of the service. I told him I was ready.

Rav Feldsher read psalms, and then Reb Yosef Mendelssohn, a gabbai who served with my father, delivered another short eulogy. Rav Feldsher read the Tzidduk H'din and I said Kaddish, then the cemetery workers lowered my parents into the ground, slowly letting out the cloth straps until each casket hit bottom with a gravelly thud. Several at the graveside wept. I had not shed a tear since that morning in the Rebbe's study and this troubled me deeply.

Burying the dead is a mitzvah for Jews, especially the deceased's closest family. In our tradition we take turns shoveling dirt into the grave until the lid of the coffin is covered. Rav Feldsher motioned for me to take the shovel first. I turned it upside down, using the back of the blade as mourners do to signify our reluctance to part with our loved ones. The hollow drumming of the stones striking the wooden lid shook me like a sudden rumble of thunder.

When we arrived at the apartment, lights were glowing warmly and the dining table was set with food. Throughout the evening, Hasidim, many of them strangers, came to pay their respects and to eat Miryam Resnick's honey cake and sandwiches. She would make a good mother to anyone, but the thought of living under the same roof as Shmuel Resnick again was not a thing I could entertain for even a second.

The crowd on that first night of shiva spilled from the apartment into the hallway. Shmuel Resnick arrived late and alone. He huddled outside the door amid other men, not showing his face in the living room or coming anywhere near me. I was no longer afraid of him. He was now my inferior, a soundly defeated opponent who had lost all authority, like an older A-player well past his prime who still imagines himself king of the courts. I despised Shmuel Resnick for his pitiful weakness.

By nine thirty most of the visitors had left. Miryam Resnick was straightening up when my mother walked in the apartment door. I swear I thought it was my mother, so lovely and youthful, full of life and the beauty Hashem had given her. I almost shouted out in my excitement.

Frayda had arrived late, the very image of my mother when she was at her best. Those remaining in the apartment went still. I could not tell if this was because the wayward Altshul girl had returned in all her immodest glory, or because Frayda's presence would have made any room go silent, even with the frowsy schmatta she wore to cover her hair.

"Zev, is that you?" she said, bursting into tears. "I can't believe it's been so long . . . You're practically a man now."

The bulging wall holding back my pent-up sorrows cracked and then split wide open, tears for our decimated family bursting from me. Frayda and I embraced like I wished we could have at our parents' graves. The visitors in the apartment stared at the modern American girl hugging the Hasid, not knowing the proper emotion to show and so showing none.

"I'm so sorry, Zevi," she said. "I tried to get here in time. Every minute on the interstate was like hell."

Frayda spoke in English using contractions, without any hint of the singsong Yiddish cadence so noticeable when many Lubavitchers speak English.

"I wanted to be with you at the funeral. I'm so sorry you had to go through it alone. How's Eema? Where is she?"

I froze, forgetting that my mother was still alive when

Rav Feldsher spoke with Frayda last. She had no idea both our parents were now dead.

"What?" she asked. "What's wrong, Zev? Is something wrong with Eema? Was she hurt too?"

I shook my head no.

"Well, what's wrong then? Is she ill again?"

I believe Frayda may have already guessed what I was unable to say out loud. I tried my best, but those first awkward words would not come. I took her by the arm and led her to my bedroom, away from the others, struggling with how to break the news. The facts of my mother's death were cold and hard, and I could not think of a gentler way to tell her.

"Eema killed herself," I said. "She did it last night. We buried both of them today."

I will never forget the look on my sister's face at that moment. I have thought about it many times in the years since. It was the most complex expression I have ever seen on another human being, a mingling of horror, grief, and shame, capped with the briefest hint of a smile. It was so fleeting, I doubted my own eyes, but I will never forget that faint flash of a smile before the tears ran down her cheeks. It was another of the great mysteries of my sister that I would gradually come to understand, as I would come to understand myself.

"I loved Eema," she said. "But stepping into this apartment and seeing those people again . . . the women standing off to themselves. I could never live like this. I knew it when I was a little girl, long before I met Paul. I had to leave, but that didn't mean I didn't love Eema . . . Abba too. And you, Zevi, I loved you. I've never stopped thinking of you all these years."

"I have never stopped thinking of you either," I replied in English, aware of how differently I had just pronounced those same words. Although I was born in Brooklyn, like so many Crown Heights Jews, English was not my first language. We speak mainly Yiddish at home and in yeshiva, and Hebrew in synagogue. Compared to my sister, I sounded like I had just come over on the boat.

She said, "I don't go by Frayda anymore. I changed my name legally to Frida, like the artist, Frida Kahlo. Most of my friends call me Free. That's how I feel being away from Crown Heights. I'm sorry if this upsets you."

I said, "It will be difficult, I mean, not calling you Frayda. Will you stay for the seven days?"

"I don't think so," she said. "I'll stay tomorrow and maybe Tuesday and after that we'll see."

Just then Miryam Resnick knocked softly and entered the room.

She said, "It is getting late and I must get back to my own children. Come, Zev, you can see Frayda tomorrow."

The tenderness I usually heard in Mrs. Resnick's voice had vanished, replaced by a dry matter-of-factness, as if she were reading from a set of instructions. My sister's back stiffened. It was plain these women were suspicious of each other, like two cold war soldiers on opposite sides of a border crossing.

"But Frayda just got here," I said. "I mean Frida."

My sister smiled.

"Can I stay here with her, please?" I asked.

"This has been decided," Mrs. Resnick responded. "Rav Feldsher explained this before already. You will get to see Frayda all day tomorrow."

I was about to reply when my sister broke in.

"That's just fine, Zevi, we'll see each other in the morning. Let's not make a big deal of it tonight."

"But I want to sleep here in my own bed."

I turned to Mrs. Resnick.

"Please, can I?" I asked again.

She sighed and said, "I can call the rabbi, but he will not be pleased to hear from me at this hour. Do you really want me to disturb him with this all over again?"

The honest answer was *Yes, I did*, but I did not object any further. I knew Shmuel Resnick would not dare lay a hand on me again after the kill shot I dropped on him earlier. I actually relished the thought of him squirming at the sight of me, and hoped he would look over his shoulder for the rest of his life in fear of a rebuke from the Rebbe.

"And you will stay here in the apartment then, yes, Frayda?" Mrs. Resnick asked, smiling feebly. "So you will know to find everything?"

"I'm sure I'll manage," she said, taking off her headscarf and mussing her hair.

Miryam Resnick tried her best to uncurl the edges of her frown, but could not disguise her disdain for Frayda's immodesty. All married Lubavitcher women wear sheitels.

"This scarf was the best I could do." Frayda smiled.

The streets of our neighborhood were full of worldly shiksas and nonobservant Jewish women in their short skirts, tight jeans, and showy haircuts. These women were no threat to Miryam Resnick, but my sister had been one of us. She was a living challenge to everything Miryam Resnick believed.

"I'm very tired," Frayda said. "So let's catch up tomorrow, Zev. Why don't we have breakfast together, just the two of us, before people start getting here. Come early."

Mrs. Resnick stood at the door with her arms tightly folded across her chest. She obviously did not approve of me spending time alone with my sister, but I sensed something else smoldering inside her. She was unusually sullen on the walk back to Kingston Avenue, and as we were about to enter her building, her displeasure finally combusted in a flash of anger.

"Enough of this already," she shouted. "Enough of this. I will speak with the rabbi tomorrow and we will find another home for you."

I was glad to hear I would not have to be around Shmuel Resnick much longer, but Mrs. Resnick continued pouring out a flood of complaints.

"Did I not take good care of you, and was I not good to your mother when she needed me in the past? I will tell you, Zev Altshul, others pushed your mother away, but I did not. I never did it! And I have always been fond of you too, and now look, here I am neglecting my own children for you. Instead of cooking for my family, I am schlepping in your parents' house, and all I hear from you is how you do not wish to stay with me. What, we are not good enough for you? I am not looking for thanks. It is a mitzvah to be of help, but I do not understand why you are so against me."

Mrs. Resnick's words cut deeply, but there was no way to explain my real reasons for not wanting to stay in her apartment.

"I am not against you," I said without much conviction. "You have always been kind to me."

This seemed to infuriate her all the more.

"Nu?" she said. "So what, then, this is the way you behave when someone has been kind to you, has taken you into their home when you have nowhere else to go?"

I was in an impossible situation. I could not tell her the truth about why I was so opposed to staying with her family again.

"I am sorry," was the only response I could muster.

I wanted to add that she should not take it personally, but felt too foolish to say such a thing. How could she not take it personally?

In part, I was trying to protect her by keeping her husband's secret to myself, but I had selfish reasons as well. To accuse Shmuel Resnick of being a thief would almost certainly bring more trouble upon me than anyone. Who would be believed, a descendent of the Baal Shem Tov, or a Shabbos-breaking handball player? I decided to allow Miryam Resnick to think the very worst of me, the ungrateful brat who is concerned only about his own comforts and whims. Tomorrow she would speak to Rav Feldsher and that would be the end of it. I would be gone and she could go on with her life.

When we entered the apartment, the Resnick children were already in their bunk beds with the lights out. Mrs. Resnick made up my air mattress on the living room floor. I offered, but she would not accept help from me. I listened to the clock ticking away and had not yet fallen asleep when I opened my eyes to see Shmuel Resnick standing over me with his fists clenched and spittle flying from his lips. I sat up and placed my hand in front of my face.

"So what then?" he growled. "Nu, you come into my house, a little hoizer gaier, and eat my food and spread your fucking chazerei to my children, to Mendie . . . you and your goyische sports mishegoss. And you accuse me of things, those things we both know I did not do. And now you upset my wife? Miryam is crying in our bedroom because of you, you son of a bitch. Crying for what? So the free food you eat is not good enough? The fucking nerve of you, dover akher! I would break your neck right now, you stinking piece of drek, you rotten piece of shit. I would break your neck right now if not from your father's memory, his death so soon . . ."

He went on railing and cursing in Yiddish and English, taking full advantage of every nuanced insult in both languages. I had clearly underestimated my opponent and should not have counted him out so quickly. I had seen broken players rally before. Just when you believe they are thoroughly down and defeated, all it takes is one quick return, a comeback point or two, and the next thing you know, they are cleaning the court with you.

He said, "I am going to speak with Rav Feldsher myself tomorrow and we will see how brave you are then. I will let him know what kind of fakaktah little orphan he has on his hands and let him take you in himself if he thinks you are so wonderful. No one will want you after what I am going to tell him, so you can go to a foster home and good riddance. I will be happy to see you in a foster home with the schvartzes. I should throw you out in the street tonight and let you sleep with the bums in Prospect Park, but this is the end of my kindness.

"You are never welcome in this house again and Miryam will not lift a finger by you tomorrow . . . I forbid it. You and that veltz kurveh sister of yours can take care of yourselves then. And I would think again before you make up any more stories by me, you son of a bitch. I do not believe you told our Rebbe a goddamn thing, but even if you did, I will speak by him also from this and then we will see if you go on speaking lashon hara from me."

Shmuel Resnick then smacked me on top of the head and kicked my pillow across the room before storming off. I retrieved the pillow and tried to compose myself, but my heart was pounding in my chest and my pajamas were clammy with sweat. Sleep was impossible after such pleasantries. I seriously considered getting dressed and returning to my parents' apartment, but it was too dangerous to be out on the streets alone in the middle of the night in Crown Heights, and it was unfair to wake Frayda because of the problems I had caused.

I lay on the air mattress trying to sort out my dilemma.

At least I would not have to live with Shmuel Resnick, but he was right, *Who would take me in?* Perhaps Rav Feldsher could find someone through one of the Chabad relief agencies, although it was hard to imagine living with total strangers. It might have been better if I had just kept my big mouth shut when Shmuel Resnick taunted me earlier in the day. Now what was I going to do?

I considered running away, but where would I go? I had spent my last sixty dollars entering the tournament, money saved from almost two winters of snow shoveling. I did not have enough left to buy even a bus ticket. Then I remembered my sneakers. I had left them in the stairwell over a day ago, and this distressed me more than anything.

I waited until dawn, packed my few things, and unlatched the apartment's triple door locks. I felt terrible about not saying goodbye or thanking Miryam Resnick for her kindness. Shmuel Resnick could rot in hell.

The dawn sky shimmered in orange-and-blue waves as I walked the length of Eastern Parkway to Lincoln Terrace. The park was deserted except for a lone jogger. The only evidence of the weekend tournament was the trash waiting to be swept up by sanitation workers. I sat in the middle of the court where I beat the big guy from the Bronx. The next court over was where Harry Rosenfeld handed me his card and told me to call him if I was serious about my game. I wondered if he still wanted to hear from me after the hole I left in the quarterfinals and maybe his wallet.

I sat on the cold, unforgiving concrete contemplating my immediate future, realizing I had none—not as a handball player nor as a Jew in Crown Heights. I had no hope for better days, with both my parents dead and my money and sneakers gone. I was likely on my way to a foster home, maybe a hellish place worse than the Resnicks'. Frayda was my only hope.

I walked directly to our apartment and took the elevator to the fifth floor and then the stairs up to the roof landing. Just as I had feared, my sneakers were gone. I hurried down to the basement, where the superintendent kept a row of metal garbage cans outside the boiler room. I took off my jacket and shirt and began riffling through the cans. A disgusting job. I turned up plenty of unusual items, including a ratty old sheitel that looked like the one worn by Mrs. Kirzner on the third floor, but no sneakers. I tried telling myself this was not the worst thing that could happen. I had played handball in street shoes before. I could do it again.

I brushed the filth from my arms as best I could, but did not put my shirt back on. I climbed the stairs to the fourth floor, hoping to avoid running into anyone who might question why a boy sitting shiva would be running around in his undershirt, up to his armpits in garbage. I knocked on our apartment door before opening it with my key.

There was my sister standing in our narrow galley kitchen with the morning sun streaming through the window behind her. She was wearing my mother's terry cloth bathrobe. It reminded me of when Eema was healthy and I would enter the kitchen first thing in the morning to find her cooking breakfast.

Frayda took one look at me in my soiled undershirt and her eyes widened comically.

"What in the world, Zevi? Look at you . . . and you stink. I can smell you from here. What, did you sleep in the street last night?"

"You look just like Eema," I said.

Frayda pulled the collar of the robe to her nose and inhaled.

"I even smell like Eema," she said. "It's the strangest thing.

51

I remember her smell, even after all this time. So many memories in this house. It's not like I thought it would be. I don't know, I sort of wish I would've come back sooner . . . maybe to visit Abba and Eema. But they wouldn't have seen me, would they?"

Frayda's eyes glistened and her voice cracked through her smile as she spoke.

"You really should go take a shower, Zev. No one's going to want to come near you like this."

"But we are not supposed to bathe until the seven days of mourning are finished," I said.

"Yeah, well, I think you're going to have to stretch the rules a little on this one. So what in the world were you doing to get so messed up?"

"I was looking for something in the garbage downstairs."

"What's so important to go through the garbage?" she asked.

I thought I noticed a slight Yiddisher inflection in her voice, as if being back in Crown Heights had stirred some long-dormant part of her memory.

"It was nothing," I said, attempting to deflect her inquiry.

I did not want to tell her the story of how I lost my sneakers, still afraid my Shabbos sins had brought this terrible judgment upon our family.

"So what was it?" she asked again. "I don't believe you went diving into the garbage for nothing."

"I was looking for my sneakers," I said, hoping this would satisfy her and she would leave it at that.

"And why would your sneakers be in the garbage?" she asked.

I intended to tell her only the sparest account of my latest predicament, just enough to satisfy her curiosity, but when I began speaking, it all came spilling out.

I said, "I left my sneakers in the stairwell so Abba wouldn't find out I played handball on Shabbos. I was going to lie to him. I left them in the stairs and now they are gone."

"So you broke Shabbos playing handball?" she said, trying her best to suppress a grin.

"Yes, and I played for money . . . in a tournament. And I was hungry so I ate treif . . . a Sabrett hot dog with mustard and sauerkraut."

Frayda laughed out loud.

"I'm sorry, Zev, your sincerity is so cute, really. It's admirable."

"This is not funny," I said.

"Well, I'm sure these aren't the worst sins Hashem has ever come across," she said.

"I did other things too. I did not go to shul with Abba and Eema."

"OK, so things happen," she said.

"But I did all this right in front of the goyim in the park. This could be a chillul Hashem."

"So then you'll ask forgiveness," she said. "Come on, Zevi, it isn't the end of the world."

"But that is not why I feel so terrible. I hate to even say it . . . I am afraid Abba is dead because of the things I did."

"Don't you ever say that!" she shouted. "What happened to Abba could've happened to anyone, you know that, don't you? And Eema has always been depressed. This wasn't the first time she tried to kill herself, you know. When you were very small . . . they didn't want to worry you. She could've done this ten years ago or a year from now; don't you see this is how life goes? It has nothing to do with you playing handball on Shabbos. You really think it's payback every time someone dies in an accident or gets sick? Hashem must be a very mean God then. Does that really sound reasonable to you?"

"There is nothing that happens without his knowledge," I replied.

"Well, that kind of stuff makes no sense to me and it hasn't for years," she said. "This whole vengeful God bullshit makes no sense at all. You really think Hashem created us and then invented a million silly rules we couldn't keep just so we'd break them and be punished?"

"They are mitzvot," I said. "They are not silly."

"Well, plenty of them *are* silly. Tell me you think it makes sense not to tear a square of toilet paper on the Sabbath? You really think Hashem cares about that? I hope he has better things to worry about than tearing toilet paper. And the rabbis debate this nonsense endlessly. You can't turn on an electric light or tie a shoelace or write a letter on Shabbos? Come on, this is crazy. It's mishegoss."

That was the first time I heard a Yiddish word from Frayda since she arrived.

"But this is how we do it," I said. "Jews have always done things this way."

"And that makes it right? So a Jewish woman has to wear a wig that looks like real hair to cover her real hair? And why is that, so a man might not be tempted with impure thoughts?"

I laughed, not because of what Frayda said, but because Mrs. Kirzner's old sheitel that I just dug out of the garbage looked nothing like real hair.

"Maybe they should make the men wear blindfolds instead," she said. "Listen, Zev, I'm not trying to change your mind about anything. You should go on living just as you are if that's what you believe; I just don't want you blaming yourself for what happened to Abba and Eema. It's not healthy for you."

Then my sister broke into a grin again.

"So you really played handball on Shabbos?" she asked.

"It was a big tournament," I replied with a certain amount of satisfaction. "I did not want to, but all the tournaments are on the weekend and I will not improve unless I play the tournaments."

"And how long have you been playing handball?" she asked.

"I played Ace-King-Queen in the backyard before you left. I think I started playing handball right after. Maybe seven or eight years."

"Yeah, and you're good at it?" she asked.

"I am pretty good at it now," I answered with false modesty, then went on to tell her about the first two rounds of the tournament and what Harry Rosenfeld said to me afterward.

"He was going to bet money on me, Frayda. This is a famous player who was going to bet money on me."

"Very good, but remember my name's not Frayda anymore," she corrected me. "I understand it's not the easiest thing when you've been calling me Frayda your whole life, but you'll get used to it."

I said, "And I have another problem I should tell you. Rav Feldsher will not be happy with me, but I cannot stay with Mrs. Resnick anymore. I need to stay here with you tonight. I have no place else to go."

She said, "I don't understand. Why can't you stay with the Resnicks? It can't be that terrible over there."

I did not tell my sister the truth of why I dreaded staying in that apartment. I let her believe the same lie I told Miryam Resnick.

"It was all my fault. I said bad things to them. I am sorry for what I did, but I cannot stay there again, not even one more night. They are very angry with me."

"Well, I don't care if you stay in the apartment with me,"

she said. "I mean, I'd like you to stay here . . . it'd be fun. We have a lot of catching up to do, but the problem is I don't think I'll be in Brooklyn after tomorrow. What'll you do when I leave?"

I knew I would ask her sooner or later. I was just waiting for the right moment and this seemed to be as good as any.

"Can I come live with you?"

My sister's eyes popped wide open again and she raised her voice.

"Zev, are you crazy? That's impossible."

I said, "But you are my only family now. I have no one else. Shmuel Resnick said they will put me in a foster home."

"I won't let you go to a foster home, but you can't live with me. You can't live like this in Urbana," she said, pointing up and down at my clothes. "We don't keep kosher. I don't know anyone who does. We have only one set of dishes. We eat pork."

"You eat pork?" I asked incredulously.

"Yes, and shellfish. I'd eat lobster every day if I could. It's delicious."

I said, "There must be other Jews there . . . where you live."

"Yes, there are Jews," she said. "But none like you. I've never seen another Hasid, and what would you do about school? How old are you now, sixteen?"

"Fifteen," I said.

"OK, so you're fifteen, and what have you learned at yeshiva besides Torah and Talmud? You can't go to public school . . . What grade would they put you in?"

"What grade did they put *you* in?" I asked.

"It was different for me. I was older and didn't have to be in school. I couldn't even point to Illinois on a map when I moved there, but I studied at home and got my GED."

"What is that—GED?"

"It's a test you take, like a high school diploma. I couldn't have survived in high school."

"So I can get a job."

"Doing what? You're fifteen years old."

"I could do something," I said. "I'll be sixteen next month."

"No one's hiring you at fifteen or sixteen looking like *that*."

As soon as those words left her mouth, I could tell Frayda wished she could take every one of them back. She picked up a sponge and began busily wiping the kitchen counter. I caught the faint odor of the dry-cleaning chemicals my father carried home on his clothes. That smell always drifted in and out of the rooms of our apartment, like the phantom trace of my breakable mother, now wrapped in old terry cloth around Frayda. The souls of my parents were like those fading scents, seeping through cracks in the walls and out onto Eastern Parkway.

Frayda stopped wiping and turned to me.

She said, "I'm sorry, Zev, I didn't mean it to come out that way. Really, I'm sorry. All I'm saying is it's completely impractical, you moving in with me. It's a different world. As much as I'd like to have you, it's an unworkable situation."

"Are you ashamed of me?" I asked, glancing down at my garbage-stained undershirt but thinking of the black fedora sitting on my head and the unruly fuzz sprouting from my cheeks. I would gladly make some adjustments if it came down to a choice between living in a foster home or in Illinois with my sister. Frayda rubbed her forehead and scrunched her eyes closed as if wishing the entire mess would go away when she opened them. The hesitation before she replied told me more than her denial.

"Of course I'm not ashamed of you," she said. "You're my brother."

Ashamed or not, she was right. Living with her in Illinois was a crazy idea. Frayda was my only flesh and blood, but we barely knew each other anymore, and in my entire fifteen years I had scarcely set foot outside of Brooklyn. I could not even name a single TV show or popular singing group, and had never read a novel. I knew almost nothing of world history, geography, or science, and my knowledge of English grammar and mathematics was only slightly better. I did not belong in high school, yet was too big to sit behind a desk in a fifth grade classroom. I was a lost boy with one foot on the handball court and the other in yeshiva, but a home in neither.

Frayda made a curious clicking sound with her tongue, something like a tsk-tsk, possibly directed at herself.

She said, "I'll have to call Paul to discuss this with him. It's an hour earlier there, but he could be up by now. I want you to go to your room so I can speak privately with him, OK? It's not fair to put him on the spot, so give me some space while I make the call."

"Really, you are going to call?"

"Go, Zev."

I thanked her and almost trotted to my bedroom, closing the door behind me. Until two days ago, this tiny room was my home; now I looked around at the stark white walls trying to find one comforting object, one item I was attached to. There was nothing. My handball gloves were still stuffed into my jacket pockets. When I dug them out, Harry Rosenfeld's card dropped onto the bed. I picked it up and read the name over and over, reciting it almost as a prayer. I pulled on my gloves and cupped my hands over my nose, inhaling the familiar smell of dried sweat and worn leather.

After quite a while Frayda knocked on the door. Her robe opened up when she sat down on the bed, exposing one of her bare legs to the middle of her thigh. I looked away.

She said, "Well, I talked to Paul and I think we must both be crazy, but he's agreed we can give it a try."

"Really?" I replied, my voice a sigh of relief.

"I want to be sure you understand we're just trying this out. This is what Paul and I agreed to. There are no promises, OK?"

"Thank you, Frayda."

"It's Frida."

"Sorry . . . thank you, Frida."

She said, "I just can't stand the thought of my only brother going to a foster home. I'm not sure how we'll deal with this. There's one synagogue in Champaign–Urbana. I've never been there, but maybe we can get the rabbi to help in some way. Maybe they'll know something about school or tutoring, I don't know."

"I promise I won't make trouble," I said.

"Yeah, I'm sure," Frida said while smirking at my handball gloves. "I'm sure you'll be no trouble at all. So you go shower now and I'll make some breakfast, then we'll go talk to Rabbi Feldsher."

"We cannot go to Rav Feldsher today," I said. "We are supposed to stay in the house for shiva."

"I can't stay here for seven days, Zev, I already told you. I'll call him after breakfast. Now go take your shower."

Frida left for the kitchen and I got undressed. We are not supposed to bathe or put on clean clothes for the seven days of shiva. There are exceptions, but I could not remember them all. I was not sure if the rules of mourning applied to someone who has been rummaging through garbage cans. I showered and put on clean underwear and socks, but did not change the white shirt or jacket I tore at the funeral or the black pants I tore at the tournament.

Frida set freshly toasted bagels on the counter and water was boiling for tea. We sat in the windowless dining room with the painting of old men dancing with the Torah hanging on the wall behind my sister's head.

"You look much better, Zevi," she said. "You know, you've grown up to be very handsome."

I may have blushed at her comment. I had always considered myself awkward looking, especially now with the sparse tufts of facial hair on my cheeks and chin. The mirrors throughout the house were all covered, as is the tradition during Jewish mourning, so I could not look to see if anything had changed. I would have told Frida how pretty she was, but I was too embarrassed, and anyway, I am sure she already knew.

"We'll need some advice," she said. "I have no idea what to do about you legally. I mean, you're underage. I don't know if you can just come live with me or we have to get papers signed or what. Maybe there's someone around here who has experience with this sort of thing."

"I don't want you to ask," I said. "They will not want me to live with you because you are off-the-derech. That is why Rav Feldsher did not want me to stay in the apartment with you."

"Well, he's not your flesh and blood, is he? Do they have a better place to send you?"

"They will not like that you eat pork and do not go to shul and that your husband is not a Jew," I said.

"Paul isn't my husband."

At first I did not understand what she meant.

"He might as well be," she said. "We've been living together since we left Brooklyn. We just never thought the piece of paper was that important."

"So you are not married?"

This was going to be an even bigger problem than I thought.

"But you asked his permission to take me."

"No, I did not ask permission," Frida replied. "That's not the way things work in the real world. We discussed your coming to live with us, how it would affect our lives and if it would be good for you. Paul and I come to decisions together. There's no asking permission. What, you think every woman needs to ask permission to breathe? Only in Crown Heights."

"I think the Rebbe will want me to stay here," I said.

"But you don't want to, do you?"

I said, "Not with the Resnicks. I do not want to live in a foster home either, but I do not want to stop being a Jew."

"How can you stop being a Jew?" Frida asked. "You can't stop being a Jew any more than a black person can stop being black. I'm still a Jew, just not the kind of Jew who's afraid to tear confetti on Shabbos. You remember that, my confetti collection?"

"I was not born yet, but I remember Abba and Eema always talking about it. I think they thought it was funny."

"Yeah? Well, it wasn't so funny to me. I remember Abba trying to explain why tearing and sorting little bits of paper on Shabbos was wrong. He cited the goddamn Talmud to a five-year-old."

It hurt my ears to hear my sister say "*goddamn Talmud.*"

I said, "The Rebbe knows I play handball and that I did not keep Shabbos. He talked to me about Sandy Koufax and the World Series. I think the Rebbe might like baseball."

She said, "No offense, Zev, but the way everyone bows to

the Rebbe around here is just crazy in my opinion. You know he eats and shits and farts like everybody else."

I tried to keep from smiling. I had never heard anyone speak of the Rebbe farting before and I did not think this was funny, but I could not help myself. I could clearly see adapting to my sister's faithless world of goddamn Talmuds and farting rebbes was not going to be easy, but I worried much more about being sent to live in a foster home with a stranger who could not care less for me.

"Do they play handball in Illinois?" I asked.

"I'm sure they do," she replied. "I don't know anything about it, but we'll find out. The U of I is a huge school. They have sports of all kinds there."

"I hope they have good players. Harry Rosenfeld says I need to play in tournaments. You know the Rebbe did not forbid me to play handball. He wants me to keep Shabbos, but he did not say I should stop playing handball."

"We'll get it figured out, Zev; now let's call over to 770."

I stood next to Frida as she dialed the wall phone in the kitchen, the only phone in our apartment. The operator at 770 said he could not connect her directly to Rav Feldsher but would locate him and have him call back. My sister hung up and said she was going to take a quick shower.

"There's no telling when he'll be getting back to us," she said. "If he calls while I'm in the shower, tell him to call again in fifteen minutes and be careful about what you say to him."

The phone rang as soon as Frida stepped into the shower. I stared at it, not sure if I should answer. I finally picked up after the fourth ring. Rav Feldsher asked how I was and I told him I was fine.

He said, "So I have spoken from Shmuel Resnick already..."

The rabbi waited for me to respond, but when I said nothing, he continued.

"So is now out of the question for you to stay by them. This makes matters more complicated . . . complicated for all of us and I think what happens next will not be so satisfactory from you. I have some people working on this now as we speak. I am hoping by the end of the day. Is a very sad situation, but you will need to cooperate. It may not be a perfect arrangement."

"I am going to Illinois with my sister," I said.

Rav Feldsher sighed into the receiver, clearly exasperated with me. He raised his voice.

"Is not a good thing! You need to live among Jews, and your sister, as lovely as she is, does not live as a Jew. The Rebbe is concerned from you. Is not in your best interest."

I said nothing.

"Hello, are you still there?" he asked.

"Yes."

"Please let me speak to Frayda," he said.

"She is taking a shower."

"So listen, I must speak with Frayda before you make such decisions. You are a minor and she is not your legal guardian. You cannot run off with her."

Just then Frida entered the kitchen, dripping wet in my mother's robe.

"She is here now," I said to Rav Feldsher.

Frida motioned for me to hand her the phone. I could hear a muffled voice through the earpiece, but was not able to make out any words. She listened for a long time, occasionally shaking her head and answering yes or no. She eventually picked up the pad and pencil my mother kept next to the phone and wrote down a number. She sounded put out when she finally answered the rabbi.

"OK, fine then," she said, "but you're not his father and

63

there's nothing on this earth that gives you or the Rebbe the right to make decisions for either of us. I'm not a child that you can order around anymore. I'll call you after I speak with the lawyer."

"Ugh," she said, hanging up the phone and rolling her eyes. "He pretends to be so nice and reasonable: *'Oh, we only have your best interests at heart, blah, blah, blah,'* but it's bullshit. He's patronizing and manipulative like the rest of them; he acts like he's speaking for God, and then has the nerve to tell me I don't have the means to take care of you. Well, he knows nothing about me."

Frida looked at what she'd written on the pad.

"He gave me the number of this lawyer, Yosef Fishbein. The guy supposedly does a lot of work on this kind of stuff. Feldsher wants me to call him, says it's to help with the legalities, things like Abba's estate, whatever there is of it. I'm going to go ahead and get dressed and then we'll call this guy and see what he has to say. We already know who he's working for, so I'm not expecting any real cooperation."

Frida went into my parents' bedroom to get dressed and I stood at the kitchen window looking down at the traffic flowing along Eastern Parkway. I remembered when I needed to stand on a chair to see over the sill. I had lived in this apartment my entire life and it was not going to be easy to leave.

Frida returned to the kitchen and dialed the lawyer. She held the receiver away from her ear this time so I could hear most of what he was saying. Yosef Fishbein offered his condolences and then explained the orthodox laws of inheritance.

"The laws are very clear," he said. "All property is divided among the male children, so whatever your father owned goes to your brother. This would include any bank accounts and insurance, if there is any. Since he is a minor, this must be placed under the control of a legal guardian, and since no guardian has been established, we must do this before the estate can be settled.

"Your father did not have a will regarding his property, and as you may know, a secular will is not halachically valid anyway; however, your father left papers at 770 regarding his wishes for your brother's guardianship. He wanted Zev placed in the care of Shmuel and Miryam Resnick, as he was when your mother was incapacitated in the past. I understand from Rav Feldsher that there is now a problem with this, yes?"

"That's right," Frida replied, shaking her middle finger at the receiver. "Just a little one. Zev doesn't want to go there and they don't want him."

"So there are other options Rav Feldsher is working on."

"My brother's coming back to Illinois with me," Frida said.

"This may not be so easy," Yosef Fishbein replied. "And I would advise against it until a court has decided. Your brother's legal status will have to be determined and the standard is always what is in the best interest of the child."

"I want to go with my sister!" I shouted at the receiver. Frida passed the phone to me. "I want to go with my sister," I repeated in a more normal tone.

"That is all very well," Yosef Fishbein said. "The courts will certainly consider your wishes; however, that has no bearing on your present status as a minor. You cannot just pick up and go wherever you please. Your sister must petition the courts to be your legal guardian, and as your older sibling, she has every legal standing to do so, but there are many other factors a judge will take into consideration. They will want evidence of your sister's parenting ability, the stability of her home . . . The courts usually try not to disrupt a minor child's existing routine. I have handled many such cases for the Rebbe. In my opinion, it would be best for you and your sister to first sit down before the beis din and work this out in an agreeable fashion, then filing with the state will be much easier."

Frida took the telephone from me.

She said, "Thank you, Mr. Fishbein, you've been very helpful. We'll call again if we need to speak with you, thank you."

She said goodbye and hung up the phone.

"So what do you think?" she asked me. "Here's another momser like Feldsher who pretends to be nice and helpful. If we take his advice and go to the beis din, you really think they'll send you to live with your unmarried OTD sister and her shaygetz boyfriend?"

I told her I didn't think so.

"So what do you want to do, Zev? We can let Rav Feldsher decide everything if that's what you want. It's up to you. When I was your age, I was sure I wanted to get the hell out of here, but maybe you don't feel that way. I don't want to be the one putting thoughts in your head; that's not fair. You can stay here, or we can go. You decide. Just tell me what you want and we'll do it, OK?"

I knew I did not want to live with the Resnicks or some Hasidic family in Crown Heights trying to do mitzvot by taking in an orphan. Frida's bitterness toward our laws and traditions frightened me, but I belonged with her, whatever tsuris that might bring me.

"So what do you want to do?" she asked.

I said, "I think we should leave now, right away. I think we should get in your car and go before the mourners get here and we have to explain anything."

"Jesus, Zev, that's not what I was expecting," my sister exclaimed.

Now this Jesus was new to me. We never mentioned the Christian god. Ever. Frida could see her off-the-cuff remark made me uncomfortable.

She said, "Forget it, Zev, we can do this. I'm totally up for it. Go pack your things and we'll get the hell out of here. Is there any money in the house?"

"Just Eema's coffee money," I said, referring to the coffee can she kept under the sink.

"Well, whatever's in there, you should take it."

"Are you sure?" I asked. "I don't want anyone to say I stole something."

"No one's saying anything, and besides, the lawyer told us it's rightfully yours. Come on, let's get going."

My school backpack was already full and I had nothing else to put my clothes in. Abba had an old suitcase I remembered from a weekend trip we made to the Catskills years earlier during better times. He told me he carried it with him on the boat from Europe. I rooted through his bedroom closet and set the suitcase on my bed. Its brown leather covering was worn and tattered. One corner was dented. It looked like it had been around the world.

I went through my dresser drawers and took out my white shirts, black pants, underwear, and socks. All my clothes looked the same. I don't know why I never noticed this before. Even my two pairs of pajamas were both blue, except one had a yellow dreidel embroidered on the front, a gift from a past Hanukkah.

I pulled two brand-new handballs from my bottom drawer along with my gloves and protective eyewear, and set them on the bed next to my tzitzit and tefillin. These conflicting objects told the story of my life. They had been pulling me in opposite directions for years, and now here they were sitting side by side on the bedspread, ready to share a suitcase, as if some truce had been drawn between them.

I unlatched the suitcase and opened the lid. Inside was a black plastic garbage bag. I lifted it out. The bag was heavy. I untwisted the top and turned it upside down to empty it. The bag was full of money. Lots of money. Bills bound with rubber bands in stacks about an inch thick tumbled onto my bed. I shouted for my sister, calling her by the wrong name again in my excitement. Frida came hurrying and stopped abruptly in the doorway when she saw the pile of money.

"What's this?" she asked.

"Money," I answered.

She rolled her eyes.

"Obviously, but where did it come from? Where'd you find it?"

"In Abba's suitcase in his closet."

"What would Abba be doing with this kind of money?" she asked.

I had no idea. I always thought we were poor. My father was constantly complaining we had no money.

I said, "Maybe this is their life savings? They never told me anything, so how would I know?"

Frida stepped to the bed and stirred the pile of cash as if trying to make sure it was real. She picked up one of the bound wads and flipped through the bills.

"How much do you think is here?" she asked.

"It looks like a lot," I said. "What are we going to do with it?"

"What do you think we're doing with it? We're not leaving it here for the vultures to pick through; we're taking it with us. However Abba got the money, it's yours now anyway, so put it back in the bag and finish packing and let's go."

I carried the suitcase full of clothes along with my backpack and the bag full of money into the living room. I set them down under the picture of the smiling Rebbe, trying not to look up at him. Frida brought out a fresh garbage bag from under the kitchen sink. She put the other bag inside it and tied the top tightly.

"We don't want this splitting open in the street," she said. "Are you sure you've got everything?"

Her question sent my mind spinning. I had taken nothing to remember my parents by. Shouldn't I go through the apartment and find a memento, a keepsake, something of theirs to hold on to? I asked Frida if she wanted to take Eema's bathrobe.

She said, "Why would I want that old thing?"

"I don't know," I replied, feeling foolish for asking. "Maybe just something to remember Eema?"

"I have my memories," she said. "We should go now. We can probably make it all the way back to Illinois in one go if we leave right away."

She unlocked the deadbolt and opened the door to the empty hallway.

"Do you think we should leave a note?" I asked. "There will be people coming soon."

"What for?" Frida said. "How many of those leeches do you think really care about Eema and Abba anyway? Plenty are only coming to do mitzvot. They're coming for themselves to score brownie points with Hashem."

I had never heard the term *brownie points* before, but knew exactly what she meant and her comment bothered me. I wondered why Frida felt such a need to lash out at our upbringing. What made her so angry?

On my way to the door I caught a glimpse of our family menorah sparkling in the breakfront. I opened the curved glass door and held the silver candle stand in my hands.

"Let's go," Frida said. "Take it if you'd like."

I opened Abba's suitcase and pressed the menorah into it, using my knee to hold the lid down while I latched it, then followed Frida into the hallway. I shut our apartment door and touched the mezuzah for the last time, saying a silent goodbye to the ghosts of my parents and my life as a Jew in Crown Heights.

We walked to Frida's car, parked a few blocks away. She carried the garbage bag full of cash and pulled her wheeled valise along. I wore my backpack and carried my father's suitcase.

A Hasidic man approached from the opposite direction. It was Akiva Goldscheider. I recognized him from shul and he was one of the visitors in the apartment the night before. He kept plenty of distance between himself and Frida, who was not wearing her headscarf. I caught him looking her up and down before he made eye contact with me.

Akiva Goldscheider was the mashgiach—the supervising inspector who makes sure all is kosher—in a slaughterhouse. He took obvious delight in his quick examination of my sister:

"No blemishes found on this one, no siree, this one is prime grade meat from only the forequarters . . ."

Akiva Goldscheider stepped aside to let us pass. He frowned at the garbage bag as if he knew what was inside it. His expression reminded me of the thin plastic masks worn by goyische children on Halloween. Underneath were the eyes of the mashgiach, whose job is to search out even the hidden faults, the condition of the internal organs.

I could almost read Akiva Goldscheider's mind:

So what are you two doing out in the street? Shouldn't you be in your apartment sitting shiva, as any good Jew would be with their parents barely in the grave? And why are you car-

rying your suitcases, running away from your responsibility as Jews, running away like two thieves?

I had seen this same judgmental expression on other faces in yeshiva and shul, the disdain for those they believe to be less frum than they are. I suddenly was glad to be leaving Crown Heights. In the middle of the next block, Frida took out her keys and pressed a button. The trunk lid of a silver car popped open. It looked very much like the car that slowed but did not stop at the cemetery. I do not even know why I paid attention to such a thing.

PART TWO

CALIFORNIA AVENUE: URBANA, ILLINOIS

The long drive was mostly uneventful, except for the truck stop in Indiana where we pulled over for a bite to eat. Frida was famished, but I was too nervous to be hungry. I had never been this far from home before. I thought Manhattan was a foreign country until we passed through the sliding doors of the gift shop on our way to the restaurant. This place was something else again.

Characters I could not imagine were speaking an American language with an accent I had never heard. Fat men in T-shirts barely covering their great bellies wore ball caps with pictures of racing cars and yellow ears of corn. There was even a green one with a deer named John printed on it. I had never seen people like this in New York City. They stared at my black coat and fedora as we passed rack after rack of cup holders and air fresheners. These men would have looked just as odd in Crown Heights as I did in their truck stop in Brookville, Indiana.

The hostess seated us and left to get our drinks. I heard laughter coming from across the room.

"Nothing in here will be kosher in the strict sense," Frida explained as I looked over the menu. "I'm just warning you now, so don't strain your brain too much trying to figure it out. I'd say if you want to be good, stay away from the barbeque or the ribs . . . Something like a tuna sandwich would be a pretty safe bet."

"What about mixing meat and dairy?" I asked.

"Like I said, nothing's kosher here. The plate your sandwich comes on probably had a cheeseburger on it right before.

Maybe we should check in the kitchen and ask the rabbi what he suggests."

"There is no rabbi here," I said, knowing she was only teasing me.

"You're catching on, Zev, so get used to your new life—here it is. This is what I warned you about. You won't be able to live like you did back home, no matter how you try."

We ate quickly and left, with Frida barely glancing in the rearview mirror as we pulled back onto the interstate. I could not help but think of the apartment and the mourners coming to pay their respects, only to find the door locked. I wondered what Rav Feldsher did when he learned we were gone. Did he inform the Rebbe, or just wash his hands of us—the OTD Altshul girl and her Shabbos-breaking younger brother?

It was almost midnight when we arrived in Urbana. I was sleeping when I heard the sound of gravel crunching under the car's tires and opened my eyes to see a weedy driveway illuminated in the headlights. Frida pulled past a darkened house and parked in front of a detached garage in need of a good coat of paint. Loud music was blasting from inside.

"That's Paul's studio," she said. "He's still working so let's go in and say hello. Just leave your stuff in the car."

"The money too?" I asked.

"It'll be safe in the trunk for now," she replied. "We have crime here, but it's nothing like Brooklyn."

She knocked on the side door of the garage and opened it. I squinted as we stepped into the bright light. Paul Griffin turned to greet us. His white T-shirt was stained with paint despite the canvas apron he wore.

"Hey," he said, coming over to kiss Frida's cheek, leaning in so as not to get paint on her. She rubbed her nose on his ear and then lowered the volume on the stereo.

"Hey, Zev, nice to see you," he said, holding his hands up to show they were in no condition to shake. "Let me clean up here and I'll meet you inside. It'll take me two minutes."

Stacks of canvases were leaned against the walls all around the studio and there were piles of drawings scattered on the floor. One tattered, overstuffed chair had been placed in the middle of the room facing a large painting in progress, maybe eight feet across and six feet high.

My eyes were still adjusting to the harsh spotlights, but I immediately recognized my sister as the woman in the painting. She was sitting in a chair in front of a dressing table in a dark and dirty room, completely naked, with her clothes draped over the back of the chair and her underwear strewn on the floor. A suitcase that reminded me of Abba's was open on a stand in the background shadows. A man's bare feet intruded from the right side of the canvas. He was lying on an unmade bed, and must have been asleep because the woman, my sister, was taking money from his wallet.

"Come on, let's go in the house," Frida said, grasping my arm and moving us toward the door.

She opened the car trunk and we carried our things inside. The kitchen floorboards creaked as Frida switched on the light. There were tchotchkes on narrow shelves everywhere, and little paintings covering nearly every inch of wall. Paul Griffin's dinner dishes were still sitting on the table. Frida picked them up and moved them to the sink to join the pyramid of unwashed dishes already there.

"He can be a bit of a slob," she said. "Sometimes, when he's in the middle of a painting, he doesn't come up for air and I'm lucky if he even comes in for dinner. That's how you have to be if you want to be a great artist."

"Do you still want to be an artist?" I asked.

"I thought I did when I left Brooklyn, but that was just

the dream of some little Hasidic girl who'd never been off the block. It's not like collecting confetti in egg cartons. You have to push yourself every day, and I just don't have that kind of drive. It comes naturally to Paul. I think he loves being in the studio more than anything.

"After I got my GED, I took art classes at Parkland and had a little corner of my own in Paul's studio; I'm not sure working next to him was such a good thing for me, though. Here I was making these pleasant little doodads . . . Those are some of mine over there next to the sink."

She pointed to a group of small paintings of bottles and cans.

"Those are really good," I said.

She blew air out between her lips and gestured as if she wanted the paintings to go away.

"Giorgio Morandi would be turning over in his grave," she said.

I had no idea who that was.

She said, "I didn't know any better. And then I had to work a job too. Paul wasn't making a lot when he was first hired and I had to pay for my classes at Parkland and help with the household expenses. I'd come home from work or class and cook dinner and then go out to the studio and Paul would be working on these monumental paintings right next to me while I was making these little nothings and all I wanted to do was talk to him and all he wanted was to concentrate on his work.

"After a few years I decided it wasn't the life for me. I still enjoy making things. I'm doing these little collages now, but I'm not an artist. It's more of a hobby and I'm probably better off that way . . . I don't know, maybe the world's better off without another half-baked dabbler. I guess I still don't know what I want to be when I grow up."

How could Frida not know what she wanted to be? At fifteen, I could hardly imagine life without handball. Could it be something I would grow out of in a few years too, a game I would play as a hobby? I had seen men in Brooklyn sacrifice everything for their love of handball, some of the best athletes in the world barely eking out a living going from court to court, hustling B- and C-players for a hundred dollars a game. If they played basketball or baseball they would have been rich and famous, yet they were unknown to anyone outside of the handball community. These were the rebbes of the street game and I wanted to be just like them.

Frida said, "Listen, don't mention Abba's money to Paul just yet, OK? I plan on telling him, but we should at least count it first and figure out where we're going to put it."

Just then Paul Griffin opened the kitchen door.

"It's time for a proper hug," he said, throwing his arms around my sister's waist and pulling her hips into him. I was embarrassed by this display, feeling like an intruder in their reunion. Then Paul came over and shook my hand, placing his other hand on my shoulder and giving it a squeeze.

He said, "Well, you've really changed since I saw you last; you've even got whiskers now."

The way he said *whiskers*, with more than a subtle hint of sarcasm, told me he was not a fan of them, but then neither was I. They were as patchy as the weeds poking up through the gravel driveway and a lighter color than the hair on my head. I knew my beard would come in heavy and dark like my father's one day, but Lubavitcher men never shave and we go through a particularly clumsy period on our way to adulthood.

Paul Griffin had changed over the last seven years too. I had met him only once. He was not welcome in our house, so Frida took me to a coffee shop to introduce us. The difference in their age was less obvious then. Now he looked much older than she did. He had put on weight and was getting a sizable bald spot on top. I was not sure what he saw in her back then, just as I was not sure what she saw in him now.

"I'm sorry to hear about your parents," Paul Griffin said, still not releasing my hand. "They weren't very nice to me, but I'd never wish anything like this on them. Having you here's going to be an adjustment for all of us, but we'll give it a try and make the best of it, OK? We can talk more in the morning if you'd like to get settled in. I have a faculty meeting at eleven and class after, but maybe we'll find some time before that."

Frida said, "I'm not going into work tomorrow. I think Zev can use a little company around here."

I told her I would be fine by myself if she needed to work.

She said, "I've just spent two whole days in a car, and I work at an arts-and-crafts store. It's not like I'm doing brain surgery; they'll get by just fine without me for another day."

Truthfully, I was glad to have her stay home with me.

"I don't know about you," she said, "but I'm really beat. Let's take your stuff up to your room."

The bedrooms were upstairs, with mine right next to theirs. Frida opened the door and fumed when she found the bed unmade.

"Damn it," she said. "I asked him to get the room ready for you. I guess this is what he calls ready. Let me get your sheets and a blanket."

She returned with the linens and we made the bed together, then she kissed me on my forehead and told me she was glad I was here.

I considered my skimpy "whiskers" in the bathroom mirror while brushing my teeth. The feathery tufts were no more attractive than the last time I saw them back in Crown

Heights. Then I realized the mirror should be covered for shiva and I should not be looking at myself. Back in the bedroom, I put on my plain pajamas, the ones without the dreidel.

I was about to slide the bag of money under the bed, but could not resist the temptation and opened it and dumped out its contents. I had never seen this much money. These were not the crisp uncirculated singles of the Rebbe's Sunday Dollars but worn bills of mostly large denominations. What was my father doing with all this money, and why was it stuffed into a garbage bag in his closet? Lubavitchers use banks just like everyone else, at least I thought we did, but Abba never discussed these matters in front of me. Perhaps he did with Eema.

It was a mistake to ponder such a mystery so late in the evening, and when I turned out the light my thoughts were still racing. I was afraid sleep would never come, but the next thing I knew it was morning and the bedroom was flooded with early sunlight. How strange to wake up without the rumbling of traffic on Eastern Parkway and the only sound the gentle warbling of a songbird perched on a tree branch outside the window.

I was unable to remember the rules for laying tefillin during shiva, but since we were not sitting shiva anyway, I decided it was OK. I got up and retrieved the blue velvet bag from the suitcase and reverently removed the arm tefillin first. I uncoiled the leather strap, then kissed the leather box and placed it in the middle of my right bicep, facing it slightly inward toward my heart. I said the Hebrew blessing and then tightened the strap around my bicep and wound it around my forearm seven times.

I removed the head tefillin and positioned the box properly above my forehead, then finished wrapping the arm strap around my fingers and palm after saying the second blessing. It felt good to be a Jew again and the mitzvah was a comfort. I recited the final blessing along with the Shema and the Amidah.

I heard pots and pans clanging in the kitchen and went downstairs to find Frida at the sink doing Paul's dishes from the night before. Three boxes of cereal and a bowl of cut fruit were set out on the table. She smiled at me over her shoulder when I entered the room.

"Hi, sweetie, did you sleep well?" she asked. "There's milk and juice in the fridge, just help yourself. Do you drink coffee?"

I told her I did, with cream and sugar, please, and she handed me a clean mug from the cupboard. I could not help noticing her breasts swaying as she walked toward me with the steaming coffee and the words SORRY I'M NOT LIS-TENING written in gold script across the front of her black T-shirt. Her nipples poked out proudly on either side of SORRY.

I felt unclean admiring any woman's breasts, especially my own sister's. We are commanded to avoid fleshly temptation, but Lubavitcher men are allowed no outlet for our urges until marriage, and I can say from my own experience this does not work very well from a practical standpoint.

"Who are you not listening to?" I asked, which allowed me to look more directly at her chest.

I am not proud of my sins. I confess them so you may see the state I was in upon beginning my new life in Illinois—the observant Jew who willfully profanes Shabbos, the son who brings judgment upon his parents, the pious one who lays tefillin and then stares at his sister's tsitskehs. This is who is telling his story. No one should feel sorry for him.

And on top of all this, I felt a growing resentment for

Paul Griffin. I told myself it is not fair to feel this way about the man willing to take a boy he does not know into his home. I said to myself, *You must bury these feelings*, but they remained bubbling beneath the surface like a pot of cholent.

Frida sat across the table from me cradling her coffee mug in both hands. She chatted away about Champaign–Urbana and Paul's recent promotion to associate professor, although I sensed she was biding her time before getting to the real matters she wanted to speak with me about.

"You remember I told you there's a shul in town?" she asked.

I did.

"There's only one, and it's reform. I don't know what they do over there, but I left a message on the rabbi's answering machine this morning."

"What for?" I asked.

She took a sip of coffee.

"I don't know, just to see if he can help us get acclimated."

"How do you mean?"

"Well, to begin with . . ." She paused midsentence and stared down into her coffee mug. "I'm not sure how to say this without hurting your feelings, but you're like a space alien here in Urbana, looking like this. People will be staring at you everywhere you go, even in shul . . . So I'll just come right out and say it. You're going to have to adapt if you expect to survive here, Zev. You can't be the same kind of Jew you were in Brooklyn. It's one thing in Crown Heights and another in Urbana, do you understand what I'm saying to you?"

I think Frida was expecting more resistance. She did not know how much I hated my unfortunate boy whiskers. I could barely stand looking at them since the day they began sprouting erratically from my chin, and when I saw them in the mirror again last night, I wished I could be rid of them. I was definitely more attached to my payos, but the side curls had always been a nuisance on the handball court. The scotch tape was unreliable when I sweat, and besides, very few Lubavitchers wore payos. My mother thought they were cute and so I never cut them.

Making a few adjustments to my appearance did not seem like such a terrible thing as long as I could continue being a Jew, but as I ate my Frosted Flakes, without kosher certification, I was uncertain exactly what that meant anymore.

"So when will we see the rabbi?" I asked. "You have to wait many months to have yechidus with the Rebbe."

Frida laughed and said, "This is not the Rebbe, and we're just asking for a little advice. The message on the machine said they'd call back soon, so we'll see. What else would you like to do today?"

I asked if there was a handball court nearby and she said we'd drive over to the university rec center and look around. I told her I wanted to buy some new sneakers and maybe some clothes, but nothing too different. She happily said we could do that too. I sensed her relief.

"And we'll need to figure out what to do with Abba's money," she said. "I think there's too much to keep here in the house, but I'm afraid a bank will have to report it and that could cause trouble."

I told her I counted it last night before I went to sleep and it was a lot more than I thought: fifty-four thousand, two hundred and sixty-five dollars.

"Jesus," she said.

Just then Paul Griffin came to the table in an old Pratt Institute sweatshirt, torn at the shoulder with a thumb-sized hole under the armpit.

"Did somebody call me?" he said.

"Paul only pretends he's Jesus because he wants to be worshiped," Frida replied.

He said, "If I were Jesus, I wouldn't have to go to that goddamn faculty meeting at eleven. What have you two got planned today?"

"I don't know," Frida answered. "Mainly some Jew stuff if the rabbi gets back to us . . . and we're going to buy some clothes. Zev's getting a makeover."

"Really?" Paul said to me. "What? Are you ditching the uniform?"

I was not crazy about Paul Griffin's sense of humor, but I have to admit I never liked people staring at my clothes, and the idea of blending in was becoming more appealing.

"I'm going to shave too," I said.

"Good choice," he replied. "I'll give you one of my razors and you can use the shaving cream in the medicine cabinet. Why don't you go on up and get started so the bathroom will be free when I get ready for work."

Frida gave me a pair of scissors to deal with my payos and I climbed the stairs to the bathroom to struggle with Hashem, still unsure about showering and changing my clothes during the shiva I was not sitting. I drew the curtain around the tub and let the hot water run over me, trying not to take too long or enjoy it too much.

I toweled off and wiped the steam from the mirror with my calloused palm, studying the face of the Hasidic boy-man looking back at me and wondering if I should also be sitting shiva for him. I held my curly right sidelock straight out. My hand was shaking as I brought the scissors to it:

"You shall not round off the hair of your temples or mar the corners of your beard."

The entire fifteen years of my life were contained in those few inches of hair, but Frida was right, I would have to make compromises. I worked at my sidelock until it came free and then set it on the lip of the sink. I did not know what to make of the lopsided face of the half Hasid in the mirror. Perhaps this was the way I always should have looked. It would have been more honest:

"You shall not play handball on Shabbos.
You shall not root through garbage cans while sitting shiva.
You shall not stare at your sister's breasts."

I removed the other sidelock and shaved my face for the first time, then put on a fresh white shirt and pair of pants and fixed my yarmulke to the crown of my head with a bobby pin. My mother had given me that card of bobby pins only a week ago. She said, "They're pretty, Zevi. They match your eyes."

I carried my keriah-torn shirt and handball-torn pants downstairs to the kitchen garbage. Frida and Paul were still at the breakfast table when I walked in and deposited my old clothes in the trash.

"Jesus," she said. "Look at you."

I wished Frida would quit mentioning this Jesus already. The Christian god scared me. The only thing I knew about him was that he was the one who turned the rest of the world against us. A Jew mentioning Jesus is like poking a hornet's nest with a stick.

Paul told me I looked better without the whiskers and got up from the table, leaving his coffee cup for Frida to set in the sink.

He said, "I've got to get ready for school. Today's my heavy teaching day and I've got six hours of class after that damn meeting. Maybe we'll have a few minutes to talk later on."

Frida said, "I guess there's no sense waiting around for the rabbi to call, so why don't I get dressed and we can do a little clothes shopping. You have any idea what sort of things you'd like?"

That was a very interesting question, something I hadn't thought about before. I never worried about what to wear in Crown Heights. Black and white was always in style. My Hasidic "uniform" made my old life so simple, just as it now made my new life so complicated.

I said, "First I would like to buy sneakers. Then maybe some shorts for handball."

"You'd wear shorts?" she said, wearing an astonished expression.

My pasty white-as-snow legs had never seen daylight.

I said, "I am the only player who wears long pants in the summer. I think I look very funny . . . Maybe I'll buy some sweatpants too, and a sweatshirt."

She said, "I can help you pick a few things out if you like. We'll need some of Abba's money, you know. I think four or five hundred should do it. And let's not mention anything about the money to Paul yet, OK?"

Frida was washing the breakfast dishes when the rabbi called and invited us to come by at eleven thirty.

"If we hurry, that should give us just enough time to do a little shopping first," Frida said. "It'll only take me a minute to get ready."

We drove crosstown to a shopping mall near the interstate, passing through Urbana and into Champaign. I could not tell the difference between the twin cities. They were equally flat and spread out beneath a Midwestern sky that seemed to be expanding outward and upward in all directions. The sky in Brooklyn was a small square overhead, contained by buildings on all sides. Brooklyn felt safe by comparison.

My discomfort subsided as soon as I put on my new Nike court shoes. They cost almost eighty dollars and were much nicer than the ones I lost in the stairwell. Frida told me to go ahead and buy some athletic socks to wear with them.

She said, "You can't wear those long ones with shorts. You'll look like an old man from Florida."

I put my leather shoes in the box and wore my new sneakers out of the store. We picked out two pairs of jeans in Urban Outfitters. Frida held up a T-shirt with the words GO AHEAD, MAKE MY DAY printed over a picture of a man in black wearing a strange helmet.

Frida said, "This is funny. It'd be pretty cool to wear something like this when you play handball."

I told her I did not understand it.

She said, "It's Darth Vader."

I told her I did not know what that was.

She said, "You know, from *Star Wars*."

I had heard of *Star Wars*, but knew nothing about Darth Vader.

"The *make my day* thing is from another old movie, *Dirty Harry*. You've never heard that expression?"

"Not really."

"It's only been around for about twenty years."

I did not like that T-shirt with the picture. I picked out some plain ones in blue, black, and gray, the least flashy colors in the store. Frida said I should get at least one with something printed on it.

"You know, to be more stylish."

So I picked out another black one with a red Nike symbol that matched the one on my shoes.

"You wanna wear your new clothes out of the store?" she asked. "I'm sure they'll take the tags off for you."

The drastic change in my appearance came suddenly, but

not easily. Every new article of clothing came with a blessing and a curse, a mixture of pleasure and regret. When I was very young, my mother dressed me in polo shirts; some even had colored checks and stripes. This was common for little Hasidic boys, but I had worn nothing other than white dress shirts, black pants, and black jackets for many years. My fedora did not leave my head outside the house except during my illicit handball games.

Imagine how I felt in my new shoes and modern clothes, walking to Frida's car through the shopping mall parking lot with only a yarmulke covering my head and my old "uniform" stuffed into a shopping bag. I now looked, more or less, like every other American boy my age, although in reality, I had less in common with them than most recent immigrants waiting for their green card. I was a part of the melting pot that never melted, the native-born stranger who never fit in.

On our way to the shul, we passed cornfields stretching all the way to the horizon. I had never imagined a world so spacious, like everything under this wide prairie sky was about to fly upward, out of control, at any minute. Even in Frida's car I did not feel secure, with nothing to anchor me, nothing to hold me down. Somewhere along an arrow-straight road we came to a modern building with a long sloping roof, wood siding, and enormous glass windows. Frida pulled into the parking lot.

If this was a shul, it was like none I'd ever seen before, and the man who greeted us in his study did not look like a rabbi. He was clean-shaven and did not wear a yarmulke. He was no Rebbe, and this was not Gan Eden Ha'Elyon. The walls of his study were lined with books, although none as ancient or scholarly-looking as our Rebbe's. The shelves and desk were crowded with tchotchkes and Judaica.

Rabbi Feinstein shook our hands and invited us to sit. He asked if we wanted coffee. I was too nervous, but my sister took a cup.

"And so tell me," he asked. "What brings you here today? I know only a little from what you shared with me on the phone."

Frida told him our story.

"So you lost both your parents only a few days ago?" the rabbi asked, rubbing his bare chin the way our Lubavitcher rabbis stroke their white beards.

"Such a tragedy," he said. "I'm so sorry, there are no words. And you say you are a Hasid?"

I did not know how to answer his question, so I said nothing. I did not know if I still was or had been.

"Forgive me," the rabbi said. "You don't look like a Hasid."

"I shaved and bought new clothes today," I said, thinking the words sounded like an apology as they left my mouth.

"And why did you do that, if I may ask?"

"I told him he'd have an easier time if he blended in," Frida answered.

"And how do you feel about that?" the rabbi asked, clearly addressing me.

I told him I didn't know.

"So you're a little confused at the moment then? That's certainly understandable considering all you've been through. So what can I do to help you?"

"We were hoping you could help Zev get adjusted," Frida answered for me again.

"Adjusted, yes . . ." the rabbi said. "And what about you, young lady? You've been here a long time already, have you adjusted yet?"

I could tell Frida took this as a confrontation, although I

do not believe it was the rabbi's intention.

She said, "I'm doing just fine, Rabbi Feinstein. I gave up on organized religion years ago and I don't miss it one bit. I'm only concerned about my brother."

He said, "First of all, please call me Rabbi Jerry. Everybody does; we're not very formal around here. So then, what are your concerns for your brother?"

"Where do I even start? He's fifteen years old and can read and write three languages and knows Torah better than anyone in your congregation, but he doesn't know who Shakespeare was, or Darth Vader either, for Christ's sake."

So now it's for Christ's sake, Frida?

Rabbi Jerry did not seem to appreciate this expression any more than I did.

She said, "And he needs to be in school somewhere, but who's going to have him? Is he supposed to sit in a class with ten-year-olds? He's never known anything but Crown Heights and it's like he's in a foreign country now. He wants to be a Jew, but doesn't know there's any way to be a Jew other than to follow the Rebbe and do what he's told. I swear the men are like robots with beards where he's from."

I did not like this either. Our father was not a robot with a beard.

She said, "So that's why we're here today. I thought you might be able to help us with some practical things and maybe help Zev sort out his Judaism. He's in a period of transition."

The rabbi shifted around in his chair. He picked up a pen and twiddled with the end cap, then set it back down and pushed it aside.

"And what is it *you* want, Zev? I hear your sister loud and clear, but you've barely said a word. I'd like to know what *you* want."

I shrugged.

"Would you like to live as a practical Jew in the world? Would you like to go to school, to get a secular education? I don't think anyone should make these decisions for you. You have to decide what kind of person you want to be and then maybe we can help, but this is not up to me or your sister."

I do not think Frida and Rabbi Jerry liked each other very much. I still did not know how to answer his questions.

"He's very quiet," Frida said.

"So then let's take this one step at a time. You want to live as a Jew, am I right?"

I nodded.

"OK. Jews here in Champaign face some unusual challenges. We're a very small minority . . . almost nonexistent the farther you get from the university. It's not at all like New York or Chicago. For example, we have only a few families in our congregation who keep anything resembling kosher. Some simply avoid pork and shellfish; others just avoid it at home. Most don't follow the dietary laws at all. The Schnuks grocery on Mattis carries a few items, but to be strictly glatt kosher is impossible here."

"Well, I can tell you right now we won't be keeping kosher in our house," Frida said.

"I don't think being an observant Jew will be a huge problem once Zev gets situated." The rabbi gestured to my new outfit. "He seems to be very adaptable. I think the bigger problem will be enrolling him in public school. It would be best for us to get some professional advice on this. He'll have to be tested, but we're fortunate to have a number of well-connected people in our congregation. I'm sure we can get an evaluation set up in short order if you like. The head of special ed at the U of I is a member here."

"Special education?" Frida said.

"I'm not suggesting Zev needs special education, but we have a special situation here, don't we? Anyway, we'll get help and find out what his needs are. To be perfectly candid, though, I'm more concerned about the trauma he's been through."

Rabbi Jerry drew a little closer to me.

"I'd like to get you in to see a counselor right away, Zev. I don't believe this should be put off. The death of a parent is far and away the most stressful event in the life of a child and you've lost both your parents; plus, there's this sea change in your environment . . . Your whole world has been turned upside down. We have some top-notch psychologists in our congregation and I'm sure one of them would be happy to talk with you to get the ball rolling."

"So what do you think, Zev?" Frida asked. "Do you understand what the rabbi's suggesting?"

I thought I did, but I was afraid to see a psychologist. I remembered what happened to my mother when she saw one.

"Would I have to go into the hospital?" I asked.

The rabbi was stunned.

"Of course not. I don't think you understand what I'm suggesting. Counselors go into the public schools all the time to help students work through traumatic events . . . to help them deal with stress and grief, things like that. This is normal, very common."

"I think it would be good for you to see someone," Frida said to me before turning to the rabbi. "We live just east of Campustown, on California, but I work and can't always be around to drive him everywhere."

"Why don't we worry about the logistics later," the rabbi said. "We have people out that way, so I don't think it'll be too much of a problem. If it's all right with you, then, let me make some calls and set the wheels in motion. I'll call you as soon as I hear something."

One thing had been bothering me since we entered Rabbi Jerry's study. I could not stop staring at his uncovered head.

"Why don't you wear a yarmulke?" I asked.

Frida looked shocked and the rabbi laughed.

He asked, "Why, do you think I should be wearing one?"

"Yes."

"Well, I do when I'm in the sanctuary or studying Torah. You know there's nothing in the Torah that commands us to wear a yarmulke, right? Reform Jews try not to let things like that divide us. Women in our congregation are free to wear yarmulkes, too, if they want. It's up to the individual. And Zev, if you'd like to attend Shabbat service, I can have someone pick you up Friday night."

We said goodbye to the rabbi and Frida took me to lunch at a place called Zorba's in Campustown. My Greek sandwich was treif, but at least the counterman said there was no pork in it when Frida asked. I had them leave off the sauce so as not to intentionally mix meat and dairy. It was a vain gesture that left an aftertaste of conviction in my mouth.

"So what's next? Would you like to go find a handball court?" Frida asked.

I could hardly have been more excited, but when we got to the rec center, we were not allowed past the front desk.

"You're not students and you don't have memberships," the girl behind the desk said.

"But my husband is on the faculty," Frida argued.

"Is he a member here?" the girl asked.

"I don't know ... I don't think so."

"Well, even if he's a member, he needs to be here in person

to sponsor you, and you'll have to buy day passes to get in."

"Just to look around?" Frida seemed very annoyed. "My brother wants to check out the courts, that's all. He plays handball."

"I'm sorry, those are the rules. I just work here, I don't make them up."

I was quickly learning how persistent Frida could be when she wanted something. She asked the girl to ring for the facilities manager.

In a few minutes a blond-haired man, probably in his early thirties, arrived at the desk. I could tell he was taken with Frida as soon as he laid eyes on her. She explained our situation and he invited us to come see the racquetball courts. There were three rooms with little glass windows in the doors. I could hear balls being hit inside.

"Where do you play one-wall?" I asked.

"Beats me," he replied. "That's pretty much a New York thing, isn't it? We have a few guys who play four-wall here, but it's almost all racquetball. There are more courts over at the Intramural Building, but it's mainly racquetball players there too, as far as I know."

"There are no outdoor courts?"

"I don't know of any," he said, glancing back and forth between me and my sister's breasts. "But listen, the courts here all have to be reserved in advance, so I'll have phone numbers. I can let you know when we get some handball players coming in."

The blond man took a card from his wallet and handed it to Frida, looking into her eyes this time.

"Why don't you give me your number?" he asked. "Is your brother staying with you?"

He handed her his pen.

Even a fifteen-year-old Hasid who had never been alone

with a girl could see where this was going.

Frida wrote her number on the back of the card and returned it to him. He puffed with confidence as he admired the handwritten phone number.

"I'll give you a call soon," the man said as we headed to the door.

Out on the street Frida explained, "You see how I didn't mention Paul to this guy? If I did, we'd never hear from him again, but now he has a pretext to call; you watch."

I realized my sister was not only persistent, but also understood the inner working of men's minds. We did not have to wait long at all for the man's phone call. In fact, by four in the afternoon I had three appointments set up. The first was a meeting with a counselor in Urbana at ten the next morning, and the second was at the university for what they called *assessment and placement testing* on Thursday. The third appointment was the only one I was looking forward to. On Friday I would be meeting two college students at the rec center for handball.

At a little after six, Paul Griffin's bicycle clattered against the garbage cans at the side door. Frida had already started dinner and I was sitting at the kitchen table in my new clothes.

"We'll be eating pretty soon, so don't go running off," she said to Paul as he walked in the door.

"That's OK, I need to chill awhile," he said. "I can see you two have done a little shopping. So how does it feel, Zev? How do you like your first pair of jeans?"

"Good," I answered.

I think he was expecting something more from me.

"Well, thanks for sharing. That was really enlightening."

Frida sighed and Paul began leafing through the mail on the table.

I liked the way the jeans looked, but they were stiff and not nearly as comfortable as my trousers. Maybe I should have told him that.

I was not sure if Frida's sigh was for my one-word answer or Paul Griffin's sarcasm. She put a big pot of water on the stove and emptied two cans of tomatoes into a large sizzling pan.

"Did Eema still make spaghetti with ketchup on it?" she asked. "I remember how special we thought that was when we were little. You remember that, Zevi?"

Of course I remembered. Eema made it for the last time only a week before she died.

Frida said, "I'm making a Bolognese sauce tonight, so we'll see what you think. It's about as kosher as you're going to get around here, so just leave the Parmesan cheese off and you'll be OK."

After dinner Paul said he was heading to the studio and asked if I wanted to keep him company. I thought this was very nice of him and Frida seemed pleased too, but when we got there he said he was going back into the house.

"I haven't had any time alone with Free in a while, so why don't you do me a favor and wait out here and I'll be back soon. You OK with that?"

I told him I was.

"There's a pile of art magazines you can look through over there, but don't mess with anything else. I won't be too long."

He closed the door behind him.

There could not have been a worse time for me to be left alone with a picture of a naked woman, even if she did resemble my sister. The painted woman's skin was smooth and unblemished, her breasts round and heavy, with nipples just as I tried not to imagine them under her T-shirt. An extended thigh glistened with a highlight along its length, and a dark triangle of hair between her open legs spread ever so slightly onto the upholstered chair she was seated on.

Hasidic boys are not taught anything about sex until right before marriage, and then only in the most rudimentary way, but we are warned never to touch our genitals, and that the spilling of one's seed is greater than any other sin in the Torah. The Talmud puts it at the very top of the list, along with idolatry and murder. Yet Hasidic boys still talk among ourselves and do what we do in secret. Paul Griffin should not have left me alone to revel in my sister's nakedness. He took longer than I had expected, giving me more time to study the painting after finishing my sordid business.

There were little details I had not noticed the night before. The woman's shoes at the foot of the dressing table had higher heels than I had ever seen. I could only imagine how difficult it would be to walk in them. On the floor a magazine was opened to a photo of a woman touching herself in the way we were warned never to do. It was partly covered by a flimsy pair of women's underpants. The clothes draped over the back of the chair must have belonged to the man sleeping on the bed. I did not know what to make of the devilish smirk on my sister's face as she riffled through his wallet.

"So do you know what it's about?"

I jumped at the sound of Paul Griffin's voice in the doorway behind me.

"I think so," I replied, trying to act as casual as a guilty man can.

"By the way," he said as he shut the door behind him. "Thanks for cutting me a break, with Free, I mean; that was nice of you. So do you know what the painting's about?"

"She is stealing from the man on the bed while he is asleep," I answered. It was not hard to figure out.

"That's right. I'm going to call it *Tit for Tat*. She's a whore and the guy on the bed's her john. It's a getting even sort of thing."

From that moment on, I wanted to get even with Paul Griffin, a man who had shown me nothing but kindness by opening his home to me.

"You're more than welcome to stay out here with me if you like," he said, "but it gets pretty boring . . . kinda like watching paint dry. You ever heard that expression? Free's probably in there watching TV if you want to join her. Either way's OK with me."

Paul turned up the stereo and started squeezing fresh colors onto his palette. I stayed for a few minutes to be polite and then went into the house. The television was on in the living room. Frida was sitting on the couch behind a portable tray with a plastic milk crate full of cut paper on the cushion next to her. She was wearing her SORRY T-shirt again over a scanty pair of gray sweat shorts.

She said, "I'm working on a collage, come and sit with me."

I must seem like some kind of pervert, the way I have been going on about Frida. This is no way to speak of one's own sister; this is no way to speak, but you must understand what I am confiding. The weight of my sins was nearly crushing me, but at the same time I was excited to be a part of this new world of rabbis without yarmulkes and women with bare legs.

I was once in the apartment of a boy I knew from yeshiva. He had a pet parakeet and opened the cage to let it out. The bird flew wildly around the room, bouncing into walls and almost tipping over a lamp before finally settling down and hopping onto the boy's finger.

What I had just done in Paul's studio was a shanda, and

what I am saying now is no excuse, but my cage door had been flung open and I was careening around recklessly in a much larger world with room for thoughts other than the teachings of the rabbis and the 613 mitzvot.

We sat on the couch and watched a show called *Thirty-something*. It was a little hard to follow because it was complicated and the people had many strange problems.

Frida said, "I hear they're taking it off the air at the end of the season. I'm really sorry about that. I like the Nancy character."

"She is the blond one?" I asked.

"That's right, the one who wants to be an artist."

"Is that why you like her?"

"I don't know, maybe. She has aspirations . . ."

Frida held a piece of cut paper up to the light.

"You know if I'd married Dov Feldsher, I'd have four or five kids by now. I can't even imagine it."

"So are you happier here?" I asked.

"Happier? I don't know, I suppose. I try not to think about it too much. Plenty of Lubavitcher women are probably happier pushing their strollers around Crown Heights. Sometimes I think it would've been easier for me.

"Just look at my life. I thought freedom was getting out from under all the rules and the rabbis, and so what kind of freedom is this? I work at a craft store, for Christ's sake. I cook and clean and take care of Paul. What kind of freedom is that?"

"So what do you want?" I asked.

"I guess that's the trouble. I don't know what I want. I've never discovered one goddamn thing for myself or thought one thought on my own. When I was a girl back in Brooklyn, I knew damn well what I didn't want, but that's not the same as knowing what you want. I thought it was then, but it's not.

And what about you, Zevi? What is it you want?"

I said, "You already know. I want to play handball."

"Yeah, well, you can't just play handball for the rest of your life. You're going to have to earn a living, get an education, have some kind of profession."

"I guess so."

"And at fifteen you can't lie around the house all day playing handball whenever you feel like it. In Illinois you have to go to school until you're seventeen. There are laws here. It's not completely our decision."

The next morning I laid tefillin, and after breakfast Frida drove us to an office building in Campustown not far from where we had eaten lunch the day before. We entered a waiting room full of fidgeting children and their impatient parents. A few sad-looking older people seemed to be trying to distract themselves from the chaos by reading magazines.

A woman at the reception desk handed me a clipboard with many forms attached and told me to fill them out. Frida signed as my legal guardian at every X. I was worried lying on the forms might get us into trouble.

"No one's going to know the difference," she whispered. "Just keep quiet about it; they'll never check."

Frida left for work as I completed the paperwork. Some of the questions were easy to answer:

DO YOU HAVE ANY LEISURE ACTIVITIES YOU ENJOY?

WHEN ARE YOU HAPPIEST?

Some questions were more difficult and I was not exactly sure how to answer them:

WHAT DO YOU WANT TO CHANGE ABOUT YOURSELF?

WHAT DO YOU THINK IS IMPORTANT FOR US TO KNOW ABOUT YOU?

The questions in SECTION 7, HISTORY OF TRAUMA

were the hardest of all to answer:

WAS ANY MEMBER OF YOUR HOUSEHOLD DEPRESSED
OR MENTALLY ILL?

DID ANY HOUSEHOLD MEMBER EVER ATTEMPT SUI-
CIDE?

HAS ANYONE TRIED TO HURT YOU, CURRENTLY OR
IN THE PAST?

I lied and answered NO to most of the questions in SEC-
TION 7: HISTORY OF TRAUMA, and then turned the forms
in at the desk. About fifteen minutes later a slender woman
with short hair came into the room and called my name. She
introduced herself as Dr. Niederhoffer, and I followed her to
her office.

At first, Dr. Niederhoffer made what I suppose might be
called small talk. She asked about my life in Brooklyn and
the differences between Champaign–Urbana and Crown
Heights. I think she was trying to put me at ease.

After a while she said she had talked with Rabbi Jerry
when he made the appointment for me, and wondered why I
did not mention my mother's suicide on the forms. I did not
have the answer to that question.

Dr. Niederhoffer asked how I felt about my parents'
deaths, and I told her it made me sad. Like Paul Griffin's
question about my jeans, I could tell she was expecting a
more elaborate answer.

She said, "You've been through a lot lately . . . some incredibly traumatic life events, and I'm sure you're feeling a bit
overwhelmed right now."

I sat quietly with my hands folded in my lap. I have plenty to say, I just do not usually say it out loud or in public.

"Can you talk about this at all, Zev? It's important for
you to try."

I nodded in agreement but said nothing.

"It's not easy getting started," Dr. Niederhoffer said with a kindly smile, "especially if you grew up in a home where no one spoke about their feelings."

Frida was the only person I knew who ever talked about feelings. The word did not exist with my parents and was not something I was interested in speaking about either.

Dr. Niederhoffer said, "It may feel safer at the moment, but stuffing everything inside isn't the answer. We're only beginning to understand the consequences of post-traumatic stress and how it can lead to all sorts of serious problems later in life . . . addictions, depression. When we shut out the bad feelings, we end up feeling less of everything. It can affect our relationships, our ability to experience joy."

A little bell chimed on the doctor's desk.

"Wow," she said. "Our time together went really fast today."

I did not think it went fast at all.

She said, "I'm sorry, we have to stop now. It can take quite a while to work through issues like these, so if you'd like to see me again, I'll be happy to make myself available . . . as one member of the tribe to another."

I'm sure by *the tribe* she meant as one Jew to another. What Dr. Niederhoffer could not understand is that we had almost nothing in common as Jews. With her uncovered short hair and slacks, she had no idea of the rules of the tribe I belonged to, or at least once did.

She came from an unkosher world of yarmulke-wearing women and bareheaded rabbis, incapable of imagining how the 613 mitzvot and teachings of the Rebbe could possibly rule every decision in a person's life, bringing both joy and misery at the same time. I did not have the language to explain this to Dr. Niederhoffer, although it might have helped her to understand how I ended up in her office.

I returned to Zorba's for lunch and ordered the same sandwich as the day before, once again leaving off the tzatziki sauce, grasping for anything remotely familiar. I did not mind eating my treif alone. The gyro meat was tasty and the missing sauce assured me I was still at least trying to be a somewhat observant Jew. It was almost one by the time I finished eating.

Back in Crown Heights, I would have been facing several more hours of afternoon Torah study. Nearly every minute of every day was accounted for there, and I was not used to having so much free time on my hands. Frida would not be home until late afternoon, so I wandered the vast U of I grounds looking for something to occupy myself. At the south edge of campus I came to a row of silvery greenhouses with a cemetery spreading beyond them for many blocks in each direction.

Inside the cemetery gates, monuments of every size and description bore testimony to the relative importance of Champaign–Urbana's dead; names like Stoughton, Cunningham, and Busey, names I recognized from streets in town. I came to a potter's field of mostly unmarked graves, the final resting place of Champaign County's forgotten poor. There were immigrants' gravestones inscribed in languages I could not read or understand.

As I continued along the cemetery path, one headstone caught my eye on account of the smooth pebbles left on top of it. Leaving small stones to honor the deceased is a Jewish custom. This was the grave of Sarah Lipman, wife of Alan. Next to it were the graves of Sophie Cohen and her husband, Saul, and next to them the Weissmans, the Shavitts, the Avners, and the Sorkins. A short distance away a little gray rabbit munched on clover beneath a monument bearing the Magen David, the six-pointed star. A momentary shadow arched across Sarah Lipman's grave and I looked up, shield-

ing my eyes from the sun. A large hawk was circling overhead, most likely seeking its next meal.

I continued past the Civil War Veterans Memorial and
the grim mausoleum, eventually coming to a break in a
hedgerow behind the University of Illinois Meat and Egg
Sales Room. *There it was*—on the opposite side of South
Maryland Drive. The Big Green Wall shimmered in the
midafternoon sun like a mirage rising in the desert, nothing
more than plywood sheets stacked four high on a wooden
frame, most likely serving as a divider between two basketball courts. Some of the sheets were splitting at the seams and
its green paint was peeling in several places. I could hardly
imagine anyone playing handball on such a sorry court, and
yet someone obviously had.

White lines, twenty feet apart and sixteen feet high, de-
fined the wall's playing surface, and court boundaries had
been laid out on the worn asphalt. Even the worst park in
Brooklyn had a better court than this, but I can hardly describe the great joy it gave me to run my hands over its uneven plywood surface. I rushed home to get my gloves and a
handball, and spent a beautiful afternoon doing what I love
most in this world.

Frida was already home from work when I entered the
kitchen at about five thirty. I went on and on, gushing about
finding the Big Green Wall. She tousled my hair and said she
was happy for me, then asked if I knew where Paul was. He
was not in his studio. She told me he sometimes stays late after class to work with his graduate students, but usually calls
to let her know. She spoke in a pleasant tone, but I could tell
she was put out with him.

"He'll probably be home before dinner," she said.

Paul called at around seven, after dinner was already on
the table. He said he would not be home until late and would

grab a bite somewhere on campus. Frida scraped his plate into a plastic bowl and stuck it in the refrigerator.

I did not hear him come in that night, even though I was not sleeping soundly, dreading the upcoming placement tests and what they were about to find wrong with me, all the things I had never been taught in yeshiva, facts any American boy my age should know.

In the morning I laid tefillin and recited prayers. I was groggy from lack of sleep and all the more nervous knowing I would not be at my best for the testing. To add to my anxiety, Frida had to be at work early and Rabbi Jerry was coming to pick me up.

"So this is the big day," he said when I got in the car, as if that might somehow relieve my nervousness. I fidgeted in the front seat all the way to the Education Building, where he parked his Honda and we took the stairs to the second floor. At the end of a long hallway we entered an office where a girl in a flowered dress rose and introduced herself as Julie, Dr. Gottlieb's graduate assistant.

"Dr. Gottlieb wants you to take very good care of this young man," Rabbi Jerry said.

"Of course," she replied. "We're all set for Zev. I even have a little snack waiting for him."

She apologized that the testing would have to go right through the lunch hour, but said we were fortunate Dr. Gottlieb could work us in on such short notice.

"Zev must be very special," Julie said.

Rabbi Jerry told me he would return sometime before two o'clock to take me for a late lunch. Julie led me to a room down the hall and sat me in a creaky wooden chair at a worn wooden desk and placed a box of sharpened wood pencils and the first test in front of me. She asked if there was anything else I needed and said she would be back to check on me in a little while.

A lot of the tests were easier than I thought, but I had trouble understanding some of the English words and skipped over many of the math questions entirely. I finished early with no idea if I had done well or poorly. I read magazines in the waiting room until Rabbi Jerry came back and asked where I'd like to eat. I told him I wanted to go to Zorba's.

"Oh, that place over on Green Street?" he said. "I haven't been there in years. Sure, let's go."

When we entered the restaurant, the counterman greeted me as if I were his best customer.

"Hey, here you are again. Let me guess—a gyro, hold the tzatziki sauce, right?"

I smiled and nodded.

"Well, it looks like you're feeling pretty comfortable here already," Rabbi Jerry said.

I nodded again, uncomfortably.

We sat facing each other in the plastic booth while the rabbi without a yarmulke tried his best to make conversation with the boy of one-word answers.

"So did you like Dr. Niederhoffer?"

"Yes," I said.

"That's good . . . Dr. Gottlieb tells me we'll get your tests back quickly, and depending on the results, she'll arrange for a graduate student to tutor you this summer."

I nodded again.

"It pays to have friends in high places," the rabbi said with a toothy smile.

I smiled too.

"You know we have a very nice oneg Shabbat at the temple tomorrow evening. I can have someone pick you up if you like."

I smiled again.

He said, "You're not very talkative, are you, Zev?"

"I am sometimes," I replied.

The rabbi poked at his Greek salad and sipped his Diet Coke through a straw. I could tell he was searching for the magic words to get me to open up.

"Did you know I come from an orthodox background, too?" he asked. "My father was an orthodox rabbi, not Hasidic, modern orthodox, but very frum. He was strict with me and I started rebelling when I was about your age, not long after my bar mitzvah. In college I turned away from Judaism altogether."

I thought his story was very interesting but could not come up with a single appropriate comment. I was afraid Rabbi Jerry would think I was rude or didn't like him, so I started a topic of my own.

I said, "I found a handball court near the cemetery yesterday."

The rabbi looked a bit puzzled by this comment that came out of nowhere but took advantage of the opportunity.

"So I take it you're a handball player?" he said.

"Yes, it is my favorite thing to do."

"Very interesting. You know I play racquetball. I try and play twice a week when I can."

Rabbi Jerry had a bit of a belly and did not seem the least bit athletic to me.

"The rules are similar, aren't they?" he asked.

"Yes, but handball is much harder."

I may have used a haughty tone.

"And why is that?" he asked.

"We have to be good with both hands, and in racquetball you have a thing this big to hit the ball with."

I formed a shape in the air about the size of a racquet.

"And you can reach two-feet farther with a racquet than with your hand. Would you like me to show you how we do it?"

"Ah . . ." He hesitated. "It's probably not a good idea today. I've got appointments coming up. Let's see what time it is."

Rabbi Jerry pondered the face of his watch.

He said, "I suppose I've got a little time."

I think he was more interested in making a connection with me than learning about handball.

"OK, real quick then, but don't we have to reserve a court somewhere?"

I said, "We can play at the Big Green Wall. I just have to go home and get a ball."

"Can we use a racquetball?" he asked. "I keep my gym bag in the trunk."

"Sure," I said. "We call that Big Ball. I don't need gloves. Here, feel these . . ."

I held out one of my callused hands. The rabbi seemed impressed, like he did not expect such toughness.

"So where is this handball court?" he asked.

"Do you know where the cemetery is?"

"You're talking about Mount Hope, right? It's more or less on my way back to the synagogue."

So this was how I ended up playing handball with the rabbi on my third day in Champaign–Urbana. He used his racquet and I used my bare hands. We agreed to go very easy, just a demonstration, but he was drenched in sweat by the end of our first game, even though I hit the ball gently and let him score a few points against me.

"You're a very impressive player, Zev," the rabbi said.

I did not have the heart to tell him he was no challenge at all. Nevertheless, this was the happiest I had been since leaving Brooklyn.

"I played in a tournament last Shabbos," I said cheerily, before realizing what I had just revealed about myself.

Rabbi Jerry placed his sweaty hand on my shoulder.

"I see," he said. "This is very complicated, isn't it?"

I nodded before I could evade his question. I had just run Rabbi Jerry all over the court, placing him exactly where I wanted with every gentle rally. He was now returning the favor.

"And I imagine you feel guilty about this?" he said.

I nodded again, almost involuntarily.

I do not mean to be disrespectful when I say this, but all rabbis are alike, from this reformed racquetball player to the Rebbe. They all love to be helpful and so much the better if they are able to dispense sage advice at the same time.

Rabbi Jerry was a cagey player in his own right. He had been setting me up since looking at his watch in Zorba's, determining what it would take to draw me out, knowing we would bond over physical activity the way men do. Now he was positioning me for the kill shot.

"This is very interesting, Zev, and I don't usually tell people this about myself . . . My father had a heart attack while I was away at college. I was a little older than you . . . twenty, maybe. He was only fifty-three when he dropped dead on the sidewalk on his way home from shul. I got the call from my uncle and returned home for the funeral the next day.

"This was during the time I'd turned my back on Judaism, and I blamed myself for my father's death. You know exactly what I'm saying, don't you? We're not talking about rational thoughts here. The guilt was so strong, I can't tell you. I know better now, but you see we are alike, the two of us. I've dealt with guilt and regret all my life. To this day I wish I'd been a better son, but we can't take these things back, can we?"

There were so many things I wished I could take back.

"We make jokes about Jewish guilt, so many it's become a cliché, but guilt isn't unique to Jews, it's part of the human condition. My conscience ached because I rejected my father, not because I rejected Judaism, but guilt is what brought me back to God, so you see it can serve a purpose, and our corporate rituals remind us we are not in this alone. That's why we reflect together as a people on Rosh Hashanah and Yom Kippur. You see the significance of this?"

The game was tilting in the rabbi's favor. He chose his words wisely and timed them to perfection, but knew when to back off and let me recover.

He said, "I really should be getting to my other appointments now, but we'll talk again soon, OK? You need to promise me one thing though . . . next time we play you'll let me reserve a court at the rec center and we'll play four-wall. I'll give you more of a run for your money then."

I told Rabbi Jerry I would be happy to play him again. When we stopped in front of the house, he asked if I would like someone to pick me up for Shabbat service the following evening and I told him I would.

Score one for the rabbi.

Frida came home from work anxious to hear how my testing went. I said it was OK and then proceeded to tell her everything about the rabbinical handball game, even little details of how I used this shot and that.

"And I am going to his shul tomorrow night. Will you come with me?" I asked.

She said, "No offense, Zevi, but I'd just as soon get a tooth pulled. You go and have fun."

"But it's not like at 770," I said. "The men and women worship in the same room together, and women can read from the Torah and wear yarmulkes too if they like."

"Gee," she said. "That's just what I've always wanted, to

wear a yarmulke like the big boys. Such high aspirations! Can I wear a shtreimel too?"

I laughed out loud. The thought of Frida in a shtreimel was so funny.

She said, "Seriously, you go. I want to see what Paul's up to."

It did not take long to find out. He came home in a horrible mood.

"You can't believe the bullshit that's going down over there," he grouched. "Cheryl's assigned us recruitment duties and I've got to go in on Saturday."

"Do you have to?" Frida asked.

"The full professors don't, but the rest of us proles do. I can't afford to be on her shit list when I go up for promotion."

Paul's frustration spilled across the table all through dinner. It felt like the house itself breathed a sigh of relief when he pushed his plate aside and left for the studio. My sister defended him as soon as he walked out the door.

"He's been under a lot of pressure lately," she said as she carried his plate to the sink and began straightening the kitchen. "He's having a show in Chicago next fall and needs every minute in the studio. I understand why this would upset him."

Neither of us went out to the studio that night. Frida fixed us two bowls of ice cream and at eight o'clock we watched a TV show called *Twin Peaks*. It was the most ridiculous thing I had ever seen.

I said, "Real people do not act crazy like that, not even the goyim."

"Oh, the goyim?" she said. "So Jews aren't crazy enough for you? I've never seen a gentile waving a goddamn chicken over his head on Yom Kippur, have you? That's so fucking crazy it makes *Twin Peaks* look like a documentary."

I always hated the Hasidic tradition of kapores. I used to cringe at the sight of the flatbed trucks parked along Kingston Avenue on Erev Yom Kippur, with the terrified birds crowded into their death cages waiting to be slaughtered. Parents brought their little children. Some of them made a game of it. I cried for the chickens giving their lives for our sins.

"And speaking of Jewish craziness," Frida said. "You don't have to worry about pre-tearing your own toilet paper before tomorrow night. If you forget, we have our own Shabbos goy in the house."

I laughed at the thought of Paul Griffin tearing squares of toilet paper as my personal Shabbos goy.

Frida left for work the next morning before Paul got out of bed. He must have stayed up late in the studio. I did not feel like waiting around to see if he was still in a surly mood, so I walked to the rec center to meet the two handball players. I arrived early and sat on a bench just inside the front door, watching the college girls coming and going in their exercise clothes. I felt more comfortable admiring them from behind the disguise of my gym shorts and Nike T-shirt, my black yarmulke the only vestige of my formerly pious life.

The blond manager who showed us around came over and asked about my sister. He said to tell her to call him. At about ten minutes before our scheduled court time, two students stopped at the front desk, obviously looking for someone. As soon as I stood up from the bench I realized the blond man had told them nothing about me. They did not try to hide their disappointment.

The taller one asked how old I was and I told him I'd be sixteen soon. The other grimaced at the sight of my yarmulke.

He said, "Are you sure you're supposed to be playing with *us*?"

They introduced themselves as Tom and Christian, and I followed behind as they proceeded to the court. We rallied gently to warm up. From what I could tell, they were average recreational players, maybe high Cs or low Bs at best. One thing was for sure though, they were not happy to be babysitting.

"We're playing cutthroat," Christian said. "You know what that is?"

I told him I did and he asked if I wanted to serve and tossed me the ball, as if I were going to need all the help I could get. I'd shown them nothing of my arsenal during the warm-up and decided to get their attention right away. I stepped into the service area and fired a line drive hard at Christian, keeping the ball just off the right side wall. He lunged and got his glove on it, but his return hit the floor before reaching the front wall, my first ace.

"Nice serve," he said.

I decided to give Tom a little taste of Zev Magic next, with a serve hugging the wall on his left side.

"Fuck," he said, after missing it completely. "Son of a bitch."

As I suspected, Tom's left was weak.

"Two serving zero, serving zero," I said.

I served another wicked ace to Christian. Very few players could have returned a shot like that, just inches off the floor and barely beyond the short line.

"Jesus," he said. "What the fuck?"

"I have never played four-wall," I explained. "I will need to learn how to use the side walls."

"Where the hell are you from?" he asked.

"Brooklyn."

"Are you a lefty or a righty?" Tom asked.

"Both," I answered.

"That's fucking insane," he said. "How'd you learn that?"

"I have always been that way. I write English with my right hand and Hebrew with my left. My teachers were amazed, but it is easier for me to do it that way."

"You have kind of an accent," Chris said, referring to my Yiddish inflection.

"Brooklyn," I repeated, determined to work on bettering my American English.

I lobbed my next serve right down the middle just to put it in play and lost service when Chris returned an inside corner kill to Tom. I found myself flat-footed during our three games, unable to accurately predict where the ball would ricochet off the side walls. There can be no hesitation in handball. You must anticipate in advance and cannot be even a stutter-step behind. Regardless, Christian and Tom were not good enough to exploit my weaknesses and I won all three games easily.

"You've got a wicked serve," Tom said as we left the rec center.

Chris said, "We usually grab a slice after the game, you wanna come with us? We can split a pie three ways."

I was uncomfortable explaining my half-hearted attempts at keeping halfway kosher to my new gentile friends, so I did not speak up at the pizza shop when they ordered a Chicago deep-dish with pepperoni. When the pie arrived, I was faced with a serious dilemma. I would not only be mixing meat and dairy, but eating pork—the *treifiest* of all treif. I had never eaten pork before.

Christian and Tom watched me pick through each slice, carefully segregating the pepperoni to the far corner of my plate. The circular depressions left behind in the cheese still glistened with rendered pork fat.

Tom said, "We could've ordered sausage if you told us you didn't like pepperoni."

"That's OK," I said, trying to sound as American as possible.

"You mind if I eat your pepperoni?" he asked.

I shoveled the offending slices onto his plate and took my first bite of unkosher pizza. It was very tasty.

I asked them if anyone played one-wall in Urbana. They said they had seen the Big Green Wall, but never anyone on it.

Christian said, "We're from the Chicago suburbs. If you want to see some really good handball, you've got to hit Rainbow Beach on the South Shore. It's three-wall and some pretty famous players show up there."

"You know who Paul Haber is?" Tom asked.

Of course I did. Paul Haber was a Jewish handball legend.

Tom said, "I met him there once. He wasn't playing, just going around shaking hands, drinking beer, and betting on games. You can't believe how much these guys bet."

Sure I could. I had seen plenty of money change hands on the courts in Brooklyn and thought some players were as addicted to gambling as they were to handball. I had never placed a bet, but in the not too distant future my livelihood would depend on it.

I asked my new friends if they wanted to learn one-wall. They did not have classes on Friday and were happy to play another game with me. On our way to the Big Green Wall they asked about handball in New York, and I described the action on my home court and Coney Island. I told them about making it to the quarters in the tournament last weekend before realizing where the conversation might be heading. I broke it off, and let them assume I lost rather than explaining why I forfeited.

We played until almost three o'clock and agreed to meet again the following Friday. Christian and I then returned to the rec center, where he sponsored me for a membership and I rented a lock and locker.

He said, "If you want to play during the week, I think there are a couple of old guys who come here in the evening. I've heard one of them is pretty good."

Rabbi Jerry called before dinner to tell me the Kotins would be picking me up for shul that evening. I was waiting on the porch at seven-fifteen when a shiny black BMW turned into our driveway. Mrs. Kotin lowered the front passenger window and smiled as I approached. She was pretty, not as pretty as my mother or Frida, but pretty. Dr. Kotin looked very dignified behind the wheel of his fancy car.

I think I might have gasped out loud when I opened the door to the back seat. There was Sharon Kotin with her short skirt partly hiked up by the seatbelt. She tugged at the hem a little when she caught me looking. Those legs. And that face: Oh, meyn Gott, such a shayna punim!

Sharon sat quietly as her parents made conversation. I answered politely, trying my best to appear at ease despite the nervous bile gurgling in my throat. These social situations are obviously not my specialty. Thank God the Kotins did not inquire about my parents or why I was living in Urbana.

Then Sharon asked what grade I was in, and whatever fragile confidence I had shattered like a wineglass at a Jewish wedding. I did not know how to answer. All I could think to say was I did not know, and I could tell by the expression on her face that was probably the worst of all possible answers. How could one not know such a thing?

What was I going to tell her, that I studied Torah and Talmud in yeshiva and had yechidus with the Grand Rebbe, but did not know any mathematics beyond long division? Should I tell her that, until three days ago, I dressed in a black suit and hat and had payos and a miserable beard that looked like fungus growing on a cantaloupe?

Frida told me I looked "cool" when I walked out the door to meet the Kotins in my new Nikes, jeans, and gray T-shirt. My black suit coat looked so different worn over jeans. "Like a hipster," Frida said. But Sharon Kotin's question reduced me to a fumfering refugee, an alien from a Yiddish planet dropped next to a pretty earth girl in the back seat of a fancy car, a strange awkward boy who does not know what grade he is in.

The Erev Shabbat service at Sinai Temple was almost totally in English. At least Rabbi Jerry wore his yarmulke at the bimah, though I could have lived without the female cantor and her guitar and blue and gold yarmulke.

The service was much more subdued than I was used to. At 770 we pray aloud—very aloud, with a lot of enthusiastic bobbing and bowing. Women do not pray with us. The men pack into shul elbow to elbow. To someone unaccustomed to our ways it is complete chaos, and when the Rebbe speaks it is like God Himself is in our midst.

Sitting close to Sharon Kotin, almost touching knees, was like having God Herself next to me in a short plaid skirt. I wished we had a mechitzah between us because I could not concentrate on anything other than her loveliness. The Rebbe mandated a partition high enough to block all views of the opposite sex during worship. I now understood the wisdom behind his decree. No one wants an erection in shul, even if he does not know the proper name for the thickening in the place of his circumcision. I positioned my prayer book carefully on my lap.

I was smitten like the patriarch Jacob when he first laid

eyes on his beloved Rachel, so enthralled with the vision that he agreed to work seven years for her father, Laban, in order to gain her hand in marriage. I was only inches from Sharon Kotin, trembling, trying to steady myself.

What madness had taken hold of me to so adore this perfect girl who probably thought me such a fool? In the midst of the service I vowed to give up even handball if Hashem would allow me to marry her, and when I stood for the mourner's Kaddish, this girl I barely knew vied with my parents for a place in my meditations. At least my erection had subsided.

At the oneg, Sharon immediately ran off to a corner of the reception hall to kibbitz with her girlfriends. They eyed me over their shoulders and giggled as I shuffled awkwardly near the food table with a plate of cookies in my hand. A short girl with curly red hair stared at me but did not giggle like the rest, which made me shuffle even more uncomfortably. There were no other boys my age.

About forty people were milling about in the reception hall. A few parents attempted to keep their young children under control, but most paid no attention as the little pishers ran around screaming and piling their paper plates high with sweets.

I felt a hand on my shoulder.

"Shabbat Shalom," Rabbi Jerry said. "It's really great to see you here, Zev. Really great."

"Gut Shabbos," I replied, using the traditional Ashkenazi greeting.

"So when can I work you over again?" the rabbi asked, wearing an enormous grin. "I promise I won't go so easy on you next time."

He gave my shoulder a gentle squeeze.

"I probably shouldn't tell you this," he continued, "but I spoke with Dr. Gottlieb this afternoon. I'm sure you'll get to meet her soon. She's been pushing your tests through and says she'll have them all back by the middle of next week at the latest. What she's seen so far is very encouraging. You're a smart boy, Zev."

I was not paying close attention to Rabbi Jerry because I was too preoccupied tracing the curve of Sharon Kotin's back, and admiring the shape of her long legs from across the room. I did not care about being smart. I cared about only two things in this world—playing handball and marrying Sharon Kotin. If only Hashem would grant me those two wishes.

"If you'd like, the Kotins will pick you up for Shabbat services tomorrow morning," the rabbi said.

Of course I wanted that. Who wouldn't want another opportunity to be near his beloved? At the same time I was absolutely certain my deficiencies would ruin any chances I might have with her. I had to devise a better way of presenting myself. I needed to learn the things a modern girl would want to talk about.

Sharon Kotin did not say a word on the drive home. She faced away from me with her forehead pressed against the side window. Mrs. Kotin turned toward the back seat and asked if I enjoyed the service.

"Yes," I lied.

I did not enjoy the guitar-toting cantor and her modern reform songs that did not belong in shul, and aside from that, I could now add idolatry to my long list of moldering sins. Hashem said, *"Thou shalt have no other gods before Me."* He wrote this with his own finger on the stone tablets given to Moses. He would not be pleased with my latest flagrant violation of his commandments, worshiping and adoring Sharon Kotin as a goddess.

When they dropped me at the curb, Mrs. Kotin said they

would be back for me at nine forty-five the next morning. I stood on the sidewalk breathing in the night air as the taillights of their BMW faded down California Avenue.

Paul was not at home, and there was a note from Frida, saying she had gone for a drink with one of her girlfriends. I gathered a stack of magazines and went straight up to my room to search for an interesting topic of modern conversation. *Time* magazine made a big megillah over something called *the Internet* and the number of computers on it reaching one million, but I was not sure what the Internet was or that Sharon Kotin would care about such a thing.

Perhaps I could talk to her about the television show *Twin Peaks*, but how would I approach her and what would I say?

"Nu, Sharon, have you seen that fakaktah goyische show *Twin Peaks*? Who do you think killed Laura Palmer?"

I could not even come up with a pretext to start such a conversation, no less finish it. My search was pointless. I was well versed in only two subjects—Torah and handball— and I knew Sharon Kotin would not care to discuss either of them with me.

I comforted myself by again recalling the fortitude of our patriarch, Jacob, in his pursuit of Rachel; how for seven years he labored, and in all that time did not touch her—no, not once. Can you imagine such devotion, such single-mindedness? But on their wedding night Jacob's father-in-law tricked him by sending Rachel's older sister into the marriage tent instead. Jacob then agreed to work another seven years for Rachel—fourteen years of servitude to claim the woman he loved!

Surely I could be patient for a few weeks or months until I learned how a modern boy attracts the attention of a modern girl. Why would I expect this to happen overnight? Only one week ago I was throwing up on Rav Feldsher's shoes. I had never been alone with a girl, no less been in love. I would have to study American speech, watch TV, and listen to music. In due time I would learn to make fascinating conversation and witty sayings to win Sharon Kotin.

I fell asleep to visions of her beautiful face and tight sweater, and in the morning woke with my blue pajamas damp and sticky in the crotch. I washed and said the penitential prayers as we are commanded to do, but did not put on tefillin on account of Shabbos. Frida was making French toast when I came to the breakfast table dressed for shul.

"Going again, are you? The oneg must've been pretty good."

I asked if she would mind me doing some laundry and she told me to just throw my dirty clothes in the hamper, but I said I had enough to do a wash on my own and loaded the machine.

After breakfast I sat on the front porch waiting for the Kotins' BMW to turn down California Avenue. They were late. I remembered the many hours spent standing in line with my father to receive a ten-second blessing and a Sunday Dollar from the Rebbe. Hasidim would wait all day in the cold and rain for only a brief moment in his presence. I would gladly wait all day for a few minutes with Sharon Kotin. Her presence was more powerful than the Rebbe's. If you are a skeptic, then you have never been in love or are too old to remember.

At almost ten, a tan station wagon pulled up in front of our house and the side window lowered. Mrs. Kotin was alone in the car and motioned for me to sit up front. I tried not to appear disappointed.

"Where is Dr. Kotin?" I asked, intentionally not showing too much interest in her daughter.

She said, "He has rounds this morning and Sharon has

practice, so it's just the two of us."

"What is she practicing?" I asked.

"She's on the tennis team."

So Sharon Kotin was an athlete too? This came as the most blessed good news, because we had something in common after all. I had seen tennis played in Lincoln Terrace Park and knew it was a game of skill and stamina. One of the famous Brooklyn players called handball *tennis for savages*. This I understood.

"I play handball," I said to Mrs. Kotin.

"Oh, that's nice," she replied.

My skills as a conversationalist do not run deep, and as usual, I could not think of what to say next. Mrs. Kotin saved me the trouble.

She said, "The rabbi tells me you come from a religious background?"

So he had told them about me.

"Yes," I replied without elaborating.

"I was raised Presbyterian," she said.

This was a shock. I thought Mrs. Kotin looked even more Jewish than her husband.

She said, "I converted when I married Irv. Did the whole mikvah thing in Chicago. You know at first I didn't think I'd take to Judaism, but I've really come to love it. It's funny, because this is the most religious I've been in my whole life. I feel like a real Jew now."

And I was thinking I had never felt less like a real Jew. Doing laundry is one of the thirty-nine labors specifically forbidden on Shabbos, and now here I was riding in a car again. The rabbis say it is better to pray at home than drive to shul on Shabbos. Of course, none of my mixed-up devotion made a bit of sense, but this was the confusing mishmash I was living.

I said, "In Brooklyn we all live within walking distance of

shul. No one drives or rides on Shabbos."

"Well, we don't keep Shabbat that way," Mrs. Kotin said. "And anyway it would be impossible here in Urbana with everything so spread out. It's probably six or seven miles from our house to Sinai Temple."

"I have not always kept Shabbos either," I said with considerable shame.

Call it Shabbos, Shabbat, or the Sabbath; I was guilty of being a serial profaner of it.

When we arrived at shul my guts were churning like the soiled pajamas in Frida's washing machine. The service had already started. At least I was in a more sober state without the distraction of Sharon Kotin sitting next to me. I could not smell her perfume or hear the sound of her legs crossing. None of her friends were there except for the girl with the curly red hair. She stood across the room from me during the oneg, looking as lonely and out of place as I did.

On the drive home, Mrs. Kotin invited me to dinner at their house on Sunday. I was not sure why she asked, but was thrilled at the chance to see her lovely daughter again. I told her I would like to come, but needed to check with my sister first. Mrs. Kotin said I was welcome to bring Frida too. I told her she had a husband, but then corrected myself.

"Well, he is not really a husband," I said. "I do not know what to call him."

"Well, please invite him too," she said. "It's really no trouble at all for me to fix another plate."

At home I read psalms for nearly an hour, but my devotions were constantly disrupted by half-delirious visions of Sharon Kotin. I do not know if pining away over a young girl makes for good Shabbos meditations, but by the middle of the afternoon I was restless and once again contemplating the beauty of handball. This should not be a surprise.

As I approached the Big Green Wall I heard the thwack of a ball being slapped hard by a gloved hand, followed by the flat thunk of rubber against plywood, an entirely different sound than the crisp bark of a ball hitting concrete. The *thwack-thunk* repeated over and over again, faster and faster, followed by silence and then a man cursing in Italian.

"Cazzo . . . Merda."

I remembered those curses from the boys I played Ace-King-Queen with in Brooklyn, and rounded the wall to see a gray-haired man getting ready to serve to himself. He straightened up when he saw my handball glove.

"Hey," he said. "You come to play?"

"Yes," I replied.

"There's never anyone out here," he said. "I always by myself."

"Are you a one-wall player?" I asked.

"One, three, four-wall. Whatever, whenever, wherever. C'mon, step up, Junior. Joe Carcone's my name.

"I'm Zev Altshul."

"You're from New York, aren't you?" he asked. "Brooklyn?"

"How did you know?"

He said, "I'm from East Flatbush, or I was a long time ago. I recognized your accent. I'd say you're from Borough Park or Crown Heights, right? Maybe Williamsburg?"

"How do you know this?" I asked, amazed by the man's prophetic powers.

"Only a guess," he said. "But the yarmulke helped narrow it down."

I had forgotten about my yarmulke.

"C'mon, let's see what you got, Junior. Easy warm-up first?"

We rallied casually back and forth, gradually putting a

little more force into it. From the effortless way he moved and positioned himself on the court, I knew I would be a fool to underestimate this older fellow. He was obviously a much better player than either Christian or Tom.

"I can see you've played before," Joe Carcone said, after delivering a crisp sidearm to what he thought would be my weak side.

"And so have you," I answered with a lob that sent him all the way to the long line.

"I was pretty good back in the day," he said, coming forward again and swinging harder on the return. "I try and keep my skills up, but there're no strong players around here to help me stay sharp."

I waited until the ball was about a foot off the pavement and then snapped off a kill too low for him to return. He clearly got my message.

"So let's play," he said.

Joe Carcone won the coin toss for serve and got right down to business. This guy must have been at least fifty years old, but he served really hard and my return did not have much on it. He set me up and won the point.

"One–zero," he said with a swagger of confidence.

"This court is terrible," I complained. "The ball sticks to the wall and drops dead like a rock."

He said, "We've barely gotten started and you're whining already? So are you ready to go back to school, Junior? I've taken shits bigger than you."

Joe Carcone was most certainly from Brooklyn. This was the kind of street talk I was used to. This is what I heard last week from the Asian kid from Queens and the big guy from the Bronx. I shut them up and in due time I would shut Mr. Carcone up too, only he proved tougher than I thought. I struggled to figure out the rebound on that damn green plywood and was down 15–10, but did not intend to let this be a walkover.

It soon became clear that stamina was the old man's main weakness, so I slowed the game down with some longer defensive rallies and ran him around a bit. Joe Carcone was an intense player, and as the tide turned, he cursed himself every time he missed a shot. I surged ahead as he tired, eventually winning 21–17. I was afraid he was upset with me for beating him and told him I was sorry.

"Sorry?" he said. "You're what I've been praying for, Junior. Finally, I have some halfway decent competition around here. You notice I said *halfway* decent, right?"

We played a second game and I won that, too. Joe draped a towel over his shoulders as we left the court.

He said, "I'd invite you to go for a beer with me, but you look like you're barely old enough to shave."

"I shaved for the first time a few days ago. I'm fifteen years old."

He said, "C'mon, let's go grab something to eat."

Joe drove us to the same pizza shop I went to with Christian and Tom. He bought us two slices and two Cokes.

"I thought you wanted a beer," I said.

"I don't drink anymore. Booze can make you do things you regret. It doesn't agree with me."

That was when I first noticed the sadness in Joe Carcone's voice. There had been no trace of it earlier on the court. I thought he must be just like me—happiest when he is playing handball.

As we ate, he shared stories of his hustling days, betting big money in New York's parks and playgrounds.

He said, "I played all over the city, letting the mugs think they were hot stuff. A lot of players have big egos. Once in a while you'll find one with the goods to back it up, but there are enough out there who think they're the second coming of

Hershkowitz. Most couldn't carry his jock."

I told him about the tournament I played at Lincoln Terrace and that Harry Rosenfeld was going to bet on me in the quarterfinals.

Joe said, "I played against Harry plenty back in Brighton Beach when we were kids . . . both of us younger than you. He was a terror as a junior, you know. By the time he was eighteen or nineteen I don't think anyone could hit as hard as he did. So how did you do in the quarters?"

I cannot say why, but all the things I had so much trouble telling Rabbi Jerry and Dr. Niederhoffer came flowing out like a water faucet on full blast. I told Joe Carcone the truth about why I forfeited the game. I told him about my father being killed, and about coming home to an empty apartment, and about my mother taking her life that same night. I explained how I ended up in Champaign–Urbana with my sister, and even confessed that I blamed myself for the death of my parents.

Why would I share these personal things with Joe Carcone? I barely knew him. He was not a Jew, but I remembered what Rabbi Jerry said about guilt.

"And all this happened within a couple of weeks?" he said. "Shit, I don't know what to say, Junior."

"And not only that," I told him. "Until last week I studied only Torah and Talmud in yeshiva, and in the fall they will be placing me in public school and I am many grades behind and do not want to be stuck in a class with babies. This worries me more than anything."

"I understand," he said.

Once I started, I could not stop.

"And yesterday I met a very beautiful Jewish girl, but I have nothing to say to her because I know nothing of the modern things she knows and I am afraid I will embarrass myself every time I open my mouth because I am so backwards."

He said, "Whoa, Junior, you're blowing my mind with all this. There's no way you can solve a shitload of problems all at once; at least that's been my experience. You've got to break it all down, deal with one issue at a time, and then move on to the next. You hear what I'm saying? So what's the most critical thing for you right now? Maybe I can help with that."

"You already have," I said. "I am happiest when I am playing handball. I want to play more handball."

"OK, then join the club. So that first one's easy. We can do that. And what's next?"

"Sharon Kotin. I cannot stop thinking about her."

Joe Carcone laughed.

"You mean your little Jewish girl? That one's much more complicated. I have to get to know you a little better before I start giving advice on your love life."

I said, "I have never felt this way. I think I am in love."

"Yeah, I hear what you're saying, but don't worry, it'll pass. I can tell you love isn't all it's cracked up to be. I can't even remember the names of most of the girls I went with back in the day. You probably won't remember this one either."

"I will," I said. "I will definitely remember her."

"I suppose anything's possible. Get back to me in about thirty years."

"Do you have a wife?" I asked.

"I did," he answered.

"So you are divorced?"

"What, you want my whole life story?"

"Yes."

Joe laughed and said, "You're a piece of work, Junior . . . So the condensed version is I enlisted in the Air Force in the sixties to avoid Vietnam and got stationed up the road in Rantoul. I met a local girl while I was a carpenter on the Chanute base. We had some pretty good times in the beginning. Let's just say I had issues, but yeah, we're divorced now."

"What was her name?"

"JoAnne. We had two Joes in the house. I called her Joey."

"Do you still think of her?"

"Jesus, Junior, what the hell else would you like to know? Yes, I still think of her. More often than I'd like."

"Where is she now?"

"Last I heard, she was remarried and living in South Bend. I haven't seen her in years."

Something very strange was happening. I had never confided in anyone this way before, and I got the feeling this was new for Joe Carcone too. I asked why he stayed in Illinois all this time.

He said, "I always figured I'd go back to Brooklyn, but I ended up getting my teaching certificate at the U of I after my discharge and one thing led to another, and blah-blah-blah, here I am teaching woodworking at Champaign Centennial for more than twenty-five years now."

"Will I go to your school in the fall?" I asked.

He said, "Not if you live in Urbana, you won't. You'll probably go to Urbana High, but you say you're worried about what grade they're going to put you in, right?"

I nodded.

"Have you been tested yet . . . you know, IQ and placement testing, that sort of thing?"

"I took many tests the other day."

"OK, good. So now we'll just have to wait for the results, but you see, you've already made progress. One day at a time. I've heard that plenty in my life. One day at a time, that's how you do it, Junior. It works if you work it . . . You wanna play again tomorrow?"

We agreed to meet after lunch and I walked home in the

fading daylight with Sharon Kotin's face rising like the pale moon over the great leafy trees. Joe Carcone said I would not remember her in a few years. I did not believe him.

Loud music was blaring from the garage as I walked up the driveway on California Avenue. Paul was working in his studio and Frida was busy cooking dinner in the kitchen. I joined her at the counter and watched her pounding chicken breasts with a wooden mallet. I must have been standing too close.

"You're hovering, Zevi," she said. "Give me some space."

I stepped back a little and picked up a bottle of cooking oil. I read the label while twisting the cap on and off. It made a clicking sound. Frida grabbed the bottle away. Next I reached for a container of black peppercorns.

"Will you please quit rattling those things?" she said. "Jesus, settle down already, you're giving me shpilkes."

I think she used that Yiddish word just for my benefit. I set the peppercorns down and picked up a shiny metal cheese grater.

She said, "So what's up with you? You're so fidgety. Something's on your mind."

I set the cheese grater back on the counter.

"What's wrong?" she asked. "Tell me."

I reached for the cheese grater again and Frida moved it farther away from me.

"There is a girl," I said, looking down at my feet.

She broke out in a huge grin.

"You're kidding, Zevi? So you're the man about town already? How exciting."

"I met her in shul. Her name is Sharon Kotin and her mother invited me to dinner tomorrow night."

"That's very nice, so you should go. What's the problem?"

"She invited you and Paul too."

Frida made enough of a face to let me know that was not going to happen.

She said, "I don't think that'll work for us, but you go yourself. Why not?"

"Because I will have to talk to her and I do not know how."

Frida laid her spatula down and gave me her full attention.

"I understand, Zevi; really, I do. It's a different world, isn't it? What can I do to help you?"

I asked how she learned to speak American so well.

She said, "In the beginning I messed up constantly. I had to concentrate on pronouncing every word, but after a while it got easier and started coming naturally. I don't even think about how to say things anymore. Getting away from Crown Heights where everyone speaks Yiddish and that fucking Yeshivish they call English. That was the main thing. Talking with Paul all the time helped too, and I watched a lot of TV when I first came out here. I talked to the TV when Paul wasn't home. It's a little weird, but it's a good way to practice."

"But how did you learn what to talk about?"

"I'm not sure what you mean. You talk about what you know."

"So what if you do not know anything?"

Frida drew closer and touched my cheek.

"Look at me, Zevi. Look at me. Please give yourself a break, will you? Everything will come in good time. For now just be the sweet and decent boy you are. There aren't too many of those out there and the right girl will see that. Now why don't you clear out of the kitchen so I can get our dinner on the table. Go watch TV and pay attention to how Americans pronounce words like *big* instead of *beeg*, the cadence of their speech, that sort of thing. You can practice while you watch."

We did not have a TV at home in Crown Heights. It was forbidden, so the question of watching on Shabbos never came up. I sat down on the living room couch, rationalizing that the remote control might isolate me enough to make the TV kosher—after all, it *is* called *the remote*, isn't it? I picked it up and pushed the POWER button.

The TV sizzled to life and I had a vision of the Rebbe, his white-bearded face smiling at me from the screen and his blue eyes twinkling as happily as the Klezmer music playing in the background. He raised a wizened index finger and wagged it gently, not more than an inch side to side. The Rebbe looked directly at me as he spoke in Yiddish:

"I have seen the sparks from your remote control all the way from Brooklyn, Zev Altshul. Nu? You have been a naughty little Yid, running off to Babylon with your sister. Now put down that muktzeh and come; we will daven together until Havdalah."

I pressed the CHANNEL button and *The Rebbe Show* vanished from the screen. I pressed the button again and again, flipping through shows of every kind, from news to nature, cooking to sports, until I found an interesting program on a Chicago station. I turned the sound lower. After about twenty minutes, Frida came into the living room.

"Dinner's almost ready," she said. "What the hell are you watching? What is this, *Soul Train?*"

I told her I liked the announcer's voice, but Frida laughed because she knew I really liked watching the Black girls jiggling and gyrating in their skintight outfits. This was something I had never seen.

"Don't be ashamed, Zevi, there's nothing wrong with it. Men like that sort of thing, you know. It's natural and you're becoming a man."

I was embarrassed that my sister knew so much about me. I changed the channel. *Soul Train* was probably not good Shabbos TV anyway, even if TV was allowed on Shabbos.

After dinner Frida went to a bar with one of her friends again and Paul Griffin went to work in his studio. He said he wanted to discuss something with me, so I followed him out there. He had made a great deal of progress on the painting since the last time I saw it. The most striking change was the blue-green paint he added to Frida's hand, the hand holding the sleeping man's wallet. It looked almost like it was under a spotlight as she removed the money.

"How're you making out so far—all OK?" he asked.

"I think so," I replied, trying not to stare at the naked Frida.

"You know I'm perfectly happy having you stay with us. That's what Free wants and you're her brother and all. I understand that, but I think you need to contribute something to the household, you know, at least until you're back in school or whatever. It's not good to be hanging out all day living on someone else's dime, you know what I'm saying?"

I did.

"Did you bring any money out here with you? I mean like savings, or from your parents or anything?"

"I have a little," was all I said.

Frida obviously had not told him about the garbage bag and I did not know how to answer. The only thing I was certain of was that I should not be the one to tell him.

"So you think a hundred a month would be fair to start with? It won't even begin to cover your food, but at least it's something."

I quickly did the math as best I could. At a hundred dollars a month I could live with Paul Griffin for the next forty years or more.

"That would be OK," I said.

"I'll be fair with you, you don't have to worry. So go back

to the house now; I've got work to do, and this is just between us, OK? Don't mention it to Free."

I watched some TV in the living room and went to bed
about midnight. I fell asleep carving a likeness of Sharon Kotin's face, sculpting her high cheekbones and modeling her
dark brown eyes. Soon I heard the thwacking of a handball
again and felt the tingling in my palms, one of the best feelings
on earth.

At about eight thirty the next morning I was in the kitch-
en with Frida when the phone rang. I could tell she was not
pleased to hear from the person on the other end of the line.

"Yes. Yes, I remember," she said.

The caller did most of the talking. Frida placed her hand
over the mouthpiece and spoke to me in a hushed voice.

"It's Rabbi Feldsher. He wants to talk to you . . . I'm not
so sure that's a good idea."

She uncovered the mouthpiece. I could not hear what
the rabbi was saying, but whatever it was made Frida angry.

"Well, that'll be up to Zev," she said. "You know he's not a
prisoner here. He's a minor, but he has rights too, and you're
not his father."

She listened in silence again, her voice a little calmer
when she replied.

"Yes, I understand what you're saying. Here, let me put
him on."

She handed me the receiver and Rav Feldsher spoke to
me in his most familiar grandfatherly Yiddish.

"You are well, Zev? I hope you do not think we have forgotten about you?"

I told him I was fine.

"You have been in our prayers already since you left. The
Rebbe has taken a special interest in you, kinehora, and he

135

wants you to come home. This is what your father would have wanted too, yes? You know this."

I did not respond, but Rav Feldsher was right. My father would be extremely unhappy if he knew what I was doing in Illinois.

"The Rebbe says you will not have to live with the Resnicks or with strangers. Yoel and Hudel Friedman have agreed to be your guardians until you are eighteen and they are happy to have you. They are the parents of one of your classmates . . . Mordecai. You know Mordie Friedman, no? So you will go to the same school and live in the same neighborhood as always. And the Rebbe recognizes your gifts. He gives you his blessing to play handball, only never on Shabbos or Yom Tov."

I admit Rav Feldsher's offer was tempting. The thought of starting public school in Urbana scared me to death. It would be so much easier to be back in yeshiva following the rules again, or at least trying to most of the time. Everything was familiar in Crown Heights. The sky was smaller there and my life would go on as planned.

He said, "We can send a car by you right now and you will be in Brooklyn with us tomorrow. Nu, shall we do this then?"

I considered what I would gain by returning to Brooklyn and also what I would be giving up. When I woke up this morning I was thrilled to look in the mirror and not see that scruffy Hasidic child-beard. I liked my new Nike T-shirt and did not miss my fedora and black coat one little bit. In Urbana I could eat pizza without making sure the cheese had been made by Jews and inspected by rabbis, even if I did have to pick the pork off it. And there was my handball game later in the afternoon with my new friend, Joe Carcone, and dinner that night with Sharon Kotin.

Ah yes, Sharon Kotin. Back in Brooklyn I would not be alone with another girl until marriage. I would not even speak privately to one until a match was arranged for me. And who would arrange such a shidduch with our family history, with my mother's suicide and my off-the-derech sister? Who would agree to a match with Zev Altshul? *"There is bad blood in that family."*

I told Rav Feldsher I wanted to stay in Illinois.

"And I am saying this is unwise," he replied less patiently. "Your sister is off-the-derech. Yes, this is her choice and there is nothing to be done by her, but you are a Hasid. You should not be living with her and her shaygetz. You will become an estranged soul too."

He then spoke to me in Hebrew—lashon hakodesh—the holy tongue. He quoted from the Book of Leviticus:

"I am the Lord your God. Do not follow the ways of Egypt. Do not follow their customs."

He said, "We want you to come home of your own accord, Zev. Frayda is not your legal guardian and you should not have run off like two dogs in the night."

"It wasn't night," I protested in English.

Then Rav Feldsher made a serious mistake.

He said, "You are a minor and your sister is a loose woman and is not a fit guardian for a young boy. There are things we have learned about her, shameful things it is disgraceful to speak of. The beis din will be told. As we speak, the Friedmans are filing papers in Brooklyn family court with the Rebbe's blessing. Crown Heights is your home, where you belong with your people."

The rabbi should never have criticized my sister like that. The beis din didn't know her. She might not have been my legal guardian, but Frida was my only flesh and blood and as fit as anyone to take care of me. She came back into my life when I needed her, and I was not about to go live with strangers in Brooklyn.

"I will be staying here with Frida," I said. "And her name is Frida now, not Frayda."

I passed the phone back to her. She held it six inches from her ear and made funny faces while Rav Feldsher spoke. I could not hear exactly what he was saying, but Frida's reply left no room for misunderstanding.

She said, "I think you have some pretty weird ideas about what it means to be helpful, Rabbi, but if that's the way you want it, you'll just have to file your papers and come get us. We'll see you in court."

She hung up the phone, shook her head, and sighed.

"What's up with that guy?" she said. "He must really want you back there."

Later that day I met Joe Carcone at the Big Green Wall. We played three games and I won them all without much trouble, as I had gotten more used to the plywood's dull rebound. As we were leaving he asked if I wanted to grab a bite to eat and I told him I needed to get ready for dinner at Sharon Kotin's. That was the second time I noticed the great sadness in him. Joe Carcone was a lonely man.

Back at the house I showered, changed clothes, and waited on the porch for the Kotins, practicing my American speech by repeating, "Hi, how you doin'?" over and over again.

Just after five thirty the tan station wagon pulled into our driveway. This time a young man was behind the wheel.

"Hey," the driver said as I approached the car. "My mom asked me to come get you."

"Hey," I replied, trying to imitate his accent.

I opened the passenger door and he introduced himself

as Richie.

"I am Zev," I said as I slid in, berating myself for not using the American contraction.

"I'm Zev," I repeated correctly.

"I heard you the first time," he said. "So you're the new Jew in town?"

He apologized when he saw the troubled look on my face.

"I'm only kidding, sorry. My mom tells me you're from New York."

"I am from Brooklyn," I answered, again regretting not using the contraction.

"So what brings you out here?"

I told him I was living with my sister, hoping that explanation would satisfy him.

"I don't know why anyone would want to come here from New York. Champaign's pretty much a corn and soybeans town. It's a shithole except for the university."

Richie Kotin spoke with an air of superiority.

"I'm up at Northwestern in Chicago," he said. "I don't plan on ever living here again."

Richie hadn't driven much more than ten blocks when he pulled into a driveway on Delaware Avenue. The houses were much larger and better kept than on California. The Kotins had a swimming pool in their backyard.

Mrs. Kotin greeted us at the door and called upstairs to Sharon, then pointed down a hallway hung with colorful modern art paintings, the kind Frida called *abstract*. She said, "Dr. Kotin's watching baseball in the family room. Why don't you go and join the boys. I'll be there in just a second."

Richie was already seated with his feet up on an ottoman. Dr. Kotin briefly looked up from the screen and smiled when I entered the room.

"Ah, here you are, Zev. Good to see you. Come in and sit down. The Cubbies are playing the Pirates."

I was glad he and Richie were so engrossed in the game because it saved me the trouble of making conversation. After ten minutes or so, Mrs. Kotin peeked in and asked if anyone wanted something to drink. I said no thank you even though I was still thirsty from handball.

"Didn't Sharon come down yet?" she asked. "Let me go see what's keeping her."

A few minutes later Sharon came in looking about as happy as Frida did when she heard Rav Feldsher on the other end of the line. She sank into an overstuffed chair and pulled her knees up to her chest after flashing me one of the most insincere smiles I had ever seen. Mrs. Kotin flashed an equally exasperated look at her irritated daughter before returning to the kitchen.

A pulse of heat climbed up the back of my neck, whether from anger or embarrassment I am not exactly sure, but it was suddenly clear why the Kotins invited me over. Rabbi Jerry had told them all about me—the sorry little Yid orphan, the Hasidic misfit who needed a place to fit in. I suppose reform Jews have their mitzvot too, but I resented being the charity case at their family dinner. I excused myself and left for the kitchen.

Whatever Mrs. Kotin was cooking smelled delicious, and my stomach was rumbling with hunger, but I asked if she would mind if I went home.

"Why, Zev, what's wrong?"

I closed my eyes and massaged my temples theatrically, trying to look as pitiful as possible.

I said, "I have a headache . . . a very bad one."

Mrs. Kotin offered me some Tylenol, but I told her I needed to go home and lie down in a dark room. I knew all about migraines. My mother had them frequently.

I said, "That's the only thing that helps when it is like this."

"I hate to see you miss dinner," she said. "Why don't you just stay for a quick bite and then we'll take you home right after."

"No . . . no thank you," I replied. "I need to go home now. I would have walked anyway if I knew you lived this close."

I apologized for the trouble and abruptly left without saying goodbye to the rest of the family. The sound of the front door shutting behind me eased my humiliation a little, but the relief did not last long.

The lawns grew wilder the closer I got to California Avenue, scraggly weeds bulging through cracks in the uneven sidewalks. A tree branch about the size of a baseball bat lay at angles in front of me, and when I stopped to kick it to the curb, the rotten wood exploded off the tip of my sneaker, sending soggy brown chunks flying into the street.

I cursed aloud like a crazy man in both Yiddish and English, raging at Rabbi Jerry for exposing the intimate details of my life. I cursed Sharon Kotin for treating me like crumbs of discarded leaven on Pesach. I cursed Rav Feldsher for trying to run my life, and Paul Griffin for trying to run my sister's. More than that, I cursed myself for being an idiot fool cursing in the street on an empty stomach instead of eating a home-cooked meal with the Kotins.

Most of all, I cursed Hashem, the source of all my troubles.

My punisher had followed me from Brooklyn and set himself against me in my new home. I cursed him for the deaths of my father and mother, for the cadence of my awkward speech, and for everything I never learned in yeshiva. I cursed him for my love of handball and my love of Sharon

Kotin. I cursed him with all my might.

I confess this even though any fool, Jew or a gentile, knows it is useless to curse God. You may struggle with him all you like; he will always get the better of you. You may cry out in your bitterness like Job, or wrestle with the angel like Jacob, but he will defeat you every time. Yet knowing this did not stop me. I continued walking straight past our house to Zorba's on Green Street, where the counterman seemed happy to see me.

"Hey, look who's here again," he said. "Let me guess . . . a gyro, hold the tzatziki sauce, right?"

I said, "I'll have a gyro, but with all the sauce this time, and also a large Greek salad with lots of cheese on it."

Take that, Hashem.

Rabbi Jerry called on Monday morning. I was not happy to hear from him. He asked how I was feeling, and the concern in his voice let me know he had already spoken with the Kotins about my odd behavior the previous evening. I did not like them discussing me behind my back. He said he had good news: the results of my tests had come in and Dr. Gottlieb wanted to meet with me on Thursday. I thanked him and got off the phone.

It was raining heavily, so I spent the morning watching game shows on TV, paying careful attention to the rhythm of the contestants' speech, their use of contractions and slang words. With Paul and Frida out of the house, I watched reruns of *Soul Train*, taking pleasure in ogling the women's round bottoms while imitating Don Cornelius's silky voice with my accent flipping back and forth between American and Yeshivish like an out-of-control Shabbos elevator.

It quit raining in the afternoon, so I practiced my serve at the Big Green Wall, waiting for Joe Carcone to finish teaching. I broke into a wide grin at the sight of him slipping on his handball gloves.

"You ready for your daily ass whippin'?" he asked as he set aside his towel and stepped onto the court.

"You can always hope," I answered.

A snappy comeback like that would have been impossible a couple of weeks ago in my fedora and black coat, but felt almost natural in my Nike shirt and shorts. My old Hasidic uniform was like a suit of armor that kept the world out and me in.

We played every day that week, with the plywood's dead rebound forcing me to swing harder and Joe pushing me to be more aggressive. He got right up in my face with his Brooklyn street swagger.

"You're giving away too much of the court," he shouted. "You make it too easy for me to get a clear line on my returns. Great players are never that polite. You've got to make the fuckers work for every point. Fight 'em for every inch. Let 'em know you're a fucking powerhouse and you're sure as hell not going to be intimidated. You don't take shit and you don't back down from anyone, got that?"

I was having one of the best weeks of my life until Thursday morning, when Frida drove me to the Education Building for my appointment with Dr. Gottlieb. The smallish woman with a pleasant face greeted us at the door with a firm handshake.

"It's nice to meet you," she said. "The rabbi has told me so much about you."

I'm sure he had.

Her sunny office was full of houseplants, and the walls were lined with framed diplomas and children's drawings. Dr. Gottlieb offered us hard candy from a jar on her desk.

"So then, let's get down to business," she said, leafing

through papers in a manila folder. "First I must tell you, you're a very bright young man, Zev, that much is quite evident. You scored exceptionally well on your IQ and Cognitive Ability tests, and your visual-motor and visual-spatial skills are literally off the charts. Honestly, I can't remember seeing more impressive scores in those areas.

"I'm afraid you did less well on your Wechslers. Those are the tests that measure things like spelling, vocabulary, reading comprehension, math . . . all areas of academic achievement. That's where your lowest scores coalesce and they suggest a serious need for remediation."

"Remediation?" Frida asked.

"This is pretty much what we'd expect from a student coming from Zev's background," Dr. Gottlieb explained. "He's clearly a gifted young man in unusual circumstances. To put it in the simplest terms, he has no trouble learning, but at the moment he's behind where a typical tenth grader should be. It's not because of any learning disabilities. We see this with a lot of homeschooled kids entering the system.

"Zev clearly has the potential to excel academically, but at this point it would be a huge mistake to put him into a class with students of his own chronological age. He's not prepared to meet the demands of the curriculum and I'm afraid it would be a challenge for him socially too. I'm sorry to put it so bluntly, but Zev's been segregated from the world his entire life. He's been raised in the equivalent of a foreign country and denied a proper education. It'll take some time for him to catch up."

"So what are you suggesting?" Frida asked.

"I recommend we begin with a comprehensive tutoring program for the remainder of the spring and summer to try and address Zev's current academic needs. We can follow up with retesting before classes start in the fall and see how much progress he's made."

Frida asked how expensive this was going to be. I thought that was funny considering I had fifty thousand dollars stashed under my bed.

Dr. Gottlieb smiled and said, "That's the beauty of being affiliated with the U of I. We have graduate students who'll do the tutoring for credit, so there's no cost except for textbooks and that sort of thing. Should be fairly minimal. I'm very busy at the moment, but Rabbi Feinstein has volunteered to help with the logistics if that's all right with you."

"That's very kind . . . thank you," Frida said.

Then Dr. Gottlieb swiveled her chair in my direction. Her deep blue eyes reminded me a little of the Rebbe's and I got the feeling she also knew more about me than was evident on the surface.

She said, "Zev, you understand this means you'll have tutoring sessions three days a week and lots of reading assignments and homework in between. You're going to be a very busy boy, but it's your best hope for being enrolled at anything close to your grade level in the fall. Are you willing to commit to a program like this? It'll be pretty intense and you'll have to work hard."

I told her I would try.

"Good," Dr. Gottlieb said. "Then I'll have my grad assistants and Rabbi Feinstein arrange things. I'm hoping we can get started right away."

Rabbi Jerry called the following morning to set up my tutoring schedule. Once everything was in order he asked if I planned on attending shul that evening. He said he could have someone else pick me up if that would make me feel more comfortable. In truth, the meal I never ate at the Kotins' left a bad taste in my mouth, but I told the rabbi I would be ready when they came for me.

Then he said, "You want to hear the strangest thing? All these years I've been in Champaign–Urbana and I've never seen even one Hasid. Now in less than two weeks I've seen three."

"What do you mean?" I asked. "Are you saying there are others here besides me?"

"I saw two men in a white van in downtown Urbana yesterday afternoon. They kept circling the block by the Illini Union. That's what drew my attention, the same van going round and round the block like that. They finally parked and got out practically right in front of me. I smiled and said hello, but they acted like they didn't hear me even though they were only a few feet away."

My first thought was that the Rebbe had sent these men to take me home to Brooklyn. I asked what they looked like, and Rabbi Jerry chuckled.

"It's funny you should ask that . . . No offense, but they looked like just about every other thirty- or forty-something Hasid—black pants, black shoes, black plastic glasses, black beards and yarmulkes. They must've left their black jackets and hats in the van, but there's no doubt they were Hasids. One was much taller than the other. A really brawny guy. I thought they might be in Urbana visiting you, but I guess not, eh?"

"No, I guess not," I said, paying careful attention to pronounce the words like an American. If they were here to see me, a visit was not exactly how I would describe it.

I hung up the phone and took a deep breath, telling myself this was probably just a coincidence and these men were in Urbana on other business. After all, why would Rav Feldsher or the Rebbe want me back in Crown Heights badly enough to send people after me? Were they really that worried about one Hasidic kid going off-the-derech?

I glanced over my shoulder all the way to my Friday appointment with Tom and Christian. I counted four white vans, three with writing on the side, but none driven by bearded men in yarmulkes. I was relieved to finally be inside the safety of the rec center.

My new friends were even less of a challenge this time. I spotted them each fifteen points and still won all three games handily. They were good sports and did not seem to mind losing to me, but things did not go so well in the locker room after the game.

I think Christian might have seen me cringe at the sight of his uncircumcised penis. I had seen plenty of penises in the mikvah, but this was the first one with a foreskin. I had been told how the Nazis rounded men up on the street and made them drop their trousers. The circumcised were either shot or sent to the camps. Christian's penis was a menacing reminder that the world is not a safe place for Jews.

The three of us went to the same restaurant for lunch, only this time Tom asked what toppings I wanted on our pizza. I concentrated on my American phrasing and pronunciation.

"How about onions and mushrooms?"

"No meat?" he asked. "What're you, a vegetarian or something?"

I told them I did not eat pork.

"Oh, sorry," he said. "I guess we should've figured that out after last week, with the pepperoni and your yarmulke and all."

After lunch we played for two more hours on the Big Green Wall. When we were done, I let them know I would not be able to keep our Friday appointments anymore because I had a tutoring session in the morning. They offered to move their rec center court time to the afternoon if that would help, but I told them we would have to wait and see. My friends returned to their dorm and I headed for home along Lincoln Avenue.

My pulse raced as I rounded the corner at California and saw the flashing blue lights up ahead. I could not tell if they were in front of our house or not. I doubled my pace, my heart racing. A single police car blocked our driveway and another unmarked one was parked across the street. I hesitated at the curb, imagining what might have happened if the two men in the white van had found Frida home alone. I gathered what little courage I had and proceeded up the driveway to find the side door kicked in and jagged splinters of the jam littering the entry.

I stepped cautiously across the threshold. The kitchen had been torn apart, with every drawer and cupboard emptied onto the floor and broken glass and dishes scattered everywhere. Frida was at the kitchen table sitting across from a policeman in a suit who was taking notes in a spiral pad. She leapt from her chair as soon as she saw me.

"Thank God you're all right, Zevi; I was so worried about you."

Paul Griffin entered the kitchen from the living room followed by a policeman in uniform.

"The whole house is a fucking wreck," Paul snarled. "Goddamn fucking shit."

The policeman in the suit asked if I knew anything about what happened in the house today. I was about to answer when Frida jumped in.

"He doesn't know anything; he's been in Urbana less than two weeks."

The policeman clearly did not appreciate being interrupted.

He said, "Please let him answer for himself," and then turned back to me.

"Did you see anything at all unusual recently, any strangers hanging around, that sort of thing?"

I told him no.

"And can you tell me where you were today?" he asked.

Frida broke in again, saying, "I already told you he doesn't know anyone around here."

"OK then," the policeman said, abruptly getting up from the table and motioning for me to follow him outside. Frida demanded to know where he was taking me.

"Since you can't control yourself, miss, I'm going to take your brother's statement in private, if you don't mind."

She said, "He's a minor, you know. You can't just question him like that without my permission."

"Excuse me, are you his legal guardian?"

"I am," she said.

"Then if you don't mind, I'd like to get a statement from your brother."

"For Christ's sake, Free," Paul Griffin shouted. "Just let the man do his job, will you."

The policeman questioned me out on the driveway. He asked where I had been all day. I told him I was at the rec center in the morning, then went for pizza, and played outside again the rest of the afternoon.

"And I suppose you have people who can corroborate your story?"

I told him I did and he asked for their names.

"Tom and Christian," I said.

"What are their last names?"

I shrugged. It never seemed like something I needed to know.

He didn't like that answer and asked again if I knew anything more about what happened in the house. He wore a very serious expression and spoke firmly.

"Listen to me, son, when we see a place totally ransacked

like this and supposedly nothing's been taken, it raises plenty of suspicions. Burglars don't usually leave empty-handed when there are stereos and other valuables lying around. You sure you haven't seen anything going on *inside* the house?"

"What do you mean?" I asked. I had never spoken to a policeman before and my hands were sweaty and shaking.

"I think you know what I mean," he said, sharpening his voice for emphasis. "Have you seen anything I should know about?"

He pronounced each word slowly and carefully, as if speaking to someone who did not understand English.

"Anything you can tell me will be helpful," he said in a friendlier tone. "Trust me, just be honest and I'll treat you right."

If I let him know about the two men in the van I would have to explain why they were looking for me and confess that Frida was not really my legal guardian. I decided to keep my mouth shut.

"What did you say your first name was again?" the officer asked without looking up, still jotting down notes in his pad.

"Zev."

"Is that short for something?"

"No."

"And is your last name the same as your sister's?"

"Yes. Altshul. Altshul is our last name."

"So where are your parents?" he asked.

"They are both dead."

The policeman stopped writing and looked up at me. He scratched his right eyebrow with the back of his pen. His tone of voice softened.

"Listen, Zev, I'm going to level with you. With a break-in like this, the perpetrators are looking for something specific, and it's a good bet there's some illegal activity going on in

150

the house . . . most often drugs. Are you sure you wouldn't know anything about that? You'd really be helping us out and might even be helping your sister too."

I told him I didn't know anything about drugs.

"Are you being honest with me? This could come back on you if it turns out you're hiding something from us."

I told him I always try to be honest, which of course was a lie.

"OK then," he said, putting his notepad away. "We might as well go back inside, but you're going to call me if you remember anything or see something I should know about, right?"

He handed me his business card: RICHARD MULHERN: URBANA POLICE DEPARTMENT, DETECTIVE CID.

The policemen wrapped up their work and left us to clean up the mess. Paul Griffin was in an even uglier mood than usual, cursing and acting like he wanted to punch somebody.

He said, "I'm going to run to the hardware store to get these fucking doors secured while it's still light out. Goddamn it, this is just what I need with a show coming up."

"Did they break into your studio too?" I asked.

"You're goddamn fucking right they did."

Frida shushed me and told me to go get the broom and dustpan, but as soon as Paul left she grabbed my arm and rushed me upstairs to my room. What little clothes I owned were tossed everywhere and my father's suitcase was sitting upside down in the middle of the floor, unlatched and empty.

"They stole Abba's money," Frida said in a panic. "They took every last dollar of it."

I was about to speak, but she cut me off.

"Whoever did this knew exactly what they were looking for, but I don't understand how anyone could've known we had that kind of money in the house."

Then I told her about the two Hasidic men Rabbi Jerry saw in Urbana.

"I thought they were here to take me back to Brooklyn," I said.

"Well, the money's gone and there's nothing we can do about it."

"But it's not gone," I said. "I still have it."

"What are you talking about? They tore the whole house apart."

I said, "The money is in my locker at the rec center. I thought it would be safer there than under the bed. I kept three hundred dollars in my socks . . . Look, it's still here."

I picked up a bulging pair of socks, unrolled them, and held the bills out.

"Thank God," Frida said. "But why'd you move the money out of the house?"

"You said we could get in trouble if we went to the bank and I was afraid Paul might come looking for it. He asked if I brought any money with me from Brooklyn and I told him I had a little. I'm sorry, I know it is bad for me not to trust him."

"Paul asked you for money?"

"Only a hundred dollars a month for food. I think that is very fair."

"That's not the point," she said. "We never discussed it and Paul didn't tell me he'd asked you for anything."

"But you didn't tell him about Abba's money either."

"Now I'm glad I didn't," she said.

The look in Frida's eye reminded me of her expression in Paul Griffin's painting, *Tit for Tat*.

I said, "Maybe those men didn't know anything about the money. You told Rav Feldsher to come get us. Maybe tearing the house up was something . . . something like a warning."

"A warning of what?" she said. "That's absolutely ridiculous. What were they going to do, kidnap you? It's absurd. And don't say anything else about this to Paul. He's upset enough as it is. You know they slashed the new painting he was almost finished with."

"Why would they do that?" I asked.

"How should I know? The cops said maybe it could've been an angry student or something. They thought it was strange too. Anyway, this whole thing is crazy, but if the people who did this were really Hasids, they won't be back tonight or tomorrow—it's Shabbos."

That's when I remembered the Kotins were coming to pick me up for shul. I did not have a number to contact them and it was almost seven-fifteen. I made it to the curb just as Mrs. Kotin pulled up in her station wagon. She was alone again.

"You're not going to temple like that, are you?" she asked, surprised to see me still in my handball shorts. Then I told her I would not be going to shul at all and her lips puckered like she'd bitten into something sour. I could not blame her for being annoyed with me, especially after the way I ran out on her dinner last Sunday.

"Our house was broken into this afternoon," I explained.

"Oh my God." Her lips uncurled. "That's awful. I'm so sorry. Is there anything I can do?"

"No thank you," I said. "We have already started cleaning."

I was not paying attention to my speech and pronounced every word like a Yiddish robot again, the boy with no personality who had never been taught to carry on a conversation in English.

Mrs. Kotin asked if I wanted to be picked up for the morning service. I thanked her, but told her we had too much work to do. I was more careful with my phrasing this time and made sure to use the contractions.

"OK then," she replied. "I'd better get going. I don't want to be late."

I said, "Say hi to Dr. Kotin and Sharon for me, OK?"

I liked the way that sounded. It came out so smoothly, I decided to venture a little further into the wild frontier of American speech.

"OK then, I'm outta here," I said, flashing a vee with two fingers, "Peace, Love, and Soul."

"Goodbye Zev," Mrs. Kotin said, unable to stifle her laughter. "You take care."

I spent that evening and most of next day picking up strewn clothing, tossing damaged household items in the trash, and sweeping up broken glass. Every swish of the broom filled me with remorse, not because I was laboring on Shabbos, but because this most recent misfortune was once again my fault.

On Sunday morning I left early for the Big Green Wall to practice before my game with Joe Carcone. Thanks to my years at yeshiva, I did not mind the repetition: *Serve–return–pick up the ball* . . . *Serve–return–pick up the ball* . . . *Serve–return–pick up the ball* . . . Not so different than examining every aleph and gimel in the Torah.

I had been practicing for more than half an hour, concentrating on hitting one spot on the wall as hard as I could, when I caught a blur of movement to my right. It all happened so quickly. I glanced up to see what I thought was a Hasidic man rushing at me. I am not exactly sure what happened next, because in an instant I was blindsided from behind and sent sprawling facedown onto the pavement.

Before I could gather my thoughts, someone grabbed the back of my T-shirt. The fabric tore as he flipped me over, and I looked up to see Shmuel Resnick's malignant grin.

"So are you happy to see me, Hoizer Gaier?"

My thoughts were in a muddle. I could not imagine what Shmuel Resnick was doing in Urbana. The man never wanted to see or hear from me again. Of all people, Rav Feldsher would never have sent Shmuel Resnick to bring me home to Brooklyn.

He dropped both knees hard onto my outstretched biceps, slamming his full weight down on them. I let out a pathetic whimper as a searing electric jolt jittered from my shoulders to my fingertips. He slapped me hard across the face three or four times, which did nothing to clear the fog from my mind, but let me know he meant business. The big Jew shouted at me in Yiddish as the other man stood over me, smirking.

"You fucking little shit, so you think we were just going to let you and your cunt sister march right out of town, eh? Where is it?"

If there was any doubt before, I now knew Shmuel Resnick was not in Urbana on the Rebbe's business and had not come to take me home.

"So where is it?" he asked again, slapping me forehand and back.

"Where is what?" I asked.

Before I had a chance to say another word, he grabbed the front of my T-shirt and lifted my head off the asphalt.

"Here, I'll show you what, Mister Smart Guy."

He punched me ferociously enough to send my head snapping back against the pavement. My eyes immediately welled with tears and iron-salty blood gurgled down the back of my throat. I had never been hit so hard in my life. I was a yeshiva student, not some Brooklyn street fighter. This should not have been happening to me.

Shmuel Resnick grabbed my shirtfront and pulled my head up again.

"Here, Mister Smart Guy, let me ask you again."

He did not ask or give me a chance to answer before punching me a second time. This one sent my nose wandering across my face. I was dizzy and gagging on my own blood.

"So where is it?" he asked again in Yiddish.

"What?" I answered in English, coughing speckles of bright red blood onto the front of his white dress shirt.

"You know exactly what I am talking about, you off-the-derech piece of shit. You need more convincing? How would you like your hands broken too, eh? You think I would not do it? Nu, I would love to make sure you do not play your fucking handball again. Tell me where it is, or you will find out how persuasive my friend Heshy can be. The fun is just getting started."

"What? I don't know what you're looking for," I said.

"Then we will see if breaking your precious hands will help with your memory . . . Heshy," he said, calling for his partner.

"This is your last chance, Hoizer Gaier. What do you say? We are not stupid. We know you and your whore sister have it. Oh, and by the way, we saw her big titties and hairy pussy on display in the goy's workshop. Very nice, showing the whole world what kind of woman she is. Your father would be very proud of both of you. We fixed the picture for him before we left. Now where is it? This is your last chance."

My arms were numb, still pinned beneath Shmuel Resnick's knees. I kicked my legs lamely, but could do nothing to resist. I told him one more time, I did not know what he was talking about.

"Enough already," he said. "You think I am fucking around with you? OK then, say goodbye to your hands, you little prick . . . Heshy."

The smaller Hasid stepped forward grinning, and without saying a word, stomped the heel of his black dress shoe hard into my right palm, turning it left and right and grinding it into the pavement. He lifted his foot and stomped a second time even harder, then three or four more times after that. The pain made me forget about my nose for a moment.

"How does that feel, schmendrick?" Shmuel Resnick laughed. "You like it? You want some more even? Now tell me where the money is, or Heshy will get started on the other one, and if you do not talk, then he will get out the magic wand. What do you say? Tell me while you still have one good hand to wipe your ass with."

The blood trickling down the back of my throat was warm and thick, making me gag. I was about to vomit when Shmuel Resnick suddenly rolled off me. I did not know why. All I remember is gazing up at the blue sky, admiring the angel-white clouds drifting serenely overhead. I turned to the left and saw my attacker lying on his side like he was sleeping peacefully next to his wife. I turned to the right and saw the man he called Heshy running away, leaving his broken glasses and yarmulke behind on the pavement.

Shmuel Resnick coughed and began to stir. Joe Carcone stepped between us and kicked him hard in the ribs. I heard his bones crack like the breaking of sticks.

Joe slipped a hand under my shoulder blades and helped me sit up. He told me to tilt my head back and pinch my nostrils. My nose was wobbly and I could hardly stand to touch it.

Shmuel Resnick struggled to his knees, leaving a small puddle of blood where his cheek had been resting on the blacktop. He spit pieces of his front teeth onto the ground. A long string of pink saliva dangled from his bottom lip and he waved at it like a drunk trying to sweep it away.

Joe Carcone stepped forward in a fighting stance, up on his toes, shifting his weight from side to side.

"C'mon, fuck face," he shouted at Shmuel Resnick. "Let's go. Get up and let's see how well you do with me. Big man, beating up a kid."

Shmuel Resnick staggered to his feet with his fists clenched. When he straightened up he was a full head taller than Joe Carcone.

"I'll give you ten seconds to get the fuck out of here," Joe shouted.

He started counting but only got to three before kicking the big Jew in the balls. Shmuel Resnick dropped back to his knees, clutching his broken ribs in agony as he retched.

"Sorry, I guess I lost count," Joe said with a smile. "Anyway, you missed your chance, asshole. And now look what you've done to our court. I should make you clean this mess up."

The way he seemed to enjoy meting out pain and humiliation frightened me. It was so at odds with the Joe Carcone I thought I knew. He helped me to my feet and placed his gym towel gently over my nose.

"It looks like I need to get you to the emergency room," he said. "You think you can walk to my car?"

I nodded, but was not totally sure I could make it.

In the meanwhile, Shmuel Resnick had crawled out of range and risen to his feet. He was hobbling feebly away.

"You want me to go after him?" Joe asked.

I told him no.

"OK then, what the hell was that all about?" he asked as we slowly made our way to the car.

"They're from Brooklyn," I said.

"No shit? And here I thought they were local farmers . . . maybe a soybean deal gone bad."

Laughing made my nose hurt even worse.

"C'mon, Junior," he said. "We need to have someone take a look at you."

"I can't," I said. "We can't tell anyone."

"No, why not?"

That was a difficult question, but I never considered keeping the truth from him. I explained about finding Abba's money and how the two men tore Paul Griffin's house apart looking for it.

I said, "You see why I can't go to the police? We already lied to them. Frida is not my legal guardian and I did not tell them about the money. I am afraid we will get in trouble."

"OK," Joe said. "I'm not sure how smart that was, but it's done. So let's go to my place and get you cleaned up and see what's what with your nose, then we'll figure out what to do. You'd better take your gloves off now; it looks like your hand is swelling."

My right hand was throbbing badly and I had a difficult time getting the glove off.

"Do you think it's broken?" I asked.

"Could be, but you won't know for sure without x-rays. You should really let me take you to the ER."

"No," I said. "No doctors."

I walked wobbly-legged to Joe's car, steadying myself on his arm. He buckled me into the front seat and drove cross-town to Champaign, pulling into the driveway of a white bungalow across from a school bus yard. He helped me to the front steps and opened the door. The house was dark despite the bright sunshine outside. It did not look like Joe ever opened his curtains.

"Sit here," he said, pointing to a chrome-legged chair at the kitchen table. "I don't want you getting blood all over the place."

He disappeared for a moment and returned with a bottle of Tylenol, a jar of cotton balls, a washcloth, and some fresh towels. He lifted the bloody towel from my face and tossed it into the kitchen sink, then wet the washcloth and gently wiped my nose.

He said, "Yeah, it's pretty crooked. I think it'd be best to have a doc look at it. You know you could end up with breathing trouble if it doesn't heal right. The guy really messed you up."

I shook my head no.

He said, "Well, I straightened my own nose a couple of times back in the day. I could try it."

"You've done this before?" I asked.

"Once or twice, yeah. My buddies and I did a lot of scrapping back in East Flatbush. We saw our share of broken noses."

Joe chuckled at the memory.

He said, "Our favorite saying was, *'You shoulda seen the other guy.'* Listen, Junior, I can try and straighten it, but I'm warning you, it's gonna hurt like a son of a bitch and you may need to see a doctor anyway. This is some serious shit."

I motioned for him to go ahead and he had me blow my nose into a towel several times. When I did, the lights in the kitchen flickered and blue sparkles danced around the edges of the room. The air hummed like an electric motor. When Joe took the towel away it was slimed with blood and mucus.

"The pain's gonna get worse now," he said. "You know the docs will give you an anesthetic before they mess with you, are you sure you want me to go ahead with this?"

I nodded.

"OK then . . . Here, turn your chair towards me."

He placed his fingertips on either side of the bridge of my nose and probed it gently like he was examining a ripe peach for bad spots.

"Now take a deep breath and hold it."

He cupped his hands more snugly around my nose and told me to exhale slowly, then gradually dragged his fingers down toward my chin. I moaned as the kitchen sizzled with brighter flashes of blue and white. I grabbed on to the edge of the table with both hands, but my injured right hurt so much, I had to let go.

Joe stepped back to examine his handiwork.

"That's a lot better," he said. "But it's still pretty damn crooked. Let me try it one more time and then we'll get some ice on you. If it's any consolation, I'm guessing your buddy from Crown Heights isn't feeling so great right now either. I'm pretty sure I broke his jaw."

I said, "I didn't see how you got him off me."

"Neither did he." Joe laughed. "My foot was on the ass-hole's chin before he knew what hit him. If Mike Ditka saw me kick that field goal he'd have hired me for the Bears."

Joe smoothed my nose again and then stuffed a cotton ball into each nostril.

"Are you OK to stand up?" he asked.

I was light-headed, but thought I could manage. Joe led me to a recliner in his living room and then left for the kitchen. The room was warm and dark. A single sliver of sunlight peaked through the drawn curtains, illuminating two framed photographs on the end table next to me. One was of a black-haired young Joe, looking very handsome in his Air Force uniform. In the other photo he was holding hands with a woman. A boy in a red soccer uniform was standing between them. The three of them looked very happy together.

"That was my family," Joe said when he returned from the kitchen and caught me looking at the photos. I thought he was about to tell me more, but he quickly changed the subject.

"I think your glove may have saved you," he said as he wrapped an ice bag around my swollen hand. "But you're not going to be playing any handball with it for a while, I can tell you that much."

He then carefully placed the other ice bag over my nose.

"You should probably stay off the court for at least a few weeks anyway until your nose heals up a bit."

I hated the thought of going without handball for that long.

He said, "Let's just lie low here until you get settled down and the bleeding stops, then I'll drive you home, OK?"

He sat down across from me on the couch.

"How did you get to be such a good fighter?" I asked. The cotton balls and ice bag made speaking difficult.

He said, "Everything's relative, Junior. I once looked like a pretty good handball player too, unless you'd seen Stevie Sandler in his prime."

"Yeah, but you just beat up two guys."

"A lot of it's mental. That's what I've been trying to tell you all along . . . Handball's no different than fighting. You don't take shit, you always go for the kill, and when your opponent's down, you finish him off. You never let him back up. Who do you think was stronger today, me or your big Hasidic buddy?"

"I don't know . . . You?"

"Well then, you'd be wrong. I coldcocked the son of a bitch when he wasn't looking, and the little shit who ran off was beaten as soon as he saw what I did to his friend. It's all in your head, that's what I'm saying. And I'll tell you this right now, Junior, life's not going to be easy for you in school next year. I'm a teacher, remember? I see it all the time. Bullies are like wild dogs, always seeking out the weakest animal in the pack. You can't let that happen to you. As soon as they sense the slightest weakness, they'll be all over you. No offense, but you'll be a target for sure with your yarmulke and the way you talk."

I said, "I hope I will speak better by the time school begins. I am practicing a lot."

"That's not going to save you, trust me. They'll find something else and no one will be there to protect you . . . no teacher, no administrator. You'll be on your own, so remember what you saw today. Don't forget it and don't take any shit. You strike first, and if you go down, you go down swinging. Even if there're ten of them, you fight back, got it? You'll get hurt, but you'll only get hurt once. If they think you're easy prey, they'll never leave you alone and you'll get hurt every day. Make a bully pay for his entertainment and he'll find someone else to pick on."

I understood what Joe Carcone was telling me, and took every word of his advice to heart.

When Joe dropped me back at the house I made sure Paul was in the studio before going inside. I wanted to get my story straight with Frida first. I did not think it would be wise to tell him two Hasids from Brooklyn trashed his house and studio looking for fifty thousand dollars we had not told him about. I needed to come up with an excuse for how my face got smashed in.

Frida was in the living room working on one of her collages when I poked my head in the doorway.

"My God, Zev," she shrieked. "My God . . . what happened to you?"

She jumped up and extended her arms, but stopped short of hugging me after getting a good look at my blood-clotted T-shirt.

"It was Shmuel Resnick," I said. "Shmuel Resnick and some other man. They did not come here to take me back to Brooklyn. They came for Abba's money."

"I still don't understand how they knew we had it," she said.

163

"He found out somehow," I replied. "The man is a thief. He even steals from the Rebbe."

"Look what they did to you. We need to go to the police."

"But we already lied to them. We will be in trouble."

"This has gotten too dangerous, Zevi. The police need to know about this. They need to have a talk with Shmuel Resnick."

I said, "I don't think he will be talking to anyone right away."

I could not keep from smiling even though it caused a bubble of pain to burst between my eyes. The room around me started buzzing again and I steadied myself against the back of a chair.

"Jesus Christ," Frida shouted. "What the hell are you smiling about?"

"I think my friend, Joe, broke Shmuel Resnick's jaw and knocked his teeth out."

"This isn't funny. They didn't get what they wanted, so what if they come back with a gun? I'm scared for you ... for both of us."

And we had one more immediate problem.

"What are we going to tell Paul about my face?" I asked.

"Shit, I don't know. Tell him you got beat up on the handball court. That much is true, isn't it? Tell him it was an anti-Semitic thing...A couple of boys made fun of your yarmulke and you got into a fight. That sounds plausible. And look at your hand. How the hell did your hand get swollen like that?"

"The other man stepped on it while Shmuel Resnick held me down. He said he was going to stomp on my left too if I didn't give them the money."

"Christ, they're fucking gangsters, those bastards. What kind of man does that to a boy? They should both be in jail."

Frida paced up and down the living room.

"I'm worried, Zevi. People get killed for less money than this."

"Well, I would rather die than give Abba's money to Shmuel Resnick. I hate him."

She said, "I'm not saying we give him the money, but the police have to know about this. There's no telling what those thugs might do next."

"But if we go to the police, what will you tell Paul? He will be mad at both of us about the house and his painting and for not telling him about the money before."

Frida stopped pacing and sat down on the couch. She rocked back and forth, working her hands together like she was kneading a lump of clay.

She said, "We need some time to think this through . . . Paul won't come in from the studio until I call him for dinner, so I guess we don't have to decide right this second. Go get cleaned up and change out of those clothes and we'll figure this out when you come back down, OK?"

I used the handrail to pull myself upstairs, with every muscle in my body crying for mercy. The biggest shock came when I switched on the bathroom light. If I had seen myself in a mirror at Joe Carcone's house, I would have let him take me to the emergency room.

Pulling my crusty T-shirt off was total agony. Even the gentle spray from the showerhead pounded my swollen nose like a watery fist. I washed my hair and for the first time felt the lump on the back of my head where it smacked against the pavement and I hated Shmuel Resnick all the more.

I seriously considered returning to Brooklyn to kill him, to pay him back for what he did to me years ago and on the handball court today. I would be doing Hashem's work. The world would be a better place without that filthy stinking rotten apple. I still had Abba's money. I could buy a gun and a bus ticket, and while I was in Brooklyn I would say hello to Heshy too.

I relished picturing the terror in Shmuel Resnick's eyes when I pointed the loaded pistol between them. The thought of it helped ease my pain as I dried off and slipped into one of my white Lubavitcher dress shirts. I had trouble fastening the buttons because of my sore hand, but wanted to avoid pulling a tight T-shirt over my broken nose again. I chose a pair of black trousers to go with my white shirt. I have to admit it was somewhat comforting to be in my old clothes again. It would be an even greater comfort to see justice done.

Monday morning, my first day of tutoring, dawned with a throbbing headache pulsing behind my swollen eyes. I had slept on my back with my head propped up on two pillows and woke with a dry scratchy throat that only added to my overall misery.

If I thought my face looked bad the day before, the one I saw in the bathroom mirror was horrifying. I had never seen such a face, like some sad distorted clown with puffy red eye sockets and two dark lumps the size of golf balls beneath them. A blackish scab was forming across the bridge of my misshapen red nose. This was not a face I recognized and I was afraid I might never see the familiar face of Zev Altshul again.

Last night Frida and I decided there was no good solution to our dilemma and agreed to take our chances by not going to the police. As far as Paul Griffin knew, my nose was demolished in a fight and he never connected it to the break-in.

"Damn, that must've been quite a brawl," he said.

"You shoulda seen the other guy," I replied, quoting Joe Carcone while holding up my bruised and swollen right hand as proof of my fighting prowess.

I recognized the unmistakable admiration in Paul's eyes

as he smiled and said, "Good for you, Zev. Looks like you gave as good as you got."

Frida sent an annoyed glance my way. I tried not to look at her.

Despite my bluster with Paul, I was barely able to haul my battered body across campus the next morning on the way to meet my tutor. I glanced left and right over my shoulder, on the lookout for white vans and angry Jews. People passing on the street stared at my injuries before turning away. At the entrance to the Education Building, a frail older woman stepped aside to hold the door open for me.

My tutor, Leeann Carter, smiled when she shook my hand for the first time, but was plainly distressed at the sight of my ruined face. In fact, I heard her gasp. It was a natural reaction, but she was embarrassed at having let it slip out.

"I'm sorry if I made you uncomfortable," she apologized. "That was really rude of me."

I said, "I know I look bad."

"No, no, it's not that," she replied, her voice trailing off to a mumble as she searched for the right words that would not come.

"I was only . . . I mean . . . ah, you know . . ."

I hope I hid my reaction better than she did. I was not expecting my tutor to be an enormous Black woman. Leeann Carter must have weighed three hundred pounds. Her chair groaned as she sat down, and I was afraid it would collapse underneath her.

"So anyway," she said, "I'll be working with you on your English lit this morning and Kevin Michalski will be your tutor for science and math this afternoon. It's going to be a full day, so let's get started."

There is no need to describe every detail of this tutoring session or the many that came after it, but of all the subjects

I studied through the spring and summer, English literature with Leeann Carter was my favorite.

We began with a short story called "The Remarkable Rocket."

"We read this in all our ESL classes," she said.

I did not know what ESL meant, but would not have been offended if I did. After all, English really was my second language, and before this I had read almost nothing but religious texts.

She said, "It's a simple fairy tale with some keen insights into human nature. It's written by a very famous author named Oscar Wilde."

I said, "Our rabbis tell us we should not read stories."

"Oh really, and why is that?" she asked.

"Because they are not true and will put foolish ideas in our heads that lead us away from Torah."

Judging from Leeann Carter's reaction, this was probably not the best way for me to begin our first tutoring session.

"That's nonsense," she exclaimed. "The Bible's literature too, isn't it? What about Cain killing Abel, and Lot's wife turning into a pillar of salt? How about Noah's ark? They're all stories, aren't they?"

"Yes, but those stories are true."

"True or not, they teach us about life and that's the same thing good fiction does. We empathize with our fictional characters. We feel what they feel. We share their experiences and learn from them."

At the time I did not know the meaning of the word *empathy*. Leeann Carter explained it to me as we considered each other's faces, hers big and black, and mine repulsive in its injury. We discussed "The Remarkable Rocket," whose main character is unaware of how others think of him and is overly impressed with his own imagined importance.

On Wednesday Rabbi Jerry stopped by to take me to lunch between tutoring sessions. He did not know about the beating and was beside himself when he saw my battered face. I did not tell him the true story of why I looked this way, or even the full lie I told Paul Griffin. I knew any mention of anti-Semitism would stir the rabbi up and I did not want him asking too many questions. I told him it was only a fight over handball.

He said, "My God, Zev, this isn't just a little scrape. You've been seriously injured. Did you report this to the police?"

I dodged his question.

"You shoulda seen the other guy," I said, pleased to trot out Joe Carcone's witty remark again. I held up my enlarged right hand as proof I had gotten in a few good licks of my own.

"There were two of them," I said, raising my chin high like "The Remarkable Rocket," enjoying the fictional role of the tough guy Yid and almost believing the story I was telling him.

"You sure this had nothing to do with you being a Jew?" the rabbi asked, already suspicious.

"No, no . . . it was only about handball," I said, shaking my head as convincingly as possible.

He said, "There are plenty of rednecks around here. We've had vandalism at the Hillel on campus . . . graffiti, bulbs broken on the outdoor menorah at Chanukah. You know, it wouldn't surprise me one bit. Are you sure your yarmulke didn't have something to do with it? How old were these fellows; were they college students?"

I dodged his questions again.

"Would you please ask Mrs. Kotin not to come for me this Shabbos? I will not be attending shul again until my face is healed."

"It's not a good idea to isolate yourself, Zev. We need the support of the community in times of persecution. When one Jew suffers, we all suffer."

I assured him again I was not a victim of anti-Semitism. Of course, I didn't tell him it was another Jew who beat the hell out of me. Instead, I played on his sympathies.

"Would you want to go out looking like this if you could help it?" I asked.

He shrugged in an expression of surrender.

"It is embarrassing and I am in pain," I added, to be sure he got the message. "I am very uncomfortable just sitting here."

"I can see that," the rabbi said. "All right then, I won't be a nudge, but you'll let me know if there's anything I can do for you, right?"

I appreciated his concern, but could not think of a single thing the well-meaning rabbi could do to help. Could he make me a new face or a shidduch with Sharon Kotin? I almost laughed at the thought of Rabbi Jerry as the unfortunate shadchan stuck with the job of presenting me as a match to Sharon Kotin's parents.

I could only imagine Dr. Kotin considering his prospective new son-in-law:

"So what does he do, this Yiddish boy? He plays handball, and what else?"

And Mrs. Kotin's kindness would be pushed to its limits:

"I'm sorry, Rabbi Feinstein, giving Zev a ride to shul is one thing, but this boy thinks Soul Train *is educational television and he can't even sit through supper."*

And what about my sweet Rose of Sharon, my Lily Among Thorns, who did not care for me even before the beating? She would take one look at me and say:

"Behold, my beloved cometh leaping upon the mountains

with his two black eyes and a nose like a squashed loaf of pumpernickel."

What a successful shidduch that would make! Oh, the absurdity of this transplanted Hasidic boy. He is a puzzle, even to himself.

The next story I read with Leeann Carter was called *The Metamorphosis*. It was supposed to be very famous. A man named Gregor Samsa wakes up from a bad dream to find he has turned into a giant insect with a brittle brown shell and many spindly legs. I had seen big cockroaches in the basement of our Crown Heights apartment house, but none as big as Gregor Samsa.

"Obviously, a man cannot become a cockroach," I said to my tutor.

"That's why we call it fiction," she replied. "So you don't care about Gregor Samsa at all?"

"Of course I care. I feel sad for him. It is not his fault he became a roach."

She said, "*Vermin* is probably a more correct translation, but that's not really important. Do you think his family treated him properly?"

"No," I almost shouted. "They abandoned him when he was no longer of any use to them. That wasn't fair. He stopped eating and wasted to death because of them. He should not have suffered that way."

"You see, Zev, fiction can be very powerful."

Yes, it was powerful. I knew what it was like to wake up in an unfamiliar body with my world turned upside down. I understood Gregor Samsa's shame, as well as his parents' shame over having vermin for a son, and I feared my own metamorphosis would come to as bad an end as his.

I read many more stories and books with Leeann Carter,

and studied almost nonstop while recovering from my injuries. I celebrated my sixteenth birthday at home with Frida as my bruises turned from dark red and blue to a purplish black before fading to pale green and dull yellow. As the swelling subsided, a new bump emerged high on the bridge of my nose, with a little kink bulging left and right. Frida said the bump gave me character. Joe Carcone laughed when I returned to the Big Green Wall in June.

"Now you look like you come from Brooklyn," he said, grasping my chin and giving it a little wiggle. "I've missed you, Junior."

I was not sure how to react to his display of tenderness. My father did not usually express affection so openly, at least not in many years. I wondered about Joe's relationship with his son. He never mentioned the smiling boy in the red soccer uniform, just as I never spoke of the stranger who came home to our apartment in the evening smelling of dry-cleaning chemicals before leaving for 770 to serve the Rebbe.

Years earlier I broke a vase in our apartment. My mother spent many nights at the kitchen table gluing the tiny pieces back together. From a distance it did not look too bad, and she returned it to its place on a little table just inside our entry. The vase would never hold flowers or water again, but it appeared whole if you did not look too closely. I believe it is like that with families too.

One evening, after a game at the rec center, Joe said he wanted to show me a couple of things in the gym. We had never gone to the gym before. I thought it must have been something to do with handball, but Joe told me to wait and then returned with two pairs of boxing gloves.

He said, "You remember the conversation we had at my place while I was fixing up your nose, how handball's no different than fighting?"

Of course I remembered.

"Well, I think it's only right I give you a little coaching in the self-defense department too. Starting school in the fall with a little confidence won't hurt you one bit."

"You're not going to hit me in the face, are you?" I asked.

"Not this time," he said, smiling. "Put on your gloves."

I was already nervous enough about starting school and now I had to become a fighter too?

"But I don't want to fight," I said.

"And I hope you won't have to. I want you to be prepared just in case, that's all. C'mon, let's go. Put up your hands."

"But I don't know anything about fighting."

"That's why we're here, isn't it? I was a lot like you, Junior ... not the biggest guy in the world, the one a bully might pick on. Being small's an advantage on the court, but not in a street fight. You've got to compensate. I earned a reputation back in the day, my brother, Vic, too. They used to say, *Don't even look at those Carcone boys cross-eyed, or they'll be all over you.*"

This did not surprise me after seeing what he did to Shmuel Resnick.

He said, "You've got to show 'em you got nothing to lose and you're crazier than they are. Make 'em think pain means nothing to you. You're a handball player; you've had a lot of practice at that already."

When we began sparring, Joe taught me how to block his punches with my forearms and move my head side to side so I would not be an easy target.

He said, "See, every time you block one of my punches there's an opening for you to counter with one of your own, unless I follow up with a flurry right away."

He threw several quick punches up high. I blocked and slipped them all.

"See what I'm talking about?" he said.

Then he threw one down low, and when I dropped my hands to block, he hit me with a hard right to the forehead, knocking me backward, almost off my feet.

"You said you weren't going to hit me in the face," I complained.

"That wasn't your face," Joe said as he stepped forward and swept my legs out from under me with his instep.

I looked up at him from the mat.

He said, "Remember, this isn't a prom dance, Junior, and it's not a boxing contest either. A street fight's a whole other animal. You use whatever you got—hands, feet, teeth, whatever . . ."

Joe extended his hand to help me up, but then let go and I fell back onto the mat again.

"And don't ever expect the other guy to fight fair," he said. "You think what I did to your buddy at the Green Wall was fair? I fucked him up from his blind side. The guy was defenseless. There was nothing fair about it. Now get up off the mat."

This time he pulled me up.

"And whatever you do, you've got to stay on your feet. I could've kicked your teeth out while you were looking up at me from down there with that dumb grin on your face. Once you're on your ass it's all over. You saw what the big Yid did to you. You've got to stay on your feet."

Yes, I had to stay on my feet. But I was not thinking so much about handball or fighting.

My love for Sharon Kotin had not faded with my bruises, but the reality of my predicament was finally sinking in. There was no way she would ever return my affection. I was up against a tough opponent with a devastating arsenal, and even the best players need to know when they're beat.

I wondered if Joe Carcone followed his own advice, or

had he been floored by the loss of the wife and boy in the photograph, the missing family he never mentioned? How often did he think of them while eating dinner alone in his bungalow across from the bus yard?

Did my father stay on his feet after my mother's illness stole her from him, or was that why he spent so much time with his dry-cleaning machines and the long nights working for the Rebbe at 770?

And what about my sister, the girl who left her home to begin a new life with a man she thought would deliver her from a world of restrictions and limitations? How long could she stay on her feet?

I overheard them arguing late one night. I could not make out the words, so I got out of bed and cupped my ear to the wall. I knew it was wrong of me to listen in on them.

Frida said, "You can't keep ignoring me, Paul. I know your work is important, but there are two of us in this house."

"No, there are three of us now," he answered. "And things haven't been the same since he got here."

She said, "You can't blame Zev for what's been happening between us. That's not fair."

"Yeah, and it's not fair for you to blame me because you don't know what to do with yourself."

Frida did not respond, but I could feel her sadness pulsing through the wall.

He said, "If you had more of a purpose in life, you wouldn't be picking at me all the time. I'm not the entertainment committee around here, you know. That's not my job, Frida. I'm sorry if I can't make you feel good about yourself."

She said, "I'm not asking you to make me feel good about myself. I'm only asking you to realize I'm not here just to cook and clean and suck your cock."

He said, "Well, you don't have to anymore if it's such an effort for you. You're not that great at it anyway."

Frida shouted curse words and then something heavy hit the wall right by my ear, causing me to lurch backward, almost falling. She slammed the bedroom door on her way out. I wanted to follow her into the hallway but was afraid that would only make matters worse.

I heard her car start and watched from the window as it backed down the driveway. I then returned to bed and stared up at the ceiling most of the night, not knowing if Frida would be coming back or what I would do if she didn't.

I did not want to be around the next morning when Paul Griffin got out of bed, so I left the house early. The sun was barely up when I arrived at the Big Green Wall. I served over and over again as viciously as I could, aiming for a small patch of peeling paint about eighteen inches off the ground, imagining it was Paul Griffin's face.

Handball always helped clear my head, but I could not get the events of the previous night out of my mind. They pecked at me during my tutoring sessions and into the late afternoon when I met Joe again. I told him about Frida leaving in the middle of the night.

He said, "I wouldn't worry too much about it if I were you, Junior. She'll probably be back. This kind of stuff happens in almost every relationship sooner or later and it's usually not the end of things. Trust me, you'll know when she's leaving for good."

Joe was a pretty smart fellow, and I was relieved to find Frida's car parked in the driveway when I returned to California Avenue around six. Paul was in the kitchen with her, and the two of them seemed more cheerful than usual, acting as if nothing had happened.

As soon as Paul left for the studio, Frida apologized for

leaving the night before. I told her I was afraid she wasn't coming back.

She said, "You're not going to get rid of me that easily, Zevi. I lost my temper. It wasn't all Paul's fault, really. I just needed to get a few things out of my system and stayed over with one of my girlfriends. Everything's OK now."

I said, "I worried about you all day. I don't know what I would have done if you left me." She gently stroked my cheek and said, "I would never do that to you, but you know better than I do that life doesn't always work according to plan. Sometimes we've got to make the best of things as they are, you know what I mean? We'll both be all right, whatever happens."

I did not like the sound of '*whatever happens.*'

Rav Feldsher called again in August, saying they had settled my father's estate and there were bank accounts—more money than I might have thought.

He said, "You should come home now for a little while. This must all be handled in New York State."

"How much is there?" I asked.

"More than ten thousand dollars."

I was tempted to tell him I had a lot more than that in my gym locker.

Frida was in the room with me. I covered the mouthpiece.

She said, "Be careful, you can't trust him."

The rabbi said, "If you do not return to claim the money, it will go to support the shluchim. These were your father's wishes. So do you want the money, or I should just sign it over now?"

"I will need a little time," I said.

"So next week then . . . if I do not hear from you by then, the shluchim will have it. You are afraid from Shmuel Resnick, no?"

I was surprised Rav Feldsher knew about my run-in with him. I had almost forgotten how things worked in Crown Heights. From the Rebbe on down, the rabbis knew almost everything that went on in our closed community.

"Nu?" he said. "You will not have to worry from him anymore. I can promise you."

Rav Feldsher wielded much authority, but I did not believe even a rabbi of his stature could guarantee my safety. Revenge would be more important than money to a man like Shmuel Resnick. He would never let such a beating and humiliation go unpunished.

"Don't trust him, Zevi," Frida repeated.

I had not covered the mouthpiece this time, and was afraid Rav Feldsher might have heard her.

"So what then?" he said. "The money is yours and this is up to you. Your father would want you to have it, yes? If you come home to take care of your business, Shmuel Resnick will not bother you."

I told the rabbi I would let him know soon and hung up the phone.

"I think maybe I should go back," I said to Frida.

"I'm telling you, you can't trust the guy. He's looking for something."

"But he is a shliach and was Abba's teacher. He has always been good to me."

"Then do what you like," she said, "but I wouldn't chance it."

A week before the start of classes, Frida and I met with Dr. Gottlieb and Leeann Carter to discuss my second round of placement tests. Dr. Gottlieb passed around her jar of hard candy again and I squirmed in my chair as she paged through the open folder containing my future. Frida patted the back of my hand and whispered for me to settle down.

"I have to congratulate you," Dr. Gottlieb said. "You've certainly risen to the occasion. I couldn't be more pleased with the results."

"He's my prize student," Leeann Carter beamed. "Zev has worked very hard."

"So now we have to put our heads together and decide what's best for you," Dr. Gottlieb continued. "I don't believe there's a simple right or wrong answer here; it's a judgment call. We have to take the total package into consideration, not just your test scores . . . there's more to it.

"Your math concept skills are a bit lower than I'd like to see, but that's not my main concern. You've already proven you can handle the work. It's the interactions with your peers that concern me most. I don't want to drop you into a social situation you're not ready for."

Leeann Carter added, "Zev has adapted amazingly well, but I'm also concerned about his social skills. I'm afraid this is going to be an obstacle for him moving forward."

I did not like having my social skills put under the microscope as if I were a cockroach like Gregor Samsa.

Dr. Gottlieb said, "I'm torn here, Zev. I want to stress this is an impressive result. Very few young men could've caught up so quickly. I'm sure you'd rather be placed in eleventh grade than tenth, that's understandable, but this decision shouldn't be made emotionally . . . I suppose I'm thinking out loud here.

"Anyway, I'm inclined to play it safe. You'd be one of the younger eleventh graders, so I feel most comfortable starting you out in tenth. We'll monitor you from here and we have some flexibility going forward, but I believe it's in your best interest to err on the side of caution just now. What do you think?"

Frida agreed at once. I struggled to disguise my disappointment. My voice cracked a little as I told Dr. Gottlieb it was OK with me too.

"Don't worry, Zev, we'll take good care of you," she said.

Her words were hardly encouraging. Miryam Resnick told me the very same thing the night my mother died.

As we left Dr. Gottlieb's office, Frida asked if I wanted to stop for a bite on our way home. I didn't, and went straight to my room as soon as we walked in the door. I took off my sneakers and lay down on the bed and did not leave my room until she called me for supper.

Paul Griffin had not come home from school yet. This time Frida did not set a place for him. She was obviously upset and I assumed it was because of Paul, but she folded the afternoon *News-Gazette* lengthwise and handed it to me.

"Have you seen this?" she asked.

"What . . . about the big Kmart closing?"

"No silly, over on the right: NAZI PROPAGANDA IN SAVOY."

I scanned the article. Someone had been slipping anti-Semitic flyers into mailboxes along Route 45, just down the road from Urbana. There were no pictures, but it described a single-page flyer with a cross and swastika at the top and the words WAKE UP ARYANS and NEVER TRUST A JEW underneath. Police had opened an investigation.

"It doesn't surprise me," Frida said, "but it's frightening to see this so close to home."

I shrugged the way I usually do when I do not know what to say. To be honest, I did not see how this affected me and was not terribly concerned. Frida took it much more seriously.

"Are you sure you shouldn't leave your yarmulke at home when school starts?"

I did not appreciate her suggestion.

"I am not ashamed of being a Jew," I said, unintentionally

implying that she was.

"Well, you don't wear your fedora and payos anymore, do you? You've made other concessions."

"I still want to be a Jew," I repeated.

"Plenty of Jews don't wear yarmulkes," she said. "You can still be a Jew, but you don't have to wave a red cape in front of every redneck in the school. You see how things are. That yarmulke might as well have a bullseye on it."

"I want them to know I'm a Jew, even if I don't keep all the commandments anymore."

Frida took hold of my arm.

"I'm just worried about you getting along, Zevi. I was so frightened that day you came home all beat up. I don't want anything else happening to you, that's all."

"Joe Carcone is worried too," I said. "He has been teaching me to fight."

"Seriously?"

"Yes, we have been boxing. I'm getting too fast for him, though."

I smiled, but in all honesty, I was more frightened about the start of school than Frida was.

Mine was the only yarmulke in the crowd of students milling about the entrance to Urbana High on the first day of class. The others all seemed so relaxed, laughing and joking, smoking cigarettes. A boy wrapped his arm around a girl's waist as she slipped her hand into his back pocket. I had never seen such things before. I stood off by myself wishing I could be at yeshiva again, totally anonymous among the hundreds of black suits and hats.

When the bell rang, a colorful sea of T-shirts, shorts, and bare arms and legs funneled through the front doors. I rode along with the wave, pretending to know where I was going as I searched the clogged second-floor hallway for my first class of the day.

Entering Room 205 was like walking down the gang-plank of a steamship into a foreign country: the rows of girls crossing their tanned legs, slouching boys with writing on their T-shirts, and a woman teacher wearing a bright red cardigan. Every eye was on me as I crossed the room and sat down in an empty seat toward the back.

"Ah, excuse me. What's your name, young man?" Mrs. Margolis, the social studies teacher, asked.

"Zev," I answered.

"Is that your last name or your first?"

This raised a few snickers from the class. She looked down at her grade book.

"Ah, yes, here you are . . . Zev Altshul, correct? We sit in assigned seats alphabetically in this class. You're right up front here."

She pointed to an empty desk closest to the door and I got up and switched seats. Some boys in the back of the room were laughing. I don't know why, but assumed it had something to do with me.

Mrs. Margolis said, "I hope you all had a terrific summer. I'm happy to see so many old faces and a few new ones, too."

She looked right at me when she said that.

"Before Principal Hauser makes his announcements, I'm going to take the roll and when I call your name, I want you to raise your hand and say, *Present*. Remember, you'll sit in the same seat every day unless I move you, OK? Altshul . . . Andrews . . . raise your hand, Mr. Andrews . . . Barrett . . . Boles . . ."

Principal Hauser then came on the loudspeaker and welcomed us to *The Home of the Tigers*. He wished us all a happy and successful school year before working his way down a long list of boring announcements, during which students jabbered and Mrs. Margolis shushed.

When class began, she had us open our civics texts to the Declaration of Independence:

"We hold these truths to be self-evident . . ."

When she got to the part about all men being created equal, one of the Black boys in the class asked why that didn't include the slaves. A white girl asked why women couldn't vote. Mrs. Margolis said our union isn't perfect and the country is still evolving. She said the Constitution guarantees our rights as citizens, and is a living document that grows and changes along with the country. Apparently the Constitution is not like the Torah or Talmud.

At this hour in Crown Heights, my classmates would be studying at long tables just as their fathers, and their fathers' fathers before them did. There were no Blacks in yeshiva. No women. We were never taught that all men are created equal, and Mrs. Margolis would never have been allowed to teach in our school.

Between classes I saw Sharon Kotin in the first-floor hallway. We briefly made eye contact while still a good distance apart, but she turned her head and pretended not to see me as we passed. A smile from any friendly face would have been a welcomed mitzvah, but this girl I sat next to in shul would not even acknowledge my existence. This hurt me as much as Shmuel Resnick's punches.

I saw her again after school on Friday as I was passing through Carle Park on my way to meet Joe Carcone. A candy wrapper skipped across the path ahead on a chill breeze that carried my first taste of the coming prairie winter. Trees cast long shadows in the late afternoon sun. Sharon was lying in the autumn grass next to a tall blond boy who did not look the slightest bit Jewish. It did not take a tzadik to see something was going on between them. She did not glance up at me as I passed.

When Joe showed up at the Big Green Wall I told him I did not love Sharon Kotin anymore. I said I did not even like her.

He put his arm around my shoulder.

"Just remember, Junior, this girl will be a small blip on your radar screen before too much longer. It won't be the last time you get your heart broken either. There'll be plenty of others. You'll probably break a few yourself one of these days."

I asked if he really thought all men are created equal. Joe snorted like it was a funny question.

"Where did that come from?" he asked.

"I don't know. We studied the Declaration of Independence in social studies."

He said, "You play handball . . . what do you think; are all men created equal?"

"No."

"Well, in the eyes of the law, we are. It doesn't mean we're all the same though."

I was not thinking of the Declaration of Independence or of handball. I was thinking of myself, and the blond boy lying in the grass with Sharon Kotin.

I attended shul on Rosh Hashanah, and again on Yom Kippur, even though school remained open both days. I did not play handball and did not watch television, not even *Soul Train*. Sharon Kotin was polite as I rode next to her in her parents' car. I did not know if she was being civil for their sake or because it was the Day of Atonement, the holiest day of the year, when Jews all over the world fast and repent of our sins.

A week later Mrs. Margolis said I would need a note from the rabbi if I wanted an excused absence on the first day of Sukkot, the Feast of Booths. I decided to attend class, but remembered this in spring when they closed school for Good Friday. I will not forget that first day of Sukkot. It was the day the Magen David appeared on my locker.

The six-pointed star was about the size of a salad plate, sloppily scrawled in black Magic Marker. I've probably drawn a hundred of them using an upside-down triangle superimposed over a right-side-up one. That's the simplest way to do it, but when I arrived at my locker at the beginning of fifth period, I knew this one was not drawn for amusement.

I got a wet paper towel from the bathroom and tried wiping it off as the other boys watched. I rubbed and rubbed, but it did not budge. Mr. Ignatovich escorted me to the principal's office, and Dr. Hauser returned with us to see for himself, then immediately called for the janitor. He asked if I had any idea who might've done this or if anyone had a grudge against me. Sharon Kotin was the only person I knew for sure didn't like me, but I did not mention her to the principal.

The janitor scrubbed the locker door, while Dr. Hauser and I watched the star fade like the dawn until it finally disappeared. The odor of the solvents reminded me of my father's dry-cleaning chemicals and I couldn't tell if my eyes were watering because of the powerful cleaning fluid, or my memories of him. The period was almost over, so I did not bother getting dressed for gym.

The next morning Dr. Hauser made an announcement over the loudspeaker. By then everyone in the school knew what had happened:

"An incident of ethnic intimidation was reported yesterday involving graffiti in the boy's locker room. We want all students

185

to be aware that the school administration takes incidents such as this very seriously and we are committed to ensuring that everyone feels safe and welcome here. Religious, ethnic, or racial intolerance will not be tolerated at Urbana High School."

Mrs. Margolis rolled her eyes at Dr. Hauser's announcement that *"intolerance will not be tolerated,"* but as the one having to tolerate the intolerance, I did not find any humor in it. Whatever hopes I had of blending in at Urbana High were doomed.

The following morning Dr. Hauser made a second announcement inviting anyone with information about the anti-Semitic graffiti to come forward. He said their cooperation would be greatly appreciated and held in the strictest confidence.

If my social circle was limited before the principal started making his announcements, it tightened even more after. I had not made one real friend in an entire month at Urbana. Before the Magen David, I was merely an oddball in a yarmulke invading their hallways. Now I was the notorious Jew, a tarnished Star of David twinkling under the principal's shining spotlight, a school celebrity for all the wrong reasons.

I did not tell Frida about the graffiti, but when I told Joe Carcone, he was not the least bit surprised.

He said, "Just be ready, Junior. These buttheads usually don't know when to quit. I'm guessing you haven't heard the last of them."

As with most things, Joe knew what he was talking about. In only a little over a week, a second Magen David appeared on my locker door, this time with a circle drawn around it and a slash—meaning NO JEWS. Mr. Ignatovich saw it before I did and I was called to the principal's office out of math class.

Dr. Hauser invited me to sit and told me about the new graffiti.

He said, "This is as distressing to me as it is to you."

I doubted that.

"If you have even the slightest inkling of who might be behind it, please tell me. Are you sure nothing else has been done to you since you moved here . . . No threats, no bullying?"

I did not mention the beating I'd received at the hands of Shmuel Resnick, another Jew.

He said, "I wish I could explain why this is happening here all of a sudden. You're not our first Jewish student, but it seems you've attracted some unwanted attention."

I wanted to tell him the unwanted attention had increased about tenfold since he started making his loudspeaker announcements. Dr. Hauser figured that out on his own right after he made the next one. It brought him as much trouble as it did me.

The following Friday, the phone rang in the early evening while I was getting ready for shul. When I picked up, Rabbi Jerry said the oddest thing:

"Is this you, Zev?"

I had no idea what he was talking about. I was sure he recognized my voice.

"Are you the boy in the papers?" he asked.

The afternoon *News-Gazette* was still rolled up on the kitchen table.

"Why didn't you tell me about this?"

"About what?" I asked.

"Was it your locker with the graffiti? I wish you'd have told me."

"I'm not the one making such a big deal of it," I said.

"Well, it *is* a big deal. You're being harassed for being a Jew and that's a big deal. It's a threat . . . intimidation. It affects all of us. And what's this about a reward?"

Earlier in the week Dr. Hauser announced a fifty-dollar reward to be given to any student with information about the graffiti. I did not think too much of it when he made the announcement at the start of first period, but plenty of students were offended by the enticement to turn in one of their classmates. Apparently some of their parents did not appreciate it either. A few of them called the newspaper and some complained to the school board.

I peeled the rubber bands off the *News-Gazette* while the rabbi was still on the phone and began turning pages until I came to the article. It was less prominent than I had expected, only a brief column buried halfway down the third page of the second section:

ANTI-SEMITIC GRAFFITI DIVIDES URBANA SCHOOL

I was the unnamed tenth-grade Jewish boy, the yarmulke-wearing newcomer whose locker had been defiled. But the main focus of the article was not anti-Semitism so much as the tactics Dr. Hauser used to put a stop to it.

A twelfth-grade girl was quoted as saying, *"I think the graffiti is terrible, but I don't think a principal should ever pay students to tattle on each other."*

A parent said, *"This whole thing's been blown out of proportion. This graffiti business would've gone away by now if the principal hadn't made such a big stink about it."*

Dr. Hauser was asked if he thought it was good policy to pay student snitches. He said, *"That's a gross exaggeration. I was trying to put an end to anti-Semitic attacks on one of our students. There's a big difference. This wasn't a random fishing expedition."*

When Frida read the article, she was furious with me for not telling her about the incidents with my locker.

"So what else are you up to that you're not telling me about?" she said.

"I'm not up to anything," I answered, pleased with how American my reply sounded. "I just didn't want to worry you, that's all."

"Well, from now on, worry me," she said, her voice reminding me so much of my mother's.

I did not tell her things had heated up even more since the principal announced his reward. It was as if a Molotov cocktail had been thrown through the front door of Urbana High and the blaze was spreading out of control.

Joe Carcone said, "Looks like Hauser's got a real shitstorm on his hands. All the teachers at Centennial are talking about it."

"He meant to do the right thing," I said.

"Yeah, I'm sure he did, but he fucked up. Paying students for information is a pretty controversial move. He would've been smart to run it by the superintendent and the school board first. I've seen principals fired over less."

"I don't want him fired because of me," I said.

"It's not because of you, Junior, don't you get that? And I'm not saying he's getting fired, but if he does, it's because of his own decisions, not something you've done. What, do you blame yourself for everything that goes wrong in this world?"

I had to think about that for a moment. I did not like the answer to his question.

The following week more graffiti appeared in a first-floor boys' bathroom—a swastika with KKK underneath it was scrawled across the tan ceramic tiles. The swastika had been drawn backward. The words SNITCHES GET STITCHES popped up in several locations throughout the school, SNITCHES ARE BITCHES in one of the girls' bathrooms.

Nobody likes a snitch, especially one who snitches for money, and though I had nothing to do with Dr. Hauser's offer, many of my classmates thought I was playing for the wrong side. I could feel their stares on my way to class, the wide berth they gave me in the hallways, and the strange allergy going around that provoked volleys of sneezes as I passed—*ah-choo* sounding much more like *ah-jew*.

If you have never been singled out like this, it is no fun at all, particularly when you have done nothing to deserve it and there is nothing you can do to stop it. I resigned myself to suffering a lonely year at Urbana High, but as long as my persecutors kept their hands to themselves, I would survive. After all, I had been through worse.

Don't forget, I spent many years with a mother who could not be a mother, and a father who loved the Rebbe more than his own son. You think I wasn't lonely then? I survived that, just as I survived Shmuel Resnick's beating. I endured the mockery of tough goys on the handball court— Brooklyn goys, not these Midwest amateurs who did not know how to draw a proper swastika.

The following week Rabbi Jerry was invited to our school assembly to address the problem of anti-Semitism. He spoke of Germany in the years leading up to the Holocaust, of Kristallnacht, and how the human rights of Jews were taken away bit by bit. I sat through the rabbi's presentation, knowing all eyes were on me and feeling every bit as humiliated as by the graffiti and *ah-jews*. The assembly did nothing to douse the fire, and the harassment continued, just as Joe Carcone predicted it would.

Dr. Hauser quit making his announcements after the newspaper article, but still took me aside every few days to ask if I could identify any of the perpetrators. I persistently told him no, even though I had my suspicions. Sharon Kotin's boyfriend, the big blond guy, was a member of the football team. I had no reason to believe he was behind any of the graffiti, but suspected at least a few of his teammates were. I had seen them laughing boisterously at the *ah-jew* sneezes, and most of them seemed dumb enough to draw a backward swastika.

I was not the only schmuck they picked on. Others were afraid of them, but Joe Carcone had trained me well enough, and I had already taken a grown man's best punch and lived to tell the tale. Shmuel Resnick was as big and strong as any of the football players. If the bullies got physical, I would fight back and do what Joe told me. I would make sure they paid a price, whatever the consequences.

In yeshiva we learned about Masada. We were taught nothing about Bunker Hill, Gettysburg, or Iwo Jima, but Masada I knew well. It was the mountaintop fortress in the Judean desert where Jewish zealots took their final stand against the Roman Empire. They held off a superior army for more than three years, and in the end took their own lives rather than surrender. It is a source of pride for our people, even to this day.

My Masada came in gym class, where the Magen David trouble first began weeks earlier. Mr. Ignatovich had been called away and we were left alone to our rope climbing and basketball scrimmages. The sounds of squeaking sneakers and bouncing balls echoed throughout the gymnasium.

I was doing calisthenics with a small group of boys and had just stood up from a set of squat thrusts when a rubber ball hit me squarely in the back of the head, sending my yarmulke flying. Frida predicted the skullcap would be a bullseye for the school's rednecks, but I did not expect it would happen quite so literally. Anyway, it was a good shot from almost forty feet away.

My head jerked forward and the ball ricocheted toward the gym ceiling with a solid recoil. I imagine it must have looked pretty funny to those watching. I might have even laughed myself if someone else had been the target. A crew of five guys standing along the baseline, all members of the football team, found it particularly amusing. One of them, a tall kid in a cut-off sweatshirt, danced around giving high fives to his buddies. I assumed he was the thrower.

My yarmulke landed several feet away. I went over and picked it up, scanning the shiny floor for the bobby pin my mother had given me. I did not want to give them the satisfaction of seeing me get down on my hands and knees to search for it. I set the yarmulke back on my head.

"Tiger Pride," one of the teammates shouted with a fist pump.

I didn't know if these were the locker room graffiti writers, but they had clearly identified themselves as our Urbana High anti-Semites of the day, and this was an escalation, the first physical assault and my moment of decision. I knew if I did nothing, it would be only the beginning, so I turned to face the enemy and replied with a middle-finger salute.

Getting flipped off by a little Yid in front of the entire gym class was a provocation these gods of the school would never let go unanswered. One of them flipped me back, and then another. I expected there would be hell to pay on my way home after school, but was not expecting what happened next and neither were they.

A kid in a maroon TIGER FOOTBALL shirt leapt from the dog pack with a fierce windup and hurled a rubber ball at me with all his might. I almost could not believe my good fortune. It was a huge mistake on his part.

The swirly-colored ball hung there in the space between us as if in slow motion, like a gift from Hashem himself, floating down from heaven. I waited for it . . . waited for it . . . and then exploded with my left, a smoking sidearm fist ball as violent as any I had ever hit. The thrower's follow-through brought him forward into a crouching position, leaving his big head the perfect target for the missile I sent rocketing back at him. His hands were down and he had no time to react.

There's less control with a fist ball than an open palm. It was probably not my best choice of returns as far as accuracy goes, but my hands were already balled in anger and you can't beat a fist ball for sheer velocity. I'd like to claim the effectiveness of my return was one hundred percent skill, but honestly, it was part luck. You have no idea how difficult it is to hit a moving target the size of a human head.

Another thing you might not know is how much damage a rubber ball can do traveling at almost a hundred miles an hour. I'd seen protective eyewear crack from hits less vicious than the one the football player took to his nose. We were both lucky. An inch or two in either direction and he could have lost an eye.

The kid immediately covered his face and his teammates gathered around him. One of them tried to peel back the kid's hands and let out a loud, '*Oh shit!*' Blood droplets spattered the hardwood and the tops of their white sneakers.

I had not forgotten what Joe told me about how he earned his reputation as a crazy man—"*Don't even look at those Carcone boys cross-eyed or they'll be all over you.*"

This was my Masada. There would be no prisoners.

I sprinted toward the group of startled jocks and the circle surrounding their injured teammate spread apart. The sight of his blood had the same effect on them as Shmuel Resnick's did on his little pal, Heshy. They were stunned and in disarray, giving me a momentary advantage, but it wouldn't last long. I had only a split second to make my next move.

Handball trains you to process information and react instantaneously. A good player knows never to telegraph his shots; either through eye movement or body language, you never give away your next move. There were five of them—four not counting the crouching fountain. I locked eyes with the biggest guy in the group and ran straight at him.

He raised his hands defensively, confusion spreading across his face. I drew back my fist while still two strides away, but at the last moment spun to the side and connected high on the cheek of the lanky kid standing next to him, the one in the cut-off sweatshirt I suspected of hitting me with the ball in the first place.

Joe taught me to punch through my target for more power, just like with a good handball swing. My feet were not firmly planted on the gym floor, but I still clocked the kid hard enough to knock him off balance before sweeping his legs out from under him with my instep. He tumbled backward onto the hardwood and I got in one decent kick to his ribs before the pummeling began.

I took a stinging fist to my left temple and another came from over my right shoulder to the back of my head, catching me behind the ear. After that, it was all a blur of flailing arms and legs, my own and theirs, until Mr. Ignatovich stepped in to break it up a moment later.

"What the hell's going on here?" he shouted at the tumbling pile of bodies. The gym teacher grabbed the biggest guy by the collar and pulled him off me. The others quickly stepped aside.

"What's wrong with you knuckleheads?" he yelled.

"He started it, Coach," the big guy said. "Look what he did to Jimmy."

He pointed to the kid I'd hit with the ball, who was still covering his nose, blood streaks on the front of his shirt. The kid I punched was picking himself up off the gym floor.

"Five on one, and you morons got the worst of it?" Mr.

Ignatovich said. "Are you kidding me? What happened here, Altshul?"

"I started it," I replied.

"Yeah, right. And you expect me to believe that? Come on, the lot of you, we're going to the principal's office. Not you, Cunningham," he said to the one they called Jimmy. "You're going to the school nurse."

"Atkins," the coach barked, and a student not involved in the melee came running. "Take this idiot to the infirmary."

As Mr. Ignatovich led us from the gym, a little Asian kid trotted up and handed me my yarmulke. Without the bobby pin, it had fallen off my head as I ran at the football players.

"Here's your hat," he said.

I was halfway down the hall before I realized my lip was split open. I poked at the tenderness with my tongue.

We waited outside the principal's office while Mr. Ignatovich spoke with him. When we were called in, Dr. Hauser was not happy with us.

"So we're brawling in gym class now, are we? Who's going to tell me what happened?"

I told him I threw the first punch.

"And I suppose they did nothing to provoke or antagonize you?"

None of us replied.

"And what happened to Jim Cunningham?" he asked.

I told Dr. Hauser I hit him with a ball.

"No, I mean what happened to his nose? The nurse thinks it's broken. What was it, a baseball?"

"No, it was rubber, just a regular ball."

The principal looked at me skeptically.

"That's what happened, really." The lanky kid in the cut-off sweatshirt spoke up, a reddish bruise already rising on his cheekbone. "He's telling the truth, but it was me that start-

195

ed it. I threw a ball at Altshul when he wasn't looking. Then Cunningham threw one and Altshul hit it back at him. I never seen a ball hit so hard, like it came off a bat. Really, it was just a rubber ball. No one was trying to hurt anyone."

"So it was all in good fun, eh?" the principal said. "Just a bunch of pals horsing around and it turned into a brawl. You really think I'm that gullible?"

There were multiple shrugs.

"And I suppose you four gentlemen had nothing to do with any of the harassment or graffiti either?"

They glanced at each other in bewilderment, shaking their heads as if they had no idea what he was referring to.

"No, of course not," the principal said. "And what about you, Altshul? So you're not speaking up either?"

I shrugged too.

Dr. Hauser tossed his pen onto the desk in disgust and declared he was sending us all home for the day and we hadn't heard the end of it.

"And Mr. Altshul, you'll be back here in my office tomorrow morning at the start of first period and you'd better have something to say for yourself by then. Oh, and the rest of you gentlemen are suspended from the team at least until after the game this weekend, or until I figure out what you've been up to."

Coach Ignatovich seemed unhappy with the principal's verdict but offered no protests.

On my way out of the building, I stopped in the bathroom to wash my face. I looked in the mirror. The right half of my lower lip was considerably swollen. I smiled, even though there would be no way to hide it from Frida.

I pushed through the front doors and descended the concrete steps on my way to the Big Green Wall, thinking there could be nothing better than getting thrown out of school on such a beautiful day. I would be lying if I said I wasn't proud of myself. I had done everything Joe Carcone told me and walked away with only a few minor bruises, but as I reached the end of the long walkway leading to Carle Park, two of the guys I'd fought with stepped from behind a group of evergreen trees, blocking my path. I glanced back toward the school. There was no one in sight and it was too late to run.

I believe every human being has only a certain well of courage and mine had gone dry, more than depleted in the gymnasium brawl. The big guy, who I think might have been the one who split my lip, took a step toward me. I knew I had gotten off too easy. I clenched my fists, ready for the beating I was about to take, but the big guy's hands were down at his sides and he did not seem angry.

He said, "You were pretty chill in there, Altshul."

I was not completely sure if that was good or bad. I took my best guess.

"No sweat," I replied, using the modern expression I'd heard so many times on the courts in Brooklyn.

"Why'd you cover for us?" he asked.

"It wasn't such a big deal," I said in my best American.

"You coulda gotten us in a shitload of trouble."

"What good would that do?" I said.

"Yeah, well, you didn't have to man up. Not everyone would've done that."

I took credit with a modest shrug. I had shrugging down to a science.

"So are we cool now?" he asked.

"We cool," I answered in my best Don Cornelius.

The big guy extended his fist. I hesitated for half a second before bumping it with my own. The other guy extended his too, then they went their way and I headed off to play handball in this new America where all men are created equal.

I practiced alone until late afternoon, so grateful to that peeling patch of paint on the wall about the size of a boy's head. I could not contain my excitement when Joe Carcone finally showed up.

"You should have seen what happened at school today," I shouted.

He laughed when I got to the part about the kid throwing the ball at me.

"Jesus, Junior, maybe you should've warned him. Next time I'll make you a sign to wear around your neck— DANGER: HANDBALL PLAYER."

"I know. I couldn't believe it. The ball just hung there waiting for me to take my best shot. I had all the time in the world, like ducks on a shelf."

He said, "I don't think that's exactly the expression you're looking for."

"The school nurse said I broke his nose. It did not look half as bad as mine though. And you should've seen the looks on their faces when I charged at them . . . those big guys . . . football players. They were afraid of me."

I described the rest of the showdown in all its glory, including my stellar performance in the principal's office.

"And two of them waited for me outside after and shook my hand like this . . ."

I showed him how we did the fist bump. Then Joe held out his fist and we bumped too.

He said, "I'm guessing you're over the hump now, Junior. So now comes the real test of your character."

"What do you mean?" I asked.

"Just don't let it go to your head, that's all. Remember you're a nice guy, not a wise guy. Now let's play some handball."

I would not understand what Joe meant until later that evening.

Frida started yelling at me as soon as I walked in the door. The principal had already called her.

"Again?" she said. "And look at you . . ."

"You shoulda seen the other guys," I answered with a split-lip grin.

She said, "Listen, that smug bullshit might've worked on Paul, but not me. Now tell me what happened. Did they beat you up?"

"Not really. There were five of them and I repaired their wagons."

"You mean you fixed their wagons."

"Yes, I fixed their wagons . . . I fixed their fucking wagons."

I knew how King David must have felt after dropping Goliath with a stone hurled from his sling. The young Hebrew was only a boy when he killed the Philistine giant. Following his victory the women of Israel came out to greet him, dancing and singing: *"Saul has slain his thousands, and David his tens of thousands."* Lying in bed that night, I pictured the Urbana Tigers cheerleaders shaking their pom-poms for me as I slowly drifted off to sleep.

I was bathing in a warm mikvah of pleasant thoughts when an overwhelming wave of regret swept over me. I had not shed a tear after Shmuel Resnick's vicious beating, but my heart now tore open like the keriah garments at my parents' funeral. I wept bitterly for the boy I injured in gym class, a salty tear for each drop of blood that fell from his nose. That's when I understood what Joe Carcone was trying to tell me earlier in the day.

News of the skirmish spread through the school as quickly as word of the graffiti and the principal's offer of cash. At the beginning of first period I was excused to Dr. Hauser's office. He asked me to come in and close the door. He'd spoken to the other students in the gym and had a pretty good grasp of what happened.

He said, "If you mention this to anyone else I'll deny ever saying it, but you gave those boys what they deserved and I'm proud of you. Sometimes the ends justify the means, but as your principal I can't tell you that. My official response is: We never resolve any issues with violence in this school. So that's the admonition I'm sending you back to class with. Remember, I'm being very clear with you. We never raise our hands to another student, right?

"I've given this a lot of thought and I've decided to drop the entire matter here . . . for the other boys too. I believe you may have taken care of the problem better than I ever could, so I'm telling the boys I'm not suspending them from the team because you interceded on their behalf. If I've made the right call, we'll all just move on from here, and if not, we'll reassess, OK? Let's keep our fingers crossed."

I returned to Mrs. Margolis's class and opened the door just in time to hear her say, *"It is better to be feared than loved if you cannot be both."*

We'd been working our way through the Renaissance and Reformation Study Unit and it took me a moment to realize she was reading a quote from a famous book called *The Prince*.

She said, "We still use the term *Machiavellian* today. Has anyone ever heard the idiom *'The ends justify the means'*?"

A few students raised their hands half-heartedly.

Over the summer Leeann Carter taught me about dramatic irony and this moment was not lost on me.

PART THREE

KINGSTON AVENUE:
SOUTH CHICAGO, ILLINOIS

So now I will explain how I ended up on Kingston Avenue again, only this time not in Brooklyn. Chicago was Joe Carcone's idea. We were at the Big Green Wall late on a Friday afternoon. It was one of the first kind days of early spring and I stayed on the court a little longer than I should have. Frida would not be happy with me charging in the door at the last minute and rushing through dinner so I could be ready when the Kotins came to pick me up for shul.

Joe still had his gloves on and did not seem in any hurry to leave.

He said, "I think it's about time we complete your education, Junior."

I was nearing the end of my sophomore year at Urbana High, but I had the feeling he was not referring to school.

"I have to go home now," I said.

"I don't mean right this second, but it's about time you learned the finer points of the game, and it wouldn't hurt for us to make a little money either . . . you know, the way we do it in Brooklyn."

"You mean gambling?"

He said, "There are opportunities . . . clubs up in Chicago, and I'm not talking this rec center bullshit. I'm talking doctors, lawyers, that sort of thing. You have B- and C-players who think they're hot shit, just begging to get hustled by a kid in a yarmulke. I'm telling you we couldn't ask for a better setup. How about we head up north tomorrow and check things out?"

"Does that mean I'll have to gamble on Shabbos too?" I asked.

Joe had seen me take plenty of liberties with the 613 Mitzvot before, but gambling on Shabbos was a new one.

He said, "You know, I think Religion confuses you, Junior. You're always caught in the middle somewhere, like you don't know whether to shit or go blind."

That was an expression I'd never heard before. I had no idea what making shit had to do with going blind. This made no sense.

"You're always somewhere between half in and half out," he said. "You need to make up your mind—either you're a black hat or you're not. Figure it out. I was all caught up in a bunch of Catholic school bullshit when I was a kid too, afraid God was gonna send me to hell if I ate meat on Friday. You really think God gives a rat's ass what you eat or whether it's Friday or Saturday?"

I did not know what God gave a rat's ass about. In shul that night I pondered everything Joe said. He was right. Religion confused me.

Frida and Paul were arguing again when I shuffled up the driveway after Shabbos services. I could hear them going at it before I got to the door and did not want to barge in on them, so I turned around and paced the dark Urbana streets for almost half an hour. The house was quiet when I returned, but I made a point of clanging the garbage cans and rattling the side door before opening it.

Paul Griffin glowered at me as soon as I entered the kitchen. He was red in the face and white-knuckling an almost-empty beer bottle. I got the feeling I was the reason for their dispute. Frida did not look up at me. I could tell she had been crying. I said good night and went straight to my room, feeling even more like the little hoizer gaier that showed up on their doorstep than when I moved in a year ago.

I was out of sorts when Joe picked me up at six the next morning despite the coffee and box of sugar donuts waiting for me on the seat next to him. He explained we would be making two stops, one at a YMCA in Des Plaines, and another at Rainbow Beach.

"Remember," he said. "We're just checking things out today, but if we *do* get to play, there's no showing off, OK? You let them see only what's necessary, nothing more, and if you don't have to dig deep, you don't. Got that?"

I fingered the roll of bills in my pocket while counting blackbirds along the interstate power lines. My mind was drifting aimlessly across the flat prairie when Joe's voice came cracking off the windshield glass like the pop of a ball against concrete.

"Did you see your rabbi had a stroke?"

I must not have heard him correctly.

I said, "That's impossible. I just saw him in shul last night."

"No, no, I'm talking about your big rabbi in Brooklyn, what's his name. I read it in *Newsweek* the other day but forgot to tell you."

"You mean the Rebbe?"

"They say he's paralyzed . . . Can't speak."

This was beyond my comprehension. The Rebbe was our Tzaddik hador, Hashem's representative here on earth. My father believed he was Moshiach. As a child I played on our living room carpet with his portrait looming over me, and his intense blue eyes had followed me ever since. He watched over all Lubavitchers that same way.

"But how can the Rebbe be Moshiach if he can't speak?" I

207

asked, more thinking aloud than expecting an answer from Joe Carcone.

"How should I know?" he replied. "It's all a bunch of crazy horseshit if you ask me."

I turned away, praying silently for the Rebbe's health. I pictured him being rolled into 770 in his wheelchair, head drooping, swaying side to side, with spittle running down his white beard. I handed Joe the roll of bills from my pocket and asked him to hold on to it for me.

After more than two hours on the interstate, we pulled into a parking lot along a dismal secondary road in Des Plaines.

Joe said, "First we'll size the place up and see what's shaking. If we can get a game, we keep it close, then we'll see who wants to lose some money. We're playing it cool here, right?"

We paid for our guest passes and climbed the steps to the viewing area above the courts. The sound of balls thwacking concrete echoed through the block corridor and the walls flickered under buzzing fluorescent tubes in the suspended ceiling. The stale air smelled like old socks in a gym bag.

At the far end of the corridor a crowd of men were bent over the viewing wall. We peered over their shoulders to see two journeymen handball players duking it out on the court below. They were in the third game of a match, a tiebreaker to eleven points. One of them was starting to crack, and his supporters shouted encouragement as he lost serve again.

"Eight–four," the stronger player shouted before firing off another ace.

"Nine–four."

"That guy's pretty good," Joe said out loud. The men in front turned to look at him. One of them smirked, as if to say, "So what else is new?" I knew Joe didn't mean it. In truth, their players were nothing special.

The tiebreaker ended at eleven-five and one of the men at the wall slipped a roll of bills out of his pocket. He peeled off five twenties and handed them to the smirker, saying, "You're buying lunch today, shithead."

"My nephew's visiting from Brooklyn and wants to play," Joe said to no one in particular. "Is there any way we can get a game?"

The men eyeballed us, looking me up and down. Joe was right about my yarmulke being a sly touch.

"The courts are booked all day on Saturday," one of them replied.

"My nephew's a good player," Joe said. "We'll buy in if you like. He just wants a little court time. We drove all the way up here from Champaign."

"Champaign?" the smirker said. "What, don't you guys have any handball courts down there?"

"Yeah, but there aren't any good players. We heard about this place and decided to come up for the day . . . Tell you what: I'll put up a hundred bucks just to get on the court. If he wins, you give it back. If not, you keep it. You don't have to risk anything. How's that?"

"So you Brooklyn guys think we don't know a classic hustle when we see one?" the smirker said.

"I already told you he's a good player and it won't cost you a dime to find out how good. We'll play doubles if that'll work out better for you."

"I've got a court at eleven," the smirker said. "My partner's not here yet, but I'll give him a call and see what he says. If he agrees, we can play doubles and I'll take your hundred."

Joe held out his hand.

"I'm Joe. This is Zev."

The smirker introduced himself as Sam.

*　　*　　*

My education in the art of hustling handball was about to begin, but I wasn't the only person getting schooled that day. Sam the Smirker would learn not to underestimate a gray-haired old man and a kid in a yarmulke. It cost him two hundred bucks after he gave back our hundred. He and his buddies then coughed up another five between them when I beat the club pro they called "Monster."

I watched them count the bills into Joe's open palm as my father and the Rebbe looked down from the observation area above us. I could almost hear them tsk-tsking as they shook their heads in shame.

Out in the parking lot Joe patted me on the shoulder and told me I did a great job.

"I don't like holding back so much," I replied. "I could have beaten them a lot worse."

"Well, you did the right thing," he said. "There's no reason for them to know you have anything left in the tank. We need to keep these guys interested . . . let them believe they can make their money back when we come up here next time. I'm surprised you never learned any of this back in Brooklyn, but I guess it's the kind of stuff your rabbi didn't approve of."

I wished he hadn't mentioned the Rebbe again. We were almost a thousand miles from Crown Heights, but the old tzaddik's voice was as strong as ever and his paralyzed arm reached as far as it always did.

Joe said, "Remember what you learned today, Junior. There're winners and losers, and that Sam's a loser. I could see it as soon as I laid eyes on him. A big ego, but he's not as good as he thinks he is, either as a player or a gambler, and that's a losing combination every time. Guys like him will bet against the sun coming up in the morning if you give them the right odds. Pretty soon you'll learn to read them. So what do you think? Not bad, eh . . . seven hundred bucks for an afternoon of handball?"

I had to agree this was a nearly effortless payday. I believe the ease of it is what gave me my taste for gambling, that and the excitement of riding into town like a Yiddish gunslinger and seeing the look in my opponents' eyes when they know they're going down and there is nothing they can do about it.

It took less than an hour to get from Des Plaines to Rainbow Beach. Joe parked his Oldsmobile along 76th Street where it dead-ends at Lake Michigan. A frigid wind whipped at us when we stepped from the car and the air felt ten degrees colder than it did in Des Plaines. He pointed to a rundown brick building at the end of the block.

"This is it," he said.

I did not see any handball courts, only metal letters on peeling blue paint announcing—RAINBOW PARK MARINE SE VICE. The R in SERVICE was missing, and red-brown rust streaks from the remaining letters ran halfway down the wall, staining the close-cropped grass below.

"It's just around the corner," he said, scribing a little semicircle in the air with his hand.

There were only three courts and a small bleacher on the other side of the building. I was expecting something a little more impressive; back in Brooklyn we had thirteen courts at Lincoln Terrace, ten at Seaside in Coney Island. I sat shivering on the sidelines until almost five, when we finally took to the court against two reasonably decent players about ten years younger than Joe. We should've beaten them easily, except I never felt less like playing handball.

I sensed the Rebbe watching my every move from the bleacher, his white beard fluttering in the wind off the lake, a look of great concern on his face. I had trouble placing my serves and digging for kills, as if my feet were glued to the concrete. Joe covered for me and was huffing like a spent racehorse. In the middle of the game he cupped his hand to my ear and said, "Will you step it up, Junior? You're gonna give me a heart attack chasing these goddamn balls around."

We surrendered the court willingly after struggling to win our first and only game. As we walked to the car, Joe said he'd never seen me play that badly. I considered making excuses, telling him I was tired from the long car ride and earlier matches, but said I was sorry without offering any explanation.

I barely uttered a word on the drive back to Urbana. Joe switched on the radio and I asked him to please turn up the heater. The cold had settled deep in my bones and wouldn't leave. We were almost to Kankakee before he finally asked what was bothering me.

"It's nothing," I said, although we both understood that wasn't true.

He said, "Well, let me know if you want to talk about it."

This was not a thing I could so easily explain to my friend who believed all religion was a bunch of crazy horseshit. How could I tell him I felt like a traitor to my people, gambling on Shabbos with the Rebbe so desperately ill? I was no longer just some rebellious Hasidic kid skipping shul to play in a tournament. I was a goy in a yarmulke. A false Jew. A disgrace to my father's memory.

Abba would be sick if he could see me, all those nights he left our apartment, sacrificing even his sleep to work for the Rebbe. I recalled packing grocery boxes with him for poor Jews on Pesach when he said, *"Nothing is more important than doing mitzvot."* I was never happier than at that moment. Now I coiled in the front seat next to Joe Carcone with my arms wrapped tightly around my chest, more certain than ever that the two worlds I'd been trying to stitch together would never mend.

Paul Griffin was in his studio when Joe dropped me off. I did not want to see him and went directly into the house. Frida was watching TV in her SORRY I'M NOT LISTENING T-shirt. As soon as I entered the living room, I saw the purplish bruises ringing both upper arms just below her shirtsleeves. My insides frothed like they did earlier on the three-wall court.

"How were your games?" she asked cheerfully.

"I did not play so well this afternoon," I said. "I do not like three-wall much."

I was very tired and my speech had turned stiff and Yeshivish again.

"You want to watch some TV with me?" she asked, patting the couch cushion next to her the way Rav Feldsher did when I returned to our apartment in Brooklyn to learn of the great tragedy that had befallen our family. I could not pay attention to the TV because I kept glancing at the bruises on her arms. I tried not to stare at them, just as I tried not to stare at her breasts the first time I saw her in that shirt. I told myself there could be many explanations for what caused those ten mottled impressions in her flesh, but I knew very well how they got there.

I told Frida I needed something to drink and left for the kitchen, only to stare blankly into the open refrigerator, weighing the consequences of going out to the studio to warn Paul Griffin to keep his hands off my sister. Threatening him was a bad idea. In spite of what Joe Carcone taught me about self-defense, I was not a fighter, and any confrontation would only bring more trouble, for Frida and for me. Later that night, in my half sleep, I saw Paul Griffin's puckery face plastered right next to Shmuel Resnick's, and from that day on, I did not feel the least bit guilty about hating him.

I called Joe the next morning and told him I would not be playing handball because I had a paper due. Like any good teacher, he said, "Schoolwork always comes first," although once again we both knew that wasn't true. I said I'd meet him at the Big Green Wall after class on Monday.

Frida and Paul argued constantly all day, snapping at each other over the smallest things, seemingly for no reason. A year earlier, when they took me in, Frida said it was only a trial and they were not making any promises. If it were solely up to Paul Griffin, I would have been gone long ago, but I wondered how much worse things could get before Frida would come to the same conclusion. There was no denying my tenancy on California Avenue had been a complete disaster.

I spent most of the day fretting about where I would go once they put me out. Maybe Frida would leave with me and we could get a place of our own, just the two of us. I did not think she liked Paul Griffin so much anymore. Maybe Joe Carcone would take me in, but he was not my flesh and blood, and Illinois was not my home. If all else failed, I could move back to Brooklyn. I still had most of Abba's money, so at least I would not be forced to live with the Resnicks or in a foster home.

Rav Feldsher promised I would not have to worry about Shmuel Resnick if I returned to Brooklyn, but I did not believe anyone could stop the big Jew from taking his revenge. Shmuel Resnick was not the type to forgive and forget so easily, and I was absolutely certain he would settle the score with me sooner or later. I still cringed at the sight of white vans and men with dark beards, and I felt his powerful hands tighten around my throat every time I saw my crooked nose in the mirror.

I left for school Monday morning hoping to find relief from the bitterness in the house on California Avenue, but my bruised sister and her abusive boyfriend followed me to Urbana High. They were accompanied by a sick Rebbe and a vengeful Hasid who took unassigned seats in my first period classroom, blocking my view of Mrs. Margolis, and mumbling to me as I slogged through the rest of the school day waiting for the dismissal bell to ring.

At the Big Green Wall, Joe asked if I wanted to drive up to Chicago again that weekend. I answered with my famous noncommittal shrug, saying I would check with Frida, even though I knew she wouldn't mind as long as my homework was done. I had not told him about the bruises on Frida's arms or that I'd been praying for the Rebbe and had vowed not to gamble on Shabbos again until he was well.

I know this must sound very foolish. How would keeping another sham Shabbos in Urbana help the Rebbe get well? Would the sound of a rubber ball pounding plywood for hours on end ascend to heaven like a prayer? Would riding in a car to Rabbi Jerry's shul and singing the cantor's peppy songs in English protect Frida from Paul Griffin? Of course, my strained attempts at piety failed once again, and we drove to Chicago that weekend, and the weekend after that, and every weekend until school let out, gambling on Shabbos as if it were the 614th commandment.

I won my first IHA tournament in Lake View later that spring, and set the trophy on my bedroom windowsill so I could see it when I looked up from California Avenue. It was little more than a cheap tower of varnished wood and plated plastic, but it sparkled in the afternoon sun like the silver crown on the Torah scrolls in the ark at 770. Abba would have been furious over that trophy. *"Like the golden calf,"* he would have groused through gnashed teeth, but Abba was not alive to see it, or to tell me how much he despised it.

In May, Joe won his age group in a tournament at Rainbow Beach. He placed the trophy between us for the drive back to Champaign, resting his hand on the head of the little gold handball player and stroking it as if it were a cherished pet. When he dropped me off at California Avenue, I told him how proud I was of him. He wore an odd expression, very hard to describe, a mixture of pleasure and pain.

I have always been good at figuring people out on the handball court—off the court, not so much. Joe Carcone was a mystery, just like my father. He kept his true feelings bottled inside. I guess the three of us were a lot alike in that way.

Memories of Abba only deepened his mystery. Who was the devout man who would sacrifice anything for the Rebbe, the gabbai wrapped in black with a suitcase full of money hidden in his closet? I never really knew my father, but did I really know Joe Carcone?

He was moodier than usual the following week. We were finishing a game at the Big Green Wall when he threw his gloves down on the asphalt and said, "You know this is shit, don't you, Zev?"

I did not know what shit he was referring to, but Joe never called me by my given name, so I knew it must be something serious.

"You're not going to get any better swatting balls back and forth with an old man every day, you know that, right?"

"I like playing with you," I said. "You're a great coach and we've both gotten a lot better this year."

"That's not the point. I've never told you this before, but you're not just a good player anymore, you know what I'm saying? You're about as good as any I've seen; at least you will be if you get some real competition. You need to go up against A-players or you'll wind up being another schoolyard bum like me."

"You're not a bum," I said. It hurt to hear him say that about himself.

"Yeah, whatever. I missed my chance. I don't want you to miss yours."

"You're still a good player," I said.

"It doesn't matter about me, my day's come and gone. You've got a chance to be one of the greats, but it's not gonna happen playing on a half-assed plywood court with me five days a week. The school year's almost over; what do you say we get the hell out of here and rent a place in Chicago for the summer? Apartments are cheap on the South Side; we can easily cover it."

I shrugged my usual shrug, the one I always use to dodge difficult questions.

He said, "I don't get it, Junior, I thought you'd jump at the chance. What's the point hanging around here all summer when we can be in the thick of it up in Chicago? We're only talking a couple of months, that's all, just until school starts again in September. Come on, it'll be good for both of us."

"But what about Frida?" I asked.

"So you're a minor and you'll have to get her permission. You think she'll have a problem with you going?"

My dilemma was far more complicated than getting my sister's permission. Joe might have understood if I had told him about the bruises on Frida's arms, but she was a resourceful girl who had forged a new life in an unfamiliar world and learned to speak American and got her GED all on her own. I saw the way she handled the manager at the U of I rec center. Frida would most likely be fine without me in Urbana for the summer. I was not so sure about Joe Carcone.

I felt his sadness on the first day we met at the Big Green Wall and had worried about him since he fixed my broken nose in his kitchen—the drawn curtains, the picture of his missing wife and son. It was a house nobody lived in, a house of spirits. On the surface he was as tough as a Brooklyn pit bull, but inside Joe was as fragile as that vase I knocked to the floor in my parents' apartment, the one with the pieces barely glued together.

"Come on," he urged. "Let's do this together. At least ask your sister and see what she says."

Frida was in the kitchen cooking dinner when I walked in the door. I skulked over to where she was chopping vegetables and picked up a saltshaker and began twirling it on the countertop. She immediately grabbed it away from me.

"Christ, Zevi, it's so freaking obvious when something's bugging you. Why don't you just go ahead and tell me what's on your mind?"

I asked how she would feel about me moving to Chicago with Joe for the summer. Her willingness made me think she was glad to be getting rid of me.

"You should go," she said. "You've been up there every weekend anyway, and Joe's a responsible guy. Just have him give me a call and we'll work things out."

"Are you sure you'll be OK alone here?" I asked.

"Go," she said. "I wouldn't dream of standing in your way. I'm happy you've got your handball. It must be wonderful to have something in your life you love so much, and anyway, I'm not alone here."

She let out a sigh, as if all the sorrows in the world came rushing out of her. I told her I would stay in Urbana if she needed me.

Frida chuckled softly, saying, "That's very sweet of you, Zevi, but do I really look like I need help?"

The truth is she did.

I said, "I can come down once a week. Joe has stuff he needs to take care of in Champaign and I can ride along with him."

She told me not to be silly.

"Then I'll call every couple of days," I insisted. "I can use a pay phone."

She said, "Cut it out, Zevi. I'll be just fine and so will you. Now stop worrying so much. What do you think's going to happen to me?"

Joe found us a month-to-month sublet in South Chicago not far from Rainbow Beach, and the following Friday night I attended Rabbi Jerry's shul for the last time. Mrs. Kotin was alone when she came to pick me up. I told her I was leaving for Chicago in the morning and would be gone the entire summer. She asked who would be supervising me. I explained that my friend was a schoolteacher and Frida had given her permission.

"Well, I hope you'll be careful," she said, sounding very motherly. "The city can be a dangerous place."

I suppose she forgot I grew up in Brooklyn.

After the service I told Rabbi Jerry I would not be back in shul again until fall. His usual benign smile stretched thin and one of his eyebrows arched like a drawn bowstring.

"So you're going to Chicago with this man and your sister has nothing to say about it?" he asked.

Rabbis have a way of asking questions that are not really questions at all so much as statements of opinion and advice.

He said, "I realize it's none of my business. I only want what's best for you."

I believed that was true. I'd long ago forgiven him for conspiring with Mrs. Kotin. My pride was hurt at the time, but I realized they meant well and were only trying to help me adjust to my new life. Rabbi Jerry was a good man.

I said, "Thank you for being so kind to me. You have been very helpful."

My American speaking was much improved, but I still sometimes forgot to use the contractions.

He said, "What good is a rabbi if not to be helpful? It's been my very great pleasure, Zev. I mean that . . . really a pleasure."

Rabbi Jerry stroked his bare chin and, after a thoughtful pause, made an unexpected confession.

"You know, I've never believed in the 613 Mitzvot."

It was shocking to hear that statement come from a rabbi, even one without a beard.

"Our whole life is a mitzvah," he explained. "Showing kindness is more a reflection of God's image than whether or not we pick up a pen or carry a set of house keys on Shabbat. We behave morally and do good because it's the right thing to do and the world is better off that way, not because of 613 laws written by a primitive tribe thousands of years ago. I can't tell you or anyone else how to live, or what's right for them, but this is what makes the most sense to me. It's what I believe God expects of me as a Jew, and how I can best do his work in the world."

The first time we met in his office, I was not even sure Rabbi Jerry *was* a Jew, but in his own way he had taught me more about the heart of Judaism than I'd learned in my years studying the intricacies of Talmud in yeshiva.

Mrs. Kotin came and stood next to us, a clear signal it was time to go.

The rabbi said, "I'll miss you, Zev. Do you have a phone

number where I can reach you in Chicago?"

"We do not have a telephone," I answered.

"An address then? Maybe I'll drop you a note."

My address was written on a notecard in my pocket and I handed it to him. He copied it down and wrote his home address and phone on the back of the card before returning it to me.

He said, "If you ever need me for anything, you know how to get in touch. It's my home number and I always pick up. Call me anytime."

We shook hands and the rabbi said, "Zei gezunt." Be healthy.

"Thank you," I said. "I hope I will see you again."

"You're making it sound so permanent," he replied. "You're coming home in the fall, aren't you?"

I smiled uncertainly because I did not know where my home was, and if I had learned anything in the past year, it's that nothing in life is permanent.

South Chicago reminded me a little of Crown Heights, only with less garbage in the streets and without all the Hasids and Moshiach banners. Our two-bedroom walkup was on the third floor of a weathered brick building, as faceless as any other on the block. The varnish was almost completely worn from the banister in the stairway and the treads creaked loudly all the way to the landing outside our door.

I quit attending shul after leaving Urbana, and no longer laid tefillin or recited the Modeh Ani in the morning. I continued wearing my yarmulke. Some might see this as another of my many oddities, but it was my way of affirming that even this off-the-derech Jew was still a Jew. Joe Carcone wanted me to wear it for other reasons.

"It's the perfect disguise," he said. "You see the way even

221

the other Jews look at you? They all underestimate you."

He even joked about me wearing my black coat and fedora to the JCC in Rogers Park for the first time. At least I thought he was joking.

We drove up to the northern suburb on a hot and sticky Wednesday night. Joe used the same line about his nephew looking for a game as before. We were told it was impossible because Wednesday was their summer league night and all the courts were booked. He offered to put up some money and one of them, obviously a macher, said, "Well, I guess he could play Little Scotty. You're going to have to spot him points, though."

I did not like the sound of this. They were making it too easy.

The macher said, "Scotty's the youngest kid in the league. He's only fifteen and he's already played one game tonight, so you're not going even-up against him."

"So what are you saying?" Joe asked.

"One game only, twenty-one points, three hundred minimum, and a fifteen-point spot."

"Are you kidding?" Joe feigned shock. "That's a lot of money and crazy points. We don't know anything about this Scotty. How do we know how good he is?"

The macher said, "You don't, and it'll cost you three hundred and a fifteen-point spot to find out. How bad does your nephew want to play?"

Joe looked over at me and I nodded, but the way the macher said *nephew* made me uneasy. He reminded me of a TV gangster with his stubbly five o'clock shadow, chomping on the butt of an unlit cigar.

Joe said, "The three hundred's probably OK, but how about we give you five points?"

"Ten minimum," the macher said.

Joe looked down at the floor, shaking his head like the guy was driving too hard a bargain.

"How about seven?" he asked.

"Eight and we're good," the macher replied.

"Done."

The macher then turned to a skinny bald guy and told him to go get Scotty. He returned in a few minutes with a not too impressive kid wearing a pair of baggy black basketball shorts. They cleared Court Three, and the whole entourage headed down there for the coin toss. The macher flipped and Little Scotty won and stepped into the five-foot-wide service zone. The side bets had already started before the entourage left the court for the viewing area.

Scotty bounced the ball and hit it low on the drop. His serve landed just beyond the short line on what he probably thought was my weak side. I was ready for it, but the ball took an erratic little hop, almost like it hit a crack on a concrete playground court. I had to check up and managed only a limp return that set the kid up for an easy kill.

"That's a point. Nine serving zero," the macher called from the viewing area, in an exaggerated official-sounding voice. I immediately regretted that eight-point spot as Little Scotty stepped back into the service zone and grinned at me over his shoulder. I knew right away the hustlers were being hustled. He ran up three more unanswered points before I finally won serve on a fly-kill. I have to admit this kid could make the ball dance.

"Side out. Zero serving twelve," the macher announced as I entered the service zone, aggravated by Scotty's smartass attitude and the fact that I had to give him eight points. I wanted to destroy the little schmendrick right then and there, but Joe's words came back to me as if he were whispering in my ear.

"We're playing it cool here, right?"

I won the next two points before losing service again. Little Scotty then won the next two points and I called a timeout and left the court with an overly dramatic gesture of frustration for the benefit of the macher and his friends. Joe met me just outside the door.

"Anything to be worried about here, Junior?" he asked in a hushed tone. "The kid looks pretty good."

I said, "He puts a tricky spin on the ball, but I've got him covered. I want you to put some more money on me now. Let's make the drive up here worthwhile."

"Just be patient," he said. "Trust me on this, there's plenty more if we don't do anything stupid. You should see these guys tossing their cash around up there. We'll do a lot better if we're patient. I'm saying maybe you should even lose this first one."

I said, "I'm not losing to this kid. Just lay down a few more side bets on me."

"Next game's where we'll make our money," Joe said. "It's not about teaching the little shit a lesson. We've got to be on the same page here."

"I'm not letting this schmuck beat me," I said.

"And I'm not putting any more money on this one, so be patient. At the very least make sure you keep it close. Let's not argue about this."

"Fourteen serving two," the macher announced as I stepped back onto the court.

When Little Scotty entered the service zone, there were no more smiles as he got down to business. He served hard down the left wall, and I think he was surprised when I returned it solidly and followed up with a ceiling shot that sent him to the rear of the court. His weak defensive return set me up and he knew it. I was perfectly positioned with plenty of time.

Joe's advice repeated as I waited for the ball to drop low enough. I started winding up, all set to humiliate the kid with a kill that would leave him seeing the sunset over Chicago with his stupid black basketball shorts down around his ankles. I wanted him to hear what the thwack of a really well-hit ball sounded like, but I did what Joe told me, even adding the embellishment of a grunt as I pretended to put effort behind a half-hearted return designed to keep him in the game.

"That's a point. Fifteen serving two," the macher called out as the kid stepped up to serve again. By this time Joe knew exactly what I was up to, setting the stage for game number two, where we'd separate the macher and his buddies from their cash.

I was not thrilled to let Little Scotty win by nine points, but it was what I had to do to milk every last dollar from the Rogers Park JCC crew. And milk them we did, leaving at the end of the night with over a grand and a half in our pockets, and me a little wiser in the ways of handball.

We stopped at an all-night diner to celebrate over burgers and fries. The guy in the booth next to us was drinking a beer. Joe watched him tip the bottle back and said, "You know, I'd love one of those right now."

"So why don't you have one?" I asked.

"There's a saying at the meetings," he answered. *"One is too many and a thousand is never enough."*

"What does that mean?"

"It means a guy like me can't fuck around. Some people shouldn't touch the stuff; it's too risky. I'll tell you one thing though: If I'm ever diagnosed with a terminal disease, I'm getting a second opinion from Johnny Walker."

"Who's that?" I asked.

"Never mind, Junior. It's a joke."

We headed back to South Chicago, having worn out our

225

welcome at the Rogers Park JCC, just as we had at the MAC downtown, and the WAC in West Allis, and in Milwaukee, Lake View, Des Plaines, Oak Park, and all the others. The nephew-in-the-yarmulke routine was great while it lasted, but we knew it could only play for so long. Our days of invisibility were over. There was no more pretending the scrappy old Italian guy was my uncle, and we would have to spot points everywhere we went.

I visited Frida in Urbana almost every Tuesday throughout the summer. We usually met for a quick bite at a diner near the craft store, but on the second Tuesday in August, she made lunch for us at the house. I felt like a stranger as I let myself in the side door. She rushed over to hug me, holding me more tightly and for longer than I expected. I sensed something wasn't right.

She said, "I'm worried, Zevi. Rabbi Jerry called yesterday to tell me he heard from one of our cousins in New York."

I said, "We don't have any cousins in New York."

"Of course not, and that's what's so frightening. The rabbi said someone from Brooklyn called trying to get in touch with you about claiming your inheritance and needed your address in Chicago."

"That's weird. Why didn't they call you?" I asked.

"Exactly. Whoever it was probably knew I'd be wise to them. The rabbi gave them your address. He had no idea what he was doing, but this means they know where you are and it scares the hell out of me."

I did not like the sound of this either, but tried to see it from another angle.

I said, "Maybe Rav Feldsher didn't give Abba's bank accounts to the shluchim after all. It's possible, you know."

She said, "Then what about this cousin business? I'm sure

Rabbi Jerry didn't make that part up. If it was Feldsher or a lawyer or some banker, why would they make up the cousin bit?"

"Maybe we really *do* have a cousin?"

"Yeah," Frida said. "Maybe we're related to the Rothschilds and they want to give you a million bucks. Get real, Zevi. Someone's looking for you, someone who means you no good. Don't you think it might be smart to report this to the police in Chicago?"

I thought about this for a moment. What would I tell them, that there are men saying they want to give me my inheritance, but they are really after my father's money?

I asked Frida how I would explain Abba's suitcase to the police.

She said, "I don't know. I just don't know, but at least you need to tell Joe about this. You both have to be careful up there."

We sat down for lunch and I asked her how Paul was doing. In truth, I didn't care a thing about Paul Griffin, but thought it might be a good way to find out how he'd been treating her. She told me he was fine without elaborating. Frida's voice dropped almost to a whisper as she said it.

"I don't know, Zevi. I just don't know," she repeated. This time I knew her uneasiness had nothing to do with Abba's money or Brooklyn Hasids.

She said, "This is a very confusing time for me, and not just with Paul, with everything . . . my job, my art, this town . . . It's all a mess and I feel almost as trapped now as I did in Brooklyn. Paul's not helping at the moment, but it's not all his fault."

"Why do you stay with him?" I asked.

Frida seemed shocked by my question. Not as shocked as I was for asking it.

She said, "I've been with him since I was eighteen, and

you just don't walk away from a commitment like that. We've been through some tough times before. We have a history together."

"But you're not married," I said.

"That doesn't matter," she replied. "We're in a relationship."

"But he's not good to you and you're not happy. I never heard Abba and Eema fight the way you two do."

"That's because I stand up for myself. Eema lived in a different world. She cropped her hair and wore a sheitel, for Christ's sake. She was supposed to defer to Abba in everything. Paul and I fight because I speak my mind."

"Well, it doesn't seem to do you much good," I said.

I was sorry for saying that. I did not mean it to sound so cruel.

"Life's a lot more complicated than hitting a ball against a wall, Zevi," she said.

I don't think she meant to sound cruel either.

"Relationships are important. Sometimes I think you use handball as a way of avoiding people."

I did not want to consider that possibility, and anyway, Frida knew nothing about handball. You can learn everything you need to know about life on a handball court.

She said, "Maybe you'll understand when you have a relationship of your own one day . . ."

Frida's eyes brightened. She had found a way to change the subject.

"A little redhead stopped by for you the other day. She didn't know you were up in Chicago and said she knew you from shul."

I said, "Curly hair, right . . . a little tubby?"

"Yeah, that's the one. I thought she was cute. Maybe you should look her up. I think she might be sweet on you."

I said, "I don't even know her name."

Frida said, "She told me, but I don't remember. I think it might be Deena, or Diana . . . something like that. So why don't you give her a call? I'm sure Rabbi Jerry would know how to get hold of her."

I was still smarting from my humiliating crush on Sharon Kotin. The little redhead did not appeal to me, but no matter, I was not about to risk another foray into the world of love. My social life was Joe Carcone and handball, nothing more. That was all I needed.

Frida said, "You know you're not living in the shtetl anymore, Zev. How about trying something new for a change?"

"I've had enough new already," I replied.

"You really should give her a call," she repeated. "Sometimes you have to take chances in life. Another may never come around."

"I'm fine like I am," I said.

"It's important to have someone who cares about you."

My sister wore a peculiar expression when she said that, almost a grimace. I did not reply, but she must have known what I was thinking.

Frida needed to get back to work and I had to meet Joe. She gave me a little peck on the cheek and told me to be careful as I walked out the door. I practically bumped into Paul Griffin in the driveway. He said, '*Hey,*' without looking up at me. I was not expecting much more from him, but his sour greeting left little doubt as to how he felt about me returning in the fall. He continued up the driveway, and I watched him open the door to his studio and disappear into the darkness beyond the threshold.

When I met up with Joe for the ride north, I told him Shmuel Resnick might be looking for us in Chicago.

He said, "Let the motherfucker come."

*　　*　　*

My summer of handball was nearly at an end and I would soon be in school again. I spent my final days in South Chicago on the lookout for suspicious Hasids and dreading the return to Urbana. I would have welcomed almost any excuse not to go back. The Three-Wall National Championships were coming up in Ohio at the beginning of September and I signed up without discussing it with either Frida or Joe first.

I had only my handball stuff and a few changes of clothes in a duffle bag when Joe dropped me off a week before the start of school. We waved to each other as he backed out of the driveway and sped off down California Avenue. I went to the side door. Frida must still have been at work, so I dug into my pocket for the key. I inserted it, but the lock wouldn't turn. I tried several more times, jiggling the knob again and again. I knocked loudly before giving up and checking Paul's studio. No one answered there so I returned to the house to try the front door.

It is impossible to describe the spiraling helplessness that washed over me when I saw my father's suitcase and two cardboard boxes sitting on the porch with a note taped to one of them. I was suddenly eight years old, with Frida gone, Eema sick, and Abba working—I was alone and on my way to the Resnicks again. My hands shook as I read the note:

Zev—Your sister has left. Your belongings are all here. I have changed the locks and do not want to see either of you again. If these things are not removed within two weeks, I will put them out for the trash. Consider this your notice.

I needed to find Joe right away. I left the boxes and suitcase on the porch and started the long walk across town to Champaign, stopping at the rec center to stash my duffle bag. When I opened the locker, I found a second note tucked into the top of the black plastic garbage bag my money was in. It was much lighter than the last time I'd lifted it. I picked up the note and read what my sister had written:

Dearest Zevi,

I know how hard life has been for you and I'm so sorry to add to your troubles. I hope you believe me when I say I had no other choice. I promise to pay back the money. I needed to get away from here and wouldn't have gotten very far on the little I've been able to save. Most of all, I'm ashamed for leaving you again, but I didn't know what else to do.

Joe has been a better guardian than I could ever be and I'm sure he will help you. This is no excuse and I don't expect you to forgive me. I will try and make it up to you someday. I'll be staying with a friend out west until I can find something more permanent. As soon as I am settled somewhere, I will find you.

Please do not mention anything about this to Paul if you see him. I am so very sorry.

Love,

Frida

I read the note again, not believing my sister would ever do such a thing, but the much-too-light garbage bag in my hand confirmed that she had. But how could she have known which locker belonged to me and how would she know the combination? Then it came to me. It was not hard to imagine her charming the manager of the rec center into helping. She was good at that sort of thing.

I stuffed the remaining bills into every available space in my duffle, then wadded up the plastic garbage bag and dropped it in the nearest trash can before continuing my sorry trek across the twin cities. Halfway to Champaign I almost turned back. I'd carried that garbage bag with me from Brooklyn. It was empty of money, but full of memories of my father, and I regretted leaving it in the rec center trash.

When I got to the bungalow, Joe's car was gone. I sat

down on the steps and read my sister's note for the third time. It was definitely her handwriting—no doubt about that. Even so, I could not believe she'd left Urbana willingly.

I remembered Mrs. Gelb from down the hall in our apartment house in Brooklyn. It was a big scandal, a real shanda. Her husband beat her, and not just once or twice. She had two black eyes when she finally pled her cause to the beis din. The rabbis tried to reason with Mr. Gelb, but he wouldn't listen and refused to grant her a divorce. He claimed to know nothing when she vanished without a trace. Mrs. Gelb disappeared, leaving everything behind, even her children. There was plenty of talk that maybe she didn't run away at all. Yossi Teitelbaum said Mr. Gelb stuffed her in the building trash compactor along with the garbage. Maybe Yossi wasn't joking.

I'd been sitting a long time when Joe's car pulled into the driveway. He looked surprised to see me hunched over on his steps with the open duffle next to me. He got out of the car carrying a single grocery bag, gave a nod, and motioned for me to follow him inside.

He said, "So it looks like we have a little problem, eh, Junior?"

"It is more than a little problem," I said, with the Yeshivish cadence I'd worked so hard to lose creeping back in like a hungry mouse.

"So vat den?" Joe asked, his mimicry coming at just the right moment to stave off an onset of tears. He set the groceries down and I handed him Frida's letter, then left my duffle bag on the kitchen table and followed him into the living room. Joe plopped down in his recliner and I sat on the couch. He shook his head as he read the note.

"You didn't see this coming?" he asked.

"Her leaving him? I could see that, yes. I wanted her to leave him. I'm glad she did, but I never thought she'd leave me too . . .

and taking the money, no, I didn't see that coming at all."

"You remember a while back I told you you'd know when she was leaving for good? Well, I think that's a safe bet now."

I thought Joe was taking this much too lightly.

"There's more to it," I said. "I'm sure Paul Griffin did something really bad to her."

"Like what?" he asked.

"I don't know . . . like hurt her or something . . . like maybe something worse. I saw bruises on her arms last spring."

Joe said, "It's probably not what you think."

I said, "Things like that happen, you know. She would never have left without me if she had a choice."

He said, "I hate to say this, Junior, but you don't know that. People do all sorts of things they shouldn't. You think your sister's the first woman to ever leave a man without an explanation?"

Joe was staring at the photo of his absent wife and son as he spoke.

"It happens every fucking day of the week everywhere in the fucking world. People do stupid shit. It's human nature. The main thing is we're in a mess now, aren't we? School's starting next week and you've got nowhere to live."

"Can I stay here with you?" I asked.

"Of course you can, for the time being at least, but we need to figure this out and do it the right way. I'm not your legal guardian, and this is the Champaign School District. You can't just move in here and keep going to Urbana High."

"So what if I keep going to Urbana like before and we don't tell anybody?"

Joe rubbed his face with both hands.

"I don't know, Junior. Personally, I don't give a shit about the rules, but I'm still a few years away from my pension and it's too risky. They'd fire my ass in a minute if we got caught.

Switching schools wouldn't be the worst thing in the world, would it? Champaign Centennial's not so bad."

The thought of being the new Jew in another school made me want to run as far away as I could. I would not go through that again. Ever.

I said, "So what if I move back to Chicago and stay in the apartment by myself?"

"What are you saying . . . and drop out of school? Are you nuts? No way that's happening. Only the worst losers drop out of high school."

I said, "You got your education and you're always saying how you missed your chance."

"Don't worry about what I'm always saying. This isn't about me. You need your high school diploma. That's your priority, got it?"

I said, "Why can't I get my GED like Frida?"

"It's not the same," Joe replied. "No employer or college looks at a GED the same as a diploma."

"I'm not going to college."

"Well, at least you're finishing high school. This is not negotiable. End of discussion."

I said, "I'm seventeen and I don't have to stay in school anymore."

"That's right, you don't . . . So what, you want to end up an old man without a pot to piss in?"

I laughed when he said that. Everything I owned in this world fit into two cardboard boxes, a duffle bag, and a ratty brown suitcase. I barely had a pot now, no less one to piss in.

I said, "What do I have to lose? I'm already making good money from handball."

"It may seem like good money now, but it's chump change. I'm telling you this for your own good, it's not a smart move. You can play all the handball you want, but you can't quit school."

I said, "You think I'm so interested in all this education stuff? I've already had more education than any of my friends in yeshiva, and I'm not changing schools again. I'm not doing it."

I never argued with Abba this way. I may not have been the most obedient son, but I always kept my rebellion to myself as I went about my rebellious business.

I said, "I've already sent in my entry for Nationals."

Joe slumped in his chair like an exhausted player who just wanted the game to be over.

He said, "You know you can still withdraw it."

I could, but I didn't want to.

I said, "So what if I go to Nationals and we figure out what to do about school once I get back? I'll only miss the first few days."

"They're not going to let you come waltzing in the door whenever you feel like it. What'll you do for an excuse? Who's going to write it for you with your sister gone?"

That was a good question.

He said, "Listen, if you don't skip school, I think we can ride this mess out for a while. Withdraw your entry and show up at Urbana the first day. You can live here for the time being. I suppose we can justify that as sort of an emergency thing while we take care of this the right way—legally, I mean. I'll call a lawyer and we can start the ball rolling for guardianship. How's that sound?"

"But I'll still have to switch schools if I live here with you, right?"

"I don't know. I suppose so, eventually."

"Well, I'm not switching schools," I shouted, making it abundantly clear this was not open to debate.

"OK," he said. "Enough, I got the message! Let me go

fix us something to eat and we can talk about this later once we've both calmed down."

While Joe made dinner, I removed the bills from the duffle bag and sorted them on the kitchen table, counting them twice.

I said, "It looks like she took maybe twenty-five thousand . . . about half of what we came here with."

"So that half was hers anyway, right?"

"Not really," I said. "At least not according to Jewish law."

"Is that fair?" he asked.

I did not answer his question.

After dinner Joe drove me back to Urbana to get my things. We pulled into the driveway to the riot of Paul Griffin's music howling at us from the garage. I got out of the car and stood like a steel pipe driven into the weedy gravel, staring at the closed studio door until Joe took me by the arm and steered me toward the front porch.

"Come on," he said. "There's no reason to be hanging around here."

We loaded the boxes and Abba's suitcase into the car and returned to Champaign.

The second bedroom in Joe's bungalow was barely larger than a closet, which was what I think he used it as. He apologized for the mess as he shifted boxes around, stacking them high along the walls to clear a path. I did not unpack my things but placed the money back into my father's suitcase and slid it under the bed.

That night I dreamed I was waiting in line with Abba outside of 770, my palm outstretched to receive a Sunday Dollar from the Rebbe's hand. Suddenly we were enveloped in a spinning whirlwind of dollar bills, and I heard the mute Rebbe reading from the Babylonian Talmud in Aramaic:

"It is forbidden for a man to sleep alone in a house,
Lest Lilith fall upon him in his sleep."

I did not understand why the Rebbe would read such an obscure verse. According to the Zohar, Lilith was Adam's first wife, created before Eve. The Kabbalists say she refused to submit to him and fled from the Garden of Eden to cohabit with the Angel of Death. They say Lilith has roamed the earth ever since, gathering semen from sleeping men.

Frida suddenly appeared in the midst of the whirlwind, as naked as in Paul Griffin's painting, clutching fistfuls of dollar bills in both hands. I turned away, but woke up the next morning unclean and stayed in bed later than usual. Joe looked up from his newspaper and smiled as I entered the kitchen. The curtains were pulled back and the room looked much cheerier with the yellow sunlight reflecting off the sparkly Formica countertops.

He said, "I was beginning to think you weren't getting up. How about some coffee?"

He poured me a cup and slid a box of Shredded Wheat across the table. Neither of us said a word while I ate. The tinkling of the spoon against the side of the bowl clanged like a fire alarm in the silence. I finally asked if he would mind taking me back to Urbana again.

"Why'd you forget something?"

"Not exactly," I said. "I want to ask Paul Griffin a few questions. He knows what happened to Frida, and if we both go maybe we can get him to talk."

"Get him to talk? What are we supposed to do, march over there like your Hasidic mafia buddies? You want to rough him up?"

I hadn't thought that far ahead.

"Jesus, Junior, you can't just barge into a guy's house and give him the third degree. That's fucking crazy."

"I need to know what happened to my sister."

Joe had run out of patience.

"You already know what happened to her. She left. Period. End of story. There's nothing you can do about it now, so get over it. She'll get in touch with you when and if she's good and ready."

Once again, I got the impression Joe wasn't thinking only of Frida when he said that.

"I'm not trying to be cruel, but she already left you once, didn't she? She took off with her boyfriend when you were a kid, and you didn't hear from her again for years until your parents' funeral, right?"

I stared into my empty cereal bowl. I hated to admit this was true.

Joe said, "It's a fact and you need to face it. We live in an imperfect world filled with imperfect people. Sometimes there's no explanation for the shit we do. Sometimes shit just happens and you've got to deal with what's been dumped on your plate. Anyway, we've got other business to attend to right now. What are you going to do about school next week?"

I'd made up my mind the night before after returning to the bungalow. I told Joe I wasn't going back to school, that I was leaving for Ohio on Wednesday and would take the bus back to Chicago after Nationals.

He rolled his eyes and exhaled sharply the way Abba did when he was exasperated with me. Joe leaned forward in his chair as I braced myself for the lecture that never came.

"OK then," he said calmly. "You already know how I feel, so there's no sense beating this thing to death. I'll meet you in Toledo on Saturday. I should be able to get there in time for the semis."

I could not believe what I was hearing.

"So you're driving to Toledo?"

"There's no way I'm letting you play your first Nationals alone. I'll bring your stuff with me and drop you in Chicago on my way back to Champaign. You'll call if you need me for anything before then, right?"

I promised him I would.

He said, "It's your novel, Junior. When you're young, you have the leeway to do stupid things. When you're older, not so much. Now why don't you get dressed and we'll go play some handball."

This was a most amazing thing. Joe Carcone, the apostate ex-Catholic, the man who said religion was horseshit, had performed an extraordinary mitzvah even the Rebbe would have marveled at.

Later that afternoon I studied the photograph in his living room again—the faded portrait of the ex-family who never called, the missing wife and son he never spoke of. I wondered why they left him and how such a decent man could end up all alone in a tiny bungalow across from a bus yard with a mixed-up seventeen-year-old as his only friend.

On the way to Ohio, I entertained glorious visions of my first national championship. I'd been dreaming of the awards ceremony since I was eight years old, imagining Zev Altshul, the wunderkind from Brooklyn, holding the winner's trophy aloft, cameras clicking away, a hundred pats on the back. But my dreams were crushed in short order as Joe arrived in Toledo just in time to see me lose to the defending champ in the semis. On the drive back to Illinois, I replayed every dumb mistake I'd made.

"I could have won that match," I said in frustration.

"The best player doesn't always win," Joe said. "You already know that. Velez has more experience and he played smarter, that's all. He showed up with a game plan and you followed it. You can't let a player that good set the stage."

"I know, I feel like such a jerk."

"Listen, you ought to thank him for what he taught you out there. He won't beat you again if you remember what you learned. Velez is on the way down and you're on the way up and now everyone knows it. You made your mark today."

Joe took me to a Chinese restaurant to celebrate. He said making it all the way to the semis in my first Nationals was a big deal, but every mouthful went down with the sour taste of a loser's consolation. At the end of the meal I opened my fortune cookie:

"A gambler will not only lose what he has, but will also lose what he doesn't have."

I did not like this fortune. I thought all fortunes were supposed to be happy.

Joe opened his cookie and read out loud:

"Go for the gold today! You will be the champion of whatever."

"Yeah, whatever." He laughed.

I asked if he wanted to switch fortunes.

Joe returned to Champaign that evening and I woke up the next morning in an empty South Chicago apartment, greeted by a dull rain spattering against the kitchen window and a sky the color of worn asphalt. After breakfast I took a bus into the city and bought a day pass to a downtown club. I practiced alone for nearly four hours and did not shower or change clothes for the bus ride home. The lady sitting next to me on the plastic seat moved as far away as she could.

It rained for three days straight, and by Wednesday afternoon I could no longer stand being alone in the apartment. I walked to Rainbow Beach in a heavy drizzle, hoping to find someone else foolhardy enough to be out on the court, but even the most compulsive handball addicts had the good sense to stay indoors. I was the only person in the park except for an unhappy dog walker huddled beneath a dripping umbrella while her pet took care of its business.

I was having serious second thoughts. If I'd taken Joe's advice and stayed in school, I would have been on my way to meet him for a slice of pizza about now instead of stuffing my soggy sneakers with newspapers and hanging my wet clothes over the bathtub in a moldy-smelling apartment. I told myself things would get better; after all, this was only the first week on my own. I would settle down. I would get used to it.

When Joe came up on Friday evening, he asked how my week went and I told him it was OK, even though it wasn't. I could not explain my discouragement. I did not understand it myself. I had no more yeshiva studies, no more high school, nothing to do but play handball. I should have been thrilled, and yet the life I'd always dreamed of felt like Rainbow Beach sand slipping through my fingers.

I waited for Joe at the kitchen window every Friday evening, just as I had once waited for Abba in our Brooklyn apartment. Looking down from the fourth floor, I had had difficulty telling one black hat from another, but my heart leapt each time that one special black hat turned from Eastern Parkway toward the building entrance. I would run to the door to greet him, praying the phone would not ring again that night so my father could stay home with us instead of putting his fedora back on and walking off into the darkness.

In mid-September I took the bus to a synagogue in Hyde Park. I was looking forward to celebrating Rosh Hashanah with other Jews, and arrived early to be sure I found a seat, but when I got to the door, they would not let me in without a ticket. I had never heard of such a thing—*buying a ticket for shul!* Families dressed in their best clothes passed me on the front steps as the shammes at the entrance wished me *gut yontif*, a good holiday, before turning me away.

Rosh Hashanah was always such a joyous holiday in Crown Heights. We celebrated the New Year with resounding blasts of the ram's horn, and after the service marched from 770 to the Botanical Gardens, where the Rebbe recited the Tashlich prayer by the lake. We shook out the fringes of our tzitzit to symbolically cast our sins into the water, and then ate wonderful meals of pomegranates, apples, and round challah loaves dipped in honey.

After being turned away in Hyde Park, I took a sullen bus ride back to South Chicago, where I shook out my handball gloves at the shore of Lake Michigan and ate a Big Mac before returning to the empty apartment. I wondered how Shmuel Resnick was observing the holiday—no doubt reveling in his position of honor in shul and sitting like a king at his family dinner table. It galled me to think of that sadistic louse celebrating the New Year with his family while I sat alone in another apartment on another Kingston Avenue a thousand miles away, with both of my parents dead.

The languid days of autumn turned wicked. The northwest wind blew mercilessly across Lake Michigan and with it came snow. I slipped a pair of rubber boots on over my sneakers to trudge the slushy blocks to Rainbow Beach with a metal shovel to scrape the frequent dustings from one of the courts. I toted that shovel back and forth up Kingston Avenue, like I did when I dug out cars along Eastern Parkway to earn enough money to pay my first tournament entry, the one I forfeited before leaving Brooklyn.

The apartment never felt warm enough after those hours in the cold. I stripped a blanket from the bed and draped it over my head like a prayer shawl as I sat at the kitchen table pressing a cup of hot tea to my chest.

At Hanukkah I set our family menorah in the middle of the table. From the time I was old enough to hold a match, Eema let me light the colorful little candles. They always brought such cheer to our apartment in Brooklyn, but the Festival of Lights did not shine so brightly in South Chicago. By then three more trophies lined the living room window-sill, but they did not shine so brightly either.

At sunset on Christmas Eve, I was standing vigil at the kitchen window, waiting for Joe to arrive. It was not quite dark when I spotted the white van circling the block. It passed by three times before pulling into an empty parking space a little way up the street. The interior lights came on and then went out, but I did not see anyone leave the van.

In Urbana, Rabbi Jerry saw a white van circle the block several times on the day before the break-in at our house. I never told him the men in the van were from Brooklyn, or that they were the ones who beat me. He had no idea those men had come to steal my father's money, or that he was putting me in danger when he gave my Chicago address to a stranger over the telephone.

I moved away from the window just long enough to turn out the kitchen light so whoever might be in the van wouldn't see me. Abba's suitcase was once again under my bed. This time the money was inside it, but I no longer feared losing what was left of my inheritance. The money was small change compared to the debt I believed Shmuel Resnick had come to collect:

"Ayin tachat ayin!" Eye for eye, tooth for tooth . . .

I only left the window for a moment and had not seen

anyone enter the building when I heard footsteps ascending the stairs to our landing, followed by a weak knock at the door. I did not open it. Joe always used his key.

My imagination ran wild as I pictured Shmuel Resnick grinning at me from the other side of the door through his mouthful of shiny false teeth, replacing the ones Joe had knocked out:

"So are you happy to see me again, Hoizer Gaier?"

I shrank under his curses as he barged his way in, spit flying as he lifted me off my feet and pinned me to the wall with his thumbs pressing against my windpipe, just as he did in his apartment years earlier. I gasped for breath before his big fist snapped my head back:

"It would be a mitzvah to kill you, Hoiser Gaier."

The unwelcome visitor knocked again, more urgently this time, followed by what sounded like a foot kicking the bottom of the door.

"Who's there?" I asked.

"Who do you think?" Joe answered. "Open up, will ya. I've got my hands full."

I quickly switched on the lights before turning both locks. Joe stepped into the room, his arms filled with two shopping bags.

"I thought you were going to leave me standing out there all night," he said. "Merry Christmas, Junior. Happy Chanukah. Kwanzaa. Whatever."

He set the shopping bags on the kitchen table and pulled a small ceramic Christmas tree out of one of them. He placed it next to the menorah I'd left out after Chanukah and lifted a wrapped box from the other bag. We had agreed to exchange gifts. This was the first time I had ever celebrated the gentile holiday, if you could call it a celebration.

I asked if he'd seen the white van on his way into the building.

"Which one?" Joe said. "I probably passed a dozen of them on the way up here."

I said, "It's parked up the street, but I didn't see anyone get out. I'm afraid it might be Shmuel Resnick."

He said, "Let's not get paranoid, but if the son of a bitch is dumb enough to pay us another visit, he'd better have upped his game this time."

Joe handed me his car keys and asked if I wouldn't mind getting a couple more bags of groceries out of the trunk.

"I don't feel like climbing all those stairs again," he said. "And say hello to your Hasidic friend while you're down there."

I did not think his joke was funny at all and did not like the idea of going out to the street without knowing what was going on with that van. I took at least some comfort in the fact that it was now after sundown on Friday. Shmuel Resnick would never kill a man on Shabbos.

Joe fixed us an Italian noodle dish he called something like *manny-goat*, and after dinner we exchanged gifts. He gave me a royal blue T-shirt with the words EAT SLEEP HANDBALL written on the front, along with a beautiful pair of white calfskin gloves with royal blue knit backs. I gave him a belated Chanukah gift—a warm wool cap with a snap-down brim. He was getting a little thin on top and I did not want him to catch cold in the brutal Chicago wind.

We sat at the small kitchen table on either side of our non-sectarian holiday shrine, drinking coffee and playing cards. It was the happiest I'd been in months, but Joe seemed gloomier than usual. We'd been playing for almost an hour when he looked up from his hand and smiled an odd sort of smile. He shook his head as if a silly thought had popped into it and he was trying to pop it back out again. I asked him what was so funny and he laid his cards facedown on the table.

He said, "Look at us. We're really a couple of loners, aren't we?"

I didn't know how to answer that question, if it even *was* a question. I'd never thought of myself as a loner before, just different than the other yeshiva boys. I was the one with the crazy mother, the one who snuck off to play handball while they were studying Torah and Talmud and dancing before the Rebbe. The other boys weren't afflicted with the same wanderlust; they didn't hear Lincoln Terrace calling to them the way I did. They'd never tasted the ecstasy of hammering a kill down the line, or felt that glorious tingling in their palms, known only to zealots of the concrete like me.

I was not a good fit in Urbana either. I may have looked like the other students, and more or less learned to talk like them, but I could never be one of them. I was the lost Magen David wandering their hallways; the half-baked Hasid who kept to himself, afraid of saying the wrong thing; the undocumented alien who, no matter how hard he tried, could never quite earn his green card.

In Chicago, I was as colorless as the cloud shadows crossing the sand on Rainbow Beach, saying almost nothing on the court or in between games. I was the withdrawn kid in the yarmulke who showed no outward emotion and was close to no one except a solitary Italian shop teacher with relationship problems of his own. I guess we really were a couple of loners.

I got up from the kitchen table to check on the white van. I could barely make it out, still parked up the block in the darkness between streetlamps.

"It wouldn't hurt for you to make some friends your own age," Joe said. "You know I won't always be around."

It sounded almost like he was writing his own obituary.

I said, "Well, you're not going anywhere right now, are you?"

"Of course not," he replied. "That's not what I'm saying. I'm just thinking of your future, that's all. You should have more of a social life."

"What kind of social life do you have?" I asked. "You're no different than me."

"That's exactly my point," he said. "You think I'm your best role model here? Just try being a little more outgoing. Make some friends. Handball's not enough for a kid your age."

The T-shirt Joe gave me for Christmas sat draped in a box on the chair between us. I read the words again: EAT SLEEP HANDBALL. The message seemed contradictory.

He said, "You're going to want a family one of these days, have you ever thought about that?"

A family? My memories of family were not so sweet. I painfully recalled my mother's constant suffering and my father working for the Rebbe on so many nights instead of spending time at home with us. I did not like the thought of Frida leaving me in Brooklyn and then a second time in Urbana. Why would anyone want a family? It was certainly not something I wished for.

Joe picked up his cards and fanned them out in his hand, then set them down on the table again, the ceramic Christmas tree lights reflecting red, green, and yellow in his eyes.

"I heard from my son," he said in a funereal voice. Joe had never mentioned his son to me before. I thought this would've made him happy.

"I send him a Christmas card every year," he explained. "I never hear back from him, but this time he sent me a note."

"So that's good, right?" I asked.

"He told me it would be best if we both moved on . . .

asked me never to contact him again. I don't know. I can't blame him for the way he feels about me."

"Was it your drinking?" I asked, startled by my lack of diplomacy. I remembered him telling me booze can make you do things you regret, but I had never spoken with him directly about his drinking before.

"My drinking?" Joe replied with an uncomfortable smile that was not really a smile at all. "Don't I wish. Maybe then I'd have some excuse for what I did to them. The drinking didn't get really bad until after they left me. I've been sober for the last twenty years or so . . . one or two minor relapses is all. No, it wasn't my drinking."

We sat together in silence as the Christmas lights glowed, the radiator hissed steam, and the wall clock ticked and tocked. I once thought Joe Carcone knew nothing about guilt. Well, I was wrong about that.

"I was a lousy husband and father," he said finally.

He spoke so softly, I had trouble hearing him.

"You can't have been that bad," I answered.

"Trust me, they don't come much worse. My little boy . . . I called it *discipline*, but it wasn't. I should've gone to jail for what I did to him . . . to both of them."

The picture this brought to mind did not resemble the Joe Carcone I knew. Then I remembered the man I saw at the Big Green Wall punishing and taunting Shmuel Resnick.

Joe must have read the curiosity in my expression.

He said, "Just let it go, Junior. I don't need to describe every bruise to you, do I? There are things you're better off not knowing."

The Rebbe said, *"Some hidden things are best not brought to light, Zev Altshul. They only distract us and cause us pain and burden our hearts."*

I remembered the Rebbe's reluctance to disclose the lurid details of my mother's suicide, and did not press Joe Carcone any further.

"Listen," he said, with a tiny spark returning to his voice. "Why don't you come back to Champaign with me? It's not too late to start the guardianship thing. It'll be good for both of us."

The words, *"good for both of us"* landed with the weight of a prophecy, and the nature of my relationship with Joe suddenly became clear. Until that moment I thought we'd bonded over handball, our shared love of the game, but that was only the most obvious part of the story. I don't know how I'd missed it before this.

Neither handball, nor Brooklyn, nor loneliness could explain our kinship—why I spilled my guts to Joe only minutes after we met, or why he took me under his wing and drove for hours to watch me to play my first nationals. There was something else drawing us together, like iron to a magnet, and I finally understood.

I was Joe's shot at redemption, his second chance to be a better father and prove to himself he was not the same man who had brought such pain to his family. I was certainly not the best of sons. I'd been a disappointment to Abba, trading my tefillin for handball gloves and serving aces instead of serving the Rebbe.

Joe said, "We can make this work, Junior. Let's give it a try."

I was tempted. Returning to Champaign with him would give us both a second chance, but the prospect of being the oldest boy in the eleventh grade in a new school poked me in the eye again.

I said, "I'll be two years behind if I go back with you now, and besides, I already have a money game set up for next week. You remember I told you about that rich guy downtown, the one who wants to go best of three with me, only a ten-point spot? We're playing on the Tuesday after New Year's. It's too good to pass up."

Joe was the one who taught me about easy handball money. Take it when and where you can.

"OK then," he agreed, "but will you at least give it some more thought?"

I told him I would.

Joe left for Champaign late in the afternoon on New Year's Eve, just before the last sunset of the old year. He pulled the wool cap I gave him low over his forehead and tugged on the brim as he opened the apartment door, hesitating at the threshold for a moment, with his hand still holding the knob. He looked back over his shoulder with a smile so tender I almost asked him to wait for me to get my things.

"See you next weekend," he said. "Call if you get it figured out before then, OK?"

I listened to the sound of his footsteps fade as he descended three flights to the street, and watched from the kitchen window as he walked to his car about half a block down Kingston Avenue. A thin cloud of exhaust steam burbled from the Oldsmobile's tailpipe as it pulled from the curb, leaving fresh tire tracks on the snow-covered asphalt. The white van that had not moved in a week was gone.

I called Joe from a pay phone on Wednesday and left a message on his machine:

"Hey, it's me. I took the schmuck for an easy eight without breaking a sweat. You'd have been proud of me. I kept it close and now the idiot's looking for a rematch. I'm still thinking about moving back to Champaign with you. We can talk more about it when you're up here this weekend."

On Friday night I listened for Joe's footsteps on the stairs, waiting for the jangling of his house keys. When he hadn't shown up by eleven, I was sick with worry and left the apartment for the nearest pay phone. I had never been alone that late on the streets of South Chicago, but it was pelting sleet and I didn't encounter another soul. I closed the door to the booth before noticing the metal cord and receiver had been ripped from the heart of the phone, leaving only a stub of dangling wires. By the time I found the next phone booth, my fingers were numb and I struggled to feed coins into the slot.

After five rings Joe's machine picked up and I left another message:

"Hey, it's me. I'm a little worried. Where are you?"

The truth is, I was more than a little worried. Joe would never miss a weekend unless something was terribly wrong. The sleet sounded like sand being thrown against the phone-booth glass and the sidewalks were already iced over.

The interstates could be treacherous this time of year. I'd seen the big semi-trucks swaying across lanes in the prairie winds, but visions of Shmuel Resnick and the white van were what most filled me with dread. I returned to the apartment and paced the floor with a dozen horrible scenarios playing over and over in my mind. I phoned several more times on Saturday and again all day Sunday, hearing only the mechanical voice of Joe's answering machine.

Many months had passed since I left Urbana, and I had never once called Rabbi Jerry. I was ashamed over my lack of thoughtfulness. Normally this would have been reason enough to keep me from calling, but I had no one else to turn to. I searched the apartment for the card with his phone number on it. I was afraid I might have thrown it away until I found it tucked in my tefillin bag at the bottom of Abba's suitcase, the last place I looked.

On Monday morning at eight I brought a pocketful of quarters to the pay phone. It was a bright sunny day, the coldest of the winter so far, and my breath rose in billows of steam as I punched in Rabbi Jerry's number. He picked up on the first ring. I could hear a TV news show playing in the background.

"Hello, this is Zev," I said sheepishly.

"Zev? Seriously? My God, I've been concerned about you. When you didn't come back to shul in the fall, I called your sister and her boyfriend said you'd both moved away. Where are you now?"

"I'm in Chicago. I have a problem and I don't know who else to call."

"So tell me. Maybe I can help."

"It's my friend, Joe . . . he comes up every weekend, only he didn't show up on Friday and he is not answering his telephone. Can you check on him for me, please?"

"Of course I can, but I'm not sure I understand. Where's your sister? Are you alone up there?"

I brushed aside his question.

"His name is Joe Carcone, and he is a teacher at Centennial High School. He lives on Harris Avenue off Bloomington Road."

Rabbi Jerry said, "I'll look into it right away. Give me your number and I'll call you back.

"I don't have a telephone."

"Then I guess you'll have to call me. How about two this afternoon? That should give me enough time to find something out."

I thanked him and hung up the phone, then dialed Champaign information and got the number for Centennial High School. A secretary answered and said, "Good morning," as if she'd already repeated the line a hundred times that day. I asked to speak to Joe Carcone, the woodworking teacher. She hesitated and I thought she might have put her hand over the receiver.

"And who am I speaking with?" she asked.

For a moment I thought about lying and saying I was Joe's son.

"This is Zev Altshul, a friend of his. I've been trying to reach him since Friday. Can you please let me speak to Joe?"

She said she couldn't do that, but would put me through to the principal's office. I waited on hold, feeding more quarters into the coin slot, but no one picked up. I hung up and dialed again. The same secretary answered. She recognized my voice right away and apologized, saying the principal had gone off to a meeting. She asked for my number. I told her I was calling from a pay phone and would have to try again later.

"Call after lunch," she said.

I spent an unbearable morning in the apartment preparing myself for the worst, imagining Joe's funeral—the dark wood casket with a bronze cross on the lid being lowered into the ground, the Catholic priest consoling the mourners with reassuring words about the resurrection of the dead, Joe's son standing next to the open grave. He'd been crying, regretting he had not made peace with his father while he had the chance. He would mourn that missed opportunity for the rest of his life, just as I mourned my failure to reconcile with Abba.

I returned to the phone booth after one, and was finally put through to the principal. I asked to speak with Joe, and he told me Joe would not be coming in.

"He's dead, isn't he?" I asked.

The principal said, "I'm sorry, we can't give out that kind of information."

"Please," I said, "I don't know what else to do. He's not picking up his phone and I'm in Chicago."

"I can only tell you there's been a car accident."

I knew it.

"He's dead, isn't he?" I asked again.

"No, he's not dead," the principal replied.

I exhaled a huge sigh of relief. So it wasn't as bad as I'd feared after all.

"Where is he?" I asked.

"Listen, you really need to be talking to the hospital or the police about this. I can get you their numbers, but I'm not sure what they'll tell you over the phone either."

"Please just tell me where he is and I'll come down . . . Please."

"He's in Carle Hospital. Anything more and you'll need to speak to them. Really, I've said too much already."

"Just one more thing . . . please. Do you think they'll let me see him?"

"I really don't know," the principal said. "It may be only immediate family."

I said, "Joe has no family. I'm all he has."

I returned to the empty apartment. There was no Rav Feldsher waiting to rest his hand on my shoulder and explain the inscrutable ways of Hashem to me. It had not been much of a comfort back in Crown Heights, and would have been even less of one in South Chicago. I did not want to hear excuses for the mysterious God of Israel, and how we must abide in his goodness no matter what miseries he sends our way. I could not trust such a careless god, and yet I prayed to him in the loneliness of the apartment, just as all desperate souls pray when there's nowhere else to turn.

I hurriedly packed a change of clothes and took the Metra downtown to Union Station. It was after three thirty when I got there and I had not called Rabbi Jerry. An Amtrak train was leaving for Champaign–Urbana at four. I found a pay phone and dialed his number. No one answered, so I left a message saying Joe was in Carle Hospital and I was on my way down.

I leaned my head against the frozen window glass in the half-empty coach car, as barren fields and dreary midwinter towns rolled by on either side of the tracks. It was dark when the train arrived at the Champaign station. I covered my yarmulke with a black wool stocking cap and pulled it over my ears before stepping out into an unforgiving January wind, with my eyes tearing from the cold.

At the Carle reception desk I asked to see Joe Carcone. An older woman in a red-and-white-striped jacket began thumbing through the pages of a printed list.

"Joseph Carcone . . . Carcone . . . Carcone," she repeated, shaking her head. "I'm sorry, I don't see a Carcone here."

I asked her to please check again and she shuffled through her pages one more time.

"Oh, here he is," she said. "He's in the ICU. Can I please see some ID?"

"I don't have any."

"Driver's license, school ID? Anything with your name on it."

"I'm sorry," I said.

"OK, let me call security and we'll see what we can do for you."

She picked up the receiver and directed me to wait on a bench across the lobby. Soon a middle-aged man in a dark blue uniform came to the desk. The woman murmured something to him and pointed over at me. The security guard eyed me suspiciously as he approached.

"So I hear you have no ID?" he said.

"No . . . I mean, yes, I have no ID."

"And why is that?"

"I don't know," I said. "I never needed one. I'm not in school anymore and I don't have a driver's license. I just want to see Joe."

"Are you related?"

"No."

"Then what?"

"I'm his friend . . . We're good friends. We share an apartment."

I might have seen a flicker of sarcasm dart across the guard's face.

"Well, everyone needs to show ID," he said. "Those are the rules. What's in your bag?"

"Just some clothes. I've come from Chicago."

"I thought you said you share an apartment with the patient."

"I do. He comes up on weekends. He has no family. I've come all the way down here and I need to see him, please."

The guard told me not to go anywhere and walked back to the front desk. I did not understand why he seemed so angry with me. After a few minutes he returned wearing the same irritated expression, holding a clipboard and a visitor pass.

"OK," he said. "Print your name and address here and follow me."

He tapped his foot and whistled softly while staring at the elevator ceiling on our way to the third floor. The doors opened and he led me down a corridor that smelled of disinfectant and other things I did not want to know about. We passed through a set of double doors and he nodded a greeting to the nurses at the ICU station.

"He's over there," the guard said, gesturing with his thumb to a bed at the far end of the room before turning abruptly and marching back toward the elevator with his rubber soles squeaking on the waxed linoleum.

I was numb and barely able to move, like when I caught Shmuel Resnick counting the money he stole from the Rebbe. The figure in the hospital bed was breathing hard, a thin cotton blanket rising and falling rapidly. There were wires and tubes running everywhere, and an annoying machine beeping in time with a graph on a screen. I cautiously approached the man in the bed and leaned forward to take a closer look, reaching for the bedrail to steady myself. My grip on it tightened when I realized the hospital people had made a terrible mistake.

The man in the bed was not Joe Carcone!

Whoever this was had an almost featureless shaved head the size of a basketball, the color of an overripe plum. A corrugated hose connected a hissing valve at the base of his throat to an outlet on one of the machines. A clear plastic tube ran from the patient's arm to a bag on a pole, and another ran from somewhere beneath the blanket to a bag of cloudy dark pee hanging from the side of the bedrail.

I was about to tell the nurses there had been some kind of mix-up when I saw the name *Joseph Carcone* printed in red marker on a whiteboard behind the bed. Below that were the letters DNR and the words SEE ADMIN.

I studied the features of the friend I no longer recognized. I had never seen a human being so utterly destroyed. I imagined what my father's body must have looked like, lying in a bloody heap on Eastern Parkway, and the trauma my mother must have witnessed, the horror that pushed her over the edge.

I sat at his bedside and wept and prayed and prayed some more. I pleaded with Hashem. I struck all kinds of bargains with him. I prayed in Hebrew, Yiddish, and English. I praised him. I cursed him. I bargained with Joe too, promising I would move back to Champaign and enroll in school if only he would get better. I told him I was sorry for all the trouble I caused.

I did not hear Rabbi Jerry come up behind me in the ICU. He squeezed my shoulder gently, as Rav Feldsher did when he told me of my father's death. When I felt his touch, I could not contain my emotions and began sobbing heavily. He did not say a word as he waited for me to compose myself.

"I'm sorry we have to meet again under such sad circumstances," he said finally. "You're obviously very close with him, aren't you?"

"Yes," I replied without elaborating.

"We can only pray for God's mercy—*baruch dayan ha'emet*—blessed be the righteous judge."

I'd heard this prayer uttered frequently in times of loss and tragedy. The sound of it filled me with anger that night, even though I knew this was unfair. Rabbi Jerry could have just as easily stayed at home with his family instead of driving to the hospital to comfort a despondent teenager. It was a miserable night. I was not one of the big donors to his shul, and had never done one good thing for him. He consistently gave and I consistently took. The rabbi owed me nothing, yet I was in no mood to entertain apologies for Hashem's dark ways.

I said, "If he is such a righteous judge, where is the justice? If he is so all-powerful and good, why does he sit back and do nothing when there is so much suffering in the world?"

I said this, knowing it was a foolish question to ask of a rabbi, but Rabbi Jerry did not respond as I had expected, as the rabbis I knew in Brooklyn would.

He said, "I'm afraid I don't have an answer for you, Zev. These are age-old questions the great rabbis have debated for years, and frankly, it's well above my pay grade. I could give you the standard answer, but I'm sure you've heard it a thousand times already with as much as you've been through in life. There's no explanation, not one that makes sense to me anyway."

I actually took some comfort in his honesty. It was easier to accept an *I don't know* than another rabbinical defense of the indefensible.

He said, "We may not be able to understand why events happen as they do, but we have choices, all of us. We can choose to believe or not. You have to decide what you're capable of accepting and which is better for you, to live with faith in a God who cares and is good, or to believe the universe is a random place with no purpose.

"There are no easy answers, and not everyone is able to believe. I choose to believe in a God who judges the living and the dead in righteousness, even if the circumstances are beyond my comprehension. Of course, it's possible none of this is true and we are only making up fantasies to comfort ourselves. But I'm afraid I would be a bitter man if I didn't have faith in his righteousness."

I said, "I am angry and I hate him."

"I understand, Zev; believe me, I do. As a rabbi, I see grief all the time. I've sat with congregants while their young children were dying. I've prayed with old people in their suffering at the end of a long illness, with spouses who will spend their last years alone. It's not easy, it's kept me up nights, but let me ask you, what good does it do to blame God? Will it make you feel any better? Will it bring back your father or help heal your friend?"

I was not able to give an answer.

At nine thirty the ICU nurse came and said visiting hours were over. Rabbi Jerry asked me to call him first thing in the morning and left for home. I asked the nurse if I could stay and she agreed and told me to keep talking to Joe, that you never know. I sat at his bedside throughout the night, rambling on about handball, reminding him of everything he had taught me since the day we first met.

I said, "When you get well, we'll go back to Brooklyn together and play doubles at Coney Island and enter the big one-wall tournaments."

All I heard in response was the sound of Joe's uneasy breathing, the hissing of the valve at his throat, and the beeping of the machine at his bedside. Sometime during the night, I fell asleep and dreamed we were at the Big Green Wall again. Winter had ended and it was the most beautiful spring day, with sunlight shining all around us like the light of heaven. Joe was practically glowing in health. He smiled and tousled my hair.

He said, "I'm so glad we could come here one last time, Junior. I hope you'll always remember this day."

I told him I would.

I was already awake when the machine stopped beeping at a little before eight in the morning. A nurse came over but did not seem to be in any hurry. She turned off the machine and told me it would be best if I waited outside.

I sat in the ICU lounge with tears streaming, my hands folded in my lap and my head bowed. I was not in prayer. There were no more prayers left in this godforsaken Jew; every one of them had ascended to an empty universe where no one was listening.

I looked up to see a man in a dark suit push through the double doors and walk straight past me to the ICU. It was Detective Mulhern, the policeman who interviewed me when Paul Griffin's house was broken into. I recognized him right away and wondered what he was doing here.

After a few minutes he returned to the lounge with one of the nurses. She pointed and said, "That's him over there," and he approached me with his notepad in hand.

"I understand you're here to visit the deceased, am I correct?" he asked.

"Yes."

"And are you related to Mr. Carcone?"

"No."

The detective's eyes narrowed like he was concentrating, trying to solve a riddle.

"You look very familiar," he said.

I reminded him that he interviewed me at the break-in almost two years ago.

"California Avenue, right?"

I nodded.

He said, "Still quite the talker, I see."

This time I shrugged.

"Can you please tell me your name again?"

"Zev Altshul."

"Altshul . . . Yeah, that's right."

He followed with a number of questions, things like my current address in Chicago, how long I'd lived there, and how well I knew the deceased. He seemed a little bored by the whole routine as he scribbled the information down in his pad, but his demeanor took a sudden turn when I asked if he thought Joe's accident had anything to do with what happened at my sister's house.

"Now that's a very strange question!" he said. "Why would you ask me something like that?"

I gripped the undersides of my thighs to keep my hands from shaking.

"Why would you think a traffic accident has anything to do with the break-in at your house?"

I said, "That is not really what I think. I don't know why you are asking me all of these questions."

To this day my speech turns Yeshivish when I am nervous.

He said, "I'm just gathering as much information as possible. It seems Mr. Carcone was sort of a loner. Not many people knew him well, and you were his friend, right?"

I nodded.

"And are you familiar with his Oldsmobile?"

I told him I'd been in it many times.

"What color is it?"

"Sort of a dark red."

He asked if I had noticed any damage to the rear of the vehicle.

I told him the car was old, but Joe took good care of it and there was no damage.

"Interesting," he said. "The front of the vehicle took the brunt of the impact where it hit the power pole head-on, but there appears to be fresh damage to the rear as well . . . a panel pushed in and white paint on the bumper. So you say there was no damage when you last saw it?"

"No damage," I repeated.

He said, "At this point we believe there may have been a second vehicle involved that left the scene. Snow covered the tire tracks, but anyway, that's what we're looking into right now."

"You mean this wasn't an accident?" I asked.

The detective did not answer. He quit writing and stared at me long and hard enough to make me squirm and avert my eyes.

"No, that's not what I mean at all," he said. "Let me ask you again . . . why in the world would you think this wasn't an accident or has anything to do with what happened at your house? I get the impression there's more you're not telling me."

I shrugged again. Shrugging is not so easy when you are sitting on your hands. I regretted not telling Detective Mulhern what I knew about Shmuel Resnick, the white van, and the money, but it would have meant explaining all the lies I had already told him and why I did not mention the fifty thousand dollars when Paul Griffin's house was ransacked, or why I did not put the money in a bank or tell anyone about it. I was afraid and confused and did not know what to do.

"So you have nothing else to add about Mr. Carcone?" he asked. "Anything more about the break-in at your house?"

I shrugged again without looking him in the eyes.

Detective Mulhern mumbled something under his breath and handed me his business card. He told me to call him if my memory got any better and left through the double doors at the other end of the ICU lounge. My hands were shaking when I slipped them from under my thighs.

Suddenly the doors swung open again and Detective Mulhern marched straight across the room to me.

He said, "So was Mr. Carcone involved with your sister or her boyfriend in any way . . . what was his name again, the boyfriend?"

"Paul Griffin."

The detective wrote it down.

"They didn't know each other," I replied.

He said, "If you're lying about any of this, it won't go well for you."

"I'm not lying," I said. "My sister talked with Joe on the phone once or twice when she gave me permission to move to Chicago for the summer, that's all."

"So why didn't you tell me that in the first place?"

"I didn't think it was important."

Detective Mulhern let out an impatient sigh as he put his notepad away.

"You're a strange duck, you know that?"

I had never heard that expression before, but knew exactly what he meant.

He said, "I'll be in touch if there's anything else I need. Don't be surprised if you hear from me again."

After he left, the nurse returned to the lounge and asked if I wanted to spend a few moments with my friend before they moved him. She was very kind.

I sat in a chair next to the body, a shomer, keeping watch over the dead. In ancient times the Shomrim guarded the deceased until burial, protecting the remains from looters and rodents. I had become Joe's guardian, a keeper of memories, the other son he never knew he had.

The nurse returned and asked if I needed to call anybody. She let me use the telephone and I called a motel a block from the hospital to see if they had any vacancies and then dialed Rabbi Jerry to tell him Joe had died. He offered his condolences and said baruch dayan ha'emmet again. This time it did not make me angry.

It was snowing lightly at six o'clock when Rabbi Jerry met me in front of the motel and asked where I wanted to go to dinner. I could not remember when I ate last. I said we could go anywhere he liked as long as he let me pay. He resisted at first, but I told him I would not go otherwise. I believe he would have liked to eat someplace nicer but did not want me to spend too much, so he suggested we go to Zorba's.

The counterman recognized me right away, but the familiar fluorescent lights and plastic booths stirred no warm memories. He asked where I'd been keeping myself and I told him I didn't live in Urbana anymore. He said that was a shame. We ordered and sat down.

Rabbi Jerry asked if I knew anything more about the funeral arrangements and I said I didn't. I told him a policeman came to the hospital today and said they thought another driver may have left the scene.

I asked, "What if Joe's death wasn't an accident?"

Rabbi Jerry looked very puzzled. I did not tell him about Shmuel Resnick or the money.

He said, "I don't know what you mean."

"OK, so what if someone else caused the accident and did not wait around for the police?"

"So hopefully there'll be a thorough investigation and they'll figure it out."

"And what if they don't find this person, what then?"

"That's kind of an odd question, Zev."

"Yeah, but what if they don't? Who takes care of it if the police don't catch the guy, how does justice get done then?"

"I'm still not sure what you're getting at. Not every criminal gets caught or punished for their crimes. It would be nice if things always worked out that way, but that's not reality."

"But justice still needs to get done, right?"

"The Torah says vengeance and recompense belong to the Lord and he will repay in due time. That doesn't mean we'll always see justice literally carried out before our eyes in this life, at least not in a way that seems right to us."

"So what about an eye for an eye? That's in the Torah too."

"Of course it is, but it's not what most people think. An eye for an eye isn't a license to take revenge, it's a call for justice, and justice belongs to the community, not the individual. Justice is dispassionate and morally correct. The law says an eye for an eye, and a tooth for a tooth. In other words, the punishment must fit the crime; you don't kill a man who steals, you understand? You see what a radical concept this was back when the Torah was written and still is today?"

"So then, it's OK to kill someone who has killed?"

He said, "That's an entirely different moral dilemma, Zev, but I'm still not sure where you're going with this."

At the time I wasn't sure either.

Joseph Anthony Carcone was buried in Mount Hope Cemetery not far from the Big Green Wall. A few of his fellow teachers came to pay their respects, but I did not speak with them. Joe's wife and son were supposedly notified but did not attend the service. I stood at the graveside in my yarmulke mumbling the mourner's Kaddish under my breath as a Catholic priest recited verses from the New Testament and the cemetery workers lowered Joe's coffin into the ground.

On the train to Chicago, I watched the Illinois prairie slowly melt into a deep violet. The lights of distant farms blinked on, dotting the endless landscape to where the sky and earth become one. I watched a lone pickup truck cut a path along a two-lane road and pictured Shmuel Resnick behind the wheel of his white van, its bright headlights glaring through the rear window of Joe's Oldsmobile. I felt the disorienting jolt as the car careened off the road and heard sheet metal tear and glass shatter as the power pole cut through the middle of it. I swore I would not forget about the man responsible for this.

It had been dark for hours by the time I arrived at the apartment. Half a dozen cockroaches went scurrying across the kitchen floor when I switched on the light. I covered the bathroom mirror with one of Joe's sweaters and began sitting a makeshift shiva for him. Under different circumstances it might have been almost humorous, sitting shiva for a lapsed Catholic with a ceramic Christmas tree still plugged in on the kitchen table, but I left it on as an unorthodox yahrzeit candle in remembrance of my friend.

I did not leave the house for the entire week of mourning as a thousand *what-ifs* piled up like the grimy snow along the curb on Kingston Avenue. If I had not left Eastern Parkway, Joe would never have met Shmuel Resnick. If I had stayed in Champaign, he would not have been out on the road on New Year's Eve and none of this would've happened. Joe Carcone would be alive today if not for me. He was right in saying I blamed myself for everything that went wrong in the world. I did, but especially for this.

I sat a lonely shiva for my sister too, just as my mother did all those years ago when Frida left us to be with Paul Griffin. Joe said she would get in touch with me when and if she was good and ready, but it had been months and there was still no word from her. Gregor Samsa slowly died alone in his room after being abandoned by his sister too. She was the only one in the family who cared for him, but eventually left him to waste away.

I hardly ate a thing all week, spending most of my time at the kitchen window wishing this were all just a horrible dream and I would wake up to see Joe's car come splashing along Kingston Avenue. My mother used to hum to herself for hours as she stared down at the traffic on Eastern Parkway, waiting for who knows what. Had I inherited that same mysterious malady, her mahalat nefesh—the mercurial uninvited guest that came and went without warning?

When the seven days of shiva ended, I removed Joe's sweater from the bathroom mirror. A sad sallow face stared back at me, more frightening in some ways than the one that greeted me after the beating I took at the hands of Shmuel Resnick. It was a deathly face that made me afraid to stay in the apartment by myself any longer.

Although I barely had enough energy to drag myself out of bed, I got dressed and took the bus to a downtown fitness club, intending to practice most of the day, but my arms and legs felt wrapped in lead and I could hardly move across the court. I quit in exhaustion after only an hour.

I had forgotten about the upcoming State Four-Wall Championships until I saw the poster stapled to the club bulletin board. I'd already sent in my entry. I don't know which I dreaded more—the prospect of being utterly destroyed in a state tournament, or rotting away in the apartment like Gregor Samsa. In my sorry condition I knew I didn't stand a chance, but the following Friday before dawn I took two buses and a Metra train to the host club in Lombard.

I entered the lobby dripping wet after walking the last half mile or so in a cold rain. Competitors milling around the registration desk wanted to know where I'd been. A masters player asked me about Joe. I told him Joe was in Champaign; at least that kept me from having to explain a very complicated story.

With only fifteen minutes to get ready for my first game, I headed to the locker room to change. A lump swelled in my throat as I lifted Joe's Christmas gifts from my gym bag and laid them out on the bench in front of me, shielding my eyes from the player standing at the next locker. I gently smoothed the wrinkles from the royal blue T-shirt before pulling it over my head and slipping on my new gloves. On my way out of the locker room I draped one of Joe's old gym towels over my shoulders. A trace of him still lingered in the terry cloth, mingling with the sweetness of the laundry soap.

I had drawn the defending state champ for my first match. He was a fierce competitor, known for his power and stamina. Going up against him would have been a good fight, even on my best day, and I already knew this was not going to be my best day. I thought seriously about withdrawing and heading back to South Chicago, but could not face that empty apartment again.

I shuffled to the court with my head bowed, feeling like

a condemned man on his way to the gallows with Joe's gym towel wrapped around my neck like a noose. The gummy air pressed in all around me as I opened the court door and stepped inside. I was sweating profusely before the match started and have no memory of winning the coin toss or shaking my opponent's hand.

No one could have been more surprised than me when I ripped off an ace that drew gasps from the crowd. My opponent was left flat-footed and never laid a glove on it, just watched it sail by. Only another player could fully comprehend the devastating beauty of that perfect serve, its power and trajectory, as it crossed the varnished floor only inches from the side wall. Hashem himself could not have returned a serve like that.

I descended upon my opponent like the angel of death, reeling off eight more aces in a row, each one as crippling as the next, switching serves between my left hand and my right. The defending champ lost the match 21-2 and 21-3. He had never been beaten that badly in tournament play— the shortest match in state championship history. I draped Joe's gym towel over my shoulders again as I left the court. The spectators went silent, as if they'd just witnessed a miracle.

Over the next two days I demolished every other opponent on my way to the state title. I had not bet a dime on any matches that weekend and returned to the apartment with nothing more than another plastic trophy for the windowsill, but news of my dominance at the States spread quickly throughout the handball world, even to the one-wall courts of Brooklyn, where the storied concrete awaited the return of its prodigal son.

PART FOUR

BANNER AVENUE:
BRIGHTON BEACH, BROOKLYN

Months went by without a word from Detective Mulhern. I figured that his investigation was most likely gathering dust in the bottom of a file cabinet somewhere. This too was my fault. The information Frida and I withheld from the police seemed innocent enough at first, but the lies had compounded disastrously, and now Joe Carcone was dead and Shmuel Resnick was walking the streets of Brooklyn, a free man on account of me.

Sonny Kaplan was one of the regulars at Rainbow Beach. He was an average player but paid his gambling debts and was well liked by all. He ran a wholesale liquor business out of the northern suburbs, but everyone knew he was connected to the Chicago mob. If you needed a little thing done, Sonny was the man to talk to.

He offered me his condolences after he learned of Joe's death. We had barely spoken two words to each other since the night I first met him at the JCC in Rogers Park when he and Little Scotty tried to hustle us. Sonny was shocked when I took him aside and asked if he knew where I could buy a gun.

"Are you crazy? What the hell do you want with a gun?" he asked, sounding so much like a Jewish Joe Carcone.

I told him I sometimes carried a lot of money around.

"Listen," he said. "We all do, but a gun is only gonna get you in trouble. Just forget it and play your handball. You don't want to get caught with an unregistered firearm. It's a felony and you can do time for that."

I told him Joe's death was no accident, and explained the

situation without going into detail about the money in the suitcase or mentioning Shmuel Resnick by name.

He said, "You're best leaving it to the cops. That's what they get paid for."

I told him I was going back to Brooklyn one way or another and would feel a lot safer if I had some protection.

He said, "Look, I'm telling you right now, you should leave it to the cops. If you need someone dead, you hire a pro. Trust me, you won't know what the fuck to do and you won't have the stomach to do it. You think it's easy? You have no idea what you're getting yourself into . . ."

Sonny Kaplan had no idea how much I hated Shmuel Resnick.

I said, "I'm sorry for asking. I just thought you might be able to help me."

He said, "I *am* trying to help you. Everyone around here knows a guy who knows a guy, and you can get anything you want in Chicago if you've got enough cash, but I'm a liquor salesman and don't get involved in any of that shit. I don't sell guns and I'm staying out of it."

A couple days later a short bearded guy in a drawn-up Cubs hoodie and dark wraparound sunglasses followed me home from Rainbow Beach. He was too small to be Shmuel Resnick, and Hasids do not wear hoodies, but I did not like the look of him. I quickened my pace and crossed to the opposite side of the street. He crossed over too, and I crossed back again, glancing over my shoulder as the man continued to follow, keeping about twenty yards back, his eyes glued to me.

About a block from my apartment I heard him trotting up behind me. My heart raced as the hooded man took hold of my upper arm. He said he'd heard I was looking for something. At first, I did not know what he was talking about. He had a brown paper bag tucked tightly under his armpit and asked if there was somewhere private we could go.

We stepped into a narrow alley between two apartment buildings and he handed me the bag. I removed a black revolver and held it up to the light, turning it this way and that. It looked brand new except the shiny black coating had been filed down to silvery bare metal along one side of the barrel and again next to the trigger.

I had never held a gun before. It was not as heavy as I had expected, but holding it made me feel powerful. I smiled at the thought of seeing the terror in Shmuel Resnick's eyes when I aimed the barrel between them.

The guy in the hoodie said, "Be careful where you point that thing. It's not a toy."

I asked if it was loaded and he took a small plastic bag out of his pocket. There were about ten bullets in it.

"You even know how?" he asked.

I shook my head no.

He took the gun from me and pressed a thumb lever next to the round thing where the bullets go, then flicked the revolver on its side so the round thing fell open.

"This is the cylinder," he said. "You put the bullets in the chambers here . . . you see these holes?"

He slipped a bullet in and snapped the cylinder closed again and spun it.

"It's a thirty-eight snubbie . . . a five shot," he said. "Idiot-proof. It'll never jam on you like an automatic."

He handed the gun back to me.

"There's no safety. You cock it by pulling the hammer back and then a light pull on the trigger will fire it. If you pull harder you don't need to cock it. Like I said, it's a no-brainer, but don't cock it unless you mean business."

He took the gun back and unloaded it, returning the bullet to the plastic bag.

"How much?" I asked.

"Eight-fifty'll do it."

I told him I would go get the money.

"I'll wait right here," he said.

I saw Sonny Kaplan about a week later at Rainbow Beach. We nodded knowingly, the way two Hasids might greet each other in a goyische neighborhood. I thanked him for helping me get what I needed. He said he had no idea what I was talking about.

The following week I packed three cardboard boxes full of household items and trophies, and shipped everything to a storage facility in Coney Island. I filled Abba's suitcase with my handball stuff and what was left of his money, then wrapped the revolver in a T-shirt and placed it in the middle of the suitcase. The next day I bought a one-way train ticket to New York.

If you were not born in Brooklyn, you may never understand what I am about to say, but just setting foot on those streets again, even in a crummy neighborhood that was not my own, was a comfort I cannot describe. *Brooklyn, Brooklyn, Brooklyn*, I repeated over and over as I left the Stillwell Avenue subway station with Abba's suitcase in hand. I checked into a cheap motel across from a salvage yard and late in the afternoon walked to the Seaside Courts at 5th and Surf. I am not telling you this because I think you need a lesson in South Brooklyn geography, but to let you know what being in Coney Island meant to me.

As a young boy I snuck off on the Q train to watch the rebbes of the concrete do battle there on Court One, not far from the Wonder Wheel and Cyclone. Back then I had to remove my fedora to peer through the chain link. The sky was the clearest blue, not hazed over like the sky in Crown

Heights. Seagulls sailed high and low on the salt breeze beyond the boardwalk, their mocking calls sounding like laughter directed at the little Yid dressed in black. At eighteen, I peered through the fence once again, this time in my shorts and Nikes.

"Hey, you're that Hasidic kid who disappeared a few years ago, aren't you?"

I instantly recognized Harry Rosenfeld, speaking from inside the chain link. I was afraid he might be angry with me.

"And I'll bet you're that four-wall player they're talking about too, right . . . the one from Chicago who tore up the States out there?"

"How did you know?" I asked.

"You're a novelty act, kiddo. Not too many handball players wearing yarmulkes these days. So what's it been . . . two, three years? What happened to your payos?"

"I cut them off a long time ago."

"And why'd you ditch out on that tournament? I had money on you."

He *did* seem a little annoyed with me.

"My parents died," I answered.

He stared at me as if trying to measure the gap between doubt and sympathy. I knew my excuse was hard to swallow.

"My father was hit by a car," I said. "I went to Illinois with my sister."

I did not feel like explaining why I was no longer living with her, or how I ended up in Chicago, so I changed the subject.

"Did you know a man named Joe Carcone?" I asked. "He says he knew you when you were kids."

I think Harry Rosenfeld may have been relieved to steer the conversation in another direction.

"Joe Carcone? Yeah, sure I remember Joe . . . I haven't

heard that name in years. Is he still playing?"

"He was my coach in Illinois," I said. "He's dead now, too."

Harry Rosenfeld seemed even more confounded by that statement and changed the subject again.

"So why'd you come back to Brooklyn?" he asked.

I did not have a good answer for that question either. Should I have told him I had a score to settle with the man I'd hated since childhood, the man I believed killed Joe Carcone? I told Harry Rosenfeld only part of the truth.

"I guess I had nowhere else to go and I wanted to play one-wall again. They only play three- and four-wall out there."

That seemed to make perfect sense to him.

"I hear you," he said. "Too bad the rest of the country doesn't get it. You ready to show me what you got?"

I told him I hadn't been on a real one-wall court since I left Brooklyn, that Joe and I had been playing on plywood.

"You trying to hustle me, kiddo?" he asked.

I really hadn't thought about hustling Harry Rosenfeld, but it wasn't such a bad idea. When handball is your only source of income, you've got to take every opportunity—a hundred here, a hundred there.

We agreed to meet at seven the next morning.

It was still light when I returned to the motel. I'd been in such a hurry to get to the courts that I hardly noticed how filthy the place was when I checked in. The room reeked of cigarette smoke and the carpet in front of the TV sported a disgusting brown stain in the shape of a chicken. Someone must have sneezed on the bathroom mirror with a mouthful of toothpaste, and there were dark curly hairs clinging to the fiberglass shower walls. That wasn't the worst of it.

The next morning, when I slid my Nikes from under the

bed, a pair of pink panties came out wrapped around the toe of one of them. They were fouled with every substance that could possibly ooze from a human body. I was afraid someone might think the defiled panties were mine, so I carefully picked them up, using toilet paper to protect my fingers, and carried them into the hallway, where I tossed them on the floor near the ice machine. I wanted to check out of there right away and find another place to live, but I had to meet Harry Rosenfeld at the Seaside Courts. He was waiting for me when I showed up at about six forty-five.

"We've got next on Court One," he said.

Court One is the big money court.

"So what do you say?" he asked. "Let's put a few bucks down. Make it more interesting?"

This was no surprise. Most of the really good Brooklyn players didn't step onto the court unless there was money on the line.

"Even-up, no spot?" I asked.

"One game to fifteen and you give me the serve. That's all I'm asking."

We both knew it was an attempt to skew the odds in his favor. In his day, nobody hit harder than Harry Rosenfeld. With a serve like his most matches didn't last very long, and I was wary, unsure of what the older guy might have left.

"How about we play to twenty-one?" I countered, thinking this would be the beginning of a negotiation.

"I've got at least thirty . . . forty years on you," he said, "and you're afraid to go even-up with me to fifteen? Give me a break!"

I searched for a comeback that wouldn't make me look like more of an idiot. Harry Rosenfeld was inside my head before I'd slipped on my gloves.

"Come on, kiddo," he said. "Let's play for a hundred.

Even if you lose it'll be worth what I'm about to teach you."

Harry Rosenfeld smiled when I agreed to his terms.

I said, "But if you want to make it interesting, then let's make it interesting... How about we play for five?"

His smile flickered a bit, along with his confidence. He asked if I had the cash with me.

"I don't want you running away on me again," he said. "I'm too old to go chasing you down the boardwalk."

I told him he didn't have to worry about that. I said I'd be sticking around and didn't plan on losing. He had no idea I had almost twenty thousand dollars and a loaded handgun sitting in the bottom of the gym bag between my feet. No way I was carrying Abba's suitcase around Brooklyn, or leaving the money in that stinking motel room.

He said, "So what happened to the little pisher with the payos who barely opened his mouth? Looks like he's grown a pair. This should be fun."

By the time our turn came a number of spectators had gathered around Court One. This was only a fifteen-point street game, the stakes weren't huge, and yet the crowd was buzzing. Apparently, many of them had heard of me. Lawn chairs were dragged over. Side bets were placed.

Sharing the Seaside money court with Harry Rosenfeld was the proudest moment of my life. He didn't know it, but I'd thought of him nearly every day since I left Brooklyn. I'd memorized every word of the advice he gave me before the quarterfinals at Lincoln Terrace, and as he stepped into the serving zone, his words replayed again:

"You're not so great at reading hooks. That's where I'd work you over."

I was ready for him.

His first serve came hard to what he probably thought was my off hand. It hooked left after taking a crazy hop just beyond the short line—a vicious serve for an older guy, as good as many A-players still in their prime. I had to reach for the spinning ball and adjust my swing, but returned it well enough to keep the rally going.

Stamina had never been Harry Rosenfeld's strong suit, so I wore him down with long rallies, making him run the court until even his killer serve lost most of its magic. After the match he patted me on the back and said I played a good game. I didn't tell him I could have been done with him a lot sooner, that I wanted to savor the moment to make it last.

He counted the bills as he peeled them into my still tingling palm. I normally enjoy taking money from my opponents, their lighter wallets reminding them of their loss long after the match is over, but I did not enjoy taking Harry Rosenfeld's money. I felt sorry for the diminished champion, and as we left the court, I asked if I could buy him lunch. He told me to look for him later.

I played two more matches, winning them both and leaving plenty in reserve, just like Joe had always taught me. I found Harry Rosenfeld finishing a doubles game at the other end of the courts near the boardwalk. I watched him from behind the long line, his sinewy arms and fluid swing still beautiful, maybe the most elegant player I had ever seen. What remained of his arsenal confirmed he deserved every accolade bestowed on him over the years.

After his game we walked to a nearby Russian place in Brighton Beach. On the way he spoke of the glory days of Brooklyn handball, of seeing Vic Hershkowitz show up at the Baths after work to play in his heavy fireman's gear, of Moey Orenstein and Lefty Kirzner playing the Sweeps at Garber Stadium, and Steve Sandler's crazy money games—hopping on one foot or carrying a folding chair as a handicap when he hustled the suckers.

"We bet on everything in those days," he said. "Basket-ball . . . baseball. We played rummy thirty hours straight with thousands on the line. We'll never see those days again. It's Little Odessa here . . . plenty of Uzbeks and Russians here, the people our parents and grandparents came to America to escape. When I was a kid, Brighton Beach was all Jews. You should've seen the Baths back then. There were forty handball courts, and Garber Stadium . . . five hundred seats packed with spectators, all watching one-wall. No place like it in the world. Now they're tearing it down to put up apart-ments."

We entered a restaurant not far from the boardwalk. The gaudy red and gold walls were lined with liquor bottles, mostly vodka. A skinny waiter with a beaky nose and a thick accent seated us at a corner table and handed us menus in Russian. We ate borscht and blintzes as I listened to Harry Rosenfeld spin his nostalgic tales of the immortal champions of old.

He said, "I'm glad to finally see another Jew coming up. It's been such a long time, I was beginning to think I'd never see another great Yid again. What're you, eighteen or so?"

I nodded.

"I'll tell you this, kiddo, if you keep this up, by the time you're twenty there'll be no one who can touch you. I wouldn't think of going up against you again unless you spot me ten or twelve in a fifteen. I might stand a chance then, but even-up or close, there's no way in hell. I might play you like the schmucks used to play Steve Sandler, if you tie one hand behind your back."

We talked for nearly two hours before I paid the check and began the long walk back to Stillwell Avenue, elated after winning my first games on the Seaside Courts and basking in the glow of Harry Rosenfeld's compliments, but reality smacked me in the face as soon as I got back to the motel and saw the soiled panties still on the floor next to the ice machine. I turned on the television just as the local news announced the death of the Lubavitcher Grand Rebbe.

At first I did not believe it, but there on the screen was his photo, followed by the video of a simple pine coffin being carried from 770, hoisted aloft by a crush of Hasidic men, thousands more pressing in all along Eastern Parkway. Many of the mourners wept uncontrollably.

The hint of a smile scrolled across my lips when I saw the Rebbe's photograph with the dates of his birth and death superimposed onto it. I do not know why I smiled. Our Rebbe had suffered greatly since his stroke and I was not happy to hear of his passing. He had always treated me with compassion, from the night he blessed me as I helped Abba pack boxes of groceries for Pesach, to the morning in Gad Eden Ha'Elyon, when he informed me of my mother's death. My inappropriate reaction filled me with shame. Then I remembered Frida's odd smile when I told her Eema was dead. That smile had puzzled me for years, but I finally understood the reason for it.

Every off-the-derech Jew is haunted by ghosts we thought we had exorcized. They whisper to us in the night and we can never quite stop our ears. Hashem and every one of his 613 mitzvot, the teachings of the rabbis, and the tears of our families continue to chasten us, whether we heed their exhortations or not. They remind us of the end of days when the ledgers will be opened and the books of our lives examined.

Frida smiled because my mother's death meant there might be one less voice echoing in her head, just as the Rebbe's death meant there might be one less in mine.

But the old tzaddik did not leave so willingly.

*   *   *

The next morning I went searching for a room to rent, and by late afternoon found one in a private house on Banner Avenue in Brighton Beach. It wasn't much more than a bed and dresser, with dark wood-paneled walls, and an overhead bulb covered by a frosted glass shade, but it was cheap and within walking distance of the Seaside Courts. Its only window faced the blank wall of an apartment house about twenty feet away across a concrete backyard—not the most cheerful place, but better than that filthy motel.

I unpacked my few possessions and set Abba's suitcase on the bed, running my hand across its worn leather, exploring the roughness of its frayed edges and probing its dented corners with my index finger. The old relic really did seem like it had been around the world. I opened the lid and stirred through the disorganized pile of money inside. At the bottom I uncovered my prayer book, tallit, and tefillin. It had been a long time since I had seen them.

I've heard it said there are reasons behind every action. I imagine that is true, but there are some actions that are difficult to explain. Perhaps I was simply reaching for something familiar in this new place, or feeling remorse over the Rebbe's death, I don't know. I put on my tallit, opened the prayer book, and recited prayers softly in Hebrew, closing my eyes and swaying as I davened between two worlds—one I could not quite grasp and the other I could not quite let go of.

When I was done praying, I slid Abba's suitcase under the bed and placed the revolver and bullets under the mattress. When I lifted the corner of the mattress, I saw a host of revolting brown bugs and their droppings and immediately rushed off to the nearby grocery.

I returned with three cans of Raid and soaked everything down well. The room was so thick with spray I could barely breathe, so I left and went to dinner at the Russian restaurant Harry Rosenfeld took me to. I like familiar places and ordered the same borscht and blintzes again.

After dinner I roamed the boardwalk, weaving my way through the boisterous crowd, young couples laughing and holding hands, the heavy salt air dripping with the smell of popcorn and greasy French fries. Coney Island's a different world at night, with a million colored lights pinwheeling on the clattering amusement rides and the screams of passengers reverberating through the darkness. I never felt more divorced from everyone and everything around me, as if whatever thin connection I once had with the rest of the world had dried up and blown away.

I walked the entire length of Steeplechase Pier, a thousand feet offshore. From there the Brooklyn coast glowed for miles in both directions. I stood at the railing listening to the waves gently shush between the wooden pilings while watching the lights of a ship blink lazily on the horizon, so far out to sea it appeared to be standing still. I thought of the unfinished business waiting for me in Crown Heights, and wished I could be on a ship somewhere with nothing but the vastness of an ocean around me.

It was almost midnight when I got back to my room. The odor of insecticide had subsided for the most part, but the landlord had taped a note to my door asking me not to stink up the house again. I got ready for bed, watching a silverfish crawl around inside the light shade on the ceiling.

I dreamed of the Lubavitcher Rebbe that night. He was reading in the holy tongue, lashon hakodesh, from Kohelet, the book the gentiles call Ecclesiastes. This was very confusing, because the Rebbe's voice was intertwined with my own and I could not tell where his voice ended and mine began.

"Vanity of vanities, says Kohelet."

"Vanity of vanities! All is vanity," said the dead Rebbe.

"What has a man from all the toil and strain with which he toils beneath the sun? For all his days are full of pain, and his work is a vexation; even in the night his mind does not rest . . ."

Then I heard the rhythmic sound of water lapping outside my window. This was very strange, because Banner Avenue was many blocks from the sea. At first I thought it might have been the sound of traffic moving along the Belt Parkway, but then the bed began gently bobbing up and down in the darkness, and I realized I was not in bed at all but on an old steamship like the kind my parents took from Europe.

Smoke billowed from the tall stacks as the wooden planks beneath my feet vibrated to the rumble and hum of the coal-fired engines. Abba was standing at the bow of the ship with his back to me. I am not sure how I recognized him because he was not Abba as I knew him, but a young boy holding a brown suitcase almost as big as he was.

The ship's wake churned behind us in a wide vee stretching all the way to the horizon. A thin ribbon of golden light illuminated the mainland ahead, but we sailed and sailed without drawing any closer to it. Suddenly a strong gust of wind slashed across the deck, ripping the little yarmulke from Abba's head. His suitcase became unlatched, the lid dropped open, and money began billowing from inside—much more than could ever have been contained in the suitcase. The bills swirled into the air like a storm at sea, until the torrent filled the entire sky, blocking my view of the horizon.

I heard the Rebbe again. He was not reading from Kohelet this time but speaking directly to me.

He said, "This ship will never reach shore because the shore does not exist. It is an illusion that will always remain on the horizon, like your dreams and the dreams of your father. You cannot hold water in your hands, Zev Altshul. It is foolishness to try."

When the money storm subsided, Abba was gone and the Rebbe was standing beside me at the ship's rail, as alive as ever, only he was wearing a white captain's uniform with shiny brass buttons down the front and a white hat with gold leaves on the brim. This was the funniest thing I'd ever seen, and I woke myself up laughing, but when I reflected on what the Rebbe had said, I did not think it was so funny anymore.

Why did he speak of my father's dreams? I never imagined Abba had any. What did he hope to find in America? Was he seeking riches, or to marry a beautiful wife? Did he hope to become a great rabbi, and raise a pious and observant son? One thing I was certain of—Abba did not dream of repairing dry-cleaning machines.

And what of my own dreams? Studying Torah was never so sweet for me. I spent most of my yeshiva years staring out the window, believing salvation waited only a few blocks away at Lincoln Terrace Park. The rabbis scolded me for my inattention, but I was not born to be a scholar. Like Sandy Koufax, I was a Jew born to sweat, and no paddle or slap could drive the foolishness from me. And now those childhood dreams were finally coming true on the courts of Coney Island. I could see them shining like gold on the horizon, a land of boundless promise just beyond my grasp, but the Rebbe's words rolled over me like sea fog:

"You cannot hold water in your hands, Zev Altshul. It is foolishness to try."

I woke up the next morning with itchy red bites on my feet and ankles, and left the room early after soaking the mattress, bedding, and carpet with Raid again. I spent the entire day at the Seaside Courts, where it seemed I had already earned something of a reputation. The largest crowds followed me to whatever court I was on, and I heard someone say, *"He's that little Hasid from Lincoln Terrace."* I am not one to show much emotion, but this made me smile.

Late in the afternoon I went up against an Italian from Canarsie. Toward the end of our game a young Hasid, about bar mitzvah age—twelve, maybe thirteen—peered through the fence on the other side of the long line. He had taken off his wide-brim fedora to get closer, watching me with more than simple curiosity. I turned to look at him before serving match point and noticed his palms flexing as if he were standing in the service zone with me.

I did not think the boy was a Lubavitcher—probably a Satmar or Skverer, come down from Williamsburg, but seeing him took me back in time. He was my past and I was his future, another off-the-derech yeshiva boy lured away from the faith by the foreign gods of handball. I took the Italian's money and afterward looked for the kid, but he was gone.

When I got to my room that evening, I found another note from the landlord taped to my door saying she would evict me if I stunk up the room again. She said this was my last warning and I would not get my security deposit back if she threw me out. I did not sleep on the mattress that night but shook out my bedding and slept on the floor. The next morning I woke up with more bites on my shoulders and torso.

I sprayed the room heavily again after taping a note to my landlord's door telling her I expected to find a new mattress and the room properly fumigated by the time I returned in the evening, and saying that if it wasn't, I would file a complaint with the board of health and report her to the housing authority for operating an unlicensed rooming house. Joe Carcone taught me the best way to deal with bullies is to show them you've got nothing to lose. *"Make 'em think pain means nothing to you."*

I loaded the revolver and stuck it in the waistband of my shorts. The handle leaned far forward, resulting in an awkward bulge even my baggiest T-shirt couldn't hide. I undid my shorts, tucked the gun barrel deep into the front of my underpants, and stepped out onto Banner Avenue with the cold steel pressing uncomfortably on the tender parts between my legs.

The morning air was heavy and a strong wind from the sea had blown up overnight, sending bits of garbage at the curb spiraling into the air. Security-gated shopfronts rattled and howled as I neared the elevated subway platform on Brighton Beach Avenue. From there I could see ashen clouds building over the Atlantic. A storm was almost surely brewing. I bought two tokens and waited for the Q to take me to Crown Heights.

When I arrived in my old neighborhood, the streets were already filled with shoppers and delivery trucks making the rounds of Jewish-owned businesses. Nearly everything appeared just as I'd left it, as if only two minutes had passed instead of almost three years. The Moshiach banners still flapped in the breeze on Kingston Avenue and pictures of the Rebbe were everywhere, with signs in so many shop windows announcing, HE IS HERE! and LONG LIVE OUR KING MOSHIACH!

On the surface everything looked the same, but I could see the great change registered on faces of Hasidim passing by on the sidewalk, their grief so raw after the Rebbe's death. Without him, Crown Heights was a community of lost souls, wandering Jews with no Promised Land or deliverer in sight. The indestructible mortar that once held all Lubavitchers together had cracked, the surety of our bond had broken.

On President Street, a yellow school bus with Ohio license plates was parked at the curb outside the Rebbe's house. He had not lived there in years, having moved into 770 shortly after the Rebbetzin died. In the time since, the house had become something of a pilgrimage site, a Lubavitcher shrine. On that morning dozens of young yeshiva students were davening in the front yard, chanting in unison:

"Am Yisrael have no fear, Moshiach will be here this year! We want Moshiach now! We want Moshiach now!"

Their teacher waved his hands in the air with tears streaming down his cheeks as he shouted, *"Long live our Master, our Righteous King!"*

Didn't they know their Rebbe was dead, or were they waiting for his resurrection like the Christians wait for their god, Jesus?

A few doors away, the Feldshers' house stood empty, with its rain gutters clogged and sagging, hedges overgrown, and shutters badly in need of paint. A FOR SALE sign tilted unsteadily from the weedy front lawn. The root-heaved walk stirred raw memories of that miserable night when Rav Feldsher unlocked the front door and we stepped into the musty vestibule. My mother's last hours were spent alone in a single bed in a dank upstairs bedroom, her final moments hanging from a rusty shower rod in the bathroom.

If I had the money, I would buy the decrepit place and knock it down. The fossilized house was nothing but a graveyard to me, and yet I wondered what had become of the gentle old rabbi who once lived there. He had always treated me well, and I was surely not the easiest boy to attend to. Rav Feldsher had been present at so many of the important moments of my life—my first lessons at cheder, the officiant at my bar mitzvah and my parents' funeral. I suppose rescuing one off-the-derech yeshiva boy became too much trouble for him and he'd given up on the idea of redeeming me.

Outside my former yeshiva on Eastern Parkway, the youngest boys in their white shirts and yarmulkes shouted foolishness to each other in Yiddish. The older boys in their black coats and hats were more composed, afraid of being chastised by a stern rabbi entering or exiting the building. They looked very studious carrying their heavy leather book bags.

I had not been there long when I spotted Miryam Resnick pushing a wire shopping cart up the opposite side of the street. I recognized her right away, even though her once-familiar face had changed more than the rest. She wore a disheveled dress with a sweater that did not match, and walked bent forward like she had aged twenty years. I wanted to feel sorry for the woman who had once been so kind to me, and yet I could not feel sorry for the wife of Shmuel Resnick.

I ran my fingers along the ridge of my bent nose, tracing the damage done by her degenerate husband who thought nothing of stealing money that belonged to the Rebbe, or choking a child, or ransacking a house, or smashing a boy's face in with his big fists. These were the crimes I was certain he had committed. I suspected there were others much worse.

Miryam Resnick did not take notice of me in my T-shirt and shorts, with the backward Mets cap covering my yarmulke. Like a proper Lubavitcher woman, she did not even look in my direction. I followed at a distance as she slowly plodded along the sidewalk behind her shopping cart. I acted on instinct, thinking only of the satisfaction I would get from seeing the shock on her husband's ugly face as I pointed the revolver at it and said, *"So are you happy to see me again, Hoizer Gaier?"* I repeated the phrase, relishing each word, as I followed Miryam Resnick to their apartment house.

I waited outside until she had gone up the elevator before letting myself into the vestibule. The heavy glass door to the lobby was locked and guarded by iron security bars. I pressed the topmost intercom button, hoping the resident of that apartment would buzz me in. When I lived with the Resnicks, I sometimes pushed all the buttons at once. It was a mischievous thing to do, but I loved listening to the tenants shout at each other— *"Why are you buzzing by me?" "I do not want to speak from you!" "So hang up the phone already!"*

When no one answered the intercom in the first apartment, I pressed the button below it. When no one answered, I pressed the third button and a crackly voice asked, "Who's there?"

I said, "It's a delivery," and the crackly voice replied they were not expecting any deliveries.

The intercom clicked and went silent.

I was about to press the fourth button when an older Hasid entered from the street and unlocked the lobby door. As I followed him inside, the man stopped short and I almost ran into the back of him. He was a kindly-looking gentleman with a fluffy white beard, but I could tell by his tone of voice, he was not about to let some stranger in a backward ball cap walk in the door to his building unchallenged.

"So what then?" he asked. "You have some business in here?"

The steel barrel of the revolver in my underpants was digging into my flesh in the worst of all places.

"So who do you know here?" he demanded from me, without the slightest hint of respect.

I was certainly not going to mention the Resnicks, so I gave him the first name that popped into my head.

"Um . . . Yossi Teitelbaum?"

My response sounded more like a question than an answer.

"There is no Teitelbaum in here," he said brusquely.

Just then two women stepped from the elevator in their sheitels and modest frum dresses. They were also troubled to see an unfamiliar shaygetz in their lobby and I heard one mumble something to the other about me being a thief. She spoke in Yiddish thinking I would not understand. They stood next to the older man in an unorthodox show of support.

"So go, then," he ordered.

I said, "I'm sorry, I must have the wrong building," and hurried off almost at a jog, feeling like a complete fool after being chased from the lobby by two yentas and an old man. I trudged back to the subway in humiliation, stopping along Empire Boulevard in front of a pest control company with a sign in the window declaring, OUR MISSION IS TO RID BROOKLYN OF BEDBUGS. I stared at my reflection in the steamed-over glass, frowning at the distorted boy in the Mets cap with an unregistered pistol stuffed in the front of his shorts. How had he come to this?

I returned to Brighton Beach to find another message from the landlord taped to the door of my room. I was expecting an eviction notice, but the note said the exterminators were coming tomorrow and a new mattress would be delivered the day after that. She said those were the soonest appointments she could get and was sorry for the misunderstanding. I sprayed the bedding and carpets again and left for the courts at Coney Island.

On Thursday night I lay on my new mattress staring up at the dead silverfish in the frosted glass shade on the ceiling of my freshly fumigated room. I dissected my first failed mission to rid Brooklyn of Shmuel Resnick, examining all the ins and outs of what went wrong, which was basically everything. I hadn't even taken the gun out of my pants, no less pointed it or pulled the trigger. Sonny Kaplan was right when he told me I would not know what to do. He said I wouldn't have the stomach for it, and he was probably right about that too.

I repeated a verse from the Book of Deuteronomy, the Parashat Shoftim reading of the Torah: *"Justice, justice thou shalt pursue . . . Justice, justice thou shalt pursue . . ."* I repeated it until I convinced myself of the righteousness of my mission and began forming a plan.

I decided to return to Crown Heights on Shabbos when I knew Shmuel Resnick's schedule. He always left for shul long before the rest of his family and followed the same route from their apartment to 770. I could wait for him between parked cars and step out at just the right moment. I briefly considered wearing my black coat and fedora to better blend in with the neighborhood, but the idea of using my Hasidic garb as a disguise did not sit well with me.

Even with the shops closed on Shabbos, Kingston Avenue would be bustling. A gunshot would attract attention, and there was no escape along the busy avenue, but Shmuel Resnick had to pass a narrow alley between Montgomery and Crown Streets on his way to Eastern Parkway. If I hid there among the garbage cans, he would suspect nothing until the moment I confronted him on the sidewalk. I could pull the trigger and drop the pistol in one of the cans, then slip away down the alley. I would not shoot the big Jew in the back. I wanted him to recognize the little hoizer gaier who was holding him accountable for his crimes.

I waited expectantly for Shabbos to arrive, not as I once waited as a child, with the intention of observing the holy mitzvot, but for the day I would execute justice on behalf of Joe Carcone. At dawn on Saturday morning I slipped the barrel of the revolver into my underwear and walked out the door to catch an early Q train.

When I left the subway station in Crown Heights, it was drizzling just enough to dampen the streets. I walked with my head down past the graffiti-covered shopfronts along Empire Boulevard. It was still early on Shabbos morning and there was almost no traffic when I got to Kingston Avenue. The kosher supermarkets, pizza shops, and bakeries were all closed. The tallit bags and mezuzah covers remained shuttered behind the locked gates of Judaica shops, and the sheitels and fedoras were resting peacefully on the plaster heads of mannequins in the wig stores and haberdashers.

A white camper van, painted to look like an NYPD vehicle, was parked just south of Montgomery Street. It was from the Crown Heights Shomrim, the official neighborhood watch. The engine was not running and I saw no one inside. I did not know if the Shomrim patrolled on Shabbos, but there was a good chance I might soon find out.

I turned from the sidewalk into the alley and waited among the garbage cans for Shmuel Resnick to pass, repeating the verse from Deuteronomy again to bolster my resolve ... *"Justice, justice thou shalt pursue ... Justice, justice ..."* I focused on bittersweet memories of Joe Carcone and the tenderness he showed me in the wake of my parents' death, and inventoried every moment I would spend without him in the coming years, charging it to the account of the remorseless criminal who pretended to be a righteous man.

I waited a long time. Too long. Something had obviously gone wrong. It was getting late and the street was now full of Hasidim on their way to shul. Miryam Resnick passed the alley with her two youngest children, yet there was still no sign of her husband. I continued to wait until the crowds thinned again. The synagogues were full, and wherever Shmuel Resnick was, I was certain I would not see him on the streets of

Crown Heights for at least a few more hours.

I stopped in a goyische doughnut shop to kill time while considering what to do next. It was not too late to go to the police and tell them what I knew of Shmuel Resnick's crimes. The 71st precinct house was only a few blocks away, but I could not very well walk in there with a gun tucked in my pants, and how would I explain why I left New York with a suitcase full of money and why I lied to Detective Mulhern in Urbana?

I was on my third cup of stale coffee and second jelly doughnut when two policemen walked in and sat down in the next booth. I fidgeted nervously in my seat and avoided looking their way, terrified that if I made eye contact, they would see right through me and know I was hiding something.

I desperately wanted to leave right then, but if I stood up, they might notice the clumsy bulge in my shorts and realize I was carrying a pistol. They stayed in their booth for what seemed like hours, and as soon as they left, I popped out of my seat like some crazy child's jack-in-the-box and headed to Eastern Parkway.

Services had ended and Lubavitchers of all ages were swarming from 770 like worker bees from a hive. Mendie Resnick passed not five feet from me. I recognized him right away among the other young Hasidim despite the patchy beard now sprouting from his cheeks. I was afraid the son of my abuser might recognize me, but he walked right by as if I were invisible in my backward ball cap. I did not want to speak with Mendie Resnick, although I was anxious to know where his father was.

That mystery was about to be solved.

"Zev? Zev Altshul?"

The voice came from a Hasidic planet many galaxies away. I turned to see an almost-familiar face. Yossi Teitelbaum.

"Nu? I thought it was you," he said in a mix of Yiddish

and broken English. "I could not believe mine eyes."

For a moment I thought he was happy to see me.

"I was staring from you across the street," he said. "I can't believe it. So look at you, like a shaygetz you're dressed?"

"It's a long story," I said in my best American.

"The rabbinim told us you was off-the-derech. They warned us is what happens when a Jew goes after treif like you, they said."

I actually felt sorry for Yossi, hiding from the rest of the world in his transplanted Brooklyn shtetl.

"You have abandoned Torah," he said with a pointed finger. "And you have no shame from this?"

"I am ashamed of almost everything," I replied.

I believe Yossi thought I might have been getting ready to repent and return to the fold. He probably imagined himself performing a great mitzvah, leading a wayward Jew back to the faith. I quickly disabused him of that notion.

"The world is very complicated," I said. "Everywhere except here."

"No, the world is simple if you obey Torah. You are an apikoros," he shouted, raising his voice so other Hasidim on the street turned around at the commotion: "Farshtinkener! A narh bleibt a narh! You should not have come back here."

"OK, OK," I said, attempting to calm him down. "I'm leaving, but please, Yossi, can you do me one small favor?"

"Why should I do a favor from you?" he asked.

"It's a small thing. Just don't tell Mendie Resnick you saw me. I don't want his father knowing I'm in Brooklyn. I have my reasons. Can you do this one thing for me, please, for old times' sake?"

Yossi's expression momentarily softened.

"So you do not know from all this?" he said. "Mendie and the rest of them lives on charity. Shmuel Resnick is in prison."

I strained to keep from grinning.

"And Heshel Gernsheimer, Akiva Goldscheider, and the gabbai, Shlomo Gittelman, too . . . all of them in jail. Rav Feldsher also, the ringleader he was. A big megillah, you did not read of it? Is in all the papers."

"I didn't see it," I said.

"In all the papers. Hasidim arrested for extortion, conspiracy, kidnapping . . . the lot of them . . . and assault too. Nu, a chillul Hashem."

Yossi ended his summation with a wagging of his head and a regretful Lubavitcher tsk-tsk.

I asked what they did.

"A big scheme it was . . . so many women coming to Rav Feldsher when their husbands refused to sign the gett."

A gett is the Orthodox Jewish decree of divorce. A woman whose divorce has been granted civilly is still chained to her husband until he gives her the gett.

"Like mobsters," Yossi said. "The families of the women paid thousands and Rav Feldsher made sure the husbands signed the gett. The rabbi says he was only trying to help the women. He says he felt sorry for them. He says he did not know from Shmuel Resnick and the others, how they did their business. They beat the husbands for hours from a warehouse by Red Hook. Heshy Gernsheimer . . . he is a shochet, you know this, yes? Heshy Gernsheimer tortured the men with a cattle prod from the slaughterhouse. *The Magic Wand*, he calls it. Can you imagine?"

Of course I could imagine it. The little butcher's appetite for torture came as no surprise to me.

"From the cattle prod the husbands always signed the gett," Yossi said with a smile. "Is good Heshy wasn't a mohel."

I smiled too, for entirely different reasons. I would be lying if I told you I wasn't happy to learn Shmuel Resnick and Heshy were locked up. I hoped they would rot in jail, but Rav Feldsher was another story. He had always been kind to me. I did not believe he was so bad.

"When did this happen?" I asked. "How long has Shmuel Resnick been in prison?"

"Is a long time already," Yossi said. "Two years, maybe. It has been very hard by the family. I will not tell Mendie because you ask, but this is the last I will do from you, Zev Altshul. You are a heretic and a shanda fur die goy and I will not speak by you again. You should never come back here. Never.

"Gut Shabbos," he said sarcastically, before spitting on the sidewalk at my feet and marching off down Eastern Parkway like a good soldier going to war. As I watched Yossi wade into the rippling sea of black, the world took a small turn for the better. Perhaps there was some justice in it after all. Trials and prison explained why Shmuel Resnick had not come looking for me and why I did not see him on his way to shul today.

The barrel of the gun in my shorts pressed harder against my private parts, reminding me of the grave mistake I almost made. Shmuel Resnick was a bully, a brute, and a thief. Today I learned he was also a kidnapper and an extortionist, but he was in jail when Joe's car hit the power pole. Shmuel Resnick did not kill Joe Carcone.

That's when the ugliest of truths came crashing down on me with the weight of all the bricks of 770. I should have seen it long ago. I did not want to believe it, but the conclusion was inescapable. My father was one of Rav Feldsher's thugs too—all those evenings working late, supposedly for the Rebbe, and the money I found in his closet. My father, the hardworking repairman of dry-cleaning machines, the respected gabbai, had been leading a double life.

The families of the divorced women paid Rav Feldsher to convince their stubborn husbands to sign the gett. Rav Feldsher paid my father and the other men to do the dirty work. It was all clear to me now, but new questions arose as soon as others were answered.

Was Abba a bone breaker like Shmuel Resnick? Was he as cruel as Heshy? Did this gang of thieves celebrate together over schnapps and slivovitz, counting the money they squeezed from a desperate woman's family after torturing her husband with a cattle prod?

And worse yet, was my mother aware of what my father had been up to? Could she have turned a blind eye to his illegal acts? The thought of my frail mother being complicit in such brutality almost made my legs give way. I steadied myself against the iron fence guarding the yeshiva, feeling like a foster child in the family of my birth.

And what of Rav Feldsher, my father's mentor, the kindly old rabbi and trusted confidant of our Grand Rebbe? Access to the money was probably the real reason he wanted me back in Crown Heights so badly, and when I refused to come home, he sent his goons to find me. Rav Feldsher was responsible for tearing up Paul Griffin's house and slashing his painting. Rav Feldsher's fists bashed in my nose. His heel crushed my fingers. How could the Rebbe not have known of the violence being done in his own community by one of his most trusted rabbis?

And what of the dirty money in the beat-up suitcase now stashed under my bed in a tiny room in Brighton Beach? Did the money even belong to Abba? Was he holding it for safekeeping, or had he stolen it from his fellow gangsters? Perhaps the money was not mine to inherit after all, and I was the one who stole it. Shmuel Resnick would likely not have come after it if the money had truly belonged to Abba. I had not even considered such possibilities before.

These questions left my head spinning like a ride on the Coney Island Tilt-A-Whirl. And then came the most devastating question of all:

Was my father's death really an accident?

Shmuel Resnick was in prison and could not have been waiting in the white van outside our apartment. He was not behind the wheel when Joe's car was forced off the road, but what about the blue Chevrolet that did not stop after striking my father?

Parts of the grille and headlights were recovered at the scene, but the car and its driver were never found, just another of Brooklyn's countless unsolved crimes. I imagined the damaged Chevy covered with dust in a Red Hook warehouse, and wondered if the police ever tried connecting the dots to Rav Feldsher and his extortion ring.

The hit-and-run could have been an attempt to shut my father up. Maybe there'd been some sort of dispute among Rav Feldsher's gangsters, or maybe Abba was having second thoughts and was about to go to the police. I preferred to believe he was not as bad as the rest of them.

I moped back to the subway station in a haze of regret, stopping for a moment at the spot on Eastern Parkway where my father was killed. There was nothing to indicate a man had once lost his life there, no stain on the asphalt, or sign of remembrance. I gazed up at the fourth floor of our old apartment house, where the new tenants had planted a row of colorful flowers in pots on our kitchen windowsill. Their beauty made me wince.

The graffiti-covered windows of the Q train drifted in and out of focus on the ride back to Brighton Beach. I was exhausted and nodded off. When I opened my eyes, a Hasidic man was standing not more than ten feet away with his back to me. The other passengers paid no attention to him, but his posture and mannerisms seemed so familiar. I was certain I knew him and strained to get a better look.

The lights in the subway car flickered and went out momentarily. When they came back on, my father, Meir Altshul, was standing over me, looking very tired with his black beard streaked in gray. I was overjoyed at the sight of him, but not so sure he was so happy to see me. Abba made that familiar tsk-tsk sound while shaking his head and speaking to me in Yiddish.

"Nu, so here you are riding the subway on Shabbos?"

This was not the greeting I was expecting, but maybe I should have been. I stumbled over my reply, having not uttered more than a few Yiddish words recently.

"But you are riding the subway too," I answered.

"Again you with the big fresh mouth already," he said. "I am here to do a mitzvah. I am dead. The same rules do not apply in the world to come."

I did not know anything about the world to come, but there were many things I needed to say to my father and so many questions I wanted to ask him.

I said, "I am sorry I skipped shul that day, Abba. I never meant to hurt you or Eema. I know I was not a very good son."

My father did not answer.

I said, "And I am sorry I did not get to say goodbye to you."

"You were off playing your handball," he replied, pouting like a child.

"But you were not so easy to talk to," I said. "And you were gone so much."

"Again with the fresh mouth," he replied. "So I am here now. You want to tell me something?"

"Only that I'm sorry."

"So I heard you three times already."

"But why weren't you ever home?" I asked.

"Nu," he said. "I had to make a living."

"But Eema needed you."

He said, "Yes, Eema needed me, but you are a big boy now. I would expect you to understand. You think mine own heart wasn't broken from her? Your mother was a very sick woman. It was painful to come home and find her in the same stinking housedress from three days already."

"But I needed you too," I said. "I had no one else, and you sent me to live with the Resnicks."

"And you think that was so easy from me? Eema was in the hospital. I had to work. I did not think it would be so bad from you by the Resnicks."

I said, "You should have known. If you'd paid attention, you would've seen I was miserable."

"So who isn't miserable these days? You think you are the only miserable Jew around here? You are not so special, Mister Big Shot. And how was I supposed to know from all this? When did you open up your big mouth to tell me? What, you think I am the Rebbe that I should know from these things, how?"

"You should have seen it."

"If you do not say something, how do I know if you are happy or sad?"

He made a good point. How would anyone know anything about me?

"Rav Feldsher said you wanted me to live with the Resnicks again. He said you left instructions."

"I never said such a thing. Shmuel Resnick is a pig."

"He choked me when I lived in their apartment."

"I would have killed him," Abba said.

303

"And he found me in Illinois and beat me up. Look what he did to my nose."

My father tilted his head to one side, as if examining a faulty piece of dry-cleaning equipment. He made that tsk-tsk sound with his tongue against the roof of his mouth.

"Such a shame," he said, "but your schnoz was not so great to begin with, Zevelah."

We both laughed out loud as the doors opened at the Avenue J station. An older woman sitting across from me appeared concerned and clutched her pocketbook tightly. I closed my eyes again.

"And look at you now," my father said, "You dress like a shaygetz. And you think this does not break mine heart and cause me shame."

"Shame?" I almost shouted. "These shorts and T-shirt cause you shame? You beat people up for money, Abba. You were a crook!"

My father raised the back of his hand.

"I should smack you, talking fresh like that. And you don't know from nothing," he said. "The men we made sign the gett was bums . . . bums all of them. The schmucks got what they deserved and the women were free to marry again. So what then if we made a little money? It was not such a terrible thing."

When put like that, my father's justification for his crimes did not seem so unreasonable, but I still had many unanswered questions.

"Abba, whose money was in your suitcase? Did it really belong to you?"

"Ah, mine suitcase . . . You found it, didn't you? And why is this so important?"

"I thought the money was yours when I took it. I thought it was my inheritance. Please, tell me who it belonged to."

He shrugged, as if to say, who knows?

"Did they kill you for it?" I asked.

My father bowed his head and stared down at the grimy linoleum floor of the subway car. He looked up just as the doors parted at the Neck Road station. We were nearing Brighton Beach and the car was mostly empty. The lady sitting across from me was gone. I closed my eyes again, but Abba was gone too.

I did not get off at the Brighton Beach station, nor at Ocean Parkway, or the Aquarium at West 8th Street. I stayed on the Q all the way to Stillwell Avenue and then followed the boardwalk to Steeplechase Pier. Dozens of fishermen—Black, white, Asian, Hispanic—lined the railings on both sides of the pier. I watched them bait their hooks and cast their lines into the ocean below, occasionally reeling in a small fish or two and dropping them in buckets or cutting them up for bait. The fish were alive when they gutted them. I hated seeing them flop around, with their bellies sliced open and the gills on their chopped-off heads still struggling for breath.

An Asian man wearing a cone-shaped straw hat pulled in a fish almost eighteen inches long. A crowd gathered around him.

"That's a fat bonito, bro," one of the onlookers said.

Another offered him five dollars for it.

During the commotion I reached into my shorts, pulled out the revolver, and dropped it over the side. I did not even hear it hit the water.

I was at the Seaside Courts when Harry Rosenfeld approached with a large manila envelope in his hand. Harry was a United States Handball Association commissioner and I thought it might have had something to do with my registration for the One-Wall National Championships.

"This came for you," he said. "It was sent to the main office in Tucson and it's taken a while to get passed along to me."

The envelope bore the official USHA logo and was addressed to him. It had already been opened. Inside I found a smaller sealed envelope addressed to me in care of the USHA. It was folded and dirty, as if it had been left in the gutter. There was no name on the smudged return address. It was almost unreadable, the ink wet and smeared, but I was able to make out numbers on a rural route in Taos, New Mexico.

I thanked Harry and left the courts for the boardwalk. The wind off the sea caused the envelope to flutter in my hands. I opened it and read the note inside:

Dearest Zevi,

I wrote to you in Chicago, but my letter came back with no forwarding address, so I guess you and Joe must have moved. I thought there might be a chance of reaching you if I contacted the handball people. I know it's a long shot, but I hope this finds its way to you somehow.

I am writing to ask your forgiveness. There is no excuse for what I did. I was desperate when I left Paul, but that doesn't justify taking Abba's money and leaving you to fend for yourself.

I've loved you since you were a baby, even though I did not always act like it. All I can say is I am terribly sorry. I know this doesn't make up for what I did and I wouldn't blame you if you are not happy to hear from me, but I want you to know not a day has gone by that I haven't thought of you. Maybe one day I will have the chance to be a better sister to you than the one I have been so far. In the meanwhile, I hope you are well and having a good life.

Love and apologies,
Frida

I had been waiting for this letter since the day I found my clothes packed away in boxes on the front porch and the half-empty garbage bag in my rec center locker. Until that moment, Frida had remained alive in my memory as the woman in Paul Griffin's painting, the one with the sly grin on her face and her hand in a sleeping man's wallet, and yet, whatever grievances I'd been harboring melted away as soon as I read the letter. Even so, it took me almost a week to work up the courage to write back. I did not know what to say, considering how we parted and all the time that had passed.

I spent the better part of an hour composing a brief reply:

Dear Frida,

You have no idea how happy I am to hear from you. I am living in Brooklyn again and still playing handball. It is my full-time job like I always wanted. Handball is not a sport where the best in the world make a lot of money, but I am doing just fine. I have so much to tell you. Too much to put in a letter. I hope you will write back and let me what you are doing.

Your Brother,

Zev

I wrote my address below that, and about ten days later, another letter arrived at Banner Avenue. I nervously tore open the envelope. The note inside was even shorter than the last, only this time she left a telephone number at the bottom of the page. Once again it took days for me to muster my courage, but I finally called her from a pay phone under the el on Brighton Beach Avenue.

The phone rang several times before she picked up, and I had to shout into the receiver to be heard over the traffic and clack of the trains above. Frida sounded far away; it was as if I could almost count every mile between us. Our conversation was awkward at first, like two equally matched players, cautiously feeling each other out at the start of a match. She did not mention Paul Griffin, nor try to explain why she left me in Urbana. I did not bring up Joe Carcone or Abba's money.

We were interrupted by an ice cream truck passing close by with a jingle blaring from its loudspeaker.

"Is that a Mister Softee truck?" Frida asked. "I haven't heard one of those in years. It's *so* Brooklyn."

I recalled Eema once scolding her for buying me an ice cream from one of those trucks because it wasn't certified kosher:

"*So, you eat treif now, Frayda? It is enough for you to live like a shiksa, you are not going to turn my Zev into a shaygetz too.*"

"*It's only ice cream, Ma. There's no pork in it. Do you really think a little ice cream is going to turn Zev into a goy? I didn't know Mister Softee was so powerful.*"

Not long after that, Frida shook the dust of Crown Heights off her feet. I did not remind her of this as I fed another quarter into the coin slot.

She said, "You should come visit, Zevi. The Southwest is beautiful and we can't really catch up on the phone like this."

I told her I would consider it. On my way back to Banner Avenue I passed a storefront travel agency and stepped inside.

It was gray and rainy when I checked Abba's suitcase at the United Airlines counter at JFK. I had never flown before and gripped the armrests nervously as the plane accelerated down the runway. I gasped at the sound of the wheels coming up and felt the thud shoot up my back.

My anxiety calmed as we passed through the gray and I saw the sun shining brightly above the cotton white clouds, the most glorious sight I had ever seen. I could not help but mutter a Hebrew blessing under my breath: "Baruch Atah Adonoi Aloheinu Melech Ha'olam . . ." Blessed art thou our

God, Creator of the Universe.

I imagined Rabbi Jerry clucking next to me in the center seat:

"You see, Zev, it's not so easy to believe in a random universe with no god, is it?"

The vast green stretching below gradually turned to a mottled tan as we headed west. The landing in Albuquerque was bumpy. I must confess, I prayed again and gripped the armrests tightly as the plane touched down. Frida waved to me from the arrivals area inside the terminal.

"Look at you, Zev, you're a stud," she gushed in a voice a little throatier than I remembered. I'd probably grown an inch and gained at least ten pounds of muscle since she last saw me.

"You have no idea," she said. "You have no idea how happy I am to see you."

"I'm happy too," I said as she hugged me tightly.

Her eyes immediately darted to Abba's suitcase. She scrutinized it suspiciously, as if I'd brought an unwelcome intruder from Brooklyn with me.

Frida said, "I'm surprised you're still dragging that beat-up old thing around."

I said, "It's the only keepsake I still have of Abba's. I don't know, I guess I'm sentimental."

She was about to say something, but kept whatever it was to herself.

I followed her to the parking lot and lifted the suitcase into the back of her old Jeep. It suddenly felt heavier, like it contained a shared weight, accumulated over years of regret and unkept promises.

I did not know quite what to make of the surrounding Southwest landscape. I recalled my uneasy reaction to the endless sky and flat prairies of Illinois, but the sky in New Mexico spread beyond my comprehension. The land here was almost completely stripped of color, tan earth dotted by scrub brush, the few trees more gray than green.

As we left the city, the highway narrowed from four lanes in each direction to three and eventually two. The Jeep's canvas top flapped noisily, and we had to shout to be heard above the roar of the tires and engine. For that and other reasons, we kept our conversation sparse on the three-hour drive. I suppose we were both hesitant to dredge up painful past histories, so we carefully navigated through less arduous territory on the way to our inevitable destination.

Frida told me she worked enough hours in the Taos Mountain Casino to pay the bills. She said men still hit on her, but she wasn't that interested anymore. I told her I won my first national one-wall title in August and was earning a name for myself in the handball world. She said she was very proud of me.

The sky contracted overhead, hemmed in by rugged hills and mountains, as we followed a two-lane state road parallel to the Rio Grande river. In an unincorporated area west of Taos, Frida turned from the macadam onto an un-paved road. After a few rough miles we came to a rutted clay driveway leading to a low adobe house. An old station wagon with peeling woodgrain on the sides was parked on concrete blocks in the yard, with an even older dog parked underneath it. The dog raised its scruffy head and sniffed the air as we pulled in, then slowly crawled out and made it to its feet.

"I'm so glad you're here," Frida said to me. "Let's bring your stuff inside . . . Come on, Bella, come, come; come in the house."

The dog waddled in after us, her body writhing happily as she wagged her tail at the sound of Frida's voice.

"Bella?" I asked. "What kind of name is that for a dog?"

"She just showed up here one day. I fed her and she never left. I named her after a friend."

Bella parked herself under the kitchen table and rested her head on her outstretched front legs. The house smelled of dog.

Frida opened the freezer and took out a bottle of vodka. She poured herself a tall glass over ice and offered one to me. I told her I didn't drink.

"Because you're an athlete?" she asked.

"No," I laughed. "Plenty of handball players drink like fish. I just never got a taste for alcohol, and besides, not everyone can handle it."

She nodded in agreement.

"I'm going to fix us a nice dinner," she said. "I hope you like Mexican food."

I told her I did.

"A lot of Hispanics play handball these days. There are always food trucks parked near the courts."

"Do you mind eating shrimp?" she asked. "I can fix something else if you'd like."

I said, "I eat just about anything now, even pork."

"Wow," she said. "You remember how hard you tried keeping kosher when you first got to Urbana? I think you felt guilty about everything you did back then."

I said, "I was born feeling guilty. I've been learning to deal with it."

"I wish I knew how," she said, the corners of her mouth tugging into an uneasy smile. "I've never gotten the hang of that one."

She placed an iron skillet on the stove and began chopping onions and several different kinds of peppers. She cooked and we talked, just like we did in the kitchen on California Avenue. It brought back memories of my struggles to become a modern

311

boy and learning to speak American from Don Cornelius.

When the inevitable finally came, Frida lowered the heat on the stove and turned to face me. She'd obviously been rehearsing the story she was about to tell.

"You didn't have a phone in Chicago, or I would've called," she said. "I wrote you a letter once I got more settled, but it came back with no forwarding address. I guess you must've moved by then."

I answered with my usual nod.

She said, "I wrote to Joe in Champaign, too, but never heard anything back from him."

I told her Joe died in a car wreck on the New Year's Eve after she left Urbana. My sister was always one for complex expressions. This one was not so hard to read.

"Then you've been on your own all this time?" she asked.

"I think I've always been on my own," I answered, before the implications of what I'd said registered with either of us. Frida turned away and stirred the pan on the stove. Her voice caught in the back of her throat.

"I tried my best, Zevi, I really did. I know it doesn't seem like it, but I tried my best and I've always loved you."

I said, "I didn't mean it to sound like that. You took good care of me when Eema was sick. I wasn't much more than a baby then, and you brought me to Illinois with you after Abba and Eema died, and I ruined things between you and Paul."

"Oh, none of *that* was your fault," she said. "We had problems long before you came to live with us. Paul was having an affair with one of his grad students, and it wasn't the first time either. I'd suspected it for a while and confronted him while you were in Chicago for the summer. Things got ugly and he said he was sick of me. We were sick of each other really, but he told me to get out and I had no money and nowhere else to go. There was no time to decide.

"Since you had money coming in from your handball, I thought you might not mind too much if I took some of Abba's. I know it was a terrible thing to do without asking you. I'm not trying to make excuses, but I didn't know what else to do ... A friend of mine had taken a new job in Santa Fe, so I packed everything I could fit in my car and went out there. I put your things in two boxes. When Paul calmed down, he said he would give them to you. I hope he did. You got your stuff, right?"

I nodded.

"I always intended to pay you back, Zevi, I really did, but I used Abba's money for a down payment on this place. They gave me a great deal and I knew I would never get another chance like this again. It may be the only smart thing I've ever done ..."

Frida's voice trailed off as if her thoughts had drifted out the kitchen window into the high desert. "You know, I'll probably never have the money to pay you back," she repeated softly.

I said, "I don't want the money. It wasn't mine anyway."

"What do you mean? Of course it was yours. Abba left it to you."

I said, "Not mine and maybe not Abba's either."

I told her about Rav Feldsher and his clan of extortionists.

"So you're saying Abba was one of them?" she asked.

I said, "There's no other explanation, is there? How else would Shmuel Resnick have known about the money? Either Abba was holding it or he'd stolen it from them. If it was just Abba's share, I don't think they'd have come after us like they did. And that goddamn Akiva Goldscheider saw us on the street carrying the garbage bag. Remember that? He was one of them. It wouldn't have been too hard for him to figure out we took the money with us when we left."

Frida said, "I can't imagine Abba being involved in something like that."

I said, "Any way you look at it, the money didn't come from fixing dry-cleaning machines, so let's just forget it, OK? The money helped us both and there's nothing more to say about it."

Frida nodded in half-hearted acknowledgment.

After dinner we sat on plastic lawn chairs in the cool desert evening, lightning flashing in the distance beyond the rim of mountains. My sister bent to scratch Bella's head as the dog lay on the ground between her feet. We talked for hours as the sky turned an inky black. I had never seen a night sky like the one in Taos, with stars like falling snow.

I recalled walking home from Lincoln Terrace Park late one fading January afternoon. I was about nine or ten at the time. Frida had left, Eema was in the hospital, and I had been sent to live with the Resnicks. It was cold and beginning to snow, large flakes the size of dimes. I held up my forearm and watched them settle gently onto my black coat sleeve. As one melted, two or three more took its place until my sleeve was almost completely covered in white. I was so filled with wonder, those snowflakes descending from somewhere on high, closer to Hashem. I recited the Modeh Ani aloud in Hebrew right there on Union Street. The stars in that Taos sky almost made me want to believe again.

Almost.

Frida and I spent the next few days seeing the sights, touring the Taos Pueblo, and hopping in and out of ceramics studios and art galleries. In one of the galleries she pointed to a small group of paintings.

"Those are mine," she said with some obvious pride. "I sell a couple every now and then."

The women in her paintings wore blank expressions and seemed to be gazing off somewhere far away. One of them was dressed in a hospital gown while the woman next to her played a violin. Another held a small bird cupped in the palms of her hands. The women's faces reminded me of Frida's, not so much physically but in the weight of sadness they carried.

On the day before I returned to Brooklyn, we bathed in a hot spring along the Rio Grande. Frida parked her Jeep on a rugged dirt road at the top of the trailhead and we hiked about half a mile down to the river gorge, where a circle of stones had been arranged to form a small pool. I took off my yarmulke and set it on a flat rock next to me, making sure the bobby pin was securely fastened to it. It was one of the last on the card of pins my mother gave me, the ones she said matched my eyes. We gazed up at the desert sky as we floated on our backs in the warm water.

"There's a lot I'd like to do over," she said. "I would if I had the chance, but the sad part is I keep doing the same stupid shit over and over again. What's that famous quote about insanity ... doing the same thing again and again and expecting a different result, something like that?"

I did not say this to Frida, but my entire life consisted of repeating the same things over and over, from reciting verses of the Talmud, to firing a hard rubber ball at a patch of peeling green paint on a plywood wall.

I could tell something was troubling Frida, like she was straining against a weight she couldn't budge.

She said, "There's some stuff I need to tell you, Zevi."

I told her it was all good between us and there was no need, but she insisted despite my reassurance.

"You remember when Abba and Eema died?" she asked. "You remember when I came to the apartment that first night of shiva and told you how hard I tried to make it to the funeral, how I wanted to be there with you, but the traffic was so bad and the interstate was all backed up?"

"I remember, so?"

"So I lied to you. I was late getting into New York, but I drove straight to Montefiore. When I saw the men in their beards and black hats gathered at the graves . . . the women standing way behind them with their heads covered, I couldn't get out of the car. I abandoned you then too. I drove off and left you alone."

This was not a great surprise. I'd suspected it years ago.

"It's nothing," I said. "It's all in the past. There's no reason to bring it up."

"Yes, there is," she said. "Please listen to me, Zevi . . . I haven't been completely honest with you. I've let you believe things that aren't true. I haven't told you everything about why I left Urbana."

"I already know why."

"You don't."

I said, "You left because Paul hurt you."

"That's not the reason. We fought like crazy, but he never hurt me, not really."

"You said he did."

"I never said that."

"But I saw the bruises on your arms. You can't tell me he never laid a hand on you."

"He grabbed me . . . He grabbed me really hard that one time while you were up in Chicago. Those were the bruises you saw. I noticed you staring at them, but I was so embarrassed I couldn't say anything to you. I can't blame Paul for that, he was pretty much defending himself. I hit him first. I lost it, and that wasn't the only time either. I have a bad temper, Zevi."

"OK, so you had your reasons and it's over, let's just move on."

"But I didn't leave Urbana because of Paul," she said. "The friend I went to stay with in Santa Fe . . . it wasn't exactly like I told you. Paul wasn't the only one who'd had affairs."

I did not want to hear this.

"I was never so innocent," she said. "I wasn't even a virgin when I left Brooklyn. I left Abba and Eema to be with Paul, and I left you to be with Bella."

I knew she was not referring to the dog.

"She was my art teacher at Parkland," Frida said. "We'd had a friendship for years . . . more than a friendship. Things were going badly with Paul and you were up in Chicago, so when Bella left for Santa Fe, I went with her."

"But you were supposed to watch out for me," I said, immediately realizing how pathetic that sounded.

She said, "I couldn't take you with me, Zevi. It wouldn't have worked out."

Those words cut deeply. I was absolutely certain Frida would never have abandoned me if she'd had a choice. I argued with Joe Carcone when he claimed people make selfish decisions all the time; he said it's human nature. As usual, Joe was right. All this time I'd believed she'd run away from an abusive boyfriend, but it turned out she was running toward a happier life that did not include me. I was just another inconvenience, an unwelcome boarder in the house on California Avenue, no different than the little hoizer gaier in the Resnicks' apartment.

She said, "I'm sorry, Zevi. I know I shouldn't have left you the way I did, but you'd already been living with Joe for a couple of months and he seemed to be taking good care of you. I thought you'd be all right, but I did the wrong thing. I don't blame you for hating me after what I've told you."

I said, "I could never hate you, but why did you have to tell me all this stuff? What good does it do either of us now?"

She said, "I don't know, maybe I'm just being selfish again, but I've been carrying this guilt around and I don't know how else to let it go."

She asked for my forgiveness.

"Please," she said. "Please say it for me, Zevi."

My sister needed to hear those words come from my mouth, so I said, "I forgive you."

I understood why the Rebbe was so reluctant to reveal the gruesome details of my mother's suicide. He said, *"Some hidden things are best not brought to light. They only distract us and cause us pain and burden our hearts."*

I wish I had not pressed him. To this day I can scarcely enter an empty room without seeing her limp body hanging by her stockings. This vision has never left me; it is imprinted on my mind and returns as an unwelcome ghost when I close my eyes at night.

And I would have been better off had I not learned of Abba's secret life. I would rather still imagine him as the helpful gabbai, packing grocery boxes for poor Jews. I was happier believing he was doing the Rebbe's work all those nights when he left us alone in the apartment.

And I am glad Joe Carcone did not go into greater detail that Christmas in Chicago, when he told me he'd done terrible things to his wife and son. I prefer to remember him as he was to me, not as he may have been to them. Sometimes the dead are best left buried, and their memory is more comforting than the truth.

Frida drove me to the airport early the next morning. The sun rose pink and orange in the rearview mirror, the colors gradually shifting to robin's-egg blue. The Southwest landscape looked more parched and brittle on the way back to Albuquerque. Not much was said between us on the highway, and the drive seemed to take much longer than it did on the way in.

When we arrived at the airport, Frida pulled to the curb in front of the terminal. I could tell she was holding back tears as we said goodbye. I lifted Abba's suitcase from the back of the Jeep, and turned to wave just beyond the terminal entrance, but the sliding doors had closed and Frida was already gone.

Top athletes are used to enduring pain. It's a gift only the great ones have. We suffer longer and more profoundly than the rest. We are able to silence the voices inside us that scream *We have reached our limit and can't go on.* I once played an entire match with two broken bones in my left hand. The orthopedist said I'd have done less damage if I hadn't tried to play through the pain. But there are wounds not so obvious as a broken nose or a broken hand, and I played through those as well. This is the special gift great athletes have.

Within two years of my return to Brooklyn, nearly everyone with a love of the concrete knew the name Zev Altshul. Like the unutterable name of God among Hasidim, many on the courts of New York held it in awe. For others, Zev Altshul was a despicable name, the name they choked on with every new victory, and stumbled over like a stone set in their path. Loved or hated, all agreed I was one of the best players in the city, one of the best players anywhere, perhaps one of the best of all time.

They marveled at my acrobatics, how I spun and pivoted with the grace of a dancer, executing shots almost unimaginable by others. They extolled the sweet music of the rubber compressing off my palms, saying no one ever hit the ball any harder. Some of my opponents claimed my power came from studying Kabbalah, that I knew where they intended to place the ball before they hit it. Such was the mystique of Zev Altshul, the eccentric little Yid on his way to the top of the hand-

319

ball world.

And I showed no emotion on the court, revealing nothing of my state of mind, no matter the situation. "A block of steel with a yarmulke" is how they described me. They did not know I was a block of steel off the court as well, only not so solid as they presumed. On the inside I was as hollow as a discarded soda can, as empty in Coney Island as I was in South Chicago, Urbana, and Crown Heights.

I played the Seaside Courts every day and tournaments all over the city, hustling players with delusions of grandeur in the lesser parks and playgrounds. It's not hard to find a wannabe A-player who thinks he can beat me with an eighteen-point spot or one hand tied to my leg. New York has more than two thousand courts scattered throughout the five boroughs, so there are always plenty of opportunities.

Of all the courts in the city, Coney Island's main rival is West 4th Street in Greenwich Village. Its three courts, pressed up against the side of an apartment house, are deceptively humble, but *The Cage* is home to a fierce crew, hungry for a piece of any Brooklyn player with enough chutzpah to invade its territory. At West 4th, I always have to bring my A-game, along with a big wad of cash.

On a sunny Friday in April, I played two money games there. After enduring the usual barrage of catcalls and a nasty bruise from an intentional elbow, I left with a fatter wallet and something else I was not expecting. I had not noticed the girl watching me from the sidewalk on West 3rd Street. She called my name as I changed out of my sweaty T-shirt and I turned to see a pleasant face pressed against the chain link.

"Zev Altshul?" she repeated. "It *is* you, isn't it? I thought you were in Chicago."

It took me a moment to realize this was not the first time I'd seen this girl. She was thinner and her red hair was darker than I remembered.

"What are *you* doing here?" I asked, regretting how those words must have come across.

"This is my neighborhood," she said. "I'm in school at NYU. I pass by here almost every day."

"Oh," I said with my usual charm, still at a loss to make better conversation.

"And what about you?" she asked. "What are you doing here?"

"Playing handball," I said.

"No, I mean what are you doing here in the city?"

"I play handball."

She said, "I mean what do you do for work or school, whatever?"

"Handball is what I do."

"You play handball for work?" she asked.

I did not tell her I made more than a thousand dollars that morning.

She asked if I wanted to catch up over a coffee, and that left me facing another dilemma—I did not remember the redhead's name, if I ever knew it in the first place. She said there was a terrific coffee shop just around the corner on MacDougal Street, one of the oldest in the city, so I followed and we found a seat at an outside table. The day was warm, so welcome after a prolonged winter. She looked kind of pretty with the spring breeze ruffling her hair.

The redhead asked if I'd like a cappuccino and I told her I'd never had one before.

"Well then," she said. "It's time to try something new."

She ordered us two cappuccinos, along with an Italian pastry to share and we made the kind of small talk I've never been much good at.

"I really enjoyed watching you play," she said. "You make

321

it look so easy."

"It's what I love to do." I smiled modestly. She had no idea how hard I work to make it look so easy and I did not tell her.

If you have never seen a game between top-level players, it is not as you might think. Handball can look like a ballet in slow motion, a beautiful dance. The best players do not scurry about. We appear to almost casually walk to the spot on the court where we know the ball will be next, then strike with devastating speed once we've maneuvered our opponent to that vulnerable position where the shot cannot be returned.

"I didn't know you could make a living playing handball," she said.

"Most of us can't. It's not like baseball or basketball, where the pros make millions. Even the best handball players in the world work other jobs."

"So why don't you?" she asked.

I tried to answer her as humbly as I could.

"I don't need a lot of money. Handball is my job; I play sixty hours or more a week."

"Is that why you're so good at it?"

"That and other reasons," I replied, again trying not to sound too boastful. "In handball you have to use both hands. Most players train themselves to do it, but they still have a weak side. Not me."

I finished my cappuccino and ordered another. The redhead seemed pleased.

She asked if I lived in the Village and I told her I lived in Brooklyn, near Coney Island. She said she'd never been to Coney Island but had read about it and seen pictures.

"It must be a really interesting place," she said. "So much history."

I think she may have been fishing for an invitation, but I

was incapable of taking the bait. I used to blame my lack of worldly social skills on my Hasidic upbringing, but I'd come to realize it was just my awkward nature.

I spent the next hour trying to get the redhead to reveal her name without me having to ask directly. I inquired about her parents, even though I'd never met them. I brought up other people we both knew in Urbana, hoping for a clue. She made a bitter face when I mentioned Sharon Kotin.

"I think she went to some party school out in Colorado. I don't know what she does now. Anyway, I don't care if I ever see her again. She wasn't very nice to me."

"Me either," I said.

She asked where I went to school and I told her I didn't.

"You didn't go to college?" she asked, unable to wipe the surprise from her face. "So where'd you finish high school after Urbana?"

"I didn't."

"You didn't finish high school?"

Although I couldn't care less about school, I was ashamed and quickly changed the subject by asking her how Rabbi Jerry was doing. She didn't know because she hadn't been home in quite a while and stayed in New York for the high holidays. She asked where I went to shul and I told her I hadn't been since leaving Urbana. She seemed even more startled by this than by me not finishing high school.

"Really? But you still wear your yarmulke . . . That's kind of weird, isn't it, wearing a yarmulke if you're not religious anymore?"

"I don't know . . . I guess, maybe."

I did not explain myself to the redhead. I simply told her I'd worn it since I was a little boy and wasn't comfortable going bareheaded. That was only partially true. I knew very well why the little circle of silk was so important to me. I knew it then and I know it to this day.

I am not a believer, yet I remain a Jew. It may not make sense to others, but I wear this yarmulke to honor the grandparents I never knew and the untold others who were beaten and killed in pogroms, and starved and gassed in the death camps. Their spirits call to me in the strangest places: a lonely Illinois graveyard, the cold concrete of a three-wall handball court on the shores of Lake Michigan, the snow-encrusted streets of a Chicago winter, and a pleasant coffee shop on a fine spring day in Greenwich Village. As strange as it may sound, this is why I continue to wear my yarmulke.

It's the same one that was on my head when I left Crown Heights, although it looks a little more careworn these days. I have trimmed its frayed edges and mended its parting seams with a needle and thread. I have sewn in small patches of black silk, sacrificed from lesser yarmulkes, to give a bobby pin something more substantial to grip onto. I imagine some might wonder why I've never replaced it, but I've won every championship with this one on my head, and although it is a bit tattered, its battle scars are no worse than those I wear on other parts of my body.

Plenty of handballers have their superstitions. Athletes in other sports have them too—a lucky pair of socks, a charm worn round the neck, a ritual of some sort. I suppose there's a bit of that in my yarmulke too, but it is more than just a lucky talisman. It stands for everything I was, am, or will be. It's an effigy in cloth of Zev Altshul, the once-Hasidic, Shabbos-desecrating apostate; the tough as a gristled brisket Jew who would rule the courts of New York.

The redhead said, "You remember that big fight you got into with those football players?"

"How could I forget?"

"Everyone in school was talking about it. I was proud of you, the way you stood up to them. A lot of us were."

I said, "I didn't have much of a choice. They would've eventually beaten the crap out of me either way, so I figured I might as well get it over with."

"Well, I think you were very brave."

I liked hearing her say that.

I had never shown any interest in her, but the redhead had this look in her eyes, like she wanted to climb inside me. I was a little frightened by that. I thought back to my crazy love for Sharon Kotin, the girl who barely said two words to me. She had trouble being civil for five minutes in her parents' car on the way to shul, and yet I would have done anything to win her affection. Maybe it was the same sort of thing with the redhead. There's no way to explain a crazy love like that.

She reached across the table and cautiously placed her hand on top of mine. The weight of her touch let me know this was not a simple gesture of friendship. I did not know how to react, and patted the back of her hand the way you might pat a small child on the head. I felt incredibly foolish for my ineptitude, but I had never learned such courting skills. Lubavitcher marriages are arranged. We are barely left alone with our prospective brides before having to make the decision to spend the rest of our lives with them. The rabbis teach us the feelings will come if we are faithful and patient.

When we got up to leave, I looked her over, trying not to be too obvious about it. She was no Sharon Kotin, but appealing enough. She wrote her number on a paper napkin and handed it to me.

"Call me," she said.

This was my big chance to learn the redhead's name. I asked if she'd mind writing it on the napkin. She gave me a funny look.

"I've got a lot of phone numbers at home," I explained. "I'll forget who it belongs to if there's no name on it."

She took the napkin back and wrote down Dana.

I said, "Oh, sorry, Dana; I already knew that. I meant your last name."

She gave me an even funnier look and wrote down Epstein, then asked for my number.

"I don't have a phone," I said. "I'm usually at the Seaside Courts near the boardwalk at Surf Avenue."

"Call me," she said again.

I gripped the napkin tightly as we walked up MacDougal Street, the thin paper wadded in my fist. I contemplated tossing it in the trash once she was out of sight, but the chocolatey taste of my first and second cappuccinos lingered on my tongue like the advice of a sister that refuses to dissipate despite time and distance.

I swallowed deeply, remembering the day Frida and I were eating lunch in the kitchen on California Avenue and she tried convincing me to give the redhead a call. She chastised me when I told her I wasn't interested. She said I wasn't living in the shtetl anymore and needed to take chances in life. She said another opportunity may never come around again.

Abba had no idea the last step he would ever take in this world would be from the curb onto Eastern Parkway. He was probably thinking about his Shabbos dinner at the moment he was struck. He would not have imagined his imminent death would be more than his fragile wife could bear, or that his legacy would be a suitcase full of tainted money, discovered by his son and shared with his estranged daughter.

Joe Carcone had no idea he had run out of second chances when he got behind the wheel of his car for the last time. He could not have foreseen what awaited him on that snowy Illinois road, and that he would never set foot in Brooklyn again, or have another opportunity to reconcile with his son, or know the loss and regret his second son would feel without him in the world.

I said goodbye to the redhead at the entrance to the subway. She gave me a peck on the cheek and I watched her walk away down West 3rd Street with the sun high overhead in a perfectly cloudless sky. I unfolded the napkin and read the name on it again—*Dana Epstein*. I smoothed the crumpled napkin and carefully folded it before slipping it in my pocket.

A GLOSSARY OF YIDDISH AND HEBREW WORDS AND PHRASES

770: Chabad Lubavitcher World Headquarters at 770 Eastern Parkway, considered sacred by many.

Abba: An endearing term for "father."

Alter cocker: "Old shitter." A derogatory term for an old man.

A narh bleibt a narh: A fool remains a fool.

Apikoros: A Jewish heretic or apostate.

The Baal Shem Tov: The eighteenth-century mystic credited with founding Hasidism.

Beis din: Orthodox rabbinical court deciding disputes and legal matters.

Bimah: The raised platform in synagogue where the Torah is read.

Bissell: A little.

B'li neder: Without a vow.

Chazerei: Something rotten.

Cheder: An orthodox preschool and elementary school.

Chillul Hashem: To willfully profane the name of God publicly by one's actions. A very serious offense.

Cholent: Traditional Shabbos stew kept warm in a crock pot.

Chuppah: The traditional tent covering at a Jewish wedding.

Das iz gut: That's good.

Daven: Prayer. Often accompanied by enthusiastic, rapid bowing.

Devekut: Dedication, closeness to God.

Dover akher: "Another thing." A back stabber. A very derogatory term

Drek: Garbage. Shit.

Eema: An endearing term for "mother."

Eruv: An artificial boundary constructed around an orthodox community to allow certain activities otherwise forbidden on the Sabbath.

Fakaktah: Fucked up.

Farshtinkener: A rotten person.

Frum: An observant Jew.

Gabbaim: Plural of gabbai, one who oversees Torah reading in the synagogue.

Gett: The orthodox Jewish decree of divorce.

Gey gesunterheyt: "Go in good health." Can also be said sarcastically.

Gonif: A dishonest or disreputable person.

Goy (pl. Goyim): A gentile.

Goyische: Non-Jewish. Of the gentiles.

Halacha: Jewish law.

Haredi: Term for "ultraorthodox" Jews.

Hashem: "The Name." A Hebrew term for God.

Havdalah: A ceremony to mark the end of the Sabbath.

Hoizer gaier: A beggar.

Kabbalah: Ancient mystical teachings popular among Hasidim.

Kibbitz: Aimless chatter.

Kiddush: A ritual blessing to begin the Sabbath and other holidays.

Kinehora: A popular blessing for good luck.

Kippah: Hebrew for "yarmulke."

Keriah: Ceremonial rending of mourners' garments at a funeral.

Kohelet: Translated from the Hebrew as Ecclesiastes, "Preacher."

Kurveh: Whore. Beltz kurveh: The worst kind of whore.
Kevurah: Burial.
Kvelling: Gushing with pride.
Lashon Hakodesh: The holy language. Hebrew.
Lashon hara: Derogatory speech that can cause harm to another.
Macher: A big shot.
Mahalat nefesh: Literally, "sickness of the soul." A Hebrew term for mental illness.
Mechitzah: The partition separating the sexes in an orthodox synagogue.
Megillah: A long story. A big deal.
Mensch: An upright man.
Meshuggeneh: A crazy person.
Meshuggeh: Crazy (adj.)
Meshumad (pl. Meshumadim): A Jew who has abandoned the faith.
Mezuzah: A small piece of Torah scroll in a decorative case hung on the doorpost of Jewish homes.
Mikvah: Ritual bath for ceremonial cleansing.
Minyan: A quorum of ten Jewish men beyond bar mitzvah age necessary for conducting religious services.
Mishegoss: Craziness, foolishness.
Mishpucha: Family.
Mitzvah (pl. Mitzvot): Commandment. A good deed.
Magen David: The Jewish star.
Modeh Ani: First prayer in the morning. Recited while still in bed.
Mohel: A Jew trained in the practice of circumcision.
Moishe Mekhuyev: One who lives off the favors of others.
Momser: A contemptible person. A bastard. Devious.
Moshiach: The Messiah.

Muktzeh: Everyday objects that may not be moved on Shabbos.

Niddah: The orthodox purity laws regarding menstruation and marital purity.

Nu: Has many meanings: Well? So?

Nudge: A pest.

Off the derech (OTD): Off the path. Describes orthodox Jews who have departed from the faith.

Oneg Shabbat: A time of refreshment after Shabbat service.

Oych a beshefenish: "Also a VIP." Very derogatory.

Payos: Long side curls worn by Hasidic men.

Punim: Face.

Rav: Rabbi.

Reb: A term of respect for a devout Jewish man.

Rebbe: The leader of a Hasidic community, used specifically in reference to Menachem Mendel Schneerson, most revered late Rebbe of the Chabad-Lubavitcher community.

Schmatta: A rag.

Schmendrick: A nonentity. A useless person.

Schnorrer: An unethical beggar who cheats others.

Schvartze: A Black person. Sometimes used derogatorily.

Shabbos: The Jewish day of rest, from sundown Friday until sundown Saturday.

Shabbos goy: A gentile who performs prohibited acts on the Sabbath on behalf of orthodox Jews.

Shadchan: A matchmaker, the way many Hasidic courtships

Shammes: One who performs the duties of a sexton in a synagogue.

Shanda: A shame. A scandal.

Shanda fur die goy: A scandal in front of gentiles. An embarrassment.

Shaygetz: A male gentile.

Shayna punim: "Pretty face." A term of endearment.

Sheitel: Wig worn by orthodox women.

Shemira: The orthodox custom of sitting with the body of a deceased Jew until burial.

Sheol: Hebrew equivalent to the Greek Hades, the abode of the dead. A place of darkness.

Shidduch: The matchmaking process for Orthodox courtship.

Shiksa: A female gentile.

Shiva: Seven-day mourning period for the dead.

Shliach: (pl. shluchim): A recognized emissary of the Rebbe, a Jewish missionary.

Shochet: A trained slaughterer of kosher animals.

Shomer: A guardian.

Shomer Shabbos: A Sabbath keeper.

Shpilkes: Agitation.

Shtetl: The tiny eastern European towns where many Hasidic Jews lived.

Shtreimel: A cylindrical fur hat worn by some Hasidic men on Shabbos.

Shul: Synagogue.

Tallis (or Tallit): Prayer shawl. Traditional fringed garment.

Talmud: A sacred commentary of rabbinical teachings on Jewish law and practice. Central to orthodox Judaism.

Tatellah: "Little man." A term of endearment.

Tchotchkes: Knickknacks.

Tefillin: Two small leather boxes containing Torah scrolls bound with leather straps on the arm and head during morning prayers.

Torah: Specifically, the five books of Moses, but also refers to the entire Jewish scripture as well as the sacred scrolls in a synagogue.

Treif: Nonkosher food, forbidden to eat.

Tsitskehs: - Breasts

Tsuris: Trouble. Aggravation.

Tuchus: Backside.

Tzaddik: A righteous and wise spiritual master.

Tzaddik hador: The most spiritual master of a generation.

Tzidduk H'din: A burial prayer recited at the internment.

Tzitzit: The prayer shawl with fringes that orthodox men wear un-der
their shirts.

Veltz kurveh: The worst kind of whore.

Yahrzeit: Memorial candle.

Yarmulke: Skullcap

Yechidus: A private meeting with the Rebbe

Yenta: A female busybody

Yom Tov: Jewish Holidays

Zei gezunt: "Be healthy." A traditional way of saying good-bye.

ACKNOWLEDGMENTS

So many people to thank:

To my readers, past and present—Gaetano Amorosi, Jim Carpenter, Javier Cevallos, Georgiana Goodwin, James Hulbert, Amy Lipton, and Sharon Scullin and Bernadette Ward. Your generous contributions cannot be overstated, and I am grateful.

Special thanks to Sharon Cooke and Sherry Cameron, who have endured more than their share of my scribblings over many years. Your honest criticism and loyal friendship have kept me going.

To my best Brooklyn friend, Jay Melvin, without whom there would be no Zev Altshul, and no *Leaving Eastern Parkway*.

Thank you to the artist, Jerome Witkin, for generously "lending" me his painting, Tit for Tat.

To Ben Van Arsdale, of Illini Handball, for introducing me to the Big Green Wall.

To my agent, Harvey Klinger. Thank you for your belief and persistence.

To Joe Olshan, my editor at Delphinium Books. Thank you for your respect and sensitivity. You are a writer's editor, and made the entire process a pleasure.

To my children, Joshua and Sarah, and their well-chosen spouses, Tara and Rob. You have been more help to me than you will ever know.

And, lastly, I must thank my wife, Barbara, who despite her better judgment, (mostly) withheld criticism while I let a forty-year art career run aground as I pursued the pipe dreams of a novice fiction writer. She is undergoing a second surgery for recurring glioblastoma as I put these acknowledgments together. I don't know if she will ever get to hold this book in her hands, but I am forever grateful.

ABOUT THE AUTHOR

Matthew Daub is an artist and writer. His career as a visual artist has spanned more than four decades. His watercolor paintings and drawings have been widely exhibited at galleries and museums throughout the United States, including numerous invitational exhibitions at institutions such as the Metropolitan Museum of Art, the American Academy of Arts and Letters, and Tthe National Academy of Design. In 1991, the Metropolitan Museum of Art featured a Daub watercolor in their annual engagement calendar, *American Watercolors*.

He has written dozens of articles for nationally distributed art magazines, as well as a monograph on the artist Carolyn Plochmann. Matthew retired after thirty-two years as a university art professor to devote himself full-time to his writing. *Leaving Eastern Parkway* is his first novel.

Printed in the USA
CPSIA information can be obtained
at www.ICGtesting.com
JSHW022219010724
65614JS00010B/14